the BELTER REVOLUTION

the belter series: book two

E.S. MARTELL

Printed in the USA
Second Initiative Press

ISBN: 978-1-948063-99-9

Editor
Adriana D'Apolito of 3P Editing
Cover Art
Aleksandra Klepacka
Typography
Kelley York of Sleepy Fox Studio
Interior Design and Typeset
Melissa Stevens of The Illustrated Author Design Services

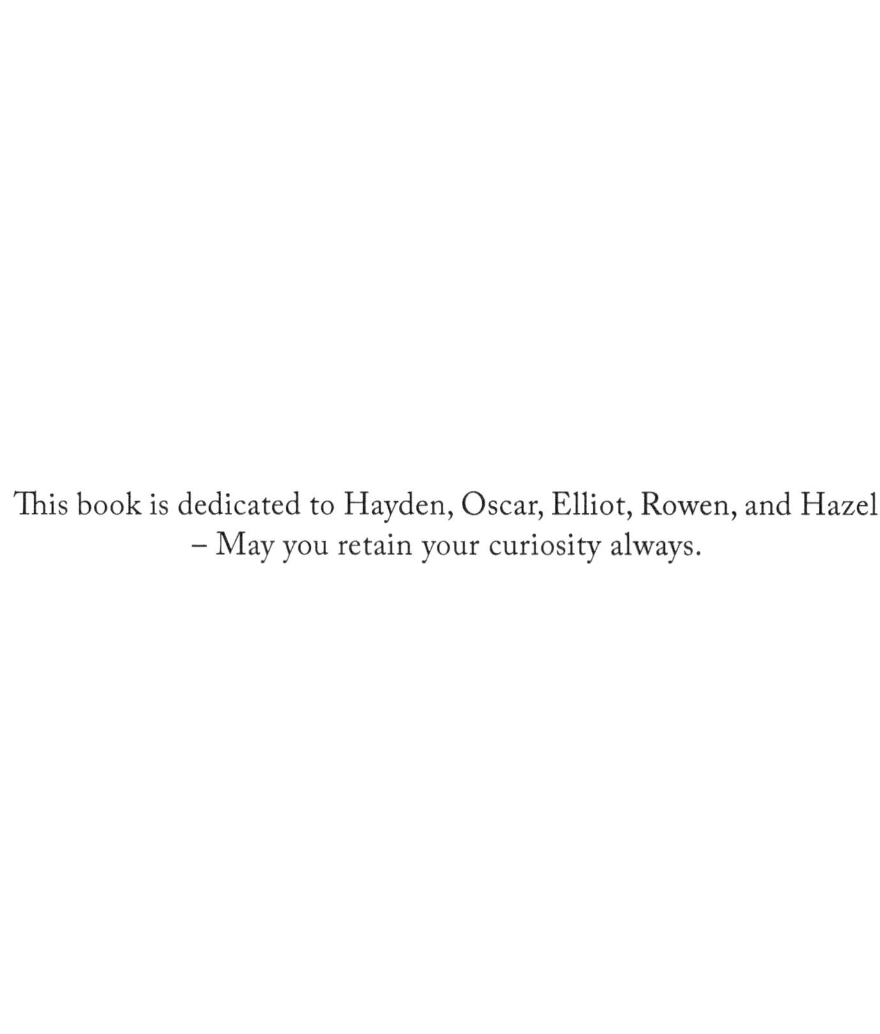

This book is dedicated to Hayden, Oscar, Elliot, Rowen, and Hazel
– May you retain your curiosity always.

BELTER TERRITORY: KEEP OUT!

All Adam wanted was his advanced degree and a girlfriend. What he got was betrayal, kicked out of University, and exiled to the Asteroid Belt. Through a series of mishaps, he became a successful pirate.

When the oppressive North American Dictatorship retaliates, Adam is thrust into a leadership role in the Belter's struggle for independence. He must reach deep to find the strength to meet the immense challenge.

His physics background and natural inventiveness play a large part in equalizing the disparity in force strength. He adapts discovered alien technology in weaponry and space drives, providing the Belters with a minimal advantage. He is a quick learner and becomes surprisingly adept in space warfare.

His girlfriend, Nile, plays an increasingly important part in his plans and in his heart. She mysteriously disappears with a Marine team member, and Adam is left wondering if she's taken up with the man, particularly since she admitted to having had a relationship with him.

What happens next is told in the story of the Belter's Revolutionary War for Independence. The story chronicles a wild conflict around the solar system, providing entertainment, adventure, humor, tragedy, and romance set against the broad background of the asteroid belt and interplanetary space.

CONTENTS

DEDICATION i
ACKNOWLEDGMENTS vii

1: THE KUIPER BELT 1
2: ERIS 9
3: ALIEN IDEAS 17
4: TITAN BASE 23
5: A NEW DRIVE 28
6: MARS AND WAR 35
7: ARMING THE D-R 54
8: COMPETITION 64
9: UNEXPECTED EVENTS 75
10: PREPPING 84
11: THE RAID 96
12: THE AFTERMATH 110
13: FINDING A HIDEOUT 117
14: RENOVATIONS 124
15: AMBUSH 137
16: TITAN, AGAIN 149
17: WAR PLANS 155
18: THE BATTLE OF EARTH ORBIT 159
19: PEACE ON EARTH 172
20: LUNA BASE 183

21: UNEXPECTED ALLIES 191

22: BAD NEWS 196

23: REPRISAL 203

24: SPACE IS BIG 211

25: THE DEATH OF THE D-R 225

26: DRIFTING TOWARDS DEATH 231

27: A RIDE 240

28: THE BATTLE FOR TITAN 251

29: THE DOCKS 261

30: TUNNELS AND DOMES 269

31: THE COUNCIL DOME 277

32: CLEANING UP 282

33: THE KISS OF DEATH 291

34: COMPLICATIONS 295

35: LEGAL PROCEDURES 300

36: THE BLOOD MOON 312

37: A MEETING 319

38: FRIENDLY – NOT! 335

ABOUT THE AUTHOR 339

BLOG INFORMATION 340

Links for my time-travel stories: 341

Link for the Gaia Ascendant Trilogy: 341

ACKNOWLEDGMENTS

Special thanks to Aleksandra Klepacka for her cover art. As always, she has captured the essence of the story in her art.

This work benefited immensely from the editorial expertise of Adriana D'Apolito of 3P Editing.

1

THE KUIPER BELT

ADAM COULDN'T SLEEP. He'd grown up on Earth in a large house with large rooms. He'd never had any problem sleeping then. The trouble now was there was too much vacant space in his tiny cabin.

The Captain's cabin on the Dire Rhea wasn't large, but then neither was the D-R. It had been built as a mining ship designed to hold a crew of six to eight humans.

The profile of the ship wasn't that of a miner any longer. The plasma shield generators and the two cannons served to reinforce the rather crude artwork on the bow. There the crew had painted a skull and crossbones just below the irritated bird's head that was supposed to represent an angry Rhea.

It was something of a joke. The Earthers had started it by calling the miners Pirates. It was a slur on people who were trying their best to establish an independent existence in the asteroid belt and space beyond. All they wanted was to be left alone and to build a civilization.

True, they had raided the government's Mars supply ships a few times, but they were desperate. The new dictatorship of the North American polity wasn't interested in giving them a break. On the contrary, the miners had always been treated like expendables, useful only insofar as they brought in desirable minerals, ferrous metals, and the odd discovery of more noble metal. There were deposits of gold on some of the asteroids, although such finds were rare.

Once the D-R's crew had heard about the Pirate appellation, they'd adopted it in self-defense. If the Earthers thought they were Pirates, well, by Saturn's Rings, they'd be the most fearsome Pirates they could be.

They were doing a pretty good job of it so far. The Belters had fought the USSN to a complete standstill, although the end result was more like a draw. Both sides had lost most of their ships, and the Belters had lost the giant hollow asteroid called the Bubble.

Now the majority of the Belters were working to build a base on Titan. One that would, hopefully, be impregnable to possible USSN attacks in the future.

Adam was nominally the Admiral of the Belter military force, but as it was composed primarily of volunteers, his position allowed him considerable leeway. He was using that freedom to explore far beyond Pluto at the moment.

His sleeping trouble was because Nile was not in bed with him. The bed felt empty without her warm presence snuggled up against him. It even sounded empty, he reflected. She didn't snore, but she did have a distinct sound to her breathing when she slept. It was a sound that he'd gotten used to, and now it felt like he couldn't sleep without it.

She wasn't far away, just keeping watch on the bridge. There were only three other people on the ship besides Adam. Nile was in charge of the alterday shift, so he and she only had brief periods between shifts to engage in advancing their relationship.

The other two crew members were Flynn, a tiny, irascible Irishman, and To'afa, a huge Samoan with a master's degree in math and a propensity for extreme violence. He usually focused that aspect of his personality on the opposition, but he had also been known to crack a few heads in bar fights.

Adam threw his arm over his eyes and rolled onto his back. Why be such an idiot? He was Captain of his own ship and the Admiral of the Belter space force. Didn't that mean that he was supposed to be sturdily independent and self-reliant?

Heading out here to the Kuiper Belt might have been a mistake. He wanted to get away from the activity on Titan. The Belter Council alternated between resenting his popularity and pestering him for his opinion on their problems.

He could do without that bother, especially when he was trying to come up with a solution to a more significant problem, one that had been bothering him since before the fierce battle with the Federal United Supreme Space Navy.

The so-called Battle of the Bubble had been terrible. Adam had no experience in space navy strategy. No one had. The attack by the Feds had been the first ship-to-ship engagement involving more than two ships in the history of the solar system. He'd had to create defenses before the engagement and improvise throughout. Fortunately, he'd somehow managed to destroy most of their superior force and drive off the remaining ships. The Belters considered it a magnificent victory, despite the loss of most of their ships.

The new settlement on Titan was progressing nicely, and the Feds hadn't made a move in their direction for several months. Both sides had been shocked by the intensity of the battle and their losses. The resulting pause and recovery period gave the settlers time to work on their habitat.

Unfortunately, from Adam's perspective, the Feds had seen his plasma cannon invention's deadly effect and had immediately devoted an enormous amount of research to good effect. Now, they had their own version of a plasma launcher.

No one knew how effective it was or whether it was as good as the plasma cannons of the Belters. There had been no engagements since the Battle of the Bubble, unless one counted the incident on Phoebe as a formal battle, rather than the attempted ambush and kidnapping it had actually been.

THE BEAUTIFUL THING about poking around in the near edge of the Kuiper Belt was that the Council couldn't easily bother him. His stated intention was to explore Eris as a possibility for an out-system base. The Council hadn't been enthusiastic, but he had insisted, so they grudgingly acceded to his absence.

Their near-Earth observers hadn't picked up any signs of the dictatorship turning its attention in their direction. Things on Earth were still in a jumble. The Non-Aligns, the countries that were resisting Elseth's rule, were continuing to fight and having some success. The USSN had used KEWs against some of the nations, but the retaliatory strikes had damaged the North American infrastructure severely.

The war, for that was what it was, had dropped from a rolling boil to a simmer for the time being. Both sides were busy engaged in building up resources and armament. The Belters benefited from the lack of attention and were working hard to rebuild their depleted military capacity.

In that way, having three opposing forces was beneficial. It was helpful in another way, also. The Non-Aligns had approached the Belters with offers of an alliance. The Federal Dictatorship had issued stern warnings in response, followed by an attempt to enlist the Belters' aid on their behalf.

That was met with flat rejection. The Asteroid Belt Mining community had been mistreated for too long by the Feds. The

Battle of the Bubble had cemented the Feds' role as an enemy to be fought at all costs and all times.

THE KUIPER BELT was full of objects, but still mostly empty space. Its best-known denizen was Pluto, but other dwarf planets were almost the same size. In Adam's opinion, Eris with its diameter of 2,326 kilometers was a good possibility for a base, whereas Pluto was not.

Pluto had a close twin that complicated navigation in the area. Eris did not. It did have a tiny moon named after Eris' daughter, Dysnomia, the demon goddess of lawlessness. Eris had a very long year of five-hundred and fifty-seven Earth years, but it rotated once every twenty-six hours, so its day was human-friendly. Its temperature wasn't. Surface temperature was known to range from a negative two-hundred and seventeen degrees C to an atmosphere-freezing minus two-hundred and forty-three degrees C.

It was a long haul out to the dwarf planet. It was located about sixty-eight AUs out, making it a little over five and a quarter hours light from the sun. That was a drawback, but also a positive. It would complicate building and supply, but the good thing was it also made an attack challenging to mount, should the Feds ever decide to try one.

EVEN WITH THE more powerful boosters, the D-R had taken weeks to reach the vicinity of Eris. Now the ship was closing in on the Luna-sized planet. They expected to arrive within the next twelve hours. That was why Nile was on duty at the moment. Adam wanted to be in charge when they arrived.

She hadn't been entirely pleased with his decision, but she understood enough to allow him that honor. He realized that he was fortunate to have found a woman who was both a fierce fighter and a considerate partner.

Meanwhile, he had a few hours to go before he was due to come back on duty. He closed his eyes and tried to visualize a new weapon.

He'd been thinking of how to one-up the plasma cannon for some time. He'd started working on the idea during the Battle of the Bubble. The plasma bursts were deadly but somewhat erratic. The plasma ablated a ship's hull erratically, sometimes resulting in quick and total destruction, and other times a disappointingly minor amount of damage.

What he needed was something that would reliably take an entire armory ship or a battleship out with a single shot. So far, the solution had eluded him.

The Feds were not above using nuclear warheads on their hyper-vee missiles, and that was something the Belters didn't want to do. Now they had their own version of a plasma cannon. The balance of power was tilting in the Feds favor, and it gave him nightmares. Right now he would be happy to take a nap, even if it involved a bad dream. He hadn't been sleeping well. Worrying had the unfortunate effect of keeping him awake.

He jerked. The comm had gone off. It was hours later than the last time he'd looked. He'd drifted off thinking about weapons.

He climbed out of bed, staggering in the Coriolis force of the D-R's rotation, pulled his clothes on, and headed for the bridge.

Nile glanced at him when he came in.

"Hi, sleepy. You look bright and ready to go. What was it? Did you stay up inventing things all night?"

"Hey, don't be sarcastic. I couldn't sleep." He glanced around. Flynn had already headed back to his bunk, and To'afa was getting some food. They were alone.

"To tell you the truth, Nile, I couldn't sleep because you weren't in bed with me."

She looked at him to make sure he wasn't joking. When she saw he was serious, she said, "That's pretty sad. You're a macho Pirate, and you need me in bed with you to help you sleep?"

He started to answer, but she immediately thought better of her words and amended her statement. "I'm just teasing. I'm flattered. I miss you, too, darling. I never never thought I would find a man that I could love, but I guess war creates opportunities for unusual happenings."

"Understood. I knew you were making fun of me. It's one of the things I like about you. You won't let me get too full of myself."

"Nope. Not gonna do that. I like my men humble."

"There you go again. Anyway, I was thinking about weapons. Maybe replacing the plasma in the cannon with antimatter, but there's a couple of problems with that idea."

She snorted. "Yeah. Like how are you going to keep it contained until you shoot it, and where does it come from?"

That was something else he liked about her. For a girl who had only a modicum of formal education, she was both remarkably intelligent and well-read.

"You're a genius. That's precisely what is hanging me up."

"Well, you'll have to solve those problems on your own time. Right now, we're close enough to Eris to start thinking about landing. Wanna sit down and take over?"

"Sure. That's why I got up. You going to go sleep some?"

"No, I'm not tired yet. I think I'll sit here and watch. Besides, in case you don't know it, I miss you just as much as you miss me. It's been lonely up here without you. Couldn't we give alterday to Flynn and To'afa?"

He thought about that as he waited for the comp to kick out a landing solution.

"We could. Flynn is a good driver. He captained a ship at the Bubble, but he doesn't work very well with To'afa."

That was an understatement. Flynn was acerbic and rude, sometimes shouting or cursing at his crew, although he was unfailingly polite to Nile. To'afa was a bruiser who liked to fight, but he was sensitive and easily hurt. All it would take was one insult too many, and he might pound Flynn's head in before he realized what he was doing.

The comp beeped. Adam checked the solution then keyed in the command that started the sequence. The D-R shuddered a little as the boosters began to brake.

The view screen showed little but empty space. The Kuiper Belt held millions of objects, but they were even farther apart than the asteroids. As Adam watched, the spot that was Eris multiplied in size. The only other object in view was the ridiculously tiny Dysnomia wending her way around the planetoid.

2

ERIS

THE DIRE RHEA was resting in the middle of a slightly rolling plain. The landscape was as flat as it could get on a planet with a radius of seven-hundred and twenty-two miles, which was to say, the horizon was close and dropped off in a perceptible arc. The low spots appeared to be filled with a foggy mixture of gas and frost crystals. They were on the night side of the planet and what little atmosphere that existed was currently frozen.

There were stones scattered across the plain, mixed with impact craters. There was no doubt in Adam's mind. Eris was an accumulation of objects that had collided over a long period. The ice in the low spots was probably methane. He guessed that if he checked, the methane would hide liquid nitrogen. There would also be a bit of water ice, but it was probably under the surface where it wouldn't leak off into space.

The gravity was close to that of Luna. That implied that Eris was relatively solid and composed of stony material.

While it wasn't strictly necessary, he wanted to step outside for a few minutes. The ship had an automatic sampling apparatus, and its arm had already scraped up some surface material that was stored for later analysis.

THE FOUR WERE gathered in the bridge celebrating. It was an historic occasion. They were the first humans to visit Eris, and as far as they knew, they were the first to visit the Kuiper belt. Of course, it was possible that some miner had preceded them and had kept it secret or died before returning. Mining was hazardous, and there were always ships going missing, plus there were wild tales told at bars when miners returned.

To'afa opened a bottle of champagne that had somehow been smuggled up from Earth. The truly remarkable thing about the bottle, however, was that it had survived long enough to make its way onto the D-R. Such items were usually consumed the moment someone got their hands on them.

The cork came out easily in the low pressure. The big man held it in place, allowing the carbon dioxide to leak out slowly rather than all at once.

"It takes a little longer to get it open," he said. "But it's a lot better this way. The stuff is so difficult to get that I don't want it squirting all over." He grinned at Adam. "Besides, the Captain would make me clean up the mess. I'd have to lick it off the deck and the overhead."

Nile made a face. "Ugh. That's seriously disgusting. Please tell me that you haven't been licking the walls or door handles or something. I'll be too grossed out to touch anything."

To'afa made a face back at her, sticking out his tongue, but saying nothing.

Flynn cleared his throat. "Hey, there's a message coming in on the tight band laser system."

Adam turned to the small man. "Let's take a look at it. They must have something important to say. It's not like we're that easy to find out this far. They must have put some effort into aligning the transmitter."

Flynn made a few keystrokes, transferring the incoming message to the vid. The four read silently for a moment, then Flynn cursed under his breath.

"Jupiter be-damned, Captain. They want us back soonest. Yesterday, if possible. Those damned Feds!"

Adam shook his head negatively. "We spent all this time getting out here and the moment the USSN shows up, they can't handle it without us."

To'afa replied, "They did lose two ships to the one we lost, but the Feds aren't going to give up easily. They seem to have recovered from the beating we gave them at the Bubble. Maybe they want another lesson."

Adam nodded. "The issue isn't settled. Our very existence gives the Non-Aligns on Earth hope that they can remain independent. The North American Union or Queen-ship or whatever it's called today really can't afford to leave us alone. Besides, they know we're going to defend our territory. We'll have to fight it out with them and come to a definite conclusion sooner or later."

He glanced at Nile. As a former USSN Space Marine, her loyalty had been to her unit and then to the marines. She didn't have any attachment to the government itself, though.

She met his eyes and nodded in agreement.

He turned to Flynn. "Would you set up the nav to get us back? While we're here, I'm going outside to explore a little bit. No way are we going to come this far without setting foot on this ice ball."

If the truth were told, Adam reflected, he wanted to go outside simply because no one had ever stepped on the surface of Eris. As far as he knew, he had been the first human to stand on Phoebe, the first on Titan, and now he had the opportunity to be the first on Eris. That was a record that would be hard to beat. Might as well go down in history as a great explorer, too.

He became aware that the others were looking at him expectantly. He looked at his hands. They were balled into fists. The Feds were going to continue until the Belters were wiped out, or...he couldn't wipe out the Earth's population. It could be accomplished with a few boosted asteroids, but it wasn't morally possible.

"Well, they'll never know if we take a little extra time. No sense wasting our trip. Nile, you want to go outside with me?"

"Yow, Adam. It's cold as the hinges of Hell a million years before the fires were lit. You'll freeze something, sure. Do you really have to go out there?"

He realized that he was flushing. She never let him get away with stupid actions. "Well, no, I don't have to go out. It's just that I want to. Do you want to come?"

"I thought you'd never ask. Let's get out there, and scratch 'Kilroy was here' in the dirt. That'll make 'em wonder."

He tried to remember who Kilroy was, then it clicked. The name had been written all over during the big war in the middle of the last century. Soldiers had inscribed the message in all sorts of unlikely places.

He laughed dryly. "Ha-ha. It might make them think, but I'll bet that those who come after us won't have a clue about Kilroy."

"Maybe not. Better wear some extra underwear. It's dark and cold and trending colder. We could have landed on the sunward side, but it probably wouldn't make any difference."

"TEMPERATURE IS A factor that we have to deal with if we're going to have a base here. We can dig in, insulate the heck out of the place, and keep an atomic fire burning."

They'd gone into the hold and were putting on insulated, skin-tight coveralls before getting into their space-suits.

She paused for a moment, and said, "I bet there isn't any life on this rock. It's too cold. Did you ever stop to think how lucky we are, living on Earth, I mean?"

He was arranging his suit before sealing it. "We're not lucky. We don't live on Earth. We live out here where everything is cold. Besides, we're children of Earth. We wouldn't be here if she hadn't been so hospitable."

THE PLAIN WAS cold, barren, and the rocks that littered the surface gave it a forlorn feeling. They bounded towards a depression that had a mist of gas floating above it, their feet making a slight crunching sound that was transmitted through the air in their suits to their ears.

Adam slowed as they approached the edge of the low spot. Now he could see that it was a shallow impact crater. Long ago, something had struck the surface here. The litter of rocks grew thicker as they approached, making it necessary to place their feet carefully.

Nile came on the comm. "My toes are getting cold. We'll have to go back in five, huh?"

"Yeah. Me too. I just want to look more closely at this hole. Hey! Look at that." He stopped and pointed.

The mist had cleared revealing something that didn't belong there.

"What is it?" she asked, her voice shaking.

He moved closer. "It looks like a created structure, but that can't be possible."

"No, it is. Look over there. That's the front of the thing. Adam, we're looking at a crashed space ship."

The hairs on his neck stood up. The thing was old. Old. It had been here for millennia if its hull was any indication. It was covered with scars and dents caused by impacts. It had been smooth when it was new. There were still some unscarred areas to be seen.

The owners would probably have kept it up when they were using it. They wouldn't have allowed the surface to become so battered. No. It had been here for a long time.

"Nile, See that protruding rock on that side?"

He pointed, making sure she saw which one he had in mind. She turned, then said, "I see it."

"I'm going to approach from that point, then I'll try working down to the ship."

"Okay, but there's some ice down at the bottom, It's probably even colder, so be careful. I'm going to stay up here where I can call for help."

He moved around the edge a couple of hundred feet, then gingerly edged down the side of a ridge. After a bit, the narrow spot widened and flattened out in a shallow curve that led down into the hole.

He estimated that it was only about ten meters deep. It probably had been deeper when the ship had struck, but the debris of ages had filled the depression partially, leaving a flat bottom from which the space ship's upper parts protruded.

Adam moved closer and inspected the ship, for that was obviously what it was, at a close distance. It was some kind of metal mixed with fibers. It looked like the builders had used the material to weave a net of some sort around the outside. What would that be?

He moved alongside the ship. The rear section sank into the ground and was surrounded by a mist. He tossed a convenient stone into the fog, and it disappeared, causing the cloud to rise in whorls. The stone's passage revealed a gray liquid at the bottom. It wouldn't be wise to step into that.

He retreated and moved around the front. The thing was about five meters high here and from the front to the point where it disappeared in the mist and liquid was about twenty-five meters.

He couldn't tell for sure, but it didn't seem to be as large as the D-R.

The front was flat, and there were the remains of a roughly cone-shaped antenna or something of the sort. It had broken during the crash, but there was enough structure for him to estimate its size. He took some pictures with his helmet cam.

Nile had been videoing the entire thing from above. She'd walked along the edge, keeping him in view.

"Adam, I'm too cold. Let's get out of here. There isn't anything you can do down there. It's going to take a team of scientists to make anything out of this."

He started back up. She was right. A few more minutes and his feet would start to develop frost-bite.

"Nile, do you realize what this means?"

"Yes, dummy. Of course, I do. We're not alone. There's someone out there somewhere, and they visited our solar system once a long time ago. I'm just hoping that they aren't hanging around somewhere. I don't care to go up against bug-eyed aliens from Proxima Centauri or somewhere."

"Well, yes. That's true, but we've got a fantastic opportunity here. If we can figure out how this ship works..." He paused, overcome by excitement. "Damn! Nile, this is an interstellar ship. It has to have a star-drive. We've got to figure it out."

"I think you're right. I can't believe it, but that's what it has to be. This will give us an advantage over the Earthers if we can figure it out."

"It'll make the entire disagreement with the Earthers irrelevant, that's what it will do. We've got to keep it quiet. Remember how Serge knew about my destination when I went to explore Phoebe? The Council probably has spies. This has to be top-secret."

She didn't answer at first, then he heard her mutter, "I'm cold."

He bounded up the slope, grabbed her arm, and started them moving towards the warmth of the D-R.

His mind was whirling with possibilities as he moved.

Take that conical antenna, for instance. It didn't look like it was designed for communication. It wasn't a weapon either if function followed form with these aliens. It must be some aspect of their star drive.

He suddenly thought of a Bussard Ram drive. This was too small for that, but what if it served a similar function.

Insight struck. That was what the mesh over the outside of the hull was for. He'd noticed that the cone and the mesh were connected. It was probably a field generator that was used to collect...what?

He stopped thinking about it. They'd reached the open lock. He helped Nile inside, and she activated the mechanism. The outer door slid shut, and the pumps thumped as the lock began to fill with atmosphere.

The heated walls kept the atmosphere from freezing on their surface. In a matter of minutes, they were free to enter the central part of the hold.

Nile's first words as she stripped off her suit were, "Damn, that's cold out there. I'm not going to be any help exploring that hulk. I'm going to get in bed, turn up the heat, and cover up my head for about a Martian year. It'll take at least that long for me to warm up again."

3

ALIEN IDEAS

THEY WEREN'T SET up to work on the alien ship. The D-R could take asteroid samples, but it wasn't designed to dig up artifacts. Flynn and To'afa were disbelieving at first, but after they'd gone out and seen the thing for themselves, they were both anxious to return to Titan and organize a work party.

"We'll have to bring all the scientists we can get from Titan. They're going to strain their brains trying to get this into their minds," the little man said.

Adam nodded. "The Council may not want to let them go, but I can't see any scientist turning down the chance to work on an alien ship."

Flynn continued. "We should go out there and dig a bit. Maybe we can find the hatch."

That wasn't feasible. The ship was partly buried in ice and rocks so that only the bow was showing. Who knew how deep they'd have to go or how much material would need to be moved to reach an access point? Who knew if the strange thing even had a hatch?

Maybe the crew beamed through the hull with some kind of matter transporter.

Adam started to answer, then paused. That front antenna thingy kept reminding him of something. He mentally shrugged, then said, "I want to dig as much as you do, but two things: First, we don't have so much as a garden shovel on this ship, and second, our suits aren't up to the task of keeping us warm. We'll need special insulation and heating circuits."

Flynn replied, "Can't we use the mining lasers. I can unlock one from their battle mount and we can..." He stopped, visualizing the result.

Adam answered the unspoken suggestion. "We could try, but do you really want to risk hitting the ship? It might have some essential structure buried just under the surface exactly where we don't expect it to be. It is an alien vessel and they might not conform to our idea of good ship design."

Flynn looked down. "I knew that, but it's the biggest thing humans have found, or the most important. Take your pick."

"I agree. That's exactly why we need to prepare and do it right. There's one other thing we need to do."

"What's that?"

"We've got to treat this discovery with top secrecy. We don't want the Earthers finding out about it."

Flynn snorted. "Those greedy Feds would want in on it, all right. No, more likely they'd want it all. We'd have another battle out here, and this one would make the Bubble look like kindergarten recess."

THE DIRE RHEA had no trouble boosting itself out of the gravity well. Eris was now receding as they headed directly for Saturn. Adam had considered taking a roundabout course, but the chance of someone tracking the ship was small. The nano-carbon coating had been re-applied to the hull, making it almost impossible to see unless the ship occluded a distant star or asteroid that someone was watching.

The voyage back would take four weeks. That seemed like an extremely long time to Adam. On the way out, he'd been excited about the prospect of going boldly where no man had gone before. He snorted at that thought. After all this time away from Earth, he couldn't resist referring to the culture.

Now that the excitement was over, he suddenly decided that Flynn needed to take alterday with To'afa as second. There was no need to give Nile more command time.

She listened to the idea then nodded. "That would suit me just fine. I'm getting tired of only seeing you in snatches as we change shifts."

Alterday couldn't come soon enough after that. The two practically skipped off the bridge as they headed for the Captain's cabin.

ADAM WOKE OUT of the best sleep he'd had for weeks. Nile's back made a pleasant warm spot against his. He was reluctant to open his eyes, but something was nibbling around the edges of his mind.

It was something in the shape of that conical antenna on the alien ship. If it was hooked up to the cable mesh that wrapped around the hull...That was it! It wasn't an antenna, it was some kind of a scoop for the space drive. It had to be.

He sat upright, thinking, not noticing that he had pulled the covers off her.

She rolled over shivering and pushed at his back.

"Hey! Don't freeze me. What is it?"

He turned and pulled the covers partly over her, but continued sitting, looking at the wall.

"Uhh, I had a thought. About the alien ship. I think I understand a little about how the space drive has to work." He paused for a moment. "But then, maybe I'm just crazy. I don't know."

She sighed and rearranged the disorganized covers, pulling them up to her chin.

"Cold in here, you idiot. Get under the covers and snuggle up to me, then tell me about it. No sense being uncomfortable while you come up with a brilliant idea."

"I don't know if it's brilliant or not, but it seems to make some sense."

He slid under the covers as she'd instructed, then tried to think about how he would explain his insight. He paused so long that she grew impatient and poked his stomach.

"Ow! Hey, that's not nice. I'm thinking."

"Oh. I thought you'd gone to sleep on me. Tell me what you're thinking about."

"The cone was distorted from the crash, and it was also broken loose from the ship. We didn't look carefully, because we were both getting cold. I wonder if we had looked, would we have noticed if that web of cabling grafted onto the hull was connected to the base of the cone."

"Makes sense to me, so then, what?"

"I think now that it generated a scoop field of some sort. It would probably have to be large to function effectively, so that means that the physical structure we saw wouldn't be the actual working part. It had to be a magnetic field. If it were, it would funnel charged particles to the cone's tip."

She pushed her face against his shoulder. "Charged particles in the tip. Mmmm."

He twisted to look at her face. Was she making fun of him? No, she seemed serious and attentive.

"Okay. You're listening. I wasn't sure. The web must transmit the charged particles across the surface of the ship to something we can't see. It's buried, probably."

Nile rearranged her arm. "Well, yeah. That's obvious. The cables have to attach to the engine at the other end of the ship. Want to bet?"

He shook his head. "No. No, that's what I think, too, but I can't figure out why the cables go outside the ship and not inside." He paused, then slowly added, "Unless…"

"What? Unless what?"

"Maybe, and I'm just speculating here, the cables generate some kind of field that either acts in concert with the drive or maybe works like our plasma shield. I can't figure that out."

She leaned back, sweeping her hair out of her eyes as she moved. "Maybe we should have tried to excavate the hull. We could have figured out some way to move the ice it's in."

"There was too much risk of damaging the wreck. We need to uncover the hull as carefully as possible. We might unknowingly damage a critical part and never be able to figure out how it works because of that."

"I guess you're right, but it would have answered some of our questions. Knowing what's under there, I mean."

He shrugged. "Maybe, but the funnel must have created a collection field, and it could collect dust particles." He shook his head negatively. They're too sparse in interstellar space unless they stored them somewhere, but the hull is too small to store a bunch of dust for ejection mass."

Nile yawned. "C'mon, either have a smart idea or let's go back to sleep."

Adam smiled down at her. She was a cute bundle of warmth against his side. Deadly, too. He shook his head slightly, marveling that she wanted him.

"Uhh. Okay. A smart idea. Here's what has been rattling around in my head for a while. The funnel field collects virtual particles, sort of the way the Em-Max does, but more efficiently. No one is completely sure. The Em-Max doesn't eject any measurable particles, but it still creates thrust, so it must eject virtual particles.

I think the virtual particles that it encounters are accelerated by the waves bouncing back and forth inside the resonant chamber. Then they are shoved away, giving the ship a bit of momentum as they are."

She yawned again. "Then what? You've told me that before."

"But, the funnel field could capture many more virtual particles. It could provide a continuous stream of the things to whatever device is located at the rear of the hull. It could be shooting a fire hose stream of virtual ejection mass for all we know. That would be enough to give it a bunch of acceleration."

Nile snickered. "Some mathematician you are. How do you quantify a bunch?"

He grinned. "It's a 'Handful' cubed. Cube a 'Bunch' and you get a 'Lot.'"

Nile lifted her head. "Alright, Adam. Now you're just wasting time. I'm going to sleep. Turn out the light or suffer the consequences."

"What are the consequences?"

She grabbed him and pulled his head down for a kiss. It lasted for somewhere between a Handful and a Bunch.

He turned out the light, then lay quietly, listening to her steady breathing as he thought about virtual particles.

4

TITAN BASE

THE D-R'S NANO-CARBON coated hull rested on a docking frame looking like a strangely shaped shadow in the reflected light from Saturn. The base was on the side of Titan that was currently facing the massive ringed planet.

Adam was conferring with some scientists and two of the Council members. The news of their find on Eris had struck the colony like an earthquake, or rather, a Titan-quake. It was the primary subject of discussion, even eclipsing speculation on what the Feds were currently plotting.

Lars Nielson was the ranking Council member of the two, and he was causing no end of trouble as far as Adam was concerned. He hadn't wanted Adam to waste time exploring the Kuiper belt, and he was frankly disbelieving about the alien space ship.

"Admiral, there's no possible way that an alien race could be so advanced that they could reach our solar system, then abandon a ship. I'm convinced that you were mistaken. It was just some odd-shaped piece of meteoroid you found. Probably drifted out there to...what was it? Oh, yes. Erin. Probably drifted out there from the asteroid belt. Maybe it was some piece of space junk the old United States launched, but it couldn't have been alien."

The man didn't even know where Adam had been. He grinned silently and restrained himself. It would only irritate Nielson if he pointed out that he'd been to Eris. There was no planet named Erin.

The bearded scientist, Miguel Acosta, stroked his beard silently, then interjected, "I beg to differ Mr. Nielson. The pictures they brought back definitely show that they discovered a ship. It might not be alien. We won't know until we get inside. It could be something from the past, but that's dubious. I've checked the archival records from the pre-dissolution period. None of the private companies launched anything like that, nor did any of the governments." He paused, then added, "At least so far as we know."

Lars responded, "Yes, but that is only so far. There were secret launches. It might be one of ours."

This was progress as far as Adam was concerned. He'd thought that Nielson was stuck on the meteoroid theory. Now he tacitly agreed that the object was a spaceship of some sort.

Adam said, "I assure you that it's a spaceship. As for human, no. We've never had the technology that is implied by the structure of the odd cable mesh on the hull surface."

Nielson interrupted him. "It doesn't matter! What matters is that the North American Dictatorship or the Queendom, or whatever they're calling themselves today, is progressing in their war on the Non-Aligns. Once they've reduced their opposition to a pulp, I can assure you that we will be next on the list."

The other Council member said, "We have to be prepared, but Admiral Maxwell's orders are being followed. The airdocks are full, and we're making additional ships as quickly as possible. I'd feel better if they weren't all so small. I think we should make some bigger ones, you know, the size of the biggest Earther ships."

She was a woman named? Adam tried to generate it, then came up with Mary Snelling. He wasn't sure about that, so he didn't answer immediately. That was a good strategy because Nielson responded.

"Mary, you know that we can't compete with them in terms of manufacturing capacity. They've got the wealth of over half the planet and millions of workers. All we've got is three airdocks and barely enough men to run them two shifts out of three."

Adam nodded at the woman. "Councilwoman, I've emphasized before that our advantage lies in the technology, not the size, of our ships. The USSN still has not emulated our plasma boosters. They can't match us in maneuverability or acceleration. They might have adopted our shield system, but theirs is not as good."

He intentionally avoided mentioning the design flaw that had been incorporated into the plasma shield generator they had allowed the Feds to acquire. The Earther engineers may have figured it out by now or not.

If they hadn't, the USSN was in for a shock when the Belters sent the disabling signal that caused the Navy shields to drop at a critical moment. If they had, well, he wasn't going to rely on the trick working a second time. It had been spectacular at the Battle of the Bubble, though.

He continued. "Besides, they have been testing their plasma weapons. Our sources have reported that they are only getting about one third the destructive effect of our cannons. I don't think they've figured out exactly how to use the Em-Max effect to boost the plasma's speed. We'll be okay unless they come up with something else."

She wasn't convinced. "But, they could, you know. They could come up with something that you, uh, we haven't anticipated. What would we do then?"

"True, they might, but that's why I'm not going to match their fleet piece for piece. There's no way we want to engage in a set battle. We're going to rely on our speed and engage in asymmetrical attacks. Hit and run, so to speak."

He held up his hand, palm outward, trying to block Nielson's next statement.

"Councilman, if you'd let me finish. That is why we need to salvage the hulk on Eris. That find is potentially the biggest discovery humankind has ever made. Those people traveled between the stars. That's something we can only dream about with our technology. We've just come out of the house and are exploring our own backyard. They've traveled, not only to the next city but to the next continent. Even farther probably. We don't know where they are from. They could be friendly, they could be extinct, they could be deadly enemies, but their ship will hold clues to technology that we may never find on our own. We've got to get it."

Acosta nodded vigorously. "This is true. We need funding for a mission. It will take at least three mining ships, and there needs to be a lot of special equipment. We'll have to excavate the ship carefully. Then we'll have to figure out how to enter. That might be a big problem by itself. For example, I can envision passages that are too small for humans. We'll need robots to explore inside, at least at first."

Nielson shook his head. "I still think we need to spend all our effort on countering the Queen's Navy."

Adam decided that he'd had enough. "Mr. Nielson, if we can get our hands on alien technology, we might not have anything to fear from the Earthers. They won't have a chance. We've got to send this mission out. I expect it to be organized and to leave within three weeks."

Nielson looked shocked. It was true that Adam had the authority to demand anything he needed for defense, but this was encroaching into the Council's power. He started to speak, but Adam spoke first.

"Besides, I've already got an idea from my inspection of the alien ship. I'll be engaging in space trials of a new device within three days. It could make a huge strategic difference for us."

Everyone in the room suddenly seemed to want to talk at once.

He held up his hand again. "No, don't bother asking. I'm not going to tell you what it is yet."

Adam turned and left. Like all meetings, this one had been mostly a waste of time. He should have just ordered the Council to send the mission, rather than trying to play nice and convince them. Sure, they could refuse, but he'd found that the threat of his retirement, of not having their winning Admiral in charge of their defense, was enough to generate massive pressure on the Council. They'd roll over in such a case.

5

A NEW DRIVE

THE IDEA THAT Adam had been working on seemed to be a logical advance based on the technology he had already developed. The funnel-shaped magnetic field was somewhat fidgety, but given that it took a considerable amount of power to start, running it took surprisingly little energy.

Once the field was in place, the metallic basket that served as the generating antenna began to act almost like a super-conductor. As such, it took little electricity to keep the field in place. Adam had a suspicion that it wouldn't work so well if it were closer to the Sun. That suspicion extended to areas nearer the intense magnetic fields of Saturn, but whether it was justified remained to be seen.

To'afa was working on the cables that surrounded the D-R's hull. The poor ship, never pretty at best, now looked like it had been caught in some kind of diabolical trap. Between the plasma generator mounts and the cables, it sported an interesting texture from a distance.

The cables were uninsulated heavy copper and were mounted on carbon fiber stand-offs that were twenty centimeters in length. It took them some time to get the wires stretched tightly so that they wouldn't contact the ship.

To'afa had proven invaluable. The big man usually pretended to be slow, but he was a wealth of ideas.

"Look, Captain, the ship normally doesn't change directions or accelerate hard enough to make these wires move, but if we had a nearby missile burst, the shock could bounce the cabling against the hull. Don't think that would be good. Do you think it would hurt anything?"

Adam nodded thoughtfully inside his spacesuit helmet. "The D-R could take electric discharge with no problem. The plasma generators are isolated as are the cannons and boosters. It might cause some of the sensors to screw up, though. The real problem is, if that happens, the mag field will go down, and it'll take all the power plant's output to get it running again. We can't afford that, especially in a battle situation. I really don't want to insulate the cables. The aliens didn't do that so neither should we, although I can't exactly say what the effect would be."

"How about we lay down strips of insulation and bond them to the hull below the cables. That way, if there is a shock that would drive the cable against the hull, it'll hit the insulation. Should fix it, huh?"

It did fix it. It was a good idea, although it took extra work and time. Adam was unhappy about the time they were spending. Sooner or later, the Council would want to see what he was doing, and he wanted to be able to present them with a finished product, not just some odd-looking wires that made the ship look worse than usual.

The major problem they had was figuring out how to route what he thought were the virtual particles that would be captured in the field into the Em-Max. Due to internal heat, the system couldn't come inside the ship. It was too warm there. The plasma boosters were conveniently mounted on the hull, though.

It took them a day to remove the plasma generator from one of the boosters and design a magnetic accelerator that would fire whatever virtual particles were captured into the end of the booster's small Em-Max unit. This was the part that required a leap of faith. As far as Adam knew, there was no way to calculate the efficiency the system would have.

Replacing the plasma generator with the magnetic field funnel might be a total waste if the device didn't deliver more particles to the Em-Max than the generator did. Somehow, Adam thought it would, but that remained to be seen.

They were ready to test the rig on the eighth day. They'd been floating with no propulsion about ten seconds light out from Saturn in the direction of Uranus. Sol wasn't visible simply because they'd positioned themselves so that Saturn occluded the Sun and, as it so happened, Earth.

That wasn't accidental. Adam wanted no possibility of his experiment to get back to the Earth government. He needed something to keep the Belters comfortably ahead of the USSN. This might be it, so he needed it to be secret.

THE D-R ACCELERATED, outbound on a vector that would pass Uranus at a safe distance. Everyone was clustered on the bridge, watching the vidscreen as Adam prepared to activate the field system.

They were moving quickly, having been accelerating for a full shift.

He looked around, his eyes lingering on Nile's face, then said, "I don't know what's going to happen, but we'd best be prepared. Get strapped in. I'm switching it on in ten."

Just before he issued the command to the comp, he checked. The other three were belted in tightly, their faces betraying a certain amount of anxiety. Adam felt the same way. There was no way of telling what the effect would be. The device he'd built might do nothing, rather than give them extra acceleration. If it malfunctioned, it might burn through the hull. Now that was unlikely, but it worried him.

He shook himself. He could sit here worrying about a million low probability outcomes and never turn the thing on. His hand convulsed and activated the touch screen. The comp obediently displayed a green button adjacent to a matching red one.

Flynn had programmed that display. Touch the green spot, and the system came on. The red one, of course, meant stop.

He waited for a second, then flicked his index finger out to the green patch.

The ship shook a little. That was simply the booster Em-Max adding to the thrust. Without the plasma serving as reaction mass, the effect was small. Then the lights dimmed. The field was building, and that took almost all the power plant's output. Non-essential systems switch to stand-by as the ship's built-in controllers rerouted electric power.

The lights stayed dim, but nothing happened. Adam took several deep breaths, waiting, then turned his head and said, "Looks like this is a bust."

Almost as if his words had been the signal, the lights brightened again. The field was in place and no longer needed as much power.

Everyone looked at the vidscreen. The adjacent monitor showed only the Em-Max's normal gentle acceleration.

Flynn swore under his breath, as did Nile.

To'afa said, "Wait. Look at the acceleration. It's going up. The field is feeding something to the booster. We've got reaction mass!"

It was true. The D-R was starting to move more quickly. However, the effect was still disappointing. The booster would have generated more thrust with the plasma generator. The mag field was working, but not...no wait.

Adam tried to figure out what was happening. Their acceleration was increasing exponentially. Suddenly it was clear.

He said, "The thing works more efficiently, the faster we're moving. Not too good when we're slow, but look at what's happening now." He thought for a moment, then added, "Maybe we have to store a bunch of particles to initially kick us up to speed."

Based on the effect, the mag field was funneling far more reaction mass to the Em-Max than the plasma generation system, and the amount increased every second.

To'afa ran a quick comp, then said, "We're doubling every three-point two seven seconds."

Flynn kicked his heels against the deck in excitement. "That means we're going to be the fastest thing in the solar system."

Adam agreed. "Yes, but it also means we're going to be able to visit other stars."

Nile was seated beside him, her eyes wide and lips drawn back in a grimace. She reached for his hand, but her arm fell back. "Adam, this acceleration is generating a lot more force than we're used to."

The force had increased gradually and so smoothly that it seemed like nothing, but it was doubling every couple of seconds. It had passed one g a few seconds ago. Now it was past four and closing in on five. Adam's finger reached for the red spot, but his hand felt like it was being pulled back. He lunged forward and touched the touch screen. The lights flickered, and the acceleration ceased at that instant.

To'afa made an alarmed grunt, causing Adam to look at him. To'afa pointed at the vidscreen without saying anything. The screen had been darkened and was set to track the Sun. There was a tiny point of light showing in the center, but that was all.

"Flynn, where are we?" Adam asked.

The small man queried the sensor suite, then swore.

"By a drunken miner's short hairs! We're just about in the Oort!"

Adam almost panicked. Coasting at this speed, they'd shortly be so far out that they wouldn't be able to return in a year. They would have to use the experimental drive again. Only this time, it would be difficult. Missing Saturn's orbit was a distinct possibility.

"Wow! We'd better turn her around and boost back. If we don't use the new drive, we'll continue outward until the Em-Max plasma engines slow us down and reverse our course. I have no idea how long I let that thing run. Anyone happen to time it?"

Flynn was looking at the sensor suite, his mouth hanging open. "Captain, unless this thing's gone crazy, we're moving at an eighth light. That's impossible."

Adam turned to the comp. A series of calculations gave him the answer. The new drive had been on for eighteen point three seconds. He keyed in their location, estimated the distance, added their outbound velocity, and let the comp crunch. The answer was eleven-point fifty-four seconds.

"Flynn, you code in a timer so that the system shuts off automatically. Set it for eleven-point fifty-four seconds according to the comp. The engine was on for eighteen-point three seconds before I shut it down. This is going to be tricky. We can't use this thing randomly. It amounts to a blithering hyperdrive. It's got to be carefully controlled, or we'll overshoot."

The maneuvering jets rotated the D-R. It was now moving backward at a velocity that would take weeks to attain using the conventional Em-Max.

Adam watched as Flynn set up the timer. It took several seconds, but that couldn't be helped. He didn't trust himself to shut the thing down manually again.

Flynn glanced at him and said, "She's ready."

He tentatively reached out, then touched the green spot on the screen. The g force built up rapidly.

Flynn was watching the sensors, and after what seemed like hours, he said, "We're moving back in. We've shed our outbound velocity. Now we're accelerating towards home."

The engine continued to fire, and they accelerated towards Saturn like a mad comet on its run towards the Sun.

The lights flickered as the experimental drive abruptly clicked off.

"Quick, Flynn. What do the sensors say?"

"We're...ah...we're at the inner edge of the Kuiper. Moving fast, but not as fast as before. Let me use the comp for a minute."

Flynn's fingers flew over the keyboard for a few seconds, then the display showed the solution. The Irishman looked at Adam and said, "If we coast from here, we've got four hours and change before we need to start slowing down. Otherwise, we'll go right past and have to turn around to get back to where we started."

Adam answered, "Okay. Let's alter course to bring us back to Titan. Set up the nav comp to fire the regular engines and boosters at the right point to slow us enough for orbital insertion. I'm going to get something to eat, then I'm going to my cabin to think this out. We've got something fantastically important here, but we're going to have to figure out how to use it without killing ourselves."

He stood and headed for the exit. Nile hesitated, then followed him.

6

MARS AND WAR

IT HAD TAKEN them seven days longer to return to Titan than it should have. The thrust generated by the funnel system was ridiculously high and fine-tuning it with the D-R's comp was apparently beyond their abilities. Adam had been forced to return to Saturn from a spot nearly within Jupiter's orbit.

The Council's secretary had informed Adam that he was urgently needed. One of the mining ships had called in. It was still stopping at Mars, using the excuse that its crew had not participated in the defeat of the USSN at the Bubble. They were bringing a small delegation from the red planet.

The Martians had suffered tremendously from the Feds' defeat. The North American government had first focused inward to suppress internal dissent and then began fighting with various of the non-aligned countries. The lack of ships resulting from the USSN's massive losses and the wartime requirements for supplies meant that the Martian colony fell into the lowest priority for the government. Supplies had dwindled, and the supply ships had almost stopped coming. It hadn't helped that the Belter Pirates had grabbed some of the supply ships for themselves.

ONCE BACK ON Titan, Adam and Nile returned to their two-room apartment. Although small, it still represented tremendous luxury compared to the banks of hammocks in which most of the population slept. It was one of the nicer perks of being the winning commander of the first-ever space battle.

Nancy, the Council's executive secretary, gave them twelve hours to rest and clean up before they were to appear in the Council chambers. They were making the most of the resting aspect. The voyage had been exhausting. There hadn't been much physical labor, although there had been enough, but the stress of using the new drive had taken its toll.

Adam realized that he exhibited a distracted air. It couldn't be helped. He was trying to figure out how to control a ship that was equipped with the drive. It had become apparent that the acceleration was not going to be a smooth geometric curve. The virtual particles picked up by the field and funneled to the drive weren't evenly distributed. Instead, they came in patches of varying density.

When they passed through a dense patch, the drive kicked them in the rear. When they moved through a sparse spot, it slacked off, often appearing to coast. The density couldn't be predicted in advance, so it seemed to be impossible to comp a data-set that would signal precisely when to shut the thing off so they could coast up to their destination at a manageable velocity.

The problem remained with him, and he found himself failing to respond to Nile's attempts at conversation at inopportune times. He also walked past their apartment without noticing where he was. He would have continued walking had not Nile snagged his arm and pulled him back.

"Hey, big guy. You've got to get your head together. We've got a few hours, and then you're going to have to perform like the Pirate I saw on Swift base. The Council depends on you to lead the negotiations. You're the only one who has a negotiating history with the Martians, and Citizen Oliver has asked for you specifically," she said.

That got his attention. "Oliver? That unctuous politician. He can't be trusted any farther than he could be thrown in a high g field."

She replied, "Yeah. I know. That is to say, he can't be trusted at all. You're going to have to be sharp, so quit thinking about that damned drive, take a shower, and let's get some rest. I'm exhausted after that voyage, and I know you are also."

He grudgingly let her convince him. An hour later, he awoke with the realization that he was looking at the problem backward. Instead of trying to calculate when the drive should be shut down based on how long it had been running, it might be more useful to try to figure how far the ship was from its intended destination and integrate that information with the instantaneous velocity. The calculations were well within the comp's capabilities. They would have to run the calcs continuously since the acceleration varied so radically, but if this approach worked, it would solve the problem.

He rolled over and leaned against Nile's warm back. The mental breakthrough allowed him to relax, and he fell into a deep sleep. The first he'd had for days.

THE ALARM RANG, and Adam grunted. Nile, who was always able to jump right up as a result of her military training, popped out of bed, shut it off, and disappeared into the small bathroom.

He stretched, then rolled over and got up with a groan. He'd been in bed longer than average, and his back muscles were tight and painful. He stretched again, then limped to the bath.

It was hot and steamy inside. The recirculation fan was working overtime to dehumidify the air. Humidity was strictly controlled, not because water was in short supply, it wasn't, but because it might corrode something that it shouldn't. There was plenty of water available since the Belters had been capturing chunks of ice and dropping them on the surface.

Nile had turned off the shower and was squeezing the last drops of water out of her short hair. Adam grinned. His hair was three times as long as hers. She felt more comfortable with short hair, probably due to her history. He really didn't care about his, but keeping it long fit the image he wanted to project—that of a blood-thirsty Pirate.

She slipped past him, fending off the half-hearted grab he made.

"No time now, buster. Besides we did that before we went to sleep."

"We've got time." He reached again.

"No. we don't. No! Now, I'm serious. Get showered and dressed. We need to be there early."

He sighed and turned the water on.

CITIZEN OLIVER HAD aged, and he was worried. Those were the first things that popped into Adam's mind when he looked at the man. Oliver had previously radiated self-confidence, and he'd looked healthy. The man sitting on the other side of the table was ten kilos lighter, and his skin sagged. When one added the stress-caused wrinkles between his eyes and the dark circles below them, it was almost enough to make Adam feel sorry for the envoy.

Oliver rose slightly and performed a perfunctory bow as Adam sat.

"Mr. Maxwell."

Adam acknowledged the greeting with a nod of his head.

"Citizen. What brings you all the way out here?"

Oliver apparently thought they had some connection from their previous meetings.

"It's good to see you, Maxwell." He stopped, apparently just noticing the eye patch. His eyes focused on it for a moment, then he looked down.

He'd seen it before, but perhaps he'd forgotten.

Adam said, "The Council asked me to attend this meeting since I'm the one in charge of defense for the Belter community."

The head of the Belter delegation cleared his throat in an attempt to get their attention. Adam glanced. It was Nielson. That was unfortunate. The man always seemed to wind up opposing Adam's positions. He'd never figured out whether it was due to a principled stand, or only animosity for Adam himself.

He sighed slightly. It would be better if they presented a united front to the Martians, although it would probably fail if Nielson acted as usual.

"Councilman Nielson, Citizen Oliver and I have met several times in the past at Swift base on Deimos. So, in a sense, we're old friends."

Nielson gave him an appraising glance, smiled somewhat nervously, then said, "Admiral Maxwell, while you were away, the Council structure changed slightly. I'm now the ranking member and chair."

Adam shrugged slightly, then thought better of it. "Congratulations, Lars. It's nice to know that the Council is in good hands."

Oliver, not to be left out, interjected, "Yes. Yes, it is. The Mars Council is pleased that your government has agreed to meet with us. We have reconsidered our previous position and would like to discuss a possible agreement with your group."

Adam leaned forward. That was interesting. Chasing the Earthers out of the Belt had seemingly given the Martians a reason to reconsider their Earth alliance.

Nielson nodded, and Oliver continued.

"The North American government has become too busy defending itself, and the Mars colony has fallen in importance to them. The new Queen believes that there is no promise in the Martian terraforming project and they've stopped sending us supplies and personnel."

Oliver spread his hands, palms up in a gesture of futility.

He continued. "We are at a critical juncture in our existence. We are almost self-sufficient, but the cessation of supply shipments threatens our ability to get over that final hump. If we do not find help, our scientists say we have five months before we will not be able to provide food for all the colonists, and that's if we reduce ration sizes to the minimum caloric content to keep people working."

Adam grunted. "That's bad. You folks are in trouble."

Oliver nodded. "I realize that we parted on less than amicable terms before, but the situation has changed for us. We now understand that we colonists, we spacers, have to stick together. The outer solar system, Mars, Titan, the asteroid belt isn't man's natural environment. It can only be conquered if we cooperate."

Adam nodded. "Yes, even something as close to Earth as the moon is a harsh mistress."

He mentally kicked himself. He just couldn't resist the impulse to be silly at the worst times. Fortunately, neither Nielson nor Oliver seemed to notice the reference.

Oliver nodded and said, "Yes. That's correct. The people on Luna should be more on our side than they are, but they're almost all military, and they rotate down to Earth often. We can't do that, so, naturally, we develop our own loyalties."

He looked at Nielson with an expression of appeal. "Councilman, I'm here because Mars is desperate. We need your help. We were afraid of losing Earth's support before, so we rejected your proposal to work together.

As it happened, Earth pulled their support anyway. We now realize that they'll never be reliable. We have to become self-supporting. For us to do that alone is impossible. We need too many things. We're prepared to sign a trade agreement with you that will hopefully be mutually beneficial."

Adam asked, "What sorts of things do you need us to provide, Citizen?"

Oliver didn't hesitate. "You offered to provide us with water ice before. We'd like to trade for that, and metal stock. I understand that you folks have started your own smelters and are manufacturing steel and other alloys. We need those, along with electronics, and any new technology you've developed."

Adam nodded. Now it came out. The Martians knew about the plasma shield technology. Earth hadn't given it to them, so they were hoping they could talk the Belters into turning it over. It was doubtful that Mars had anything that the Belt needed now. Previously, Mars had seemed like an oasis full of growing foodstuffs, but that was due to the shipments from Earth. Now that the Belter's farms were producing, the likelihood was that Mars would need their products, rather than the other way around.

The technology issue was a foregone conclusion. He'd made the decision that he couldn't withhold the plasma shield for humanitarian reasons, although it seemed out of character for an acknowledged Pirate to feel that way. On the other hand, the new weapons technology, the plasma drive, and most certainly the newly discovered hyperdrive as he'd taken to calling it, were things the Martians didn't need.

He could support providing them with the plasma shield so that they could protect themselves against radiation. Giving them faster spaceships and state-of-the-art weapons would simply mean that there would be two powers besides Earth. Things were complicated and dangerous enough with Earth opposed to their fledgling attempt to establish themselves as an independent and free entity. Adding a third party to the mix would definitely be a bad idea.

He smiled. Oliver was in for a bit of a shock. He started to speak, but Nielson chose that precise moment to assert his importance.

"Citizen Oliver, what you propose is totally unacceptable. Your Council refused to aid us when we most needed assistance. You asserted your loyalty to Earth, specifically to the North American government, then the Dictatorship. Now that the Queen has dumped you, you choose to come to us, hoping that we'll make up the slack and provide you with luxuries."

Oliver opened his mouth in protest, but Adam forestalled him.

"Councilman, I think you've made your point. Indeed, Mars wasn't in a position to help previously. When I last parted from them, it was apparent that Earth was applying all the leverage it could exert to coerce them. If things had been different, I fully believe they would have helped us. For that reason, I think we should work out an agreement to help them."

Nielson flushed. "No, Maxwell. I've made up my mind. They don't deserve our help."

This was irritating. Nielson was following his previous pattern perfectly.

"Look, Councilman, I understand your position. The Belter community has struggled to provide for itself, but now we're gradually becoming self-sufficient. We have plenty of water ice and the means to get it to Mars. We also have more than enough iron ore along with other metals. Our smelters are cranking out more bar stock than we currently require for ship-building and for habitat construction. There's no reason we cannot trade some of our surpluses to our fellow humans."

Nielson shook his head. "No. They don't have anything to trade in return. How will that work? He says they won't be able to feed themselves. Are we to give them all our food too?"

"In fact, Mars does have something we need. They have excess population. We need willing workers."

Adam could see that Nielson wasn't really listening. He was obviously thinking of his next rebuttal point.

"Councilman, think this over. We're a tiny community. Even if all the mining ships came together and joined us, we number less than two thousand people. There are, what? Forty or fifty-thousand people on Mars. From the standpoint of the genetic pool alone, we need to merge our populations. Otherwise, our children's children will come close to fitting the old definition of a redneck. Their family tree will be closer to a straight line than not."

Nielson started to say something, but then stopped. Adam had made a good point.

Sensing an advantage, Adam continued. "Lars, let's look at this from a different perspective. You represent the Belters in the form of the Council. Now the Council doesn't really dictate to the rest of the group. You know that."

He looked at Oliver. "The miners are too independent to take much by way of orders. They cooperate because they see the necessity, but they'd balk if the Council started ordering them around."

He turned back to Nielson. "That goes for our navy also, Councilman. They follow my orders. You needed my lead to win at the Bubble. The rest of the defense force is committed to me, not the Council. Now, I'm not threatening you, so don't get your hackles up, but what I am saying is that it's my personal and professional opinion that we need to help Mars. We need to help them now because our long term goal should be to incorporate Mars into our group."

Nielson said, "Well, the genetic pool idea is something I hadn't thought of. More workers would be good, too. We're behind on domicile construction, even though we've got plenty of materials. You're correct in that there aren't enough workers."

He had been looking at Oliver, but now he looked directly at Adam, and there was a glint in his eyes that betokened further conflict. "I do have to let you know, Admiral, that your position and the associated title is honorary. If Earth keeps its current focus and leaves us alone, I can't see that we'll need much of a defensive force."

That was it, then. Nielson thought he'd simply dump the informal Belter navy.

"You're well within your rights to withdraw any title you've bestowed on me, Nielson. I don't care about that. What you're forgetting is that I'm a Pirate. All the miners are basically Pirates, too, and they follow me. So do a majority of your fellows on Titan and in the other habitats. They don't expect me to order them around and I won't until it's absolutely necessary, but they do respect my judgment. If you want me gone, I'm happy to oblige. Then you can see how far the Council control extends."

The Councilman paled slightly. "That's... that's...uh..." He swallowed, and his cheeks flushed.

Adam couldn't tell if it was anger or embarrassment. His next action showed that it was the latter.

Nielson looked apologetically at Oliver. "Well, you see how it is. We don't always agree on ways and means out here, but we still find a way to cooperate. I've considered your proposal and Admiral Maxwell's input. I'm prepared to...uh, go to the full Council and recommend that we develop a working arrangement with Mars. We'll go slowly. If it works out, we can expand our aid. If we feel we're being taken advantage of, we will terminate the agreement. Understood?"

He finished up with an almost belligerent tone. He'd apparently regained some of his attitude during his speech.

There was one more thing. The plasma shield. Adam said, "Citizen, I've got some schematics for you. I made a decision some time ago that the plasma radiation shield that I developed had to be distributed to all spacers. It's the only proper course of action. There are drawbacks to that strategy, though. We leaked the invention to Earth, and they used it against us during the first conflict. We still won."

Oliver nodded and said, "You somehow surpassed them in weapons development, and that made up for the difference in force strength." He had obviously studied the battle.

Adam nodded in agreement, then continued. "We'll give you the shield technology, even though Earth did not see fit to pass it on to you. We won't give you our weapons tech, though. We're currently ahead of Earth, although I'm sure they're working overtime to catch up on that. If we give it to you, I'm afraid that there will be too great a chance of it eventually filtering its way to Earth. Your population is too large to vet thoroughly."

Oliver shrugged apologetically, his eyes gleaming. "I fully understand. That's just the way it is. We've never been allowed to check the colonists closely enough to tell if any are spies. However, we're grateful for the shielding." He looked around the table, then continued. "If I could ask a personal favor, would you consider installing the shield tech on our courier ship? I'd like to avoid any additional radiation exposure. Coming out here exposed me to far more radiation than I feel comfortable with."

Adam laughed. "I'll make sure that the plasma generators are installed on your ship. You won't have to worry about the radiation issue, and you'll find that the shield works well against space junk, meteoroids, and dust. It'll keep your hull intact unless you're hit with something really massive."

NIELSON LEFT TO attend the afternoon Council meeting, and Oliver headed for his ship, stating that he had to send a message to the Mars Council.

Nile had remained sitting against the wall throughout the meeting. Now she asked, "Do you really believe we can make our own civilization out here?"

That was a good question. Did he? He thought it over for a moment. Then a vision opened before him. It was satisfying. Humans could live in the Belt and on many of the moons. The total land area was far smaller than Earth, and their population would never equal that of the home planet, but they could survive and build their own lives. It was going to be up to him to ensure that they avoided the ancient trap of government and force that humans had always suffered under.

He turned to Nile. "I'm hungry. Let's go get some food. Yes, I think we can do it. Have our own civilization, I mean. I want it to be as free as possible. The old US Constitution was an imperfect vehicle, but the older document, the Declaration of Independence, affirms the right to fight for freedom. Maybe we can go that one better and come up with a means of living together that ensures liberty without coercion. We have to cooperate because of the environment. That's challenge enough. We don't need to be forced by some Council or government. Especially one that has no idea what's going on at the extreme distances we have and what local actions are required to ensure survival."

She looked up at him. "I hope you're right. If you think it can be done, I'm right here beside you, and I'll give it my best. It's worth working for. That's for sure, but I've got to tell you that you're going to have your hands full. There will be so many nay-sayers for every point you propose that it will seem like everyone is against personal freedom."

Lunch was a let-down. Adam had somehow lost his appetite.

THE INTERNAL DISSENT in the North American Dictatorship flared up again, and this time it was worse. The Belters heard about it from the ships that were monitoring the developments on Luna.

There was open revolution in many cities, and the military had been called in to suppress the population. The military suppression wasn't done with a light hand. According to some estimates, as much as twenty percent of the North American civilian population had been liquidated by direct conflict, mass executions, or by starvation.

It was terrible and getting worse. The Non-Aligns, the countries that were attempting to maintain their independence, saw an opportunity and began a series of attacks that rapidly escalated into a global conflict. Queen Elseth responded with space-based assaults on the opposition. Cities were subject to railgun barrage, and in some cases, the USSN dropped a few KEWs. Those did far more damage than a twenty-kilo railgun slug. Rio had been decimated by a massive KEW.

The only restraint displayed by the Dictatorship was that Elseth had not yet resorted to nuclear weapons. Of course, that was probably because the use of atomics wasn't essential. A large KEW could create an equivalent amount of devastation.

From the Belters' viewpoint, it was a mixed blessing. On the one hand, everyone hoped the Dictatorship would fall and that the Earthers would leave the Belter community, including Mars, alone for the foreseeable future. On the other hand, it looked as if things were getting out of control. No one would benefit if Earth was allowed to commit suicide, and the population was reduced to a fraction of its former size.

The situation on Earth provided plenty of scope for discussion, but there was no real motivation to get involved. People seemed disposed to take a wait-and-see approach. Meanwhile, the Belt's relationship with Mars had gelled.

Many of the miners had repurposed their explorations. They now were actively looking for water ice rather than the elusive big score of precious metals. Because dropping the ice on Mars was a risky enterprise due to the possibility of hitting a surface installation, the Martian Rainmaking Company had been chartered.

The MRC, as it was commonly called, took delivery of chunks of ice from the asteroid miners, installed computer-controlled engines on the chunks, then remotely guided them into high Mars orbit. There, the ice was broken into smaller pieces and launched toward the surface. The launches were carefully timed so that no colonist or installation was in danger.

Although thin, the Martian atmosphere was still thick enough to ablate most of the incoming ice chunk. This injected the water directly into the atmosphere in the form of vapor. The vapor froze immediately, of course. It was somewhat similar to throwing a pan of boiling water up into the air on a sub-zero day on Earth. The water formed ice crystals and those formed clouds. The clouds were gradually growing thick enough to keep the surface from radiating what heat there was into space.

The frozen clouds were now beginning to form at lower elevations, and there was a rumor that the MRC was predicting that there would be rain on the surface sometime in the next six months. This was eagerly anticipated by the Martians. It was a milestone in their effort that indicated they were on the way to success.

With the help of the Belters, the Martians had expanded their farming efforts. They had plenty of workers, comparatively speaking, but they had not been using the advanced techniques the Belters had developed. This was due to the control that had been exercised over the Martian colony by the bureaucrats on Earth.

While well-meaning, the Earth-bound administrative process had failed to adapt to the specialized requirements on the red planet. Told that they had to raise crops in a certain way, the Martians had simply tried to do their best while following instructions. Due to the way they were recruited, most of them were not experienced farmers and had no better idea than to follow directions.

The base in the Swift crater on Deimos had become a major port, with people traveling in both directions, to the surface, and outbound. Belters were always heading to Mars to provide technical assistance, but most of the travelers were workers outbound to the Belt and Titan.

The demand for labor was so high that recruiting had become very competitive. That situation had forced the Belter Council to come up with a monetary system hastily. They had initially used the North American Amero, but since their relationship with the Dictatorship was permanently severed, it had been deemed essential to come up with a means of exchange that was unique to the Belt.

The end result was a wholly digital currency. Some young hackers had seen the opportunity and developed a system that used incredible cryptography, far stronger than the old digital currencies on Earth. The new money was immediately adopted, and commerce was now booming. The net result was that Belters and Martians were beginning to feel that they might have control over their own future.

In addition to travelers passing through Swift, freighters dropped large amounts of metals there. For the most part, the metals were refined and shipped from smelters located in the Belt. The Martians had hustled to build a lander that was suitable for more cargo than they'd had to deal with in the past, and it was kept busy bringing construction materials down from the little moon.

ADAM HAD BEEN keeping a low profile for weeks. Once he'd gotten the Council to admit that there might be some advantage in helping the Mars colony, he'd backed out of the situation. His strategy seemed to be working. Nielson was now acting as if setting up trade with Mars was all his idea and taking all the credit for the venture's success.

Adam used his time carefully. He and Nile worked out, then rested, then he devoted hours to research. He didn't fully understand how the alien drive worked, and that mystery nearly drove him to distraction. The problem was a huge challenge in that it forced him to work through cutting edge quantum physics, particle physics, and astrophysics. The material stretched his mind. He'd studied it in school, but this was a crash course that delved into extreme detail.

He was pondering the interaction of the drive's collection field and virtual particles when another idea came to him. What if…

Nile was sitting on their bed, reading quietly. He turned to her. "Nile?"

She looked up, her finger holding her place on the tablet screen. "What?"

"Are you busy?"

"You mean, can you interrupt me? Yes. I'm just reading some pulp science fiction story. It can wait. What is it?"

"What if I changed the collection field? If it were the opposite polarity, it seems to me that it would attract positrons, rather than electrons. Positrons are scarce in normal space, but theory seems to imply that they should be more densely distributed in the quantum plenum. If they—"

Nile put her tablet down and held up her hand in a stopping motion.

"Whoa. Whoa there, partner. What precisely is a positron? You're going too fast for this marine."

He grinned at her. "Don't play dumb with me. I know you better than that."

"No, really. I mean it. What precisely is a positron and why aren't they found in normal space?"

"You know electrons, right?"

"Of course, Silly. They're some of my best friends."

"I'm trying to be serious, not silly. Anyway, a positron is an electron with a positive charge. It's the opposite of an electron. Anti-matter, so to speak."

"Oh. Oh, wait a minute. Wouldn't that be dangerous? Anti-matter, I mean. It would meet up with normal matter, and the two would cancel. Would that mean they'd explode or something along those lines?"

"Something like that, I guess. A positron colliding with an electron would result in mutual annihilation, and considerable energy would be released. So, yeah. It would be an explosion. Although, if there were only one of each, it wouldn't be a big explosion."

"Okay, so you change the trap field and collect positrons. What then? How do you handle something that will wreck the normal matter of our ship? Oh, and wouldn't there be other anti-particles that you'd get too? What about those?"

"There are antiprotons too, but if the field were adjusted to capture positrons, it would repel antiprotons. There is probably also antihydrogen, too, but an antihydrogen atom would have zero charge, so we wouldn't get any of those either. I could fix it so that we collected positrons only. The way to store those is a kind of magnetic bottle called a Penning trap. That way they won't erode the normal matter in the ship."

She looked quizzically at him. "But, dearest, most fierce Pirate, you haven't told me why you want positrons in the first place. What good are they? Will they make the drive more efficient? More thrust or something?"

He shook his head. Once again, he'd gotten ahead of himself.

"No. I had a completely different application in mind. The drive works well as it is. Even though I don't fully understand how it works, we can use it. The major problem with it is to control the thrust and not to overshoot. I've kind of already fixed that."

"What? You didn't tell me that! We can use it, then?"

"Yeah. I've worked out a computer program that will calc the thrust on a moment by moment basis and adjust the velocity by shutting the Em-Max on and off rapidly in such a way that the acceleration will be fairly smooth. It will shut the engine down when we reach the correct velocity for a turn-around. Then we can start to decelerate at a rate that will stop us near our destination without any overshooting and clawing our way back. It's easy."

"Maybe easy for you, but it sounds complex to me."

"Well, the comp will handle it, so it will seem easy. The positrons, though, are another matter."

She looked critically at him.

"Are you making some kind of pun about antimatter?"

"Huh. No, I hadn't thought of that, but it was kind of punny in a way. No. The positrons are going to be our next advance in the way of weapons. If the Dictatorship comes after us again, I want to be prepared to beat them so thoroughly and so quickly that they'll get the message that we aren't to be messed with."

She moved and sat on the side of the bed with her hands resting on the edge beside her hips.

"Now you've got my attention. I like weapons. I know what to do with them. Generally, I point them at people I don't like, and the weapon removes the problem. What about this new weapon?"

"If we can store a bunch of positrons in a Penning trap, then open one end of it and accelerate the particles as they come out, it will amount to an antimatter gun. Shooting a stream or a bubble of antimatter at a normal matter object like, say an enemy spaceship, would make a fine weapon. It'd burn through a hull almost instantly. Best of all, it could be scaled so that we could vary the effect. Fire a small amount of antimatter and make a little hole. A big amount and..."

She laughed aloud, then said, "A big amount and BOOM! Right?"

He shook his head. "I think boom, but we'll have to experiment with the idea."

She looked sober. "That brings to mind another thing. Why haven't you released the alien drive to everyone yet? You've downplayed it at every opportunity. When you got the scientific mission organized to go after the alien hulk, you didn't mention the drive, just the opportunity to get our hands on alien tech."

"The control issue, remember. I didn't want to get everyone's hopes up, besides what I told them was enough to send them off with their tongues hanging out. Remember Dr. Berlin? He couldn't get moving fast enough. It's a sure bet that they'll have the alien ship out of the ice and towed back here as quickly as possible."

"I guess you're right. No one has mentioned how quickly we got back, though, and that bothers me."

"That's probably because they were too intent on the Mars problem. I want to have the control for the hyperdrive worked out, so when they get around to asking questions, I'll have a complete solution for them. That means that we're going to take the D-R out where no one will be around. I don't want any observers while we work on the drive control problem. The positron gun idea, too, but I want to keep that a secret until I think about it more. You wanna give Flynn and To'afa a call?"

7
ARMING THE D-R

THEY HAD TAKEN the Dire Rhea out beyond Neptune. The Council had set up a ship registry that kept track of the Belters' ships. This helped greatly in operations. The purpose wasn't to control where the ships went, instead it was to facilitate shipments, services, and emergency rescues. Knowing that another ship was within a reasonable distance could make the difference between life and death for a crew in a disabled vessel.

The registry kept track of most of the space ships operating in the belt. Of course, there were still some miners who were too independently minded to cozy up to the Belter community. The Council generally left those people alone to follow their own paths. It was thought that the independents would eventually join up with the greater community on their own.

In any event, no known ships were operating within several light minutes of the D-R's location. This isolation was precisely what Adam wanted. He'd ordered and taken delivery of a Penning trap and a variety of other devices that he hoped to assemble into the weapon. The computer program was already resting in comp storage. He'd worked on that on the way out from Titan, and now Flynn was working through the code, looking for bugs. Adam had come to trust the Irishman in that respect since he seemed to have a natural knack with computer instructions.

They hadn't used the alien hyperdrive with computer control. Adam's was waiting for Flynn to finish debugging the program before they tried. Then they would test it with short hops. That way, if the code failed, they wouldn't have to travel far to get back to their point of origin.

While Flynn muttered under his breath, the others worked on Adam's theoretical weapon. The capture field was the easy part. It required only a small modification. When they were finished, it could be switched from capturing reaction mass for the hyperdrive to pulling in positrons only.

The hard part was switching the system over from routing particles to the drive to shuttling positrons into the Penning trap. They had to construct a device that had some of the elements of a particle accelerator. It was necessary to keep the positrons from contacting ordinary matter, so they had to be transferred to the trap in a magnetic field within a tube.

The trap was another major engineering feat. It amounted to a magnetic bottle that could be opened to receive the incoming positrons, closed to store them, and then opened to release them into the weapon's firing port where they would be shot out by a magnetically propelled field.

Adam's original idea of using the same mechanism as the plasma cannon proved impracticable. There was no way to inject the positrons into the Em-Max drive. They would simply ablate the housing and release high-powered microwaves all over the place.

It was a tedious job. They were working on the transfer mechanism when Flynn stomped in triumph on his face.

"Arr, Captain! I've got the code checked. You had some bad parts in there, but I fixed them. We're ready to test the hyperdrive control."

The three of them were engaged in a tricky mechanical assembly at the moment, and none of them even looked at Flynn, although Adam grunted as a response.

Flynn frowned, then kicked To'afa's foot. "You got cotton in your ears? I've got the hyperdrive ready to go, and I'd like to test it sometime before I reach my dotage. I intend to spend me final years in Finnegan's Pub drinking stout and pinchin' the barmaid's cheeks. I don't have time for your foolin' around.

Nile looked up at him. "Wait one. We're about finished with this part."

At the same time, To'afa shoved the tube he was supporting into place. The big man slid back on the floor from the reclining position he'd been forced to assume, and said, "You're going to pinch the barmaid's cheeks, huh? Which ones? Top or bottom?"

Flynn laughed and slipped into a more jovial mood. "Why, whichever ones are nearest to hand."

Nile joined in the banter. "Speaking of hands, you'd better watch the barmaid's. If it were me that you pinched, I'd likely use the back of mine on your own cheek."

Flynn grinned. "Aye, I suspect that you'd try, at least, but I'm fast on my feet, so you'd surely miss."

She laughed and retorted, "What? And you in your dotage? I wouldn't think an old man would be so quick."

"Well, I'm not going to be a normal old one. I get faster, the older I become."

Adam stood up and brushed his hands on his pants. "Sort of like the Universe, huh. The older it gets, the faster it expands, but that might mean you'll simply expand and get so fat you can't move."

Flynn looked at Adam, obviously not tracking.

Adam shook his head. His sense of humor was a little odd. It had gotten him into difficulties on numerous occasions. He walked toward the door, motioning the others to follow.

"Okay, Flynn, let's go test the drive."

THE FIRST TWO attempts exposed a problem. The comp control was fast, but not fast enough to allow them to use the drive if the distance was under a light second. They invariably overshot before the software reversed the drive.

After a little tinkering, Flynn realized that they'd run headlong into a hardware problem.

"The bloomin' processor speed is too slow. By the time the computer reaches the monitor loop, we've already gone past where we wanted to be. This hyper-alien-whatzit is crazy quick."

Adam nodded. "I guess we'll have to restrict it for longer hops. Let's try for twenty seconds light and see how close we get."

Nile was checking the local area. "There's a smallish asteroid at about that distance. Why don't we head for it?"

Adam looked at the screen to see what she was talking about.

"Okay. That's a go on that idea. Let's set it. Just a minute. Alright. I've got it lined up. Hold your seats lady and gentlemen, here we go."

He pressed the actuation button on the screen. The drive kicked on, then kicked off after a couple of seconds, then back on in the reverse mode. The acceleration was brutal, and the decel was worse.

When he could speak again, Adam said, "We'll have to fix our seats so they'll reverse. I don't like the feeling that my guts and my eyeballs are having a contest to see which can come out of my body first. That slow-down was awful."

They stopped the testing until the seat problem could be solved. To'afa and Flynn went to work on it, while Adam and Nile went back to the weapon development project.

THE TWO WORKED well together. Adam found that Nile was attuned to his thinking to the point that she would hand him a tool almost before he realized that he needed it. They labored over the trap assembly, then the particle routing apparatus for several hours.

Adam pulled away from the assembly, straightened, and scanned their work.

"It looks like everything is together. We still have to tune the magnetic fields, though."

"Why aren't we using the Em-Max to accelerate the particles?" Nile looked puzzled.

"The Em-Max is a closed unit. The positrons would dissolve a hole right through the endplate, then we'd have microwaves bouncing all over the place. The other thing that would happen is even worse."

"What would be worse than microwaves everywhere?"

"Uh. Antimatter contacting normal matter. Lots of hard radiation. Probably gamma rays, but maybe B mesons or W and Z bosons would be the immediate negative result."

"That wouldn't be good, would it? Would we survive?"

"Maybe, if the override shut it down quickly enough, but we most likely wouldn't be healthy afterward."

"Let's not do that then. Okay?"

He nodded. "Most certainly okay. I would still like to use the same basic setup with the Em-Max, but I'm afraid that I'll have to use a mag field and that's going to take a lot of power."

She brightened. "What if you built an Em-Max around the containment tube?"

He thought that over. "Mmm. I hadn't thought of that. I'll have to think about it a bit. It sounds like it might be a solution, though."

She stretched. "I'm hungry and tired. Can we take a break?"

"Yeah. Let's get some food."

NILE'S SUGGESTION WAS a good idea. It just took time and was work-intensive. After the Em-Max chamber had been modified to provide an integral magnetic containment guide, the path for the positrons was unobstructed. Adam's theory was that the antimatter particles would be accelerated by entrainment with the microwaves passing around them.

The magnetic guide was designed to accelerate particles, so the device didn't rely solely on the microwaves as a driver for the positrons.

After working overtime for a week and a half, Adam announced that they were ready for a test.

Everyone was gathered on the bridge, watching a smallish asteroid directly ahead of the D-R. The projector was elaborate and had to be fixed in place on the ship. Adam had designed it so that it was aimed directly forward, parallel to, but under the axis of the ship. They'd have to point precisely at their target to have any effect.

That didn't seem to have much downside, though. In Adam's experience, space conflict usually provided opportunities to face directly towards opposing forces.

"Ready?" Adam's hand was on the interlocked fire control button as he looked over his shoulder at the others.

"Give it a try, won't ya? I can't wait to see the next Fed ship that wants to blow us out of space. They're going to have a surprise." Flynn was practically gyrating in his seat with excitement.

Nile nodded in agreement.

Adam said, "Here goes."

A nearly invisible flame seemed to lick out from the D-R. There were sparkles along its path as positrons struck bits of space dust and annihilated them.

The beam struck the asteroid with a flash. The brilliant light continued on and on, eating its way through the target. Adam's hand trembled for a moment, then he released the switch.

"That's enough for a test." He increased the magnification on the viewer, and there was a collective gasp.

"Jupiter! Look at that!" Nile's face was pale.

To'afa had been grinning, but his expression changed to one that might be interpreted as horrified.

Flynn started to curse, then faltered. "Jeshua, uh, Mary, and…I, I can't think of anything to say."

The positrons had shredded the asteroid. There was a slice all the way through. The rock had been rotating slowly, so the beam had cut a wide hole as it burned through. The antimatter's destruction had extended out in a random pattern from the point where the beam had initially struck.

The asteroid began to break into pieces as they watched.

Adam said, "The positrons must have spread out somehow. Let's play the vid back in slow motion for a better view."

They clustered around the screen to watch. In slow speed, the video revealed a series of sparks along the beam's path. The flash when the asteroid was struck was impressive. Rather than a single explosion, it was composed of many tiny flashes as each positron met an ordinary matter particle in mutual destruction.

To'afa said, "Look! It's kind of pretty, really. All those sparkles are like a…a holiday of some kind."

Flynn snorted. "You'd think holiday if you was close to that. There's probably a sleet storm of hard radiation being released in those cute sparkles."

Nile made an incoherent sound to attract their attention. She was looking at the monitor focused on the asteroid. The rock had suddenly shattered into thousands of fragments that were drifting lazily away.

"Gods! What would that do to a spaceship?" she whispered.

Adam shook his head, disparagingly. "I really don't want to find out, but I suspect that we'll eventually have to use it against the USSN. That Elseth has her hands full with things on Earth right now, but if she can get the population and the Non-Aligns under control, she'll turn in our direction without waiting even a millisecond."

Flynn cackled gleefully at the thought, then said, "Yeah. Those arses will have a real surprise when we hit them with this thing. Hey, what'll we call it?"

He scratched his head, then said, "How about Doctor Doom? I like that."

It was Adam's turn to snort. "Come on, Flynn. That's like some old sci-fi name or something. Let's just call it what it is: an antimatter gun."

Flynn shook his head. "No. You can't go calling it that. The instant the Feddies hear that name, they'll go rabbiting off with a bajillion credits to fund research, and we'll be facing the business end o' their version of the thing."

Nile interjected, "He's right, Adam. We've got to keep this secret. The instant it gets used, and if, that's a big if, there are any survivors, they'll report back to the Feds, and they will absolutely get to work on their own version."

"Hmm. Well, we call the Dire Rhea the D-R, so how about referring to it as the D-D for Doctor Doom?"

Flynn nodded in a pleased manner, but then thought of something.

"Hey, how about the double-D. No one will be able to make anything out of that name. If anything, it sounds like a bra size. A nice big one, too."

Then Nile shook her head in amazement. "Boys will be boys. Flynn, you're incorrigible, but it probably isn't a bad name. I agree. Double-D sounds good to me."

Adam nodded. "Okay. That's what it is. The thing is, we don't want to say anything about it. I'm not even sure right now if we should put it on our other ships. Somebody would talk for sure, so we all have to keep this totally quiet. It's essential."

"In the Marines, we learned that the only way a secret remains secret is if only one person knows it and keeps it to themselves. We're already at a disadvantage," Nile said.

Flynn had been thinking of another element required to keep the secret. He asked, "Can you reduce the size? This mess you've cobbled together is pretty obvious. We can't have any visitors. The way this looks, they'd be askin' inconvenient questions for sure."

Adam said, "That already occurred to me. I think I can reduce the size, but the magnetic containment system just takes space. Unless I come up with a way to make it more efficient, there's not much I can do to compress it."

The particle guide extended from the bow back to the engine room, then looped forward again to the opening of the barrel at the front of the ship. Adam envisioned the path of the particles as they moved from the collection funnel down the magnetic guide.

Suddenly inspiration struck him. There was no reason to configure the magnetic tube the way he had. He'd been thinking of a conventional linear particle accelerator, but the small size of the D-R meant that a spiral path would use the space more efficiently. There even might be a way to make better use of the magnetic field given such a configuration. His mind went off into a mad whirl as he thought of different ways to set up the magnets.

Nile pushed at his shoulder. "Adam? Hey, Floof! What's the matter with you?"

He turned to face her without speaking. The alarmed look on her face instantly faded as she recognized the state he was in. She turned to the other two. "He's half-way to solving the size problem. Probably won't return to his normal stupidity for at least an hour or two. Don't try to get him to make sense right now. He's not communicating on a human level."

Flynn nodded. "I've seen him like this a little." Then he looked at her and asked, "What was that? Floof? That sounds like some kind of kinky bedroom name." He leered at her, waiting for her answer.

"No. You guys are all alike. I just thought of it, but now that you brought it up, I'm going to start calling him that, and I'll make sure he likes it." She raised her eyebrows at Flynn and nodded for emphasis.

Flynn's imagination was apparently working overtime because his mouth dropped open.

Adam had come back to himself just in time to get the last part of the conversation, but he was momentarily caught up in the idea of her making sure he liked to be called Floof. He tried to restrain his urge to laugh. She'd have to work hard at it. He tried to imagine some of the things she'd do.

Flynn finally thought of something to say. "That's the most outrageous thing –"

She raised her finger in mock anger, shutting Flynn off in mid-sentence, then snapped, "But only when we're alone and don't you use the word again. I'll find out, and I'll be pissed if you do. I'm the only one who can call him that."

Flynn backed up, an expression of alarm on his face. "Okay. I'm not going to get in the middle of your private affairs. I'll be good."

8

COMPETITION

THEY ARRIVED BACK at Titan prepared to present the new drive to the Council. Adam had not brought up the antimatter projector, so it was not on the agenda.

The boarding tube connected to the D-R's airlock with a clash as the grapples locked on and sealed to the hull of the ship. That was followed by the sound of the outer lock opening. Their ears popped as the pressure adjusted to the slight differential. It seemed to be impossible to get the pressures matched precisely. Ships almost always kept the minimum pressure for humans to function well. Lower pressure was safer in case of a meteoroid strike.

The pressure in the Titan habitat was higher. The atmosphere, such as it was, made it marginally more comfortable to hold higher pressure, and a meteor strike was also less likely. The problem was that the habitat, by its very nature, couldn't control the pressure precisely. That meant that the official PSI amounted to an estimate. It was never precisely what the docking official said it was, and that meant their eardrums always had to suffer.

The docking tube was frigid, and the humidity in the air condensed immediately on the cold surfaces covering them with a thin layer of frost crystals. The underfoot was slippery despite its corrugated surface. What made it worse was the railings were far too cold for bare skin. Even with gloves, human skin would freeze if the contact was more than momentary.

They moved carefully down the tube, sniffing the different odor in the air. Ships quickly took on a characteristic smell caused by cramming humans into tight quarters without much opportunity to wash. The habitat air was strange. It smelled like a combination of industrial chemicals and human cooking, with a background of some kind of air freshener. It was different, not better, just different.

Once through the tube, they passed through the double doors of the habitat lock, an easy matter, since there was no pressure differential.

Adam flinched as he exited the lock. There was a clamor as several reporters vied to shove microphones in his face. Humans still devoured news, and the Belter community was no different. Unfortunately, he hated the notoriety and always felt ill-at-ease in front of a camera.

"Admiral, were you successful? Did you solve the hyperjump problem?"

Hades! That was supposed to be a secret. He pushed through the reporters. They seemed to have multiplied. The last time in, there had only been five or six, now there were more. Some of them undoubtedly were bloggers. The Belters didn't distinguish between formal news businesses and private bloggers. Any source was fine as long as it was accurate. Inaccuracy wasn't tolerated. Made-up stories would lose viewers and potentially get the person responsible in trouble.

There was a tall, muscular man standing behind the reporters. Adam didn't give much attention to him, other than automatically evaluating him for threat potential. The man was imposingly muscled and looked like he knew how to handle himself. It would be best to be aware of where he was at all times.

Nile, coming out of the lock behind him, suddenly called out a greeting. The tall man waved at her, and a huge smile lit up his face. Adam's trouble sense spiked. What was this? He turned to Nile, but she'd already pushed past him and was hugging the muscular man. He was hugging her back and bending to kiss her.

She avoided the kiss and brushed her lips on his cheek. That was a little better, but Adam could feel his face beginning to flush. Who was this guy?

As if in answer, Nile turned toward him, still wrapped in the guy's arms and said, "Hey, Adam. This is Jason Klingfeldt. He was in my old unit."

Adam moved forward and extended his hand. Jason's grip was crushing, and he bore down hard. It was a display of status that Adam particularly disliked. Rather than squeeze in return, he yanked his hand back, pulling the taller man toward him.

Jason released his grip with a smug grin.

"Sorry. Don't know my own strength," he said.

Adam drew a breath. He was angry, but his instinct told him to calm down. "That's okay."

The formalities over, Jason returned his attention to Nile. He hadn't let go of her during the introduction.

"Nile, baby, it's been ages since I saw you. What have you been doing? You know you're looking better than ever. Longer hair suits you. I liked you when you were barely covered, but now you're gorgeous."

Nile saw Adam's face and worked her way out of the big man's arms.

"It's nice to see you, too, Jas. Say, whatever happened to Sergeant Hewitt?"

He paused, looked up and to the left, then said, "Aw, that ol' reprobate! He finally retired. Last I heard he was drinking Scotch and chasing tail at Shannon's Bar. He can't seem to get farther away from the base than that. You know, you can get out of the Marines, but you can't get the Marines out of you."

Nile nodded, then said, "Yeah, I know. What are you doing here, Jas?"

"I got tired of being cannon fodder. They're constantly fighting on Earth, now. Anyway, I jumped on a ship out of Luna, ended up on Mars a few months ago. That didn't suit me. They're pretty stratified there. Scientists lording it over everyone else, and their Council...whew, talk about pompous asses! I got my fill of construction work, then caught a shuttle for Deimos. From there, I signed on to a mining ship that was short-handed. One of their crew had an accident, and they needed to go back out. They were coming this way, so here I am."

Adam asked, "Do you have a job yet?"

Jason ignored him and placed his hand on Nile's shoulder. She allowed it to rest there for a moment, then moved just enough to dislodge it. She repeated Adam's question. "How long have you been here? Are you employed?"

The black-headed man said, "Got here a couple of days ago. No job yet. I'm still learning what's what. This is a real going deal you Belters got set up, that's for sure." He reached for Nile again.

Adam suddenly felt tired. He'd had enough. The guy might be Nile's friend, but he sure acted possessive of her. He was also a first-class jerk. Adam turned and started off without saying anything. He could hear Jason starting to say something else to Nile, but the background noise blurred the words.

He was partly down the hall when there was the sound of hurried feet behind him, then Nile grabbed his arm.

"That wasn't nice! Walking off like that. What's the matter with you?"

Now that she asked, he was embarrassed. "Uh, I was, I'm tired, I guess. I wanted to get to our apartment and get cleaned up. The D-R's bath can't compete with the one here."

She came around and stood in front of him, looking up at his face. "You're jealous, aren't you?"

"Do I have a reason to be?"

She looked down for a moment. Adam's heart sank as he intuited her response.

"Jas and I had a thing for a short time, but that was a long time ago. It was nothing."

She looked up, her eyes wide and deep. "Nothing. I never knew what I was missing until I found you. Just forget him. He's pushy, but he's one of the good ones. He's a good fighter, and he's reliable."

"Didn't sound too reliable to me. He walked out of his unit. Didn't he say that?"

"Yeah. I can't quite figure that one. I wouldn't have thought he'd go AWOL." She was silent a moment, then added, "I think you should get him a job somewhere."

Adam was trying to be reasonable, but his voice was curt. "He can go down to the employment bureau like everyone else. I don't know him despite your attestation to his character. I could put him somewhere, I guess, but I'd rather he prove himself somewhere away from me."

Her face flushed. Now he'd done it. He could tell that she was getting angry.

"Look, Mister Pirate, just because I dated him for a couple of weeks doesn't mean you can get angry with me. That was way before I even knew you existed, so you can't claim that I was cheating on you. Get over it and grow up!"

She turned and strode down the hall. Adam followed, gradually accelerating until he began to catch up.

Gods, she was beautiful. Even angry, she made his pulse speed up. He'd have to do something to make it up to her.

"Nile, I'm sorry. I guess you're right. Seeing the way he latched onto you and something about his general attitude set me off. I'm not angry with you."

She stopped short and turned, bringing them face-to-face. "That's better. He's okay. He's my friend, not my lover. Let's forget it and go get cleaned up. You're right. Our apartment is a lot more luxurious than the D-R. C'mon."

She grabbed his hand and tugged. He followed without speaking, even though he was far from reassured.

TO'AFA REMAINED ON the D-R ostensibly to handle routine maintenance. In fact, his primary purpose was to ensure that the positron projector was unobserved.

Adam had worried excessively about the weapon getting out. It was a sure thing that news of it would leak to the Earthers once it was known to exist. Since his inventions were, at least in his mind, merely common-sense extensions of already existing tech, he figured the Feds, as he called them out of habit, would come up with their own version once they realized it was possible.

He feared that Earth's resources and money, once applied to the problem, would result in a more efficient and powerful version of the weapon. That would bode ill for the Belt civilization.

The Council was another problem. The meeting with them involved some basic schmoozing, but they needed no incentive to dedicate resources to the new hyperdrive. That was an advantage that no one could afford to ignore.

As usual, the belt community was quick to embrace the idea. Within two days, there were at least three new companies chartered to build components and install the new drives. That was a good thing, since the number of ships that wanted it rose as quickly as the ship owners and crew heard about it.

He estimated that it would be less than a month before that invention was the subject of intensive research in physics labs on Earth. It couldn't be helped. He justified letting it go in much the same way he had justified releasing the plasma shield system. It was for the benefit of all of humanity. One group couldn't justify keeping it for themselves.

On the flip side, when the Earthers had hyperdrive capability, it would make it far easier to attack the belt community. It was a problem that he'd created, and he had to accept responsibility for it. His only option was to remain ahead of the USSN in offensive capability. They had far more shipbuilding capability than the Belters at present.

That would eventually equal out. There were more resources in the belt, and they were easier to get at. Everything on Earth had to be boosted into space or travel up the Ribbon.

Now that was a thought. The Ribbon. It was Earth's main conduit to orbit. It was an attractive target, once one got over the initial revulsion at the concept of destroying a civilization changing installation. Of course, the USSN maintained a defensive shield of ships near the Ribbon station.

They probably didn't expect the Belters to attack the Ribbon, but it was definitely possible that one of the Non-Aligns would sabotage the base station. The North American Socialist Monarchy, as it was currently being called, was continuing its effort to destroy all opposition to its attempt to absorb the rest of the globe. Adam shook his head at the thought.

Elseth had proven to be far deadlier than her late, unlamented father. He was thankful that he hadn't gotten any deeper involved with her than he had. It had been a disaster for him, but it had resulted in one good thing: the development of the Belter civilization.

He most likely wouldn't have survived the intrigue that the woman surrounded herself with. He was lucky that she'd basically dropped him. She was toxic.

That thought brought him to Nile. He loved her. He felt surprised that it was so easy to admit. It was a good feeling, but now the presence of Jason made him unaccountably upset. The man kept showing up whenever they were out. It was almost as if he was stalking her.

The worst thing was that she seemed genuinely happy to see the jerk. It was enough to make his stomach churn. As a result, he appeared to be making things worse. Nile accused him of being alternately moody or grumpy at least three times a day.

He tried to make it up to her, but the business of reducing his jury-rigged drive to a functional unit that could be mass-produced and installed quickly on the various types of space ships that frequented the belt conspired to get in the way.

He worked as hard as possible, and that made him tired, which made him more grumpy. He felt he was driving her into Jason's arms.

THINGS CAME TO a head at the end of an alterday shift. Adam had been called out of bed to confirm that the first installation of the hyperdrive was correct. Nile remained in the apartment. The two were to meet and have breakfast when he finished.

He confirmed the installation was correctly installed, gave the ship's Captain some last-minute instructions on what to expect and how to fine-tune the system, then left for the cafeteria.

He arrived thirty minutes before he had told Nile he would be there.

The first thing that he saw was Nile seated beside Jason at a table across the room. The two had their heads together and were conversing. Jason laughed, then put his arm around her and leaned closer.

Adam hadn't waited. As the big man leaned close to Nile, he approached from the other side. She saw him, and her eyes went wide. She started to say something, but by that time, Adam had Jason's arm and had yanked him backwards onto the floor, scattering chairs in the process.

Jason yelled in anger and started to climb to his feet. Adam used a foot sweep to take his legs out from under him before he managed to stand.

Klingfeldt yelled again and rolled. Adam moved closer, ready to knock him down back.

Adam was focused entirely on the big man when there was a solid slap on his left cheek. He jerked and turned.

Nile was standing there, her face red with anger.

"What the Hades do you think you're doing?"

Her attack confused him. "I wasn't going to let him kiss you. I—"

She interrupted. "That's not what...oh, you won't believe me. He was trying to tell me about something suspicious. We were worried about being overheard."

Adam shook his head. "That's not what it looked like. You're right. I don't believe it."

He turned to walk away just as Jason's fist connected with his temple on his blind side. Because he was turning, the punch slipped partially.

Adam staggered but didn't go down.

He spun around and dropped into a guard position, then stretched his neck from side to side, causing a cracking sound from his vertebrae as he loosened the muscles.

"Alright, big guy. You missed. Give it your best shot."

Jason started to move forward, but Nile jumped in front of him.

"No, Jason. You can't beat him. You don't understand what you're up against. He's incredibly well trained in some form of fighting I've never seen. Just back off. Go. Now!" She shoved Jason's chest.

The black-haired man looked over her meeting Adam's gaze. Something he saw in Adam's eye caused him to move back a half step.

"Okay, one-eye. Nile says not to fight you. You're important here, and I'm not. You'd probably have me in the cage as revenge. Maybe some other time." He turned and strode out.

The other customers were just beginning to rise out of their chairs. It had happened too quickly for them to understand what was happening, let alone respond.

Adam shook his head. There was something warm on his cheek. He felt it and looked at his hand. He'd been cut and was bleeding. He picked up the nearest napkin and blotted the dampness.

Nile looked at him, anger apparent in her stance. She didn't speak for a few seconds, then she said, "That was uncalled for. He wasn't trying to kiss me. You should know by now that you're the only one I care for."

Adam was shaking with stress in the aftermath of the fight. He lowered the napkin, glanced at it, then said, "I expect I'll need some stitches for this. You distracted me just in time to give him a chance."

Her mouth dropped open in surprise, then she said, "If that's what you think, maybe you'd better find someplace else to sleep. I don't want anything to do with you until you come to your senses."

That practically tore his heart in two. He gasped, then the residual adrenaline in his body converted his hurt into anger. "Fine. That's what I'll do. Why don't you go after him? I'm certain he needs comforting."

He turned and strode off before she could respond.

IT WAS ABOUT an hour later when he checked in with To'afa on the Dire Rhea. He'd stopped at the medic, gotten six stitches, then grabbed some coffee and a muffin. His head hurt, and the D-R seemed like an excellent place to lay up for a while.

To'afa took one look and wisely kept quiet about what he saw.

Adam asked, "Any trouble here? Anyone wanting to inspect the ship or anything like that?"

"No, Captain. The service crew wanted to clean up, but I ran them off. I'm the only one here, and no one has come by."

"We've got to keep the new weapon, uh, the D-D quiet. I guess I'm overly worried about it, but we can't afford to let her Queenship get hold of it."

"Roger that."

To'afa turned to the monitor. Adam looked over his shoulder.

There were several ships in orbit, but that wasn't unusual. The Belters were independent and came and went on their own schedule.

"Been keeping an eye on all the traffic. We're getting to be a regular stop for all the miners, Belters and independents, plus the Martians. That's a Martian ship there," To'afa said, indicating a vessel that was in a high orbit.

"Yeah. Well. Uh, I'm going to rest a bit in my cabin. They had me up at an unearthly hour this morning. Tired. Check with you later."

To'afa didn't say anything. When he heard Adam move away, he looked at his friend's back. Whatever it was wasn't good. Adam slumped and looked beaten.

9

UNEXPECTED EVENTS

ADAM BURIED HIMSELF in work, retreating to the D-R in his spare moments. Nile didn't show up. He was hoping that she'd come and apologize, but perhaps he owed her an apology. Thinking it over, he gradually came to see that he might have been mistaken.

After four miserable days, he decided to find her and set things right.

He was on the way to their apartment when the public announcement system blasted out an alert. The system was in place primarily for meteoroid strikes and other similar natural emergencies, but this time the message involved a stolen space ship.

Adam didn't hear the entire message due to background noise, but he listened to enough to turn and head for the docks. His presence would be required. The Council always wanted his involvement whenever something happened that related to defense in any way.

BY THE TIME he'd arrived at the dock, security had figured out what had happened.

Adam was shocked at first, then angry and greatly saddened. It appeared that Nile had signed Jason through and the two had gone out to one of the nearer mining ships. It was a smaller ship, but it had been upgraded and was outfitted with everything but the antimatter weapon.

It was also fully fueled, awaiting its Captain and crew. Now the crew was beginning to straggle into the staging area where they were interviewed by security. The consensus was that the ship's Captain, one Dennis Hofstrau, had been waiting on the ship. They were due to leave in twelve hours. The crew had been taking the last moment of liberty available, while the Captain planned their voyage.

This was often the case. Captains, particularly miners, often kept the details of their voyages secret. The two had boarded the ship, using rocket packs, and apparently, the Captain had let them through the lock.

This action would typically not have alarmed anyone. People visited ships at times. The rapid departure of the Mole Rat had attracted attention. It had attracted more attention when the alterday nav showed up and raised a fuss about where her ship had gone.

THE MOLE RAT had used the hyperdrive and was now so far away that it couldn't be sensed. All in all, it was a perfect theft. What Captain Hofstrau thought of it was anyone's guess. What Adam thought of it didn't lend itself to polite company. He was furious, and the more he thought it over, the angrier he became.

It seemed that Nile had taken up with her old flame, dropped him like a hot potato, and then the two had stolen a ship with almost all of the Belters' new technology. The drive alone would be worth more credits to the Feds than any human could ever spend.

Nile's knowledge of the positron weapon would be equally valuable. The two would have enough to spend the rest of their lives in luxury on a private beach.

It was almost too much to bear. How could he have been so naive a second time? The worst was, he really loved Nile. It wasn't even difficult to admit. He had thought he was in love with Elseth, but really, there hadn't been anything that was on the level of what he felt for Nile. He hoped she hadn't abandoned him, but it certainly looked like it.

No one was demanding his attention at the moment. He looked around, then headed for the men's room. Once inside, he locked the door and stared at himself in the mirror. He thought about tears, but his eye simply glared at his reflection. After a moment, he realized he was furious, and his anger had burned the sadness out of him.

She'd better have a good explanation of her actions when he caught up to her. Meanwhile, the loss of their drive secret had to be overcome in some fashion.

Someone was knocking on the door. Adam turned and unlocked it, trying to control his anger as he turned the bolt.

"Admiral, there's news from Earth. The Council asks you to attend an emergency session as soon as you can get to the chamber." The speaker was one of the port security men. He looked young, almost immature. Adam had a moment of insight. The man was probably about his own age. Experience made a huge difference.

He brushed past the guard. "Let them know I'm on my way."

THE COUNCIL WAS in an uproar when Adam entered. He stood by the door for a moment listening. They were debating whether to take action against the North American Federal Dictatorship. The more he heard, the worse it sounded. Elseth had taken the unprecedented step of dropping nukes from orbit.

The Chinese had pushed too hard in the South Pacific, sinking many Fed ships, then investing the Philippines. Mindanao had fallen, and now the Chinese navy was headed towards Hawaii.

Elseth had responded. Beijing was now a pile of rubble with an estimated ten million dead. There had been sporadic missile launches from China, but they had all been intercepted by space-borne laser defenses. China had been unable to successfully hit back so far, but the analysts seemed to think that there was a chance that they would eventually launch a mass attack on the North American continent.

The discussion in the room was heated and loud. The consensus seemed to be trending in favor of a military response.

Adam, tired of the shouting, abruptly stepped forward.

"Quiet! We can't allow humanity's home planet to rip itself apart and that's going to happen unless we step in. Her Queenship has bitten off more than she can chew with this step. China will never allow the destruction of Beijing to stand without striking back. Those fools down there are on the verge of all-out war, and it's going to be nuclear this time. KEWs are one thing, but poisoning the planet with radiation will render it uninhabitable. If we don't do something, we might be the only humans left. Despite our big talk about being independent, we need the larger gene-pool. We've got to stop this before it gets out of hand."

He looked around. Most of the Council members were nodding in agreement.

Nielson asked, "But, what can we do? We don't have the manpower to launch an invasion to stop their war, even if we wanted to intervene."

Their course was evident to Adam. "The nukes were dropped from orbit. So were the KEWs. The USSN has had a field day without any major opposition in space. The Non-Aligns have had to make do with surface launches to boost things into orbit. Their ships are vulnerable on the climb out of the well, as we've seen. Their missiles were all destroyed before they could reach orbit. We have to equalize the situation. That's all that is needed. If the Feds no longer have an advantage, then maybe they'll back off."

The president looked pale. "You're talking about destroying the Ribbon, aren't you?"

Adam thought about it for a moment. It would amount to setting humanity back years in the space effort. The way things were going on Earth, it might even mean that the Ribbon would never be rebuilt. It was a fantastic resource, and he was proposing to destroy it. Humans would suffer from the loss. Was that morally acceptable? Could he do that and still look in the mirror?

Then a cold feeling washed over him. What did he owe humanity? He wasn't a Pirate by choice. He'd wanted to be a physicist. Then he'd wanted to live his own life by his own terms. Most recently, he'd been dumped by the one person he cared more about then... well, just about anything. Destroying the Ribbon might mean that she wouldn't be able to sell her knowledge to the Feds. They'd probably be too busy with the war they'd started on Earth to have any resources left for space drives.

That consideration tipped his moral balance. He crossed his arms and nodded. "That's the root of the problem. It's the key to the Feds' dominance."

The room erupted as the Council members began arguing the merits of the idea. There was self-interest in keeping the Ribbon intact. All of the Earth goods that filtered to their community initially rode into space on the device. Cutting it would force them to move far more quickly towards self-sufficiency.

It might even place them in mortal danger. Without Earth-grown plants, without vitamins, medicines, and nutrients that hadn't yet been synthesized in space, survival would become more difficult. Could they form a trade treaty with the Chinese or the Russians? Such a step might let the fox into the hen house. Neither of those political entities was trustworthy. Both were out for all the power they could gather. The only thing that had worked to keep them out of the Belters' lives was the Fed Dictatorship. They were too busy resisting incorporation into its sphere of influence to give space much attention.

Adam was getting bored and thinking about leaving. It might be more satisfying to simply cut the Ribbon himself, rather than wait for these politicians to decide on the step. It would certainly be quicker.

THE COUNCIL DEBATED the issue for another hour, paying almost no attention to Adam. He sat in a chair at the side of the room and listened when he wasn't occupied by his depressed thoughts of Nile.

"Admiral? Admiral?"

He jerked, then jumped to his feet. He'd been drowsing. "What?"

It was Nielson. The man stepped back, alarm on his face. Adam was still angry, and it showed. He looked at Nielson, trying to orient himself. He'd been daydreaming about Nile and her new boyfriend. He had been prepared for a fight with Jason, his fists clenched as he loomed over Nielson.

He looked around, slightly confused. It was the Council chambers. Nile wasn't here. He nodded and stepped back.

"Excuse me, Councilman. I was thinking about strategy, and you startled me."

Nielson took a breath, then said, "No matter. No matter. We've decided that destroying man's path into space would endanger all of us. Cutting our supply line like that is too risky. We can't—"

Adam interrupted. "If you don't cut it, Elseth will bomb the rest of the world into the stone age. We need supplies, but we don't want them to be so radioactive that they can't be used. If the war escalates any further, the Non-Aligns are sure to use their nuclear arsenals. They'll release all of their missiles at once. The Feds' space defenses won't be adequate to stop all of the nukes. North America will take a huge hit. When that happens, the remaining navy ships in orbit will retaliate."

He glanced past Nielson. The rest of the Council was staring at him, dismay on their faces. He continued. "Don't look at me like that. It's the most logical outcome to the conflict. North America is wiped out, then the USSN wipes out just about all of the rest of the world. Even if the Ribbon is still intact after that, there will be no one left to use it. How long do you think it will remain active with zero maintenance? It's an expensive system, and it's complicated as all get out. It'll break down quickly. Besides, there won't be any transportation left on the surface. All of the shipping is by drone, you know. The EMPs from the bombs will knock out the power grid and drone electronics. There will be no trade and no supplies from Earth."

Nielson stuttered, "B...but, they can't leave us without the things we need for survival."

"C'mon, Nielson. Think about that. We've been stealing our supplies from them for a long time. Trading with Mars has alleviated some of our problems. The Feds cut that supply line. They were going to starve us to death sooner or later. There's no reliable trade with them, Ribbon or no Ribbon. Destroying it won't have much impact on us, but it will leave the Federal Dictatorship with no means to resupply their own ships. That should mean the end of their global conquest aspirations. The only other thing we'll have to do is to contact the Non-Aligns and let them know that we will enforce a cease-fire. If they try to nuke North America in revenge or for any other reason, we'll whack them hard enough to convince them it wasn't a good idea. We have to preserve the planet. We don't have to maintain any political entity."

Adam's patience had finally worn out. "I'll be in my apartment if you have any additional questions." He strode out. He could hear the conversation increase in volume as the door closed behind him.

IT WAS MID-MORNING in MainDay when Nielson messaged him. It was a copy of an official Council decision that all ships were to stay far away from Earth. The Council had decided that the Belter community would remain completely neutral in the conflict on Earth.

There was a specific set of instructions for him. He was to ensure that the Belt space force was prepared to defend against any raids by the USSN or any other Earth force.

That was it, then. The Council had committed them to increase their independence. Perhaps they hoped to resume trade with the winners of the war, he didn't know, and the message didn't say.

In his opinion, it was a stupid decision. He had become more convinced that his prediction of complete destruction was correct.

He sat at his desk, thinking. There was really only one thing to do. He'd probably be considered an outlaw, but that was no worse than considering himself a Pirate. The D-R would have to cut the Ribbon to save the Earth. The space elevator could be rebuilt far more quickly than the planet could recover from a nuclear holocaust.

Odds were poor, even given the hyperdrive and the positron weapon. The USSN kept a squadron of ships near the Ribbon Station. In fact, that was the force that had been dropping KEWs and bombs on the surface. There were even more ships at Luna. The Feds had continued building, even though they were limited in resources by the conflict.

He wasn't sure, but there were at least twenty ships in Luna orbit. Those combined with the Ribbon squadron would make it difficult to get close enough to bring the Ribbon down. He needed help. There was no other option.

His friends would have to be part of the effort. There would be too much risk to allow less familiar people to know what he intended. It wouldn't matter, once they left on the mission. The hyperdrive would ensure that they couldn't be caught in time. The only question about that was whether Klingfeldt and Nile had turned the drive over to the Feds yet.

Recruiting people and getting ships to help would be the risky part.

10
PREPPING

AFTER CAREFUL CONSIDERATION, Adam checked to see if Jem was on Titan. It so happened he was. It was pure luck, actually. Jem spent most of his time at the second asteroid base. It was smaller than the Bubble and not as comfortable as Titan, but he'd made his home there and was busy providing for his little family.

He was on Titan delivering a small cargo of gold ore. He'd found an asteroid that was paying off in a big way. Its location was a secret since he wanted no competition for his personal source of wealth.

The two agreed to meet at one of the new restaurants. Adam arrived slightly early, only to find that Jem was already there.

"Adam! It's good to see you. Been a while. Jupiter, that patch makes you look sinister."

Adam gripped his friend's arm, laughed, and said, "Sinister? Never been called that before."

Jem said, "Well, maybe not too sinister, but it gives you a certain air that seems to speak of danger."

Adam became serious instantly. "That's the problem. I can't seem to get out of the frying pan, and even if I do, all I've got to look forward to is the fire. They seem to go out of their way to find excuses to keep me involved."

Jem asked, "The Council, you mean? Ah, I can see that. Your reputation is too good. You've been too successful, and now they need you to be the force behind their politics. You know you'll never get away from them unless you run away somewhere."

Adam sighed. "Yeah. I know, but they have no one else. At least no one that I trust to do as good a job as me."

The two found a table and ordered. Adam leaned forward. "Jem, I've got something I've got to do that requires secrecy. Something dangerous, too."

Jem drew back, scratched his head, then said, "Man, you get right to the point. How about asking me how my wife and child are doing first?"

That was embarrassing. He'd practically forgotten that Jem was married.

"Uh. Sorry. How are they, then?"

"That's not very sincere, but since you asked, they're doing well. The kid is a natural at low gravity. I think he'll be a great miner."

Adam thought that over. "Probably. It's because he's known nothing else."

Jem frowned. "That's my fear. I worry that growing up solely in low-g conditions may do something to his body. It has to, really. He's not developing musculature the way an Earth-born would."

"Well, we're founding a new culture out here. I think we'll find that our population will diverge from that of Earth within a couple of generations. Maybe we're in at the start of a new species."

"Maybe." Jem stretched, his right arm almost knocking the drinks out of the waiter's hands. The man had come up unexpectedly from Jem's right.

"Oh. Sorry, man. Didn't mean to hit you that way."

"No harm done. The cups have lids. Here's yours."

Once the food was delivered, Jem took a bite, then said, "Okay. That's enough socializing. What do you need me to do?"

Adam looked around. The Belters valued their privacy and eschewed voice recognition systems along with video cameras. That aversion was a direct result of the loss of privacy on Earth. Here in this restricted environment where all-encompassing surveillance would be easy, no video cameras were recording public interactions; no hidden microphones either.

There was no one near at the moment. Adam cleared his throat and said, "I need another ship for a raid."

Jem looked puzzled, then asked, "A raid not approved by the Council, right?"

Adam snorted. "Those idiots are going to fool around and let Earth be destroyed. We've got to take some action to cool things down before the Earthers blow the whole place up."

Jem looked away, considering. "I heard the news. I agree. It doesn't sound good. The dictatorship started using nukes. That's hard vacuum."

"Huh?" Adam was puzzled.

Jem laughed. "It sucks." He shrugged, then added, "My wife uses it. It's about like everything else around here."

Adam nodded in agreement. "Yeah. Hard vacuum is pretty appropriate for my life right now, too."

"What happened to your girlfriend?" Jem looked curious.

"That's what I meant. I don't exactly know, but I have a bad feeling about her going off." He looked around, then muttered, "There's just no privacy around here, even if we aren't being recorded."

Jem looked serious. "Don't feel too bad. I heard from To'afa. He says she left with an old boyfriend. That right?"

"You don't have to throw it at me like that. But, yeah. It looks like it. I can't figure what she was doing and..." Adam looked down at his lap to see if that was where his heart had fallen. "I...it can't hurt to tell you. Jem, I really thought she was the right one. I miss her more than I can say."

"That really is hard vacuum, then. Sorry." The older man forked at the remains of his food. "Well, let's change the topic. I'll help you, at least tentatively. I want to come back to my kid, you know. I promised my wife when we got married that I'd be extra careful from then on."

"That isn't something I can promise you if you go with me on this one."

"Yeah. I figured that's what you'd say. Well, promises were made to be broken, but old friendships, that's a different story. What are we going to raid?"

Adam looked straight at Jem. "The Ribbon."

To his ears, it sounded grandiose—like a child bragging about how dangerous he was. The concept was daunting, partially because he hadn't entirely convinced himself that he could destroy mankind's greatest achievement. Cutting the planet's only space elevator was an act that could easily be viewed as totally evil, no matter how good his reasons were.

Jem drew back, frowned, then said, "Damn, you don't do things by halves. That's probably the only place more defended by the Feds than Luna base. Why are we going there, and what are we going to do when we get there?"

Adam explained. It took some time before Jem could see the necessity of cutting the launching Ribbon. The older man kept coming back to the enormity of the idea. The Ribbon was the cumulative result of humanity's effort to get into space, and destroying it seemed almost sacrilegious.

Jem was resistant to the idea that there would be no humanity left unless the Earth-based conflict was stopped but finally agreed that it was at least a possibility. The two talked for a while longer, then decided to wait until the morning to meet on the D-R to discuss ways and means.

THERE WERE FOUR people on the bridge of the D-R.

Jem had eased his ship into a parallel orbit less than thirty minutes previously, and now The Lazy Hooker was resting only a few hundred yards away from the D-R.

Flynn had come out from the surface of Titan late in alterday watch. To'afa was already on board since he'd been crewing the ship, doing various maintenance tasks and playing backgammon at an online casino with a wide variety of gamblers. So far, he was up over ten thousand credits, and he was pumped up as a result.

Adam was non-committal on the backgammon issue. It was To'afa's money, and Adam didn't feel that it was any of his business. Good idea or not, it was better than the drugs that To'afa sometimes took.

"The basic idea is simple," Adam said. "We circle around and come in from closer to the Sun. If we arrive from a Sunward direction, it won't automatically implicate the Belt. I'm assuming that we'll be successful, but there is a chance that they will recover enough to attempt a reprisal."

Flynn shrugged. "We beat 'em once. I'd like to see 'em try again. They'll get the same result."

That was probably true, but the smaller man was ignoring the damage, loss of life, and ships that resulted from the battle of the Bubble.

"Maybe we can beat them again. They've had plenty of time to build more ships. There are quite a few in lunar orbit and more on the surface. I haven't seen a recent report, but I wouldn't be surprised if they outnumbered us by at least two to one or more. We need to create confusion. Keep them guessing. Once the Ribbon is down, I'm hoping that the Feds will back off on their bombing. They won't be able to resupply easily at a minimum."

To'afa grunted, then commented, "They might blame the whole raid on the Non-Aligns and intensify their bombing instead."

That was a bothersome possibility. "Yeah, that's something I've been worried about. If they drop more bombs, we'll have to go back and take out some of their ships directly. Once we do that, they'll figure out we're from the Belt. I don't want that to happen, but it may."

Flynn swore, not an unusual event since he did so in almost every other sentence he uttered. "By Hades, I hope that's the case. We should let them know upfront that we're from the Belt. It would keep them from blaming someone on Earth."

Adam hadn't thought of that. It would undoubtedly distract the Feds. They'd be crazy to fight a war on two fronts, especially when they'd lost their primary means of resupply.

"Maybe you're on to a solution. I don't like it, but if we're going to step in, we should take responsibility. The only thing is, I'm reluctant to drag the rest of the Belt into the thing."

Jem nodded in agreement. "They're not going to like it much. On the other hand, I get the feeling that you've been unhappy about being so popular with the Council. Dragging them into a war, especially when they voted against intervening, will probably cure their infatuation with you. We all might end up as outlaws."

Flynn laughed. "Then we could go back to being Pirates again. It sounds good to me."

To'afa nodded, too. "I'm in."

Adam looked at his friends. They were ready to back him, even in something so crazy as this.

"Alright. The D-R has a new weapon. We need to put it on both of your ships."

Jem asked, "What is it? You always seem to come up with good stuff."

"I've been keeping it quiet. We call it the D-D, I'm afraid to name it, since secrets don't stay secret, even out here. Anyway, it's a game-changer. Far more deadly than the plasma cannon, but it won't work well in an area with a lot of dust."

Jem looked puzzled. "What's to stop them from dumping a hold of dust particles as a defense?"

That would be a problem, but the Feds wouldn't figure it out until too late, if they could keep the positron weapon secret. "Nothing and that's one of the reasons I'm keeping it quiet."

Flynn looked down at his feet. "I, uh, I don't have access to a ship right now. The owners of the one I was captaining basically fired me. Said I was too resistant to their orders."

That brought laughter. Adam said, "You've never been one to follow an order that went against your judgment. We'll just have to locate a spare ship for you. I'll work on that. It shouldn't take too long. I know this Admiral, see."

To'afa groaned. "Don't make a joke about it. Flynn has been smoldering inside about being stuck on the rock. He's had a taste of being on his own, and I think he's addicted."

Flynn snapped, "At least I like to be on my own. You seem to be stuck working for Adam."

To'afa responded, "He's good. He knows what's going on, and I figure my chances of surviving are higher if I'm with him than on another ship. I'm happy here. Besides, he needs me if it comes to hand-to-hand."

A brief memory of To'afa swinging his ax and chopping through a spacesuit passed through Adam's mind, then he said, "Okay. That's settled. I'll see about a third ship for Flynn, then I believe we'd be better if we went off to Jem's home base. We can work on adding the new weapon to both ships there with less interference."

Jem nodded. "I'm intrigued by this new thing. How does it work?"

"Oh, let's just say it's interesting. It involves alien technology and does something we hadn't thought was possible.. Seriously though, I'll fill you in once we get away from Titan. Better get your fill of civilization tonight. We'll probably be ready to go by late mainday tomorrow."

ADAM KNEW OF two ships that were currently under construction. They were located around the horizon on Titan. A new shipbuilding company had been formed and was just starting to crank out smaller ships that were based on the standard miner pattern.

The significant difference was that these were designed with the plasma systems and the new hyperdrive as an integral part from the beginning. No retrofitting required. He'd kept it quiet, but he had encouraged the shipyard owners and had invested the majority of his battle stipend, awarded by the Council, in their business.

A brief comm discussion revealed that one of the two was complete and ready for a shake-down cruise.

"Listen, Bob, why don't you let me take it out. I've got an experienced Captain, and I'll make sure that it gets checked thoroughly."

"Yes, Adam. I'm sure you will, but the Sagittarius Combine has put a down payment on it. Knowing you, I'm not sure it will come back in one piece. Can you guarantee that you'll return it within a week?"

"You know that there are no guarantees when it comes to space, Bob. I need it for a specific purpose, and I'll have to have it for at least a month. I can guarantee you that it will come back with some equipment installed that will make it far more valuable than it currently is."

"By the dust of Mars, Adam! I can't go around disappointing my clients. I'll get a bad rep, and no one will be putting in orders. Right now, I've got more than I can handle, but I've got to think long term."

"Bob, Bob, listen to me. I've got another invention that is going to prove to be at least as important as the plasma cannon. I've been keeping it secret, but I will eventually need someone to manufacture it and install it on ships. Other business owners would space their mothers to get hold of this. I'm offering it to you with two conditions. One is that you let me have this ship, and the other is that you pay me ten percent of the net on the units you sell for ten years. No more than that."

Bob was apparently tempted. "Maybe. The terms you're offering sound too good to be true. They are way below market, especially if your invention is as good as you say. What are you getting out of it? Why are you doing this?"

"The ship. I need that ship. If I can't get it from you, I'll go elsewhere. There are others available, you know. It's just that I want one of yours. Not having to contend with the retrofitted plasma system and power lines running all over the place will make it a lot easier for me to install my new mod. However, if I have to use an older ship, I can work around the retrofits. I've installed the system on the D-R and know it will work."

"It's on the D-R? Now?"

"Yes, but don't get any ideas. You wouldn't recognize the system if you were able to get past To'afa. To help convince you, I'll provide you with a schematic and engineering plans for the new system when I pick up the ship from you."

Bob cursed, "Phobos and Deimos! Fear and Terror! You know this will make me very unpopular with Sagittarius."

"Okay, okay. Can you refund their money?"

"Sure, but it's not that, it's the inconvenience they'll experience."

Adam sighed. Things were always tricky, but there was always a way. It seemed that it usually involved him compromising on things that he'd rather not compromise on.

"How about you explain to them that you're going to upgrade their ship at no cost. You can give it to them with the new weapon, uh, modification, when I return it."

Bob's hearing was excellent. "Did you say 'weapon'?"

"Ah. I misspoke. Don't spread it around."

"Look, Adam here's what I'm willing to do. You fly out here in the D-R, give me a demo of this new wea—, uh, modification, and, provided I like it and it works, then I'll let you have the #001. The first ship out of our yard. You'll have to give me the other stuff you mentioned when you take the ship, though."

Adam chuckled. "You're a good friend, Bob. Also, you're a sharp businessman. I'll see you in about two hours."

TWO DAYS LATER, Flynn, captaining the 001, now named the Double-Zero-One, rendezvoused with the Dire Rhea and the Lazy Hooker as they neared the second asteroid base.

Once they'd eased their ships to a relative stand-still a few hundred yards from the slowly rotating rock, they jetted over to check in with the Mayor of the place.

There were less than one hundred people now living in the cavern. The Fed attack on the Bubble had persuaded most of the Belters that populating an asteroid with a large number of people was dangerous. Most asteroid bases now held only two or three families to limit their bases' strategic value.

There were a lot of bases spread around, however. The population had grown and was still growing, although the outflow from Earth had stopped. Most of the new people were from Mars. They had not fit in well with the tightly controlled society the Martians were creating and had been encouraged to leave for the freedom of the Belt.

Mayor Tansy was not overly warm to Adam. She made it clear that his presence always seemed to be associated with some sort of conflict.

She was blunt about it, too. "We don't want any Feds or fighting out here. This rock isn't easy to defend. It's no Bubble, that's for sure. The main opening to the cavern is just too large. Promise me that you're not going to get a war going here."

"That's the last thing on my mind, Mayor. We're only going to enjoy your hospitality for a short time while we modify two of our ships. We might need some machining done, and I know you have a good machinist. Otherwise, we have the parts and workers we need to do what we want to do."

"You'll pay going rates plus forty percent for the inconvenience you're giving us if you take our machinist. He's almost always booked completely."

It was probably better to complain, just to make her think he wasn't desperate to get the work done.

"C'mon, Elsie. That's robbery. We'll pay going rate, sure, but forty percent more? That's..."

She interrupted. "That's what it'll take. I'm serious about that."

It wasn't actually unreasonable. There was no other real machinist available unless he returned to Titan. The actual need for the man's services would probably be small, too.

"Alright, Elsie. It's a deal. How about food? You going to charge us forty percent more if we visit your restaurant?"

"No. Food's getting cheaper, what with the asteroid farms and the produce that's getting shipped from Mars. We've got a good cook, too."

Her image on the comm screen looked around the bridge. Where's that girlfriend of yours. I thought you'd be married by now."

That hurt. "Uh, she's off on another job. I'm not quite sure where she is at this instant." He paused, then added, "She'll be back fairly soon."

That last was more to raise his spirits than to convince Elsie.

The Mayor had to go and remind him of Nile's absence. He'd processed it over and over, finally convincing himself that she had been kidnapped, despite the look of the thing. That explanation seemed weak whenever someone else asked where Nile was. Now he'd be in for some more sleepless nights agonizing over the apparent betrayal.

THE FIRST INSTALLATION went well. The Double-Zero-One was designed so that the modification was far easier than it had been for the D-R. The second installation was complicated. The Lazy Hooker was a jumble of patches and jury-rigs.

Jem was a competent Captain, but his ship was old and had been worked on by numerous crews. He'd been gradually cleaning up the mess left by the various engineers, but there was still a lot to do.

Adam almost gave up a couple of times, but the necessity of having a third ship with a complete complement of weaponry kept him going for the extra week needed to get the positron gun in place.

Earth was currently on the far side of Sol, but that fit into their plans. It would make it more difficult to tell precisely where they'd started.

A week and four days after they'd arrived at Valhalla, the three ships set off, heading out of the ecliptic on a course set to curve around the Sun and bring them back in near Venus' orbit.

11
THE RAID

THE HYPERDRIVE MADE short work of the lengthy trip. They ceased accelerating when they reached a point that was eight minutes light from the sun. The ships coasted for a day, then reoriented and accelerated towards Venus' orbit.

Earth grew larger as they reentered the solar system. Tension grew at the same rate. They'd be in position to start their attack run within seven hours.

Adam had told the others to reduce comm power so that the signal was feeble. They were moving in close formation, and a weak signal was adequate for ship-to-ship communication. Even a weak signal would persist, however, and there was a chance of interception, so they kept contact to a minimum.

All three captains were engaged in computing the individual vectors they were to take. The plan was for each of the three ships to come in on a straight pass from a different angle. The vectors would allow them to cross the target position separated by only a minute. Flynn was to strike first, then Jem, then the D-R would finish, cleaning up whatever needed to be cleaned up.

Adam hoped that the Ribbon would be cut by the first ship, the first shot, really, but there was no way to ensure that would be the case adequately. The positron weapon was too new.

Both the positron gun and the plasma cannon would be brought into play. Positron first, followed by a plasma shot. The hyperdrive had to be shut off to charge the positron holding chamber, so the ships would coast through the intersection with the Ribbon.

The timing was critical. There was a minor chance of collision if they were too close, but the possibility of flying through the remains of a positron shot or a plasma bolt was distinctly higher. It was an exercise in geometry and timing to come up with the optimal vectors. Each Captain ran their own calculations, then used short-burst encryption to send the results to the D-R where Adam carefully plotted the attack vectors.

He was satisfied. His tiny squadron of three ships diverged and headed to the starting point for their attack vectors.

The ships at both Luna and the Ribbon Station were now showing on the sensor suite. That information was the critical piece. He hadn't been able to tell what ships were near the Ribbon until this point.

If there were too many ships there, the chances of a successful attack dropped. They would need to maneuver to avoid hostile fire, and that would complicate aiming. He wanted each shot to hit the vulnerable point directly below the Ribbon Station. Getting away afterward would also become difficult.

The sensor-suite clicked to itself, then displayed a picture that made Adam's stomach churn. Nearly half of the Luna fleet was resting near the Ribbon Station. Thirty-four ships were in position to immediately respond to their attack.

He grabbed the comm system microphone, punched the keyboard for encryption, then said, "Plan two."

There was a pause, then the comm clicked twice as Jem signaled assent, then three times as Flynn replied.

The Navy ships used an auto-broadcast identification system that allowed them to keep track of each other. It could be turned off if the ship's Captain wanted to run incommunicado.

Adam hoped that the silence his group had maintained, and the lack of response by the resting ships meant that they hadn't been automatically identified as enemies. Now each of the three Belter ships turned on a broadcast that was intended to spoof the Navy ID system.

They broadcast ID numbers that belonged to actual Navy ships. The problem was that one or more of the ships ahead of them might be the true owners of the ID or know that the ship with that ID was not supposed to be near the Ribbon Station. If that happened the ID spoofing would fail, an alert would be broadcast, and they'd be facing a foe that was ready for them.

THE D-R WAS approaching the start of its attack vector. Flynn was slightly ahead according to plan. He was to take the first shot. Jem's Lazy Hooker, the second, and the D-R would be last, following a few seconds later to finish the task. With any luck, the Ribbon would part with one or two shots. There was tremendous stress on it, and it should rip apart when weakened.

The Ribbon Station massed megatons and served as the counterweight spinning at the end of the Ribbon and holding it in place.

If the Ribbon was cut, the Station would quickly drift away from Earth. The Ribbon itself would slowly begin to fall. There would be time to evacuate the buildings that surrounded the attachment point, or at least, that was what Adam hoped.

He observed that his hands were shaking with a fine tremor. He was about to become the most hated person in the history of humanity. They would call him terrorist and worse. The Ribbon was not only the sole space elevator, but it was also the symbol of the ascendance of humankind.

A cold wave went over him. It had to be done. Those idiots on the ground had let Elseth and her backers push them into a war that threatened the very survival of the planet. What was a human artifact, even one as impressive as the Ribbon, worth in the face of the destruction of humanity's Mother?

Flynn came on the comm with an encrypted short-burst.

"Approaching. They've started to react. We're being hailed on the military laser band. What should I say?"

For the Irishman to ask what to say, betrayed the stress of the moment. Flynn was never without an answer.

Adam replied, "Maintain comm silence. They'll hear our short-bursts, but even if they break the encryption, it will be too late. You're clear to final. Go for it!"

Flynn came back on immediately. "Got a problem here. The positron storage is only at point three-two cap. It was full, but it's leaked out somewhere. Whoever installed this system was a bloody idiot."

Despite the bad news, Adam grinned slightly. Flynn had done at least half of the installation on the Double-Zero-One.

"Switch to plasma. Do your best, then scramble."

Flynn's mike button clicked in acknowledgment.

A moment later, the comm broke up with the characteristic static as the plasma cannon was discharged. The D-R's sensor suite flashed red, then the monitor showed a bright glow on one edge of the Ribbon about a thousand meters below the mass of the Station.

The resting warships began to break out of their formation.

To'afa said, "That's trouble. It's like poking a beehive with a stick. They're going to be on us pretty quick."

Flynn's ship accelerated away as he boosted with the hyperdrive.

Adam ran a quick scan looking for Jem. The Lazy Hooker was on target, but a few seconds behind where it should be. It would take at least seven seconds before Jem was in a position to fire. Adam ground his teeth in frustration. Jem's ship had no problem keeping up on the voyage to this point, but now it was behind for whatever reason. He grabbed the mike again.

"Jem, what's the hang-up?"

The reply was chilling. "Capacitor bank is acting up. I slowed a bit to give us time to reboot the controller. Didn't work. I've got no plasma, and the antimatter gun is only about half charged. I've got positrons, just not going to be able to fire them at high velocity."

Adam wiped his hand over his eye. The raid was turning into a disaster. He reached for the comm, then the sensor suite caught his eye.

"Jem, multiple plasma bursts and missile launches in your direction. It looks like some are going to intercept your path possibly. Veer off."

Jem replied, "Not before I shoot what I can."

He apparently fired as soon as he finished the sentence. The comm broke up with static, then the sensor suite alerted to the positron burst.

Adam adjusted the D-R's course slightly, while he watched the target with an intent glare in his eye.

Unlike a plasma bolt, the positron cloud was almost invisible in a pure vacuum. The only thing that gave its position away were tiny flashes as individual positrons annihilated dust particles in their path.

Suddenly the Ribbon glowed red, then bright yellow. Jem's shot had struck. Adam held his breath watching the vid. That would show the result more definitively than the sensor suite.

The yellow glow faded, revealing a long rip in the Ribbon fabric. The antimatter cloud didn't depend on velocity to do its damage. The Ribbon was partially cut, but the remainder seemed to be strong enough to hold against the Station's pull.

Adam clicked the mike button. "Jem, scramble now. Change vectors and scramble."

Jem's voice came back. It didn't sound right to Adam. Jem usually was laconic, but his voice was tight and clipped now.

"Power is failing. Can't activate hyperdrive. Cap bank is back up, though. I'm shooting plasma at the rest of it now. Then I'll have to rely on Em-Max to get me out."

That wasn't going to work. He wouldn't be able to accelerate quickly enough to avoid the missiles, even if he successfully dodged the plasma bursts that were coming in his direction.

The comm dissolved in static as Jem's plasma bolt was released. The vid showed it clearly as it tracked across the distance toward the Ribbon.

Adam advanced the D-R's speed, in his desire to be there instantly. The ship closed in on the Ribbon quickly.

The extent of the damage clearly showed as they drew closer. The Ribbon was still holding, although only about one-quarter of its fabric remained. The shots had taken out a wide swath of the middle, leaving the two edges attached.

The left edge flared as Jem's plasma arrived. When the glare died, the Ribbon was still attached. The right edge was about a quarter of the width, although only the extreme left side was holding.

With two widely separated targets, the situation grew more complex. Adam would have to use the plasma gun to take out the narrow left edge and then hope the antimatter would finish off the right side.

The Lazy Hooker was turning hard towards the surface of the Earth. It looked like Jem was suicidally heading directly into the mass of USSN ships, trying to ram them.

There were two small flares from the Hooker as both onboard missiles were fired. Neither the plasma nor the antimatter had any hope of recharging so quickly.

Jem came back on. "The power is back. I'm activating hyperdrive."

His ship began to move, diving directly through the massed warships, then accelerating away at an angle that would take him past the outermost edge of the atmosphere.

Adam watched half his attention on the D-R's course, the other half on the Hooker. He opened his mouth in an ineffectual warning cry. Jem was flying directly into a cloud of plasma. Three of the warships had predicted his path, and their shots were in the perfect position to hit.

Adam snapped his teeth together with a click.

The Hooker was bathed with red fire. There was a flash, indicating that something had blown over there.

There were more flashes from the massed warships as the hyper-vee missiles from the Hooker impacted. Adam hoped they would do a lot of damage.

Jem's ship appeared out of a surrounding cloud of small debris. It was obviously out of control, heading directly for Earth. There were already signs that it was entering the atmosphere. Superheated bits of metal and composite flew off as the friction heated the hull.

To'afa started to sob. "My friend! Jem, what have you done? Jem."

Adam snapped, "Pay attention. We've got to make this count. Jem would want us to succeed."

The D-R was now in range. Adam waited a moment, checking the complex trajectory before he pushed the firing button. It looked good. The interior lights dimmed as the capacitor bank discharged sending the antimatter on its way.

He switched to backup power and kicked the reactor, routing all output to the cap bank. The charge needle climbed quickly. The bank didn't need to be at full potential for this, but every joule would help.

It was challenging to keep his mind on targeting. He wanted to watch for the positron impact, and a distracted part of him found it difficult to look away from Jem's fatal plunge. The navy ships were complicating the situation by taking shots that were roughly directed at him. His plan for the three to come in on different vectors had almost worked. The enemy was having a difficult time re-targeting, but they were narrowing in on his trajectory.

The D-R was almost too close to the Ribbon Station for a clear shot.

Adam veered slightly to bring the left edge into perfect alignment, then he fired as the aim crossed the target.

The far edge flared as his positron cloud enveloped the nano-carbon chains that made up the Ribbon. The flare grew as the matter and antimatter mutually destructed. Before he could see the result, his plasma bolt struck directly on the thin strand that connected the parts of the left edge.

The strand grew bright red, then disappeared. The massive Station instantly began to swing up and away.

Adam switched the reactor power over to the hyperdrive collection net, turned on the drive, and waited for the system to collect enough virtual particles to kick the D-R out of danger. For a moment, it seemed as if nothing was happening.

The flares of a mass of missiles approached. The navy had finally fixed on his position. The hyperdrive needed to kick in now, or the shield would be overwhelmed.

The glowing right edge of the Ribbon abruptly flicked out. The positrons had done their job. There was still some Ribbon left over there, and the full mass of the Station swung against it, pivoting around and changing its path. The remaining Ribbon parted, and the miles of fabric below began to draw together as it started falling.

Adam's mind seemed light minutes away. He noticed that two of the navy ships were in the way of a fold. They accelerated, but the fabric was too large and moving too quickly. The ships were pushed together and enveloped by the falling Ribbon. It meant nothing to him, other than a dull sense of partial revenge.

Jem's ship was almost over the horizon now, a blazing ball of fire that could have no survivors. Adam had a stray feeling of dismay. What would he tell Jem's wife and child? What could he say that would make up for the loss?

The missiles were closing in, only moments before impact. The hyperdrive began to move the ship, accelerating at an exponential rate.

One second the D-R was directly in the path of the missiles, the next, it was far away, gaining speed with every moment. Leaving the missiles and even slower navy ships behind.

He called Flynn, "Where are you? I lost track of the Double-Zero-One in the confusion."

He waited for a response. Their separation was rapidly increasing, and the signal transit time made for a slight delay.

Flynn's navigator, George, came on a few seconds later.

"YOU JUST WAIT a minute. Captain's looking at a minor problem with the output gain control in the engine room."

Adam grinned wryly. Flynn had taken George on at the last moment and the man was skilled at his job, but not socially adept. He had been known to answer the comm with profanity if he felt the incoming call was an interruption of whatever he was attempting to do.

That attitude was more or less endemic, though. The belter community was informal to the point of rudeness at times. People were expected to focus on their jobs and not worry about extraneous things like manners. The convention had a way of keeping susceptible individuals from getting too prideful. He didn't care. His rank was earned by his performance and not just awarded for political expediency.

After a moment, Flynn came on.

"Heading for Venus again, but the hyperdrive is hiccuping. I think I need a new transfer module. What happened back there?"

He couldn't speak. There was a strange tightness in his throat that seemed to paralyze his vocal cords. Finally, he croaked, "Ribbon's gone. So is Jem."

"What? Those miserable ground rats! Shootin' at us when we're trying to help them."

Flynn was uncharacteristically calm sounding and to Adam's ears that indicated that the Irishman was furious.

"Flynn, continue on planned course. I'm right after you. We're done here. Now, what's happening with the hyperdrive?"

"I'm only getting about twenty percent of nominal output. I'm thinkin' that somethin' hit the collection funnel. Whatever it is, I'm barely faster than a full-on Em-Max."

"I'm going to try and keep them focused on me. With any luck, they'll forget about you. Keep going on the planned course. Out."

The answer came back in terms of two clicks on the comm. Adam adjusted the D-R's course slightly. He was heading straight out at ninety degrees to the ecliptic. It was a noncommittal course that betrayed no information about his ultimate destination.

The USSN ships had finally gotten organized and were at full boost behind him, but there was no way they could keep up. He'd shut the hyperdrive down and had the Em-max at only fifty percent. If the navy could see him, they might keep after him and ignore Flynn.

Once they were far enough out, he'd activate hyperdrive again and effectively disappear. His pursuers would be left wondering where their target had gone.

To'afa chose that moment to make an alarmed sound.

"What?" Adam was temporarily distracted as he glanced at his friend.

"Ships on an intercept vector from Luna." The big man pointed at the sensor suite.

Adam glanced. He'd been so involved in watching the pursuing force that he'd ignored the sensors' warning. One glance was all he needed. The solution was simple: go hyper now to avoid the interceptors.

He shook his head in frustration. That action would get the D-R out of the crosshairs, but Flynn's drive status possibly put him in danger. Something would have to be done to keep the Feds focused on the D-R.

That, too, was an easy decision. He altered course slightly to put the intercepting force more nearly in front.

The ships closed quickly. Adam bit his lip. It was pure bad luck that Luna was where it was. The commander of the ships located there had been more ready than the USSN's history indicated. The man had gotten his flotilla organized quickly.

The antimatter gun was fully recharged. Their speed added to the gun's ejection velocity meant that the positron cloud would be moving faster than usual. That took a moment of calculation on the comp.

The answer appeared. He was almost too late to shoot. He twitched the D-R's nose a few degrees to bring the aim into better focus, then fired.

The D-R shook unexpectedly, then something outside clanged against the hull.

The instruments hadn't warned of any incoming ordinance. Adam looked at To'afa. The big man looked blankly back, then said, "What was that?"

A second inspection of the instrument boards showed nothing. Adam replied, "Don't know. Maybe we hit something. I'm recharging the antimatter weapon now. We'll know the result of our shot in a few seconds. I want to be ready for a follow-up if we didn't get all of them."

The recharge procedure was simple. Check the reactor for power, key the comp to reroute the funnel's output to the storage chamber for the weapon, then wait until the readout said it was at capacity. It was inconvenient since the energy funnel's entire production was required, and that left nothing for the hyperdrive. They could either escape quickly or load their new super-weapon for another shot. Those were the only two choices.

There was something wrong with the comp. Adam keyed a diagnostic routine. In response, the board lit with red grabbing his attention. The display showed the magnetic containment field had failed as the bulk of the positrons were in the barrel. The antimatter contacting the ordinary matter of the tube created a rupture.

That was what they'd felt. Some of the antimatter particles had burned through the side of the barrel. The rupture was on the side away from the hull, but that was the only lucky thing about the failure. Now they could only rely on their plasma weapons and shielding. The USSN ships had comparable weapons with the added advantage of their railguns and hyper-vee missiles.

His hands flew as he switched the funnel output back to the drive system. Suddenly, the strategy of turning towards the intercepting ships didn't seem so smart. He changed course, re-vectoring as quickly as possible. The fabric of the ship groaned with the gees. His vision darkened with the force.

To'afa let out a loud grunt. "Hey! Too sharp, Captain. Too sharp."

He relaxed the turn just a bit, and the gee force dropped slightly. They were now pointed ahead of the USSN ships, but the numbers and relative positions were against them unless the hyperdrive kicked in soon.

A check of its status showed that the flow of virtual particles was building, but not to the point where the drive would activate and boost them past the enemy. Adam checked the plasma cannon. It was ready to go, but they were still too far for an effective shot at this high speed.

There was a sudden flash among the intercepting ships as one vessel exploded. The debris struck two more, spinning them out of control. A second vessel exploded, and some of the others suddenly developed gaping holes in their hulls. The positron cloud had done butcher's work, but there were still some ships intact.

The sensor suite blared alarm. The enemy had released a flight of missiles that were now entering their boost phase, coming directly at the D-R. They were off at an angle and re-vectoring to compensate for their target's velocity.

Adam ran a targeting solution on the comp, made a slight adjustment in the D-R's orientation, then fired the plasma cannon. The lights dimmed as the cap-bank discharged. He could see the glowing mass of plasma recede quickly, heading directly towards the missiles.

The guidance computers in the hyper-velocity missiles were programmed to avoid solid objects in their path to their assigned target. They were not programmed to steer around a plasma cloud. The flight of missiles exploded with a brilliant flash, betraying the presence of nuclear warheads.

When the vid screen recovered, To'afa said, "I'm glad those were off our course. I'd hate to fly through the mess of hard radiation they left."

Adam nodded, still watching the collection funnel's performance numbers. It had reached the point where there was enough collected mass to activate the hyperdrive. He set the timer for a five-second boost, then reached for the activation button. There was a screeching noise as something hard ripped along the outside of the hull.

"Damn Feds must have shot a bunch of railgun slugs at us before they launched the missiles," he snapped.

He activated the drive. There was a blur followed by a sensation of smoothly increasing gravity as the D-R accelerated. The drive cut off five seconds later, precisely on time. It was a relief to have it cease. The acceleration was becoming painful.

The Navy ships and Luna were far behind them now. They were moving at high speed directly out of the system, heading for empty space.

When Adam looked at the Earth and Moon in the vid, the solar system was tiny and rapidly shrinking. The USSN ships were not visible.

"That was good. I wonder what we looked like when you hit the Go button," To'afa said.

He thought about that. It must have been impressive to watching Navy personnel.

"Let's hope that they didn't get the chance to figure out our drive. That Klingfeldt hasn't given it to them yet. Right now, it's the main advantage we have over them," Adam answered.

To'afa said, "You're forgetting the D-D."

Adam snorted, "That was unexpected. I'm going to have to figure out what went wrong. We can't have it blowing up in every engagement or after just a few shots. Luckily, the blow-out was away from the hull. Otherwise, we'd be in vacuum right now."

To'afa shook his head but said nothing.

After a moment, Adam continued, "We'll wait a few minutes then alter course and head home."

12

THE AFTERMATH

FLYNN WAS AT Titan when the D-R coasted into orbit. He'd taken a more direct route and beaten them in by twelve hours. His ship had some minor damage from the raid, but nothing compared to the hull damage inflicted on the D-R by the rail-gun slug.

The blown-out barrel of the antimatter weapon was another issue. Adam was anxious to get on that right away since he thought it was critical in the situation that was now developing.

Both the Belter community news and Earth's news stations had been available to the D-R, but Adam made it a policy not to watch what he characterized as propaganda and lies. However, he had made an exception and turned on the Belter news station as the D-R was approaching Titan.

The Federal Dictatorship, Elseth had changed the name again, was furious about the Ribbon. It didn't help that the rest of the Earth, including the Non-Aligns, was also angry. The Ribbon had served as a symbol for all of Humankind, despite their conflict.

Elseth had initially blamed the Non-Aligns for the raid. Her surviving ships had immediately intensified their bombing efforts. Now, many Non-Aligns cities had been destroyed, and to all accounts, there was a considerable casualty toll.

The surviving Non-Aligns were counter-attacking, using a combination of smuggled vest-pocket nukes and submarine-launched missiles from a fleet of subs that no one had known existed. The North American continent was suffering almost as much as the Non-Align cities.

An old weapon had been used for the first time. Drone submarine-based nuclear bombs had devastated most of the coastal cities on North America.

. These were detonated deep in the off-shore waters to create tsunamis. The resulting massive waves had wiped Miami completely off the Florida peninsula, and most of the Eastern seaboard cities had suffered similar damage.

Some enterprising Belter had hijacked video from a ship in Earth orbit that showed some of the damage. Titan news was showing the video every few minutes. When Adam saw it, his spirits sank. The Earthers were doing precisely what he had hoped to prevent.

Glowing pools of hard radiation could be seen from space as soon as an orbiting ship crossed to the night side of the planet. Adam was horrified. His plan, rather than stopping the destruction, had induced the combatants to go even farther towards mutual destruction.

That wasn't the least of his problems. The Belter Council was on the warpath and wanted his head. They had issued an order for his arrest on the charge of treason.

Flynn hadn't landed on Titan after receiving that news, although the Council seemed unaware of his role in the raid. At least, they hadn't issued an arrest order for him so far.

When the D-R coasted up near Flynn's ship, and they'd established a closed laser comm-link that was unlikely to be intercepted, Flynn warned Adam immediately.

Flynn ignored a greeting in order to get directly to the point.

"I've been here a bit longer than you. It would be best if you hightailed it out of here right now. The officials down there are out for blood. They're saying you're a traitor and an enemy of all of mankind. Maybe knocking down the Ribbon wasn't such a good idea, huh?"

Adam hesitated before responding. It had made perfect sense. Cutting the Ribbon meant that Elseth's space force couldn't resupply. They would only have a limited number of nukes in orbit and on Luna. As far as he was aware, there hadn't been any new nuclear weapons created for years. The USSN had to be using old ones that had been transported up

While there had been some radioactive material found in the asteroid belt, it was rare. The few discoveries had been publicly announced, too. He didn't think it was likely that the Feds had been able to amass a significant supply of bomb-making materials.

He punched the comm button. "Hi, Flynn. Good to see you, too. It looks like we precipitated the final stage of their dirty war. They don't seem to know it was us, the way they're fighting each other."

"Yeah, but Admiral, maybe we should let the Earthers know that we did it. Maybe they'd stop killing each other then."

Adam had already thought of that. "If we tell them, they'll do something about it. They will have to save face. I'm afraid that they would try to bomb Mars and Titan both. I don't want that on my conscience."

"Couldn't we watch for ships and intercept them before they got out here?"

"Possibly. Maybe we could, but it would be difficult. Space is big, and we have a limited number of ships. How long do you think the average miner is going to stand watch before he decides he needs to go back to searching for his next big score?"

It took Flynn a moment to respond. "Right. We can't stop them until they get out here and get close. We'd have to keep a close watch on incoming ships. Not let them get into orbit, I guess."

"It's worse than that, Flynn. They could release a missile to coast in silently on a direct course. Once it got close enough, it could boost. We probably wouldn't have time to stop it, particularly if there was more than one."

They were interrupted by the broadband comm. The Council had just heard that the D-R had arrived, and they had dispatched a shuttle with orders to the crew to bring Adam back to answer questions.

To'afa grunted when he heard the announcement. "Ugh. That's bureaucrat-speak for 'we are going to lock you up.' I've heard that kind of stuff before."

Adam nodded. "Yes. I believe you're correct about their intentions. I think that we'd be better off somewhere far away, at least until they've had a chance to calm down."

He looked over at his friend, then continued. "I've still got some hope that the Earthers will find some sense, but if they don't, then we're going to have to make another pass at them. Make them quit somehow. I haven't figured that out yet, but we can't stand by and watch them destroy Earth."

To'afa nodded, then turned to the nav-comp. "Maybe Valhalla would be far enough? We need to head out there and see Jem's widow."

He looked depressed, then added, "Man, I'm not looking forward to that meeting, but it has to be done."

It was Adam's turn to nod in agreement. After a moment, he agreed. "Set up the course. We'll leave before the shuttle gets out here."

Flynn was informed of the decision over the closed-link laser. The Irishman agreed that they'd all be better off somewhere else.

"Look, Adam, uh, Admiral. We can't let them get their hands on you, and I don't trust them not to take their anger out on me. Let's get moving. We need to leave in the next ten minutes. That shuttle's not wasting any time boosting up here."

"I agree, Flynn. We're powering up now. Oh, and stop calling me Admiral. They'll pull that title as soon as they remember they gave it to me. It didn't mean much anyhow."

Adam's fingers slid over the control board, and the D-R responded. A low hum, almost subsonic, permeated the ship as the reactor began charging the banks.

"To'afa, we'll have to check that out. Sounds like one of the transformer windings is working loose again."

"Sure thing. I've got 0.96% on the reliability scale, though. I don't think it's going to cause problems for a while."

Adam nodded, then touched the Initiate Boost pad. There was no sound as the Em-Max engaged, but the vidscreen showed Flynn's ship sliding out of the center.

The sensor suite had started flashing orange with a proximity alert for a recognized-friendly craft.

To'afa said, "That'd be the shuttle with the cops. It looks like they're trying to get in our way."

Adam nodded. "That's a stupid thing to do. They can't stop us and a collision would destroy their ship, but not ours."

To'afa agreed. "Yes, but it might damage our collection funnel. Maybe they were ordered to stop us at any cost. Without the hyperdrive functional, the Council can get some other ships up here."

"Good thinking. You're probably right."

He didn't want to use the hyperdrive so close to the other ship, but it looked like it was the expedient thing to do.

"Hold on. Acceleration in five."

Both men checked their belts, then Adam engaged the hyperdrive. The storage was about half-full of virtual mass. He had made it a rule to always keep mass in reserve, just in case of emergency. This situation showed that it was good practice.

Titan abruptly grew smaller. There was an outraged mixture of commands and curses from the shuttle, but the reception was spotty. The hyperdrive disrupted normal comm channels.

He checked the vid lock on the Double-Zero-One. It was still showing the ship centered on the display.

Flynn was moving, also. The vid showed his ship, but it was slightly blurred due to the disparity in velocities.

To'afa sighed. It came out as more of a pained grunt. They were still accelerating, and it was becoming painful.

Adam switched the drive off, leaving them coasting. The sense of acceleration vanished, then the Em-Max restarted, and it came back but at a barely perceptible level. They were on their way to Valhalla, but after that, where? The future seemed confused. If both Earth and the Belt Council wanted them, they were truly outlaws. He grimaced. Not outlaws—Pirates.

The comm alerted, signifying an incoming tight-beam laser short-code. The system chirped, then expanded and decrypted the transmission.

A man's face appeared. He looked blankly at the screen for a moment, then said, "Admiral, I'm the president of the Independent Miners Association. We have told the Council that we disapprove of their attempt to arrest you. We were not in favor of cutting the Ribbon, but we agree with you. Something had to be done. Regardless, we believe that you were acting in good faith, so we decided to support you. Most of us are ready to back you up if you decide you need to take more action. Just call me."

The comm clicked off. Short-code messages were not interactive by their very nature. The header of the message contained originating ship information. To'afa tapped on the comm system's keyboard, storing that data for later use.

The comm alerted, then Flynn's face appeared. It was slightly distorted, but his voice was clear enough.

"You sure gave those buggers a thrill. When you ripped past them, their shuttle actually bucked then rolled. I think they were a little irritated by you leaving so quickly. D'ya think they'll follow us?"

"Not in that shuttle. They're probably watching our departure vector, trying to figure out where we're headed. We'll need to change direction a couple of times while they can see us easily. That'll slow them down a bit."

Speaking was accomplished at the same time as acting. Adam reoriented the D-R and boosted off at an acute angle. The gee-force grew unpleasant for a moment, then eased off.

Flynn's face blurred, but his voice came in, suddenly stronger, "See ya there, Captain."

13

FINDING A HIDEOUT

THEIR ARRIVAL AT Base Two, as it was still uncreatively called, was not pleasant. Jem's wife, Katy, had already heard the news that he hadn't returned from the raid and she was devastated.

"Damn you, Adam. You were the only man he looked up to, and you dragged him off and got him killed. What am I going to do? I've got two children and one on the way. No Belter is going to want me and my family. I can't work. Pregnancy always makes me nauseous, and it's worse in zero-gee. The kids are good kids, but they are too young to be on their own, so I need daycare, that is even if I could work and—"

Here she broke down and began sobbing. "None of that is important, it's Jem. I can...can't believe he's gone. He was so careful and such an experienced spaceman. Nothing was going to kill him, no accidents, except you, got him in a war that couldn't be won. I...I—"

She bowed her head, her shoulders shaking silently.

Adam didn't know what to say, but he felt that he had to defend his position and, for some reason, Jem's good name.

"Look, Katy, I know things are going to be hard for you. I miss Jem too. He was the first member of the D-R's crew that I met." He thought about that. Maybe it wasn't a good idea to mention that the first time they had met. Jem had jammed a twelve-gauge sawed-off shotgun against his neck and threatened to blow his head off.

"Jem died doing what he thought was right. It shouldn't have happened, but it did. His ship was far superior to the Navy ships we were fighting. He just was unlucky, that's—"

"That's exactly what I'm talking about!" she interrupted bitterly. "He was never unlucky. He was too careful, and it isn't luck that keeps you alive out here, it's knowing what you're doing and being methodical. You got him killed...and I don't know what I'm going to do."

At least he could help with part of her problem. "You know that I've got part interest in several businesses? And, that I also hold patents on the shield tech, the plasma cannons, the new hyperdrive, and..."

He stopped there. The positron weapon was still a secret. Or it was supposed to be. He felt that the longer he could put off people knowing about it, the more of an advantage he would have in any conflict. When a new weapon was used in a fight, it was often only six months before the other side showed up with their own version. He currently had no ideas about other inventions and secretly worried that he might have exhausted his lifetime store of creativeness. What if he never came up with another invention?

He had been successful to this point largely because he'd been able to invent new tech faster than the Feds. That could change. Maybe it already had. If the positron gun was his last invention, he wanted to keep it out of the hands of his enemies as long as possible.

"Katy, what I'm saying is that I'm going to give you a monthly stipend that will allow you to raise your children without having to worry about anything. I can't replace Jem. I wish with all my heart that I could have him back again, but it isn't going to happen. He believed in what he was doing, and he did a magnificent job until his ship was too damaged to continue fighting. He was a hero, and if someone ever wrote a history of the Belt, he will have an important place in it."

She snuffled and nodded, then gulped, trying to recover her composure. "It's just that I miss him so much. It's one thing for him to go off on a voyage somewhere. I know he'll come back eventually. Now I've got to figure out how to live without him. I...I don't know what I'll tell the kids. Oh, Adam, I'm not angry with you. I know you've got our best interests at heart. I just wish..."

"I know," he said. He leaned forward and pulled her into an embrace. She hugged him back, then pulled away, her eyes shiny with tears. "I'll take your money. It's the only way I can be sure that Jem's children will survive. They're the only part of him I've got left."

He made a mental note to set up a trust for her, provided that his bankers would still deal with him as a wanted man. They'd better, he thought. It would do no good for their reputation for it to get around that they had frozen his accounts.

Katy cleared her throat, and he looked at her inquisitively. She said, "We got a message before you arrived. The Council has dispatched five ships to come here. They aren't sure where you were going, but they suspect that Valhalla might be your destination. You've got maybe two days, so you'd better head out. They're Em-Drive vessels. No hyperdrive yet."

That was unwelcome news. He had intended to stay there and begin to rebuild the D-R and the Double-Zero-One leisurely. Both had some battle damage and needed repair. Besides, he wanted to rethink the best use of the ships and their role in space combat. Now it looked like he would have to go elsewhere.

"That's too bad. I was hoping to stay here."

She shook her head, vehemently. "No, you can't. The Council cops will get you, and we don't want them penalizing us. Valhalla isn't self-sustaining, and we can't afford to be cut off. We're a small community and don't count for much in their eyes. You know that they'll come out here looking sooner or later, that is, if they haven't figured out, you're here already. You can't stay." She paused, breathing heavily, then added, "There is a spot that Jem discussed with me, though."

JEM HAD LOCATED an asteroid that might make a good base. It was near the outer part of Jupiter's orbit, so it was remote, and he'd never told anyone other than Katy about it. Several other significant rocks surrounded it. The mass of the group meant it would be easy to disguise the presence of two ships. As long as they weren't emitting active signals, they would be almost indistinguishable from the drifting rocks until the searchers got close enough for fine visual details.

KATY WAS RIGHT. The Council members weren't dummies. It was a sure bet they'd investigate Valhalla. Adam took a deep breath, trying to overcome his frustration. Establishing operations on a barren rock was something he was getting tired of doing. On the other hand, he had plenty of experience at the task. With that in mind, he printed a list of components that his small group would need and went shopping.

There were only two merchants in the community. Fortunately, they both carried a wide assortment of necessary and valuable objects, although most of it was second hand. On close inspection, Adam found that some of the merchandise couldn't reasonably be distinguished from junk.

His credit was good, at least until the Council got smart and froze it, so he bought two of everything using the general principle that some of the items wouldn't work, so a backup would be needed. There were still some critical components that he would find necessary, and he didn't know where he'd find those, but at least this was a start.

Once the electronics, metal, composites, and food were loaded, the D-R and the Double-Zero-One departed. They headed in the general direction of Neptune, which was currently nearing apogee and directly anti-sunward from Valhalla. They planned to re-vector once they were far enough away to make it difficult for any observers to see them.

TO'AFA WAS WATCHING the vid when Adam came into the bridge. He paused for a moment, peering over the bigger man's shoulder. When To'afa partially turned, Adam asked, "What's going on?"

The station was some rebroadcast news. These days it was difficult to tell what the original source had been. News broadcasts were picked up and retransmitted from one settler's low-powered station to another. Sometimes the station identifiers were stripped from the digital packets; sometimes they were not.

"Ahh, it's those ground pounders on Earth. They're still tearing up the place. The Feds have ceased dropping stuff from orbit, but they've launched surface-based attacks. The Non-Aligns haven't given up. The ones that aren't totally destroyed are fighting back. There's been an exchange of nuclear missiles, but not too many. At least, not yet. I hope somebody down there has some sense."

This was not the best news. "I guess they are going to need another lesson. We've got to get established and make the necessary repairs. I don't want the antimatter gun to blowout again. Besides we've got a slow leak in cargo compartment four where that cut nearly penetrated the hull."

"Yeah. I'm with you, Captain. What about Flynn's ship?"

The Double-Zero-One had suffered some damage from a nearby missile explosion. There were several shield generators out and, unlike the D-R, there was a bad leak in the hull. The hull outside Flynn's cabin had been struck hard, and there was a chunk of metal sticking through.

The jagged piece had actually gone through the mattress and bunk floor. Flynn made light of that, saying that he hadn't found the bed all that comfortable to start with, but the fact that his cabin was in total vacuum made him angry.

"I've been thinking about the order of the repairs we'll make. You and Flynn and George can handle the hull damage and install new shields at the same time. I'm going to devote my time to fixing the positron gun. I've got a couple of ideas about modifying the mag-field that might make it less apt to fail."

To'afa shook his head. "I'll leave that to you. The hulls are going to be simple, and I like simple." He grinned, showing white teeth. "You can keep that complex crap to yourself."

Adam smiled back. "Thanks a lot, Buddy."

TO'AFA WAS PROBABLY right. The hull damage was relatively straightforward to repair. It just involved a lot of work, both inside and in vacuum. Keeping the positrons under control was a different matter. He had an idea about redesigning the coils that generated the magnetic field. The antimatter had ablated the gun barrel and then blown out explosively on the last shot, so the stators weren't doing their intended job properly.

It wasn't as if there was any muzzle pressure to overcome. The main issue was simply imparting momentum to the particles and keeping them tightly grouped until they left the gun.

He'd used the Em-Max principle to entrain the things, but the mag fields hadn't kept the stream of particles separated from the actual matter in the weapon. That was a recipe for disaster, and they were fortunate the blowout had directed the antimatter away from the hull.

That thought linked to another idea and Adam was off in a fugue state, his mind filled with visualizations. He didn't precisely think in mathematical terms, but more in images that were bounded by math-defined parameters.

To'afa looked at his Captain and grinned to himself. The look on Adam's face was one that he recognized. Something good was going to come out of his friend's mind shortly. He just had to keep quiet and let it incubate until it was ready.

He went back to watching the news feed. It hadn't gotten any better during their conversation.

14
RENOVATIONS

THE ASTEROID THAT Jem had discovered was not perfect, but it would do. It was actually composed of a tight cluster of boulders, some larger than others. The rocks seemed to be held in a relatively stable formation by micro-gravity. There was one sizeable irregular chunk that was the heart. The others moved slowly around it in a stately dance.

The movement made for an uneasy relationship. Adam figured that it would take only a small disturbance to nudge one of the rocks out of its path. If that happened, the others would move also, and that would probably lead to collisions. Parking the two ships in the middle of a bunch of rebounding rocks didn't seem to be the best idea.

After thinking about the problem for a little, the solution occurred to him. Under his direction, both ships moved into a parallel path on the backside of the rocks. This placed a significant obstacle between them and any potential observers. A mining ship might come out this far by chance during an exploration run, and it would certainly discover the outlaws, but it was unlikely that either a Navy or a Belter Council ship would happen by. There was nowhere to go along this vector.

The next step was to begin work, and that was quickly started. It was going to be a long process. They had the onboard machining tools, welders, 3-D printers, and such, but the lack of workers was the limiting factor.

Another problem was Adam's mental state. He had taken to thinking about Nile during the voyage, and his imagination had made him depressed.

He could envision her in bed with that friend of hers. It wasn't a pretty picture. It gave him a sick feeling in his stomach, and he became morose. It got so bad that To'afa took note and tried to cheer him.

The only problem with that was that To'afa had never had a serious relationship and couldn't quite comprehend what Adam was going through. He seemed to think that Nile's absence meant that Adam now had the freedom to explore other opportunities.

"When we get back in some civilized place, I'll take you bar hopping. There are always women that are interested in miners. They think we got credits." His teeth flashed in a grin as he spoke, apparently remembering some event.

Adam shook his head in frustration. "Not what I want big guy. Nile is one of a kind. I only want her." What he left unspoken was his fear that she might not want him any longer.

To'afa shook his head wonderingly. "You got it bad, man. I don't know how to cheer you up. At least you've been working on our problems full out."

That was the only good side to the issue. Working helped keep her off his mind.

THE HULL REPAIR was moving along quickly. To'afa and Flynn had worked as a team before, and George was quick to catch on. The rips and punctures were repaired in a few days, and now the three were installing the shield generators plus a few antennas that had been knocked off in the general melee.

Adam's problem went more slowly, partly because he was rethinking the antimatter projector from scratch. That part speeded up on the third day when he came up with a new shape for the mag field generators. Then he modified the Em-Max that boosted the stream of particles.

Rather than a single Em-Max unit, he split the task among five parallel installations, then merged the greatly accelerated stream of antimatter back together by forcing it through an intense magnetic field.

The end result promised to be an antimatter bolt that had far more velocity than before.

The need for more velocity on the shot bothered him until he came up with the insight that another Em-Max could be installed near the end of the barrel for an added final boost. By that time, he'd used all of the spare components on the D-R, so he raided Flynn's ship for two more.

This brought a complaint from the Irishman. "Adam, how are you going to fit my ship up with a better gun? You've used most of the spare parts on yours."

He nodded absently, distracted by a kink in the timing circuitry that was causing problems. "Yeah, uh, well... let's see. First, I'm making a prototype that is going to be superior to what we have now."

Flynn interrupted. "What we got now is superior to anything the Feddies got. Why mess with that?"

It was a rhetorical question. Flynn knew the answer. He was as well aware as anyone of the speed of weapons development fostered by the hothouse of war.

Adam didn't answer directly. Instead, he addressed Flynn's real question. "Once I get this thing working correctly and reliably, we'll head back to location two and scrounge some more parts. If we can get what we need there, we'll jump back out here and fix your ship up with the new and improved version."

Flynn was satisfied with that promise. "Ah. I can get behind that plan. You know I'm just worried about our next clash with the USSN. I can see it's coming soon, especially if they don't stop fighting down there."

"That was the next thing I wanted to discuss with you. If they haven't ceased fire by the time we're ready, we're going to go on another raid. We'll broadcast a demand that they stop all hostilities, and we'll be prepared to enforce it."

"Look, Adam, they won't just roll over that easily. How are we, just the two ships, going to make the powers on Earth do anything?"

"That's been bothering me, too. The best I can come up with is we fly in, shoot enough of their ships, so they learn not to mess with us, then we go into orbit and broadcast our demand. If they don't agree, then we'll see if an antimatter beam can get all the way to the surface through the atmosphere."

That was possibly a stretch. The positrons would annihilate electrons in the atmosphere, destroying atoms and creating a void, much like a lightning bolt. The air would rush back in, creating a thunderclap. If there was enough power in the beam, it might last long enough to reach the surface and do damage there, provided it got through before the air pressure could begin to refill the void.

The calcs he'd run indicated it was possible, theoretically, at least. Whether it would work in practice was another question.

"If we can't reach the surface with antimatter, we can for sure shoot up the lunar base and any ships we meet. Something will eventually get through to them."

Flynn didn't respond immediately. When he thought it over, he said, "We should broadcast on all bands so that our message gets through to the general population. If we tell them that we're trying to enforce a cease-fire, we should get their support, and that might help a lot."

"That's not a bad idea, Flynn. I don't tend to think in terms of psychology. I'm afraid my education was more oriented towards math and matter. Anyway, let's do that. Why don't you see about coming up with a script for the broadcast? Maybe you'll be able to use that Irish gift of blarney on them.

Flynn reluctantly agreed to work on a speech, provided Adam would deliver it.

TWO SHIFTS LATER, the new and improved positron cannon was ready to test. Adam was exhausted since he'd worked through both shifts without more than a fifteen-minute nap. He had reached the point where his imagination about Nile kept him from sleep. Work seemed to be the only thing that distracted him from the topic.

Flynn and George jetted over to the D-R, leaving the Double O-One floating silently. Neither of the two wanted to miss the test of the new weapon.

The first step was to recharge the positron containment field. That meant the ship had to be moving with the collection field extended. The system was more efficient, the faster they went, so Adam kicked the ship into a few seconds of hyperdrive. When they were at a tenth light, he switched the drive off and shifted the field to funnel positrons into the tank.

They coasted towards Neptune's orbit for fifteen minutes or so collecting antimatter, then hit an area where there was some kind of discontinuity. The antimatter was thick in space, so the field topped off in less time than usual.

The D-R revectored and began to accelerate back towards the clump of rocks they'd named The Nest. There were a few outlying meteoroids nearby that would do for test targets. Adam planned to use the load of antimatter they'd harvested sparingly to allow for three shots.

A combat situation would require higher power, but this was a test, and he wanted more than one shot to check his field readings.

They slowed and matched the velocity of The Nest, then picked out a target. It was a thousand-ton chunk of metal ore and rock that was leading The Nest in orbit by about ninety kilometers.

Adam glanced at the others. They were alternately watching him and the vidscreen, which was focused on the innocent rock rotating solemnly on its eons-long journey.

"Ready?" They nodded. "Firing on three, two, one."

He clicked the trigger and listened to the capacitor bank discharge. The lights dimmed a bit, flickered, then regained their normal brightness.

The bolt shot out from the D-R far more quickly than the previous gun had managed. It left a streak of sparkles trailing behind, making it easy to track.

The sparks were individual atoms and pieces of dust flaring as the antimatter struck them. The actual sparks were brief, but they were so bright that the afterimage glowed on the humans' retinas, making it appear that the flashes persisted.

The target rock flared almost instantly, wiping out the tiny sparks in its brightness.

The flare glowed for a moment, then faded. There was nothing there.

George gasped, "That thing was big. As big as a small ship and it went 'poof'! Even a cruiser would have no chance against us."

Adam nodded solemnly. "For the next test, I want to install a shield generator on the target. Let's see how well a shield will resist antimatter."

The setup took an entire shift. The main issue was that his proposed test required a source of power. Not wasting the spare auxiliary generator was a consideration. George's suggestion to float the power supply nearby, but not on the rock, then to extend cables to the shield generator was implemented. There was a slight chance that some of the positrons would miss the rock and strike the generator, but it was the only solution they could think of.

This test, too, was successful. The antimatter reacted with the plasma, creating a sparkling effect as it burned through the gas atoms. Once the positrons reached the shield generator and burned into it, it exploded, dropping the shield. Then the rock went poof, just like the first one.

"It looks like we'll have to concentrate on hitting right on top of one of their shield generators for maximum effect. The sooner we can take one out and bring down the shielding in that area, the easier time the antimatter will have getting through to where it can do significant damage."

Flynn's observation was merely common sense, but Adam realized that it helped to put the result into words that could take the form of a combat strategy. He nodded, not saying that the conclusion was obvious.

Flynn was touchy and resented any implication that he wasn't brilliant. Adam and To'afa nodded, closely followed by George, who was taking his cues from them.

Flynn seemed to glow in pride, then added, "We should make that part of our strategy manual. Maxwell's Space Combat for Pirates sounds like a good title? Don't you think?"

Adam said, "I'd need to give you credit, you know."

Flynn replied, "I'd be satisfied with a fifty percent share of the book royalties."

"Considering that we'd probably sell about two copies before the information was stolen and incorporated by every Captain out there, that wouldn't amount to much," Adam said, smiling.

Flynn frowned. "Faith. You're right. Those people are Pirates of the worst sort." Then realizing what he'd said, he added, "But, so are we. I guess we won't be getting rich out of that idea."

"No. It's not the pot of gold at the base of the rainbow," Adam answered.

SATISFIED WITH THE new and improved version of the antimatter weapon, they headed back to Valhalla to get the additional parts needed to install a similar gun on the Double-Zero-One.

The problem they encountered there was that there was a Council ship at the base. It wasn't immediately apparent. Miners came and went in irregular patterns, and Valhalla was the base for seven or eight ships. The count varied depending on discoveries, loads, and the need for supplies.

A Captain would come in to unload, record a new asteroid that showed exceptional promise, or to resupply. It was difficult to predict things in the asteroid belt. People and ships were where they were because of business, not externally imposed schedules.

Externally, the Council ship was just another mining ship. It did have a Council logo painted on the side, but the art was so small that it couldn't be identified without a telescope from one hundred meters away.

Adam could count five ships near the irregular rock. There had been three when they had left. Accordingly, his two ships were on approach, gradually slowing under Em-Max drive as they glided towards the base.

To'afa alerted him that something was amiss in the middle of his night shift.

"Captain, we've got a tight beam laser signal. Not an encoded burst. It's live. Lag-time is only a few seconds. You'd better get up here and take a look. They want to speak to you."

He couldn't seem to get a good sleep. If it wasn't an engineering problem to solve that kept him awake, it was horrible dreams about Nile – nightmares, really. Now it was somebody that wanted to talk.

He sighed, unhooked the restraining straps, and threw the covers off.

To'afa looked worried when Adam entered the bridge, and his speech betrayed his anxiety.

"Captain, it's Bertrand. He's asking for you."

Bertrand was another Captain. He'd started out as a miner, but he'd risen in the quasi-military organization that the Belters had adopted.

Adam wasn't particularly familiar with the man, but he had a reasonably good reputation. The one thing that Adam knew was that Bertrand was now directly employed by the Belter Council.

He had a feeling of trepidation as he sat down in front of the vidscreen. A keystroke activated the link, and the frozen image of Bertrand moved slightly, then responded after a few seconds, obviously seeing Adam for the first time.

"Admiral Maxwell," he acknowledged. "I'm both pleased to see you and unhappy about it at the same time. I've got bad news to give you. The Council has issued an order for your arrest, and as one of their agents, I'm supposed to carry out their orders."

That was what he'd expected. The Council couldn't excuse his independent actions, particularly since he hadn't managed to stop the conflict, apparently making things worse.

"Captain Bertrand we haven't previously met, but I've heard good things about you." He paused and waited for the signal to reach out the few hundred thousand miles to the other's ship.

Bertrand eventually nodded, making a gesture that somewhat resembled a bow. "Thank you, Admiral. I should actually call you Captain since the Council has rescinded your title, but there's a rift that you should know about. The independent miners had a loose association. I think you know that." He paused, waiting for a response.

Adam nodded in turn. "Yes, I'm aware of the group."

Bertrand continued. "They've formally organized. They're now the Asteroid Independent Miners. Regardless of their name, most of them either know you personally or owe their lives and livelihood to you or owe money to one of your companies. They've voted to protect you. The Council is issuing orders right and left, but the AIM is ignoring them. You've created complete anarchy on Titan. No one seems to know who is in control."

Adam's spirit fell. He couldn't seem to get a break. Nile was gone, Earth was still fighting, he was wanted, and now this mess was also being blamed on him.

"That wasn't my intention. The Council ordered me to leave Earth alone, but I couldn't stand by and watch our home world be ruined. I didn't ask the AIM as you call it to stand up for me. My actions are my own, but I intend to work for the good of all humans, even if they're enemies of the Belt community. I'm going to continue my efforts in that regard. The question is, are you going to try to stop me?"

Bertrand leaned forward. "That's what I've been directed to do. Stop you, even if I'm required to fire on your ship."

Adam waved his hand at To'afa. The big man nodded and said quietly, "I've got the shields ready to switch on, and hyperdrive is charged and ready to go."

The words were spoken softly, but Bertrand apparently heard them. "It won't be necessary for you to flee. I doubt that my ship would stand up to a direct fight with the Dire Rhea and, uh..." He looked aside at something. "Oh, yes. The Double-aught-one. That's Flynn, isn't it?"

Adam nodded. "It's a good bet that your ship isn't a match for us, but we don't want to fire on you. Perhaps you could simply tell the Council that you didn't see us. We'll leave quickly."

Bertrand shook his head negatively. "No, that won't be necessary. I'm thinking I'm going to make the Council very angry with me. I'm convinced that you're in the right." He amended his statement. "The AIM membership has mostly decided that you're right. For my part, I am convinced that you're right. We have to do something about the conflict on Earth."

That was welcome news.

"Captain, I'm pleased to hear that, but you must know that I intend to make another effort to stop the conflict. That might modify your view of me."

"Admiral, I assure you that it won't. I'm going to transmit an encoded message to the Council resigning my position. I'd like to volunteer to assist you. The Rift Voyager may not be equal to the D-R, but it is a capable ship, and I think we can help. We are, at least, willing to try."

"Bertrand, I'm very pleased to hear that. The last thing I want is a disagreement out here. The Belter community has too many challenges for us to fight among ourselves. I wouldn't have fired on your ship. We would have simply left under hyperdrive. With any luck, you wouldn't have been able to track us."

"Acknowledged." Bertrand nodded. "I'm placing myself and my ship under your orders, Admiral. Now, what would you like us to do?

Adam thought for a moment. He had heard good things about the man, but there was still a measure of doubt. Giving him the improved antimatter weapon would not be a useful action. Even letting him know about it would increase the odds that the USSN would find out.

"Captain, I'd like you to act as my eyes on Titan. I can't afford to have the Council organize a force that might interfere with my plans. I know asking you to spy for me is an imposition, but will you do that for me?"

Bertrand's face drew down slightly. "Ah. I'd rather do something else, but I guess I could watch them for you if that's what you need."

Adam smiled slightly. "Let's not call it spying. It's nicer to call it intelligence gathering. Anyway, it will only be for a few days. I've got some additional preparation to accomplish, then I will be ready for action. You can relay a message to me through Valhalla. They don't want me around, either, but they will hold messages until I pick them up. Once I'm ready, I'll contact you directly. I can use your help, Captain. Two ships are not much of a force. Your Rift Voyager might make all the difference between success and failure in what I'm planning. Welcome to the Belt Pirates Club. It's a small group and quite exclusive."

Bertrand grinned, then responded, "You ought to know that the AIM membership has been referring to you and Flynn as The The Belter Revolution. A lot of the Captains would like to join up with you. You're popular right now." He grinned, then added, "Except in the Council offices."

"Well, I guess as far as the Council, and the Feds are concerned, we are Pirates. They'd probably hang us if they ever caught us. Our status will be determined by whether we're successful or not. It's like the old saying that 'history is written by the victors.' If we win, we'll be heroes.

If not, we'll be hiding from both the USSN and the Council for the foreseeable future." He looked at the other man's image on the screen.

"Does that prospect make you want to change your mind?"

Bertrand shook his head. "No. I meant what I said. We're with you."

"Alright. How soon can you be ready to return to Titan?"

"They expect us to be away until we either find you or run low on food. I think I might find that some of our supplies are spoiled if I looked closely. That would give me an excuse to return sooner."

"Do what you must, Captain. I need to know if the Council is going to organize a more thorough search for me. If they do, I'll need to know where they're looking and the force they've raised against me."

"They've only sent out two ships besides mine so far. They're limited to sending out ships as they come in. Besides, they don't have that many captains to do their enforcement work. There are only four others, and two of them are busy with mining work. The Council doesn't pay that much, so we've all got to work at mining to keep going."

Adam nodded. "Yeah, I know what you mean. I don't pay well, either. In fact, this is a voluntary effort, but I'll see what I can do retroactively, that is if we succeed in stopping the fighting on Earth."

THE D-R AND the Double-Zero-One braked, slowing their approach even more, but continuing directly towards Valhalla.

Bertrand's ship began to move within five minutes after their conversation. It maneuvered away from the rotating rock, then boosted away using the Em-Max drive's gentle acceleration. The Rift Voyager receded as it gained velocity, heading in the general direction of Titan.

15

AMBUSH

VALHALLA, THE MISNAMED second base of operations set up by the Belter community, was out of direct sight. All hands were busy full time on the weapon, and Adam trusted the sensors to alert them. They did not monitor the comm bands directly.

The residents of Valhalla were more welcoming this time around. Bertrand's position had been made known, and the fact that the AIM was supporting Adam went a long way towards alleviating the fears that Katy had expressed.

Valhalla was too vulnerable to serve as an adequate substitute for the old Bubble habitat due to its structure. The Bubble had benefited by a narrow entrance to its large internal cavern. In contrast, Valhalla was cursed with a wide opening to a shallow crevasse where the residents had constructed rooms that clung to the rock in a way that reminded Adam of swallow nests on an overhanging cliff. Construction was complicated, and there wasn't much room for many dwellings.

Consequently, it had never sheltered many people. The first wave of Belters passed through, then quickly moved to the surface of Titan as soon as the decision was made to settle there.

The few people, who remained in the Crack, as the shelter was known, were forced to live a marginal life, subsisting on minor trade, emergency repair of damaged mining ships, and a limited mining operation. None of these enterprises brought in much by way of credits.

The primary resource was a rather large scrap yard. As Adam had observed, the two merchants carried a wide variety of miscellaneous parts, most of which had been salvaged from the scrap yard. The origin of the junk was due to one Jack Westphal, who had towed several destroyed hulks from the vicinity of The Bubble after the great battle.

Captain Westphal didn't live to benefit from the salvage yard he was apparently building. He'd gotten trapped in a hulk when a bulkhead had shifted due to centrifugal force. His comm had been damaged, and no one found him until many hours after he'd run out of oxygen. Now his memory was commemorated by the junkyard that was known as Jack's Heap.

Adam and Flynn had spent some hours poking through the miscellaneous salvage. It had been a profitable search. They had come up with enough spare parts to fit the Double-Zero-One with the improved positron weapon.

Now that the weapon's modifications had been worked out, Adam calculated that the installation would only require a few days. However, he still felt the need for the security that only distance would provide, so they left for Jem's hiding place as soon as they were loaded. Once there, they set to work on the installation of the second improved antimatter weapon.

The two ships remained in hiding in the cluster of rocks with their sensor suites to alert if anyone approached while the four men worked on the installation.

THE INSTALLATION WENT quickly to Flynn's delight. The Irishman was worried that an enemy would find them before his ship was ready, and he worked hard and long hours at the task. His complaints, when he thought one or more of the others weren't working as hard as he had begun to get on everyone's nerves.

Once the positron gun was finished, Adam insisted on working over the plasma shielding for both ships. He'd dreamed up a modification that allowed the generators to operate with ten percent less power while outputting fourteen percent more plasma. This meant the system could work longer while generating a more resistant shield.

After due thought, Adam had the men remove most of the conventional armor from the hulls. With the stronger shield in place, he thought that the ships were adequately protected. The side benefit was that the vessels were much lighter. This made them more responsive to the maneuvering jets and increased their acceleration.

Even the relatively staid Em-Max engine shoved them faster than expected, while the hyperdrive made them appear to vanish from sight instantly.

While the armor removal was going on, Adam came up with yet another wrinkle on the plasma generator idea. He fooled around with a spare unit until he got it to spray plasma jets in multiple directions at once. The idea was to use it as a point-defense weapon. It could be fired as a missile neared and need not be precisely aimed. The plasma jets shot out like a shotgun, or more accurately, like a lawn sprinkler, blasting anything that was within a kilometer of the hull.

Both ships now sported several of these systems, arranged so that there was no unprotected sector left open for a missile to sneak through.

IT WAS WELL into the third week of work when the modifications were complete. Adam wanted to test the new weapons, but the need for secrecy meant that they'd have to move somewhere they couldn't be seen. The cluster of rocks that Katy had revealed to them seemed to offer the needed security.

Accordingly, they eased away from the rocks, accelerating sedately under Em-Max power. Once they were twenty kilometers away, the Em-Max drives were cut off, and the ships re-oriented to target their previous hiding place.

The nest of rocks was hanging in space engaged in its slow-motion game of bumper cars. George had estimated that, on average, two of the rocks would collide every hundred years. Overall the cluster was remarkably stable. It'd been moving along in much the same way for millions of years.

Flynn's antimatter gun worked perfectly, requiring no additional adjustments. Adam wanted to test the plasma spray point defense, but it could not be fired if an allied ship was close. It wasn't designed to distinguish between a friendly ship and an unfriendly piece of ordinance.

While Adam was trying to calculate the minimum safe distance for friendly ships when the point defense was active, To'afa came up with a suggestion.

"Why don't we link the ships' comps? If we have a network of allied ships, the comps can be used to coordinate point defense for the entire group. That'd be far more efficient."

Adam agreed. He'd been so focused on making a single ship impervious to damage that he hadn't thought of a group strategy to this point. The idea was valid, and it didn't take a tremendously long time to create the software linkage and arrange for the point defense sprays to fire only in the desired directions when both ships were moving in formation.

He spent two hours working on encryption for the network. It wouldn't do to make it easy for an enemy to hack into the communications linkage and screw things up.

Once that was done, they moved both ships into the boulder nest, then activated the point defense sprays. Chunks of rock flew everywhere, some striking the plasma shielding that protected the hulls while other pieces rebounded from collisions like pool balls on the break. The boulder nest would never be the same, but the test was spectacularly effective.

The two ships moved off, heading for Valhalla. Adam was in no particular hurry to arrive. He needed time to plan his next move. The conflict on Earth had intensified and showed no signs of resolution.

The North American Free Dictatorship—it had changed its name once again—was continuing to drop objects on cities belonging to the Non-Aligns. The destruction had failed to induce surrender and had, in fact, hardened the resolve of the various non-aligned countries.

The NAFD's ministry of news was reporting that all was going well in the war. Some countering broadcasts were slipping out from the Non-Aligns that seemed to indicate otherwise. The old Russian Union was rumored to have dug up a store of antique nuclear warheads that were being fitted onto modern missiles in preparation for a massive counterattack.

Meanwhile, ground fighting along the borders of the Non-Aligns had reached a stalemate. The NAFD no longer had the surface military dominance that had been enjoyed by its parent country. The Earth-based military had been systematically gutted of funding over the past few years.

The common rationale was that all future conflicts would be in space, with the corollary assumption that KEWs dropped from orbit would be sufficient to quell any surface conflict. Now that the NAFD's space force was finding it difficult to resupply, thanks to Adam's action, the Non-Aligns were having an easier time of massing forces to fight off incursions.

Adam was gradually coming around to the conclusion that he would have to take direct action against the surface to have any significant effect. The loss of the Ribbon had slowed the bombardment but hadn't stopped the conflict.

In his mind, the problem revolved around Elseth. The woman had turned into more of a threat than he'd ever dreamed. She was a natural political schemer with a fanatical lust for power. It wasn't likely that she'd just quit and let things settle down.

As much as he didn't want to be remembered as the Belter who had struck Earth, he could see no other option.

He was still mulling over possible actions when they neared Valhalla. There were several mining ships parked near the asteroid, and that was unusual, but it sometimes happened. No one could tell when miners would need repair or resupply. The new business would probably keep Valhalla eating for some months.

Bertrand's information had relieved Adam's worries. It didn't seem likely that the Council would be able to mount an adequate search for him. Neither did it seem likely that any miner would risk a ship trying to capture him. The odds were too much in favor of the D-R. It had been more than a match for any mining ship before, but now it had become a heavily armed warship. It even looked like a warship.

The D-R had started with a slimmer profile than most of the mining ships. That was due to its age. It had been designed by one of the early ship architects, back when humans' conception of space ships involved a sleek shape.

The extra armor had been grafted on, giving the ship a clunky look, but now that it had been discarded, the sleek look was back, accentuated by the obvious point defense turrets and the plasma cannon barrels. The antimatter gun topped off the look. The muzzle protruded past the base of the collection funnel, making the ship look pugnacious.

The two Pirate ships moved through the resting miner ships and slid into a parking orbit near the asteroid. The other ships were spread out in a rough line. There was a single ship near Valhalla, while the others were farther away. The gap where the D-R and the 001 had pulled in was the most convenient open space.

To'afa got on the comm and requested a news feed. Valhalla would be more up-to-date than the D-R, due to its larger antenna array, which was continuously linked to Titan. The news feed began to download for later review, and To'afa asked for Suzy.

Instead of Jem's widow, a rough-looking man came on the vid.

"She's not available, so you'll have to speak to me," he said.

Adam came over and looked over To'afa's shoulder.

"If I have to speak to you, I'd like to know who you are," he responded.

"Captain Baumer. You've probably heard of me."

"No, sorry. Your name isn't familiar."

"That's good...uh, not important." The man hesitated, then someone handed him a slip of paper. He glanced down at it, then raised his head and grinned maliciously at Adam's image.

"I see that you're parked where we expected you to stop. Look around. You'll see that my ships have you bracketed. Any attempt to escape will result in your immediate destruction."

Adam glanced at what had suddenly become a tactical situation. He was indeed surrounded, and he noted ruefully, it was his own fault. He turned back to Baumer.

"Who sent you, and what are your intentions, Captain Baumer?"

The other man sneered again.

"As long as you're trying to be polite, I will explain rather than shoot. We're here from Earth orbit. I've got a letter of marque from the NAFD. It gives me the right to stop all ships and to take possession of any ship hostile to the NAFD. I think we can both agree that you have proven to be hostile, Captain. I'm sending a boarding crew over. You're my captive."

Adam shook his head in disbelief. The man was a privateer operating with a thin layer of legality.

"What do you intend to do with us?" he asked. Might as well play for a little time.

"Her Majesty has requested your presence. She didn't exactly say whether you should be alive or dead, though, so cooperate."

What Baumer didn't know was that Flynn was monitoring the conversation and had already initiated the newly designed battle software. Now the two ships were linked through the network. To'afa was ready with the weapons console, watching Adam for instructions.

Adam nodded at the Samoan and the shields flicked into high power. The command signal activated the 001's shields at the same time.

Baumer's instruments told him the story. He swore, then gritted, "You think your plasma shield is going to protect you? We've got advanced plasma cannons on all ships. They're more than a match for a shield. Don't you try to leave, either. We'll fire at the first sign of acceleration."

Adam shrugged, trying to appear indifferent, even though his nerves were screaming at him. "If I were you, I'd back off, Mister. You're not going to survive this action."

Baumer laughed and said, "It's not likely you'll survive, you mean. You can join the recent population of this nasty little rock."

"What do you mean by that?" Adam's blood pressure began to rise. He could feel his face flushing.

"If you'd had any kind of caution, you'd have seen the bodies floating away. We spaced them all. This asteroid is our new base. I'm in charge now."

Adam paused. He looked down at his hand. His fist slowly clenched until the fingers turned white from the pressure. When he looked up at the vid, there was an expression on his face that must have shown something of his anger to Baumer. The man drew back and said, "What?"

Adam took a breath, trying to control himself. "You're in the Valhalla comm center?"

Baumer didn't answer directly. "I'm renaming it New Antwerp. I've got to put some decoration on these walls. It's far too plain. Got any suggestions? Maybe your head?"

He didn't have time to say more. To'afa set off the point defense on both ships and bolts of plasma reached out, touching the nearby privateer ships. Their first-generation shields were overmatched. The bolts passed through easily.

Two ships exploded outright. Two others vented atmosphere in large gouts, leaving their crews dealing with hard vacuum and unlikely to pose a threat.

The other three ships fired their plasma cannons directly at the D-R and 001. Space lit up as the plasma beams clashed with the point defense beams. Glowing beads of metal streamed off the privateer ships. The D-R's shield flashed, and the interior lights flickered with the power drain.

Adam's fingers were flying as he activated the hyperdrive. The battle network took charge of Flynn's ship, and both Pirate ships accelerated rapidly. The remaining privateers probably thought that they'd vaporized their targets. One moment they were there, the next they were gone.

The two ships flipped out of hyperdrive quickly, then, coordinated by the encrypted battle network, they revectored back towards Valhalla. They were still moving away from the rock, but slowing with Em-Max power.

"Flynn? You get all that?" Adam asked.

The comm showed the little man. His face was bright red with anger. "Those rotten, no good, dirty...I'm at a loss for words."

"Let's take the rest of them out," Adam snapped.

Flynn's face cleared and he nodded. "Let's get 'em. The rock too?"

"Baumer's inside. He's going to get a big surprise. Yes. The rock too."

Both hyperdrives snapped on, and the ships sped towards the asteroid. The positron guns fired as they got into range. The beams spread slightly with the distance striking both of the remaining privateer ships and the asteroid itself.

The privateer hulls sparkled for a moment, then winked out of existence. The asteroid was another matter. Its greater mass absorbed all of the weapons' output without being destroyed, although pits and chasms suddenly appeared in the surface.

The cavern entrance was currently on the other side of the rotating rock, so the locks hadn't been struck. That meant it was likely that Baumer was still alive.

The D-R's hyperdrive briefly flicked on and off, bringing the ship to a near standstill beside Valhalla. Adam maneuvered until he was looking directly at the rock. It rotated slowly, gradually bringing the cavern entrance into direct alignment with the waiting Pirate ship.

"Baumer? You still in there?" Adam asked.

The vidscreen cleared, showing the privateer's strained face. "You worthless piece of used toilet paper! What did you do to my ships?"

"I'll take that as an affirmative. I destroyed your ships, and I'm going to do the same to you just as soon as I finish talking."

"Ha! I'm inside millions of tons of rock. No plasma cannon is going to reach through this. You'll burn your generator out before that happens."

Adam's finger hovered over the trigger. He was angry, and Baumer deserved to suffer.

"You signed your death warrant when you killed the people there. They were my friends, and I'm not going to let you escape. I want you to watch closely. Oh, and you'd better be in a pressurized room. I'd like you to live a little longer so you can appreciate what's going to happen to you."

He adjusted the power on the gun to a lower level, then pressed the trigger. The Valhalla entrance lock, doors, frame, and all vaporized. A massive gust of atmosphere flew out, filled with loose debris. The low powered charge faded before it did more damage.

Baumer's face bulged. The comm center was vacuum proof, but there must have been a leak somewhere. The man's eyes were open wide with terror. His voice was different in the rapidly thinning atmosphere.

"Damn you! We'll get you. If not me, then the rest of us. You wait and see. I'm going to get into a suit, and I'll be your worst nightmare. I'll never give up until I see the color of your guts."

The positron weapon spoke again. This time the power was full strength. The vid went black as the entire interior of the cavern was destroyed in a brilliant flash.

Baumer was gone, but so was Katy, Jem's two children, and twenty-four other people that he'd counted as friends. Adam had a sad feeling that it was his fault. He had too many enemies. He'd been worried about the Council and had all but forgotten about the Earthers. Now he refocused.

He had to take action and stop Elseth. The woman was going to destroy Earth, and probably the Belter community while she was at it.

HE WALKED INTO the tiny bathroom adjacent to his cabin. His reflection in the mirror served to remind him that he had no one to blame but himself. He couldn't get an even break in life. He'd failed to graduate due to getting involved in Elseth's crazy scheme; he'd been run off Earth by her father, the late, unlamented Senator Worthington. Then he'd fallen in with Suarez and sort of accidentally found that he was considered a Pirate. Then he'd been partially blinded. Now, Nile was off with some guy and…he paused, looking at his single eye. It was shining in the light.

His chest hurt, and he felt miserable.

He really loved that woman. He'd realized that he was willing to do anything to get her back. If he only knew where she was, he'd go after her. No question about that. On the other hand, maybe she didn't want him. She'd seemed awfully pleased about her good-looking friend.

Perhaps she had dumped him for Klingfeldt. He thought about that for a while. Then he thought about the friends he'd had who had been killed.

That brought him full circle to the Valhalla residents. If the NAFD sent bounty-hunting privateers after him, he'd endanger everyone who might know where he was. Everyone he cared about would become an unsuspecting target.

The image in the mirror became blurry. He wiped his eye with a towel, then frowned. Feeling bad about the situation wasn't going to have any effect. He had to keep moving forward. The only hope was for him to win or to die in the attempt. He grinned mirthlessly. Hopefully, it would be winning. Dying didn't fit into his plans at the moment.

16

TITAN, AGAIN

THE TWO SHIPS were half a second light away from Titan. It wasn't much, just enough to make the laser link to Captain Bertrand irritating. The delay was just long enough that it interfered with putting a coherent sentence together.

The Rift Voyager was currently in orbit around the moon. Bertrand was using the private laser system to report on the overall attitude.

"The average Belter views you with approval. That goodwill has spread some, too. A few of the Council members have gone on record saying that they might have been too hasty in condemning your actions. The main problem is Nielson. You made him look like a fool. Don't say anything. We all think he is one, but your action damaged his self-importance. He's still ready to tar and feather you."

"I don't have time for his ego. Elseth is sending out privateers, and a group of them killed everyone on Valhalla. They tried to take me prisoner, too."

Bertrand's eyes widened in shock. "Everyone? They killed the women and children too?"

Adam nodded slowly. Even acknowledging it hurt. "I'm afraid so. The place isn't habitable now."

Bertrand wanted details. Adam still didn't want knowledge of his advanced weapons and speed to get out, so he provided a sketchy outline of the fight. It didn't sound believable in his ears, but Bertrand apparently thought it was.

"So, they ran into a buzzsaw between you and Flynn. This will go a long way towards convincing Nielson to rescind his arrest order. For one thing, once it gets out to the populace, he won't dare to arrest you. It'd cause a general revolt."

"That would be one revolt too many. We can't afford to let the USSN know that we're fighting among ourselves. They'd try and take advantage for sure," Adam said.

Bertrand's response came a few seconds later.

"There's no one currently in orbit that can match the D-R. I think that you should come in and broadcast the news about Valhalla on the broadband comm. Nielson won't like it, but it's probably the best way to swing the entire community over to your view."

He was right. Shortly after the news went out, Nielson initiated a laser link. The D-R was close, so there was little delay.

"Maxwell, you've put me in an untenable situation. I don't want to overlook your insubordination. You disobeyed a direct and lawful order from the Council. Unfortunately for me, I seem to have no choice but to reinstate you as Admiral of the Belter Defense force. They're outside my office right now trying to break down the door. It won't hold forever, and I'm going to need your support to keep order down here. Will you help?" He looked desperate.

Adam considered. He was fully prepared to make another attempt to stop the carnage on Earth with just the two ships, but Titan couldn't be allowed to deteriorate into warring factions either.

"Okay, Councilman. I'll broadcast an appeal for order and let everyone know you've reinstated me, but I'm going to demand that you work with me to stop the NAFD's war on the Non-Aligns. Will you do that?"

Nielson looked over his shoulder, then hastily said, "Yes, yes. Of course. Now make that broadcast."

IT TOOK A few hours for things to return to a semblance of normal, but the rioting calmed almost immediately when the message got out that Adam was back.

They had waited until mainday morning to make plans. Now Adam was engaged in a wideband conference with the entire Council and all of the AIM Captains that were present.

He looked at the comm screen. Windows showed each of the participants.

"Gentlemen, I've agreed to resume my duties as Admiral of the Defense Force with a contingency. I'm asking that every Belter do their part to stop the war that the NAFD is waging. We simply cannot afford to destroy our home planet. We need more people out here, and we need the biological resources of Earth intact, even if we're mostly self-sustaining at this point."

He paused and scanned the windows. Heads were nodding in agreement.

"We'll detail two fleets. One to guard Titan and other resources in the Belt, while the second carries out an attack on Earth. We will move in on Earth and Luna and stop the NAFD's use of KEWs against the surface. If necessary, we will provide safe escorts for the Non-Aligns to bring their own ships into orbit. I want them to form a peace-keeping force that is equal in strength to that of the Feds. We'll monitor the situation and ensure that the two parties cooperate."

One of the windows flashed, and the man there asked, "What if the NAFD won't listen to reason? What if they continue their efforts to dominate the surface?"

Adam shook his head. This was what he most feared. "Then we'll have to take more severe steps. If we have to, I'm prepared to teach them a harsh lesson. We will have to disable the Dictatorship somehow, and that will create havoc, but it's not like such things haven't happened on Earth before. I've been thinking that we might leave the Non-Aligns to impose order. We haven't the personnel to do that ourselves. We'll have to monitor the situation and make sure that no one group is taken advantage of, and no group tries to step into the power void and take over. That's something I believe we can and should do."

Another window flashed. This time the question was about relative forces.

"Admiral, the USSN has a lot of ships. We don't know how many they've got on the lunar surface, but the number of ships in orbit has increased since shortly after your first raid. We hypothesize that they have intensified their ship-building to make up their losses. Do we have the numbers, the power to stop them? Will this be a protracted war? Is the outcome certain, or is there a possibility that we might lose?"

Adam chuckled. "Captain Clark, that's a lot of questions to ask at once. Let me see if I can reassure you. First, I agree. We don't have as many ships as the USSN. However..." He held up his index finger, interrupting their questions. "However, our ships are more capable. We don't have time to rebuild every ship in our fleet. Besides, I don't believe it is necessary. We don't need an armada of warships. We mostly need independent miners with general-purpose mining ships."

He paused again and scanned the screen. They were watching him expectantly. "Our fleet has several ships with advanced arms. Since the Battle of The Bubble, several ships have installed plasma cannons. Everyone has at least a level one plasma shield. Our big advantage is that we now have two ships that are superior to anything the USSN has by several orders of magnitude."

That might be a bit of an exaggeration, Adam thought, but the stunned looks on the massed faces on the screen told him that they'd follow his lead.

"The Dire Rhea and the Double-O-One have been extensively modified. These two ships are better shielded, better defended, faster, and more maneuverable than before, plus I've invented a new weapon that will cut through the USSN's shielding easily. I expect them to stop fighting after a single engagement. They're not fools, and they'll see that continuing to oppose us is futile."

The screen erupted with flashes as everyone tried to ask questions. Eventually, the system caught up, and one of the Council members was highlighted.

"Admiral, what is this super-weapon?" she asked.

"That information is restricted," Adam said. "This conversation is probably being monitored by spies. I'm not giving any clue as to the basis of our superiority, only that we are superior and they will regret resisting us."

An AIM Captain asked, "Can we count on that?"

Adam nodded, considering. "You know that any weapons advance that is used in battle is likely to be duplicated by the opposing side within a few months. We have only this one chance to settle this thing once and for all. I'm not going to give them a chance to meet us on anything like even terms, but I will tell you that not one of the privateers that killed the folk of Valhalla survived. We destroyed them all with no damage to ourselves. We can do the same to the USSN's ships, if necessary. Is that adequate?

The Captain looked uncertain for a moment, then his face cleared. "I'm willing to believe you. You've been successful to this point, and you do have a record as a weapons inventor. Yes. I believe you."

THE MEETING TOOK more time, but that statement was the determining factor. The participants were in agreement on the fundamental issue. They would attempt to impose peace on Earth. The subsequent discussion was along the lines of how and when they should proceed.

17

WAR PLANS

THE BELTER FLEET stopped at Deimos to pick up additional crew. The Martian governing Council had asked for experienced spacers to volunteer. Mars was not willing to be left out of what Citizen Oliver had characterized as a historic action to save Earth.

Adam was getting sick of the phrase. It seemed like everyone wanted to "Save Earth!" For his part, the two words seemed to heap more pressure on him. Both the Belters and the Martians expected him to pull some miracle out of vacant space. He had discarded almost all of his ideas on the upcoming action for one reason or another. It seemed like everything he thought of had some fatal flaw.

He didn't want to be known as the man who had killed millions trying to stop a war that was killing thousands. The problem was that the NAFD would undoubtedly resist the curtailment of their orbital operations. That would mean they would have to fight, and that would create lots of debris to fall on the surface.

Dropping thousands of tons of destroyed spacecraft on Earth was going to be almost as bad as the KEWs that Elseth's forces were currently using. People would be killed. Innocent people, or as close to innocent as people could be these days. That didn't sit well, and it was becoming hard to sleep.

What little sleep Adam did get was disturbed by dreams of firey objects shooting across blue skies and creating massive explosions as they impacted on schools and hospitals.

He was sitting in the galley looking at a half-eaten sandwich when To'afa poked his head through the hatch.

"Captain, the Martians are all on the ships, and all crews are fully manned. We're ready to leave."

Adam sighed. So it begins, he thought. "Alright. Give the order to head directly to Earth. I want all ships to arrive in their assigned positions. We don't want the Feds to have the chance to pick off someone who gets separated without backup."

"Aye, Captain. Oh, and Flynn says for you to take a sleeping pill. We're limited by the slowest ships, so we've got a couple of days before we arrive. You should get some rest."

"Maybe, but the Earthers are going to see us coming. They'll take some kind of steps, and I'm going crazy trying to predict what they'll do."

To'afa shrugged. "We've got sixty-two ships. What can they do? We're going to kick butt and take names, and they'd better behave."

Adam smiled at the statement. The big man had a way of putting things that made light of problems.

"I wish that were the case, but we don't know how many ships from Luna are ready to fly. They could outnumber us. As it is, both forces are almost matched. They only have a few less than we do. If the Luna ship-building facilities have been busy, they might have far more ships ready. Besides, we've only got Flynn's ship and the D-R with the advanced weapons and shields."

To'afa nodded, then said, "Maybe, but the D-R is a match for about a hundred conventional ships."

"That's exaggerating our capabilities. We can still be destroyed by a lucky missile strike or maybe even a railgun slug if it slipped through our defenses at the right moment."

To'afa shrugged again. "But that won't happen."

Adam had another thought. "How about the installation of the battle network on the other ships? How's that going?"

"I think we're nearly done. Most of the installation is software. It's being done remotely. The last I checked, there were only a handful of ships that were having trouble getting the system running. I think they had some older equipment that wasn't compatible."

Adam rubbed his forehead in frustration. "Check on it for me, please. I'd like every ship to be in the network. That will go a long way towards coordinating maneuvers."

It was To'afa's turn to rub his head. "Well, yes, but the lag factor bothers me. If we're too widely separated, won't that cause problems? Everything bogs down if the info isn't current."

"Yeah. That's a problem, but the software should account for it. I've increased the refresh rate so that the data-link is as close to real-time as it can get. If two of our ships get too close and are in danger of collision, the system will override their steering and revector them."

To'afa's face cleared. "That sounds good. Now listen to me. It'll be fine. We're going to get the job done. You always do."

THAT WAS THE problem. Everyone was relying on him.

Adam cursed silently to himself, then rose and headed for his cabin. He wasn't needed, and maybe Flynn's suggestion was a good one. He could use some uninterrupted sleep.

HE WOKE IN the middle of mainday night. An idea had slipped into existence in the context of a dream. He lay in the dark, thinking it through.

He'd planned for the Belter ships to arrive in a single formation and then to spread out in low Earth orbit locating and capturing or destroying the USSN ships there. The operation was going to have to be done quickly before any ships from Luna could interfere.

He knew that his plan was overly simplistic, and it worried him into a state where he couldn't sleep. As a result, he turned on the light and made a series of notes.

His force would be split into three equal groups. One would strike at the ships dropping KEWs from low orbit. The second would go directly to Luna to interdict any reinforcements from that source. The third group would circle around and approach from sunward, arriving after the first two groups had begun the operation. This third group would serve to reinforce either group one or two, depending on who needed help when they arrived.

Once the rough outline was on paper, Adam snapped off the light and fell asleep. For a change, his dreams were not about the upcoming conflict.

THE BELTER FLOTILLA had split into three groups. Two were now headed directly towards Earth, while the third looped far out and around to arrive from sunward. Adam had selected the quicker ships for that purpose. They had to travel a greater distance and would have to go faster to be there in time to cover any problems.

18

THE BATTLE OF EARTH ORBIT

THE TWENTY-ONE SHIPS that were to approach from sunward were long gone. They'd left earlier and were traveling as quickly as they could. The comp had calculated that they would arrive in Earth orbit within twenty minutes of his group.

Group Two had diverged from Group One and was currently closing in on Luna. The scan showed only a few ships in Luna orbit, but there were probably plenty more on the surface. The Belters wanted to begin their attack as soon as they got close in the hopes that surface-based USSN ships would be destroyed before they were able to launch.

Adam was miserable. He was eaten by indecision and insecurity. He'd made his plans, but now all he could think of was how something might go wrong and get a lot of his friends killed.

An old quote kept passing through his mind. It was something about battle plans only lasting until one met the enemy, and he was beginning to find it irritating. If only he could think of something else.

He slapped his forehead. That last thought somehow reminded him of Nile. She was something else to think about. He wondered where she was. It would be awful if she were in one of the USSN ships that he intended to destroy.

He tried to find comfort in the thought that he was doing his duty for the Belter community and for Earth in general. The NAFD was entirely out of control, and Earth was suffering. People in the Non-Aligns were suffering. Elseth was bombing them daily. They had to be suffering, and he had to do something about it. He shook his head. Why did it have to be him, always him?

He was really just a student, not the blood-thirsty Pirate and space battle strategist that everyone thought he was. All he really wanted was to find Nile, straighten things out with her, hopefully in a way that involved her moving in with him. After that, his desires became somewhat fuzzy. He thought they might prospect some, maybe homestead an asteroid, but that seemed distant and unreal.

The sensor suite alerted, snapping him back to the upcoming conflict.

He glanced at the display. They were closing in on Earth, and there would likely be a navy ship or two posted to challenge incoming traffic.

His eye opened wider, and all thoughts of Nile vanished. The display showed a fleet of ships, so tightly packed that it was difficult to distinguish one from another.

The spherical formation was at one of the LaGrange points and seemed to be stationary. It didn't make sense unless the navy had foreknowledge of the Belter force approach.

Assembling that many ships and arranging them so closely wasn't done in a matter of hours. It would have taken days. Adam rubbed his forehead. He had to assume that there had been a leak, and the USSN was prepared to fight.

They'd obviously pulled all of the ships from Luna, and that meant that Group Two was not going to meet any resistance. He pondered calling them back, but the NAFD's Luna shipyard was a vital piece of the puzzle. If the Belters could take that and turn it over to the Non-Aligns, or possibly manage it themselves, it would serve to make the whole system safer. Elseth couldn't be allowed to continue to build up a fleet solely for her own purposes.

The other puzzling thing was why the Feds had elected to form a sphere. Adam realized that he had limited tactical knowledge and what he did know was based on his own experiences. There were plenty of military tacticians on Earth. It would have been good policy for Elseth to set them to war-gaming out space battles.

He suddenly felt less confident. What if the two antimatter cannons were not enough to tip the tide?

The sensor suite beeped. The Belter flotilla had been slowing all the while. They were now about one hundred klicks from the ball of ships. Not counting the ones on the far side of the formation, which were obscured, there looked to be roughly one hundred and fifty ships of various configurations in the globe.

He could see converted mining ships, cruisers, and at least two that were much larger. Those were probably Main-Battleships. They would be heavily armored and shielded.

The Belter's ships were linked by the new battle control system. Adam's fingers flicked against the screen rearranging his ships into two equal groups that began to diverge.

They could pass on both sides of the enemy formation, firing as they flew by. He increased the flotilla's speed. No sense giving the navy ships any longer than necessary to take pot-shots at them.

Shields on the Belter ships began to flare, and some of the vessels veered out of formation. They'd flown directly into a swarm of railgun slugs. The chunks of metal were difficult to detect at any distance. The sensors were set for ship-sized objects.

The Belter's upgraded shields were generally adequate to deal with rocks and railgun slugs. This time was no exception. The ships that had veered trying to move out of the way of the oncoming fire slid back into position.

The comm beeped, the screen blurred, then cleared to reveal a navy officer. Adam thought the insignia was that of an admiral, but he'd never studied the navy and really didn't know.

"Invading ships, this is Earth command. You are encroaching on restricted space. Slow to a relative halt and prepare to be boarded. We're impounding your vessels," the man ordered.

Adam was so startled, he laughed. "I'm sorry. What was that? You think we're going to give you our ships?"

The officer frowned, then said, "If you do not stop, we'll be forced to destroy your fleet."

Adam laughed again, this time with a sarcastic tone. "You've already tried to shoot us out of space with your railguns. You know that we're shielded against plasma and missiles. How do you propose to stop us?"

The officer opened his mouth to respond, but Adam continued. "Never mind answering. You can't defeat us. We're not invading. We're here to stop you from destroying the planet. If you had any sense, you'd immediately join with us."

The officer spluttered, then said, "You're Pirates. We don't recognize your authority. You're subjects of Her Majesty, and she's ordered us to either capture you or destroy you."

Adam patiently explained. "Her Majesty, as you call her, is a megalomaniac. Her lust for power is going to destroy the planet's biosphere. We can't afford to let Earth be ruined. You must stop. I'm asking you to take your ships to Luna and land there, then await our arrival. We're going to enforce peace on the planet. You can either be with us or against us."

The screen flicked again as the officer's visage disappeared. Elseth's face appeared against a magnificent backdrop. She was sitting at a desk in what was apparently a throne room. She looked out impatiently, then recognized Adam.

"Adam, dearest, I've missed you. Now I see that you've missed me too. You've come visiting. Let's not fight. Meet with Admiral Johnson and turn your ships over to me, then come down to the

Capitol. I'm anxious to see you. We can take up where we left off. I need a man I can depend on, a royal consort. I know you, and you'd be perfect."

He shuddered. Her voice sent chills up his spine. He'd thought he was over her, but there was something about the blasted woman that still had the power to attract him. A fleeting picture of Nile passed through his mind activating his conscience.

"No, Elseth. That time is long past. You lost me when you bedded Serge. He's dead, by the way."

"Ah, Adam, you just don't understand. If you killed Serge, you did me a favor. He was becoming a bore. He was demanding more and more power. I sent him out to bring you back, but not as an invader. Now be a good boy and come on down so we can resume where we left off." She smiled.

The smile did it. Adam suddenly saw her as a vindictive spider, spinning a web of intrigue designed to pull all power in the solar system into her hands. The last vestiges of his infatuation with her vanished at that moment.

"No, Elseth. I won't do that. We're here for one purpose. If you want to survive, you will immediately stop bombing the Non-Aligns. Order your fleet to Luna base and have them await our orders. We're going to stop the war on Earth. The planet is the primary biological resource for humans, and we've got to protect it. You're killing people and ruining the biosphere in the process. It must cease. Humans need Earth."

Her face changed to a scornful frown. "You wouldn't recognize necessity if it bit your ass. You were always naive. I see that you haven't changed. I'm the sole power in the universe, and I won't have any competitors. Once I finish bringing the rest of the planet under my control, your little group of self-inflated asteroid miners will be next. My space navy will track every one of you down."

She turned away and spoke to someone offscreen. "Tell Johnson to destroy all of them." She turned back with a wicked smile.

"Now take your medicine, Adam. It's goodbye for you. I've been as patient as I can, but you see, I'm the Empress. I'm not going to wait forever."

Adam was caught by one detail. "Johnson? Wasn't he the one I defeated at the Bubble? I thought he was dead."

She laughed. "I don't know about any bubble, but I assure you, Admiral Johnson is very much alive, and he's shortly going to ensure that you aren't. Goodbye, Adam."

The comm blacked. Adam drew a deep breath. What was it about that woman that got to him in such an unpleasant way? She'd been his first lover, but that was lost in time and treachery. Nile had come along and...he paused for an instant. Yes, Nile was all he wanted. If he only knew what had become of her.

THE BELTER SHIPS were now in two tight groups separated by several hundred klicks and moving at a speed, which would put them in firing distance of the navy ships within five minutes.

Something was going on in the globe of enemy ships. The mass was splitting apart, leaving a tunnel through the center as the surrounding ships moved outward. It looked at first as if the enemy was moving to intercept the two Belter squadrons, but then the sensors picked up a single ship that remained squarely in the middle of the hole.

Its distance was odd, though. Adam checked. It was positioned significantly behind the Navy ships. The shape was weird, like nothing he'd ever seen.

He turned to ask To'afa if he could guess the purpose of the cylindrical ship when there was a brilliant flash. Neither of them had been looking at the video display at the time.

Adam whirled around, but the vid display had dissolved into a swirling mass of static.

"That looks like a nuclear blast. Why would they do that? They haven't launched any missiles," he said.

His speculation was interrupted by the comm. It was from Flynn.

"Adam? Something happened. I don't know what. It was like a bright light that went through us. None of my ships are left. They're...they're gone."

Adam asked, "How about your instruments? All we saw was a flash like they exploded a nuke."

Flynn didn't sound like himself. His voice was shaky when he responded. "My radiation counter is off the charts. We're passing through an intense radiation field, or my reactor has a leak."

Flynn paused, then continued, sounding alarmed. "I'm bleeding. My nose is bleeding. My skin is..." He abruptly stopped.

Adam called, "Flynn? Flynn? What's going on over there?"

Flynn came back on, his voice faint. "We've been hit with intense gamma rays. George is worse than me. He's bleeding everywhere. Eyes, mouth, nose. And, his skin is sloughing off. Blistered." He paused, then said, "It's been great knowing you, Adam. I'm done for. The luck o'the Irish has failed me. I'm going to use my antimatter weapon on them rats. It was some kind o' laser, I think." Flynn broke off with an odd noise that sounded like a combination gasp and sob.

Adam knew that he should feel something. His friend was dying or dead, and he had lost half of his squadron.

He searched inside himself. He felt numb with no regret. There was nothing but anger and a thirst for revenge.

He marveled at himself. How could he be so cold? He remembered getting choked up at movies. Now a movie, no matter how sad, seemed trivial. This was life and death, and it required all of his attention.

The battle network was just now catching up. The blast had disrupted it unexpectedly. Adam noted that he'd have to try and engineer around that problem. The Double-O-One was hundreds of kilometers off towards Luna at the moment. That distance was all that had saved Adam's half of the flotilla.

Whatever had struck her was something Adam didn't want to face.

The Feds had some kind of superweapon. The thought crashed through Adam's feeling of invincibility. A superweapon! Flynn had said laser, but the tubular ship had apparently exploded. Adam racked his brain, trying to understand.

Then he remembered. There had been some research on a so-called fission-pumped laser system way back in the last century. A scientist named Teller had proposed it.

Adam thought it had been dropped due to the basic insanity of placing numerous nuclear warheads in orbit where they might be hacked and turned on their surface-bound owners.

There were also technical problems with the idea. The laser or lasers couldn't be focused in the split millisecond before they were destroyed by the blast that powered them.

That was it, though. It had to be. The Feds had figured out how to pump an x-ray laser with a nuke. The fact that it was only a single shot mechanism, destroying itself, didn't make it any less fearsome. It had enough power to evaporate ships. Flynn had apparently been caught in the fringe of the beam and fatally irradiated.

From the sound of it, he wouldn't survive, even if they reached him immediately to provide anti-radiation treatment. As that thought occurred, the sensors alerted. Flynn had fired an antimatter shot at the Fed ships.

Adam called Flynn, but there was no answer, so he waited to see what effect the positron beam would have. The Belter ships were moving quickly past the stationary Fed formation. Flynn's dead ship was on the other side of the Fed ships, moving just as fast. The radiation hadn't slowed it down as it passed through the plasma shield and hull.

The plasma shield! Adam focused the sensors on the Double-O-One. There was no sign of its shield. The beam had disrupted the entire system, possibly damping the ship's reactor as it passed through. It was a wonder that the reactor hadn't gone critical instantly. Maybe that was what had happened to the other ships.

Without power, how had Flynn fired his cannon? Adam went through the system mentally. There was probably enough voltage stored in the cap bank to get off one shot. The containment field hadn't failed. If it had, the entire Double-O would have dissolved as the antimatter escaped.

To'afa grunted. Adam looked at him, then looked where he was pointing. The vidscreen showed a sudden hole in the Fed fleet. The antimatter blast had struck and taken out three ships while another one was spinning out of control.

In response, the navy ships on his side of the formation opened up with their railguns, simultaneously launching hyper-vee missiles. Adam re-vectored his command slightly, hoping to bypass most of the inertial slugs.

The missiles were a different story. Their guidance systems adjusted to their targets' new course.

"Plasma cannons. All ships. Use plasma on the missile swarm."

Space glowed as the ten ships fired their weapons. Adam added the output of his antimatter gun to the barrage.

Missiles exploded ahead of them. None were nuclear, fortunately. The Feds had used nuclear warheads before, but these were conventional high explosives.

The plasma cannon cap bank and the antimatter tank were recharging. That was a problem that needed to be dealt with, assuming he survived. The weapons wouldn't fire quickly.

Adam calculated they'd be by the expanding sphere of navy ships before he was ready to fire another shot. His fingers touched the control screen. In response, the Belter ships began to re-orient. They'd be prepared to accelerate back towards the navy formation when their weaponry was ready to fire.

He looked at To'afa. The big man had a grim expression, and he was clenching his fists.

"Let's get 'em, Captain," he said.

Adam said, "I don't want to break out of formation, but the antimatter weapon will recharge better at high vee. We've got to use all the advantages we've got right now."

He called the other ships. "I'm going to hyperdrive for a moment. Continue on past. Accelerate back at them and engage. I'll probably be there before you're ready to fire."

The D-R seemingly vanished as he activated the hyperdrive, the collection funnel gathering virtual particles. He flew back along the same path they had just taken. If he were lucky, his other ships would serve as a distraction, holding the Feds' attention while he attacked from behind.

The mass of navy ships was cooperating with the idea. The enemy ships had changed their orientation to follow the nine remaining Belter ships.

Adam shook his head. Instead of this being a triumph where the Belters destroyed the USSN with few losses, it was turning into a major defeat. He had to do something creative. Flynn's face passed through his mind bringing a wave of anger with it.

The laser comm suddenly beeped. It was Group Three arriving to reinforce his depleted squadron. They were coming as quickly as they could and were now about ten minutes from engagement distance. The Feds hadn't located them so far, but it was just a matter of time before they'd show up on the navy sensors. They were stealthed, but that only went so far.

The D-R re-vectored towards the back of the mass of ships. There was another bomb-laser ship deploying away from the main body. They were going to use the same weapon. The hyperdrive went to full thrust for a second, causing the two humans to strain under the gee force.

They were still receding, coasting away from the enemy, but that would change in a few seconds. Adam fired his plasma cannon at the bomb-laser ship, hoping that it would strike before the laser fired.

It did, and the hull of the weapon flared. Molten metal sprayed off of one side causing the ship to spin on its axis, then the entire thing vanished in a nuclear explosion.

The vid instantly scrambled into a distorted mess of static. Adam shut off his engines immediately. He had to be able to see before he could decide what to do next.

When the vid cleared, it showed a Fed fleet with a gaping hole through it. The plasma strike had spun the laser barrel towards the massed ships just before the bomb ignited. He gritted his teeth in a snarl. It was only just that the Feds got to enjoy the effects of their own weapon.

The remaining Belter ships were firing plasma bursts at the other side of the formation. Adam picked out one of the battleships and let go with the antimatter gun. The colossal ship shuddered, sending off a vivid flurry of sparks that resulted from antimatter and matter particles dancing in mutual destruction. Half of the battleship vanished as the antimatter struck. Just beyond it, the remains of the antimatter burst, those particles that had missed the battleship and continued on, cut through a cruiser causing the reactor to let go with a burst of nuclear-powered flame.

At this point, the D-R was moving past the navy formation on one side, while the other Belter ships were moving directly towards the formation from what had been the back. Together they formed an ideal kill zone. Adam could fire without fear of hitting friendly ships, and he was out of the line of fire of their guns.

He fired a long burst of positrons. The D-R's antimatter cannon sucked up the rest of the stored antimatter particles, emptying the containment vessel. The extended shot burned through three of the navy ships. The other Belter ships were firing plasma, but the small force was still outnumbered five to one.

Adam yelled at To'afa, "Hyperdrive again. We'll go to their other side and attack from there."

The two men groaned as the ship accelerated out and around the larger formation, recharging the positron containment vessel as it went.

The shields flared, and the D-R shook violently. They'd flown right through a field of railgun slugs. The problem with the slugs was they continued on a straight line without losing any velocity, and they were difficult to detect. The navy ships had apparently fired a burst at where they thought the Belters would be, but the only ship to be struck was the D-R.

To'afa checked the status board. "All okay. No major damage. We've lost two of the plasma generators though. They're both on the port side, so try to protect that from incoming fire."

Adam nodded, "Affirmative. Keep our starboard towards them as much as possible."

Group Three was approaching from behind Adam's position. He hoped they'd allow for that and not try to shoot him by mistake.

The D-R slowed, easing the gee forces. They were nearly in position on the opposite side of the navy ships.

A globe of plasma whizzed by, heading at the enemy. Group Three had arrived and was joining the battle. The odds against them were reduced with the addition of the twenty-one ships. Now the enemy outnumbered them by about two to one.

The Belter's plasma bolts did their work on the inferior shields of the Navy ships, and the positron cannon burned through two or three ships with every shot.

Suddenly ships were flying in all directions. The Fed formation had been broken. The individual vessels were accelerating away from the battle. The Belters pursued, shooting indiscriminately at their enemy.

The next minutes of battle were chaotic. Belter ships chased Navy ships shooting at them and were in turn chased by Navy ships trying to burn through their shields with plasma or unleashing a stream of railgun slugs.

After ten minutes, it became apparent that the surviving navy ships were headed for Luna. Adam broke off the pursuit, organized his seventeen remaining ships, and headed towards Earth orbit.

A comm message from Group Two came through.

"We found only token resistance around Luna. We lost two ships, destroyed three cruisers and several scouts and shuttles. The shipyard is empty. No hulls there. It looks like they had everything they owned up and flying at us."

Adam replied, "We're on our way to settle things on the surface. Watch for some navy ships coming your way. They're pretty well shot up, but they might have some fight left, so be careful."

"Affirmative. We'll watch for them. Unfortunately, we had no luck on the surface. The place is hopping with marines. They chased our landing force back into space, and we lost several men in the process. The Feds still hold the shipyard."

Adam shook his head. The place was key. With it, the NAFD could rebuild its navy. If he controlled the yard, and at least that local part of Luna, the resources could be put to work expanding the Belter fleet. New mining ships and possibly some cruisers would be very welcome in the Belt. Something would have to be done there, but he had more immediate problems at the moment. He sighed, then turned his attention to the next part of the problem. Earth was ahead.

19
PEACE ON EARTH

THE BELTER SHIPS settled into high Earth orbit. Adam had made use of the time, resting while To'afa got the reduced fleet into the desired position. There had been some radio traffic back and forth. Adam trusted To'afa to handle it.

The big man poked his head into the Captain's cabin.

"Captain, I've got a conference set up with the heads of the Non-Aligns. It should start in five minutes. The NAFD isn't speaking to anyone at the moment. I tried, but I can't raise them. You can handle the conference from here or the control room."

Adam sighed. "The control room. It'll make it look like I'm prepared to take immediate action if my demands aren't met."

To'afa nodded, then disappeared from the doorway.

RATHER THAN TAKE questions from the various governments, Adam decided to make a simple statement with his requirements.

There really was no option that he'd allow. They'd either have to fall in line, or the Belters would have the unpleasant task of enforcing their will.

HE LOOKED AT the main vid screen. It was broken into numerous windows. There were nearly two hundred political entities on Earth, but only seventeen of them were really large enough and prosperous enough to count. Each of them was represented on the screen.

He inspected the faces in front of him, waiting until the scheduled moment. This pause gave them time to evaluate him. He hoped he looked serious enough to impress them but feared that he did not.

He was far younger than any of the seasoned politicians in his audience. His eyepatch probably made him look somewhat sinister. He knew for sure that his expression was not pleasant.

The time had come.

"Gentlemen, thank you for meeting with me on such short notice. You've probably been apprised that we're from the Belt. We've been watching the conflict on Earth, and we have come to the conclusion that it cannot be tolerated any further.

I realize that you have had little choice. You've been attacked by the NAFD, and some of you have suffered tremendous losses. We have defeated the USSN, and the remainder of their fleet is heading to Luna as we speak. They will have a surprise when they get there. We have destroyed their ships and taken their base. They will have to surrender, run, or fight.

They will not survive a fight. We've just demonstrated that the Belter ships are more durable and better armed than the USSN ships. They attacked with a new superweapon, but we overcame that. Your countries each have a minor presence in space. Many of the asteroid miners originated in the Non-Aligns. We want no conflict with you, but you are now required to follow our instructions exactly. There is no latitude for changes or improvisations on your part.

I expect you to form a governing Council that will be responsible for the planet. Each of the seventeen countries that you represent will have one representative. All actions will be approved by a majority vote, and no one can abstain. I'll have no deadlocks from you. Understood?"

They were quiet for a moment, then the Russian representative asked, "What about the American government? Will they have a place on the Council?"

Adam's lips drew back slightly, making him look fierce. "Not at this time. As far as I'm concerned, they've forfeited their right to self-representation. However, I will leave it up to you to decide to admit them to the Council at any time in the future that you think appropriate. Just be advised that the Council must always have an odd number of members, so there will be no tie votes."

He scanned the faces. Some appeared bewildered, while others seemed to be calculating.

"Gentlemen, please pay attention to this next part. I'm dead serious about it. You will disarm. Everyone will disarm. I'll have no nuclear weapons, no railguns, no death lasers, no weapons capable of inflicting damage on other countries. All disputes must be negotiated or adjudged by the Council.

If there is any sign of war at any time in the future, be assured that we will return and the conflict will be settled harshly. Those responsible will be punished summarily."

Adam felt it was going well. Many of the men were nodding their heads. He started to speak again, but To'afa grabbed his shoulder.

"Missile launch, Captain. We've got to move."

He looked at the sensor suite display. Well over one hundred missiles were climbing upward from North America, and some were already arching over towards their targets in other countries.

Adam addressed the faces on the vidscreen. "We'll resume this discussion later. Be advised that we've detected a missile launch from the NAFD. They appear to be aimed at your countries. Those of you who have a missile defense system, activate it now. We are going to destroy as many of the missiles as we can from space, but some may slip through.

I will have no reprisals from you, though. Do not think to attempt to launch an ICBM targeting the NAFD. Their rulers deserve it, but most of the people there are innocent, and we're not going to allow them to suffer."

As he spoke, his fingers were flickering across the battle system control screen. The Belter fleet broke out of formation and dispersed, each ship moving to intercept one or more missiles. Plasma bursts were already being fired, destroying the missiles and causing spectacular flares in the upper atmosphere.

A few of the missiles slipped through to be met with anti-missile missiles. Three nuclear blasts occurred near the surface. One of these decimated the majority of Paris, and another wiped Istanbul off the face of the globe. The third was higher when it was ignited by a plasma bolt.

The EMP from that one darkened Hong Kong totally, taking the power grid down.

Adam wondered how many people would die as a result of the power loss. It would probably take months to rebuild the power grid. The large transformers were not items that could be purchased at any store. They had to be hand-built according to individual specifications.

The last missile was burned out at the midpoint of its trajectory within thirty minutes of the initial launch. Adam wanted to continue the meeting since he hadn't detailed all the conditions, but it looked like that would have to wait. Most of the faces on the screen were gone with the exceptions of the Australians and the Chinese.

He'd have to arrange a new schedule. That was irritating. He disconnected from the two remaining men with a brief thanks and turned to To'afa.

"That went somewhat well, despite the interruption. Did we get all the missiles?"

To'afa said, "Two got through, and a third caused an EMP. There are going to be a lot of people dead from just those three. There—"

He stopped as the comm chimed, announcing an incoming call.

Adam flicked the screen. It cleared to show Elseth's angry face.

"You naive ass!" she spat.

Somehow that statement activated Adam's sense of humor. He laughed in her face.

She drew back slightly, eyes narrowing in a calculating manner, but before she could reply, he said, "I was going to call you. Thanks for saving me the trouble. Your missile launch was mostly ineffective, but three warheads got through. You'll have to indemnify those countries. I don't expect that it will be cheap."

She spluttered for a moment then apparently got control of her thoughts.

"Indemnify them? You're even stupider than I thought. I'm the Empress. I own Earth. All humans are my subjects. You Asteroid Pirates are going to regret the day you rebelled against me."

Adam's humor faded. He'd suffered enough at her hands, and it was going to stop.

"Shut up, Elseth," he said. "You've got everything wrong. My force just destroyed the majority of your space force, then we took out most of your missile launch. You have nothing that we can't counter. Now you're going to cease all hostilities towards the Non-Aligns."

She drew in a breath to retort, but he cut her off. "Not only that, but you're going to be under their direct supervision. I've set up a governing body made up of your main competitors. They are going to be responsible for enforcing peace. There will be no more acts of aggression from the NAFD. In fact, I'll be surprised if they don't imprison you for the rest of your miserable life."

"You truly are an insufferable ass. I made a mistake not having Serge kill you immediately. You don't know what you're talking about. I've got thousands of additional missiles even if you temporarily set my space navy back. Oh, I'll have some officers flayed alive for that, but that's for later.

I'm going to complete my conquest of the resistance here on Earth and rebuild my magnificent space navy, then I'll have them track you down, even if you flee the solar system. They'll find you wherever you are. Then I'm going to bring you down here for a long and painful session with me."

How had he ever thought he was in love with her? She hadn't shown any signs of this level of insanity back then, but the seed of it must have been somewhere in her personality. He shook his head in acknowledgment. He knew that she was right. He was a naive ass.

"I'm going to explain this slowly, Elseth. That way, you'll be able to process it. We've won. You've lost. You must pay the price. You will announce that you're stepping down and appoint someone else to rule in your place. They'll only be temporary, but I'm going to leave that up to the new Council."

He looked at her, noting the background of the video. She was in the oval office, or that was what it looked like to him. The décor had been changed to a disgusting shade of pink, and there were gold sconces on the wall behind her. It looked like some child's version of a throne room.

He continued, "I'll expect the announcement of your resignation within the next hour. We're monitoring from space and will tolerate no more aggressive acts. After that, I don't care what you do. You might try to hide, but I expect that they'll catch you eventually."

Her voice suddenly changed, becoming that of a younger girl. She'd spoken to him in this tone when they first met, and it was one that he had thought appealing. Now it seemed grating and out of place.

"Adam, don't be so harsh with me. Everything I did was because you rejected me. I messed up. I didn't really want Serge. It was just... just to try and make you love me more, find me more desirable. My father is dead. I have no one here I can trust. Please reconsider. We could rule the world together. I promise that I'll listen to you and follow your wishes. Please."

He wavered a bit. She looked so helpless, he felt the same old urge to protect her. That feeling faded almost as quickly as it came. She was responsible for untold deaths. He shook his head as if he was shaking off a magic spell.

"No. I'm not going to help you. You got yourself into this, and you'll have to suffer the consequences."

She snarled, "It's that damned woman, isn't it? Your little runaway marine. I know all about it, and I'm having her dealt with. No one gets away with insulting me! You'll see!"

A note of steel entered his voice. "You haven't hurt her, have you? If you have, you're going to regret it."

She laughed wildly. "Oh, I wouldn't hurt her. Physically, that is. I gave her to my psychologists. They reoriented her, giving her a new sense of duty. She's been a good little marine serving her country since they finished. I don't know where she is right now. You might have killed her if she was in any of the ships you destroyed. That would be poetic, wouldn't it?"

Adam's heart chilled. He wanted to hear no more. He lifted his hand towards the screen to switch it off.

She flinched at the movement as if he were threatening her in person. He lowered his hand, contemplating it for a moment, then said, "You have your orders. Resign or face the consequences. I'll make you if I have to."

She snarled, making a feral sound. "Right. I'll face the consequences if I do or if I don't. My chances are better while I'm in power, don't you think?"

He shrugged. "I really don't care either way. You're out of power, and that's it."

He raised his hand to terminate the call. She snapped, "I'm going to order ten thousand more missiles launched. Your foreign friends are going to be a Council presiding over an atomic wasteland if they survive."

He terminated the call, then activated the battle-link with an all ships message.

"Possible mass missile launch from North America. Try to intercept at low altitudes. Use KEWs on all launch sites, active or not. Do not leave them with any aggressive capacity. None whatsoever."

He turned to To'afa. "Vector us over Washington and get a targeting lock on the White House."

The big man looked at him with an alarmed expression. "Do you really want to be the one that destroys the Capitol?"

Adam's conscience twinged, but then the deaths he'd seen, the losses he'd experienced, the injustice converged in a fiery heat to anneal that twinge. His anger faded quickly, but it left him with a hard edge that seemed unreal, but somehow fitting.

"No, I don't. She's leaving me no choice."

The D-R was over the Atlantic near the equator at the moment. Getting over Washington would take fifteen minutes or so. Adam adjusted their altitude, and the ship began to descend. He wanted to be as close as possible. The atmosphere would attenuate the antimatter bolt, so the less air the shot had to pass through, the better.

A FEW MINUTES later, as they were passing over the city, Adam's finger hovered over the activation pad of the gun. He delayed almost too long, but a memory of Flynn laughing over a beer suddenly struck him. He triggered the positron gun. The air sparkled and flashed as the antimatter and ordinary matter particles destroyed each other.

Far below, the White House was suddenly outlined in a coruscating radiance. The after image remained for a few seconds on the retinas of those who happened to be looking. When it faded, there was no building there.

Under high magnification, the vidscreen showed a slumped hole in the ground. The beam had eaten into the ground. Probably a good thing, Adam thought. He recalled hearing about basements and sub-basements.

It would be just like those politicians to have a bolt-hole deep in the ground, but he had given them no warning unless telling Elseth that she basically had no choice counted.

To'afa was less analytical. "You did it! The NAFD is gone. They didn't get away. She didn't getaway. There wasn't time. Man, I've been living for this day. The trouble they put me through."

He leaned over the vid and shouted, "How'd you like that? Huh? Payback time from the big, bad Pirates in the sky!"

Adam shook his head in amazement. He knew that To'afa had been through a lot, but this display showed a side of the man's character that Adam had thought had been discarded.

To'afa straightened with a triumphant smile and turned to Adam. Whatever he was going to say was forgotten as the vid signaled an incoming call.

They both looked at the device as if it had grown horns, then Adam slowly leaned forward and accepted the call.

The screen showed a USSN officer, an admiral apparently from the insignia. "I'm Admiral Jessimine. As far as I can determine, I'm in charge of the government at this point. You seem to have taken out everyone else. I'd like to talk about terms with you. We've got little choice at this point."

To'afa swore under his breath. Adam couldn't make out what he said, it was so soft, but then he added, "Spoke too soon. I never get a break."

Adam smiled to himself, but Jessimine took it as directed towards him. "No need to gloat, young man. You've beaten us, and

I'm prepared to take whatever steps I can to get you to call off your attack. Whatever you hit the White House with has gotten our tech people really upset. They say we have no means of countering it. Now, what do you want?"

What did he want? He'd gotten tired of telling people repeatedly, and now this alleged Admiral was asking him again. He frowned, then snapped, "What I want, Admiral, has little bearing on the matter. What the Asteroid Belt population wants is for Earth and specifically the NAFD to cease all hostilities. We will not allow you to continue to wreck the planet in the fashion you've been doing. It's too great a resource for all humans for us to let you waste it in that fashion."

Jessimine was apparently taken aback by the fierceness of Adam's speech. He leaned back slightly, his eyebrows raised.

When Adam had finished, Jessimine leaned forward again. "I understand your point, and I must confess that it's one that has worried me. However, I was constrained by the chain of command. I can promise you our cooperation at this point."

Adam was suddenly overwhelmingly tired. The whole thing was beyond his job description as far as he was concerned.

"Look, Admiral, I want you to take what steps you can to cease all missile launches. Stop all aggressive action, then prepare for representatives of the Non-aligns to dictate terms to you. They now have a governing Council responsible for Earth. You'll have to abide by their decisions."

"What gives them the right to say what we do? The NAFD is a free and sovereign nation. We have—"

Adam cut him off. "You have nothing if you can't enforce your will. Right now I'm calling the shots, and I'll take another shot with my weapon if you don't believe me. The next one will be on my next pass over Virginia. I think perhaps the Pentagon would be a good target."

The Admiral's eyes showed alarm, and he looked over his shoulder. Adam smirked in response. He'd guessed correctly. The Admiral was currently in the Pentagon.

"Uh, no need for any additional action," Jessimine said. "We'll follow your orders. All our forces will stand down, and I'll wait to be contacted by this Council you're telling me of. Will that be adequate?"

Adam leaned back. "For now. I'm sure they'll have other requirements for you. Meanwhile, I'm going to have my forces take over your shipyard on Luna. You can save me some trouble by calling them and telling them not to resist. I'd like the yard to be intact when I get there. If they resist, it will not be in that condition, and I'm likely to come back and take out my frustration on more ground targets. Understood?"

Jessimine nodded earnestly. "Yes. Completely." He bit the word off as if it was sour.

"Good. It's been a pleasure speaking to you, Admiral." Adam disconnected.

To'afa said, "Man, did you ever put that guy down. I never saw the air let out of a stuffed-suit so fast."

"Yeah. He may do what I asked. I hope he will. I really don't want to have to come back here. Now, let's get the Luna situation attended to and then head back home. We're so close to the sun in here, I'm afraid I'll get a tan."

To'afa laughed harder than the weak attempt at humor warranted.

20

LUNA BASE

THE D-R WAS just leaving orbit when the second force that Adam had sent to attack the NAFD base on the Moon showed up, figuratively dragging their tails behind them. The action in and around Earth had been so intense and quickly paced that he'd practically forgotten about Force Two. He remembered talking to the commander, but other than thinking they had things basically under control, he couldn't quite remember the details of the conversation.

Lucas Rigby was a miner who was highly respected for his ship handling. Adam had assigned Force Two to his command, expecting that he'd be able to keep the USSN ships out of the fight near Earth. They had done that successfully, only losing a couple of ships in the process.

Lucas had then sent a landing party down to secure the shipbuilding facility. That had proven to be a huge mistake. He'd told Adam that they'd been kicked off the surface, but that had been a gross understatement. His landing party had been composed of the crews of five ships. Force Two ships were carrying extra men since the raid had been planned from the beginning, so the landing party had thirty men.

They'd run into heavy resistance from a platoon of USSN Space Marines that had been assigned to guard the place. Rigby hung his head, looking down at the console as they spoke through the vid.

"I'm sorry to tell you, Admiral, but we lost twenty-seven. The remaining three were barely able to make it back to the ships. They brought just one back. We had to leave two on the surface and the others in orbit. Those marines are well-trained and tough."

The twenty-seven men had all been killed. There was no such thing as a minor wound in a vacuum. A hole in a suit was as good as a death sentence. So far, no one had come up with a really good and durable emergency patch. Adam shook his head, reflecting that was something that had to be remedied.

"Look, Rigby, no one knew the place was guarded by marines. I know they're tough. This is my fault more than yours. You knew we needed to capture the shipyard and you did your best. It just wasn't enough, but that's not your fault. I haven't given up on the idea of capturing the place. We can make good use of it. The dictatorship won't need it any longer, and I'm not going to turn it over to the Non-Aligns. I trust them to look after their own interests on Earth, but I'm suspicious of what they'd do if they got into space in force. The Belt is too resource-rich and makes too tempting a target. The next thing we'd know would be we'd have to fight them. I want no more threats from Earth."

Rigby looked up. "But, we are going to have to beat those marines still, if we're going to take the place. I...I don't have anyone left."

Adam cut him off. "I know you don't. I'm leaving five ships in low Earth orbit to ensure there are no more missile launches. They've got instructions to drop a rock on anyone who raises his head too far down there. The rest of us are going back to Luna with you to see what we can do about the situation."

Rigby nodded but said nothing.

Adam asked, "What happened to the navy ships that we chased out of Earth orbit? Did you intercept them?"

"We didn't see anything. I don't know where they went."

"Hmm. The last I saw of them, they were headed directly for you. They must have deviated after that."

"Yes, Sir. Perhaps Luna Base warned them."

"Perhaps. I guess we'll have to look out for them. Fortunately, there weren't too many that got away."

THE REMAINING BELTER ships left orbit, joined up with the remnant of Force Two, and headed towards Luna Base under Em-Max power. There was no need to hurry. The base wasn't going anywhere, and Adam wanted a few hours to come up with a plan.

He was in his cabin, thinking when To'afa came to warn him they were nearing Luna orbit.

"We're getting into range of their railguns, Captain. Whatever you've got planned, we need to get it going shortly."

Adam grunted. Nothing like being in demand. It was just that it was a heavy load, and right now, he didn't feel like he was really up to it.

"Okay. I think we're not going to fight them. They're probably dug in and ready for us. We're going to use psychology on them instead."

"How's that going to work?" The big man was curious.

Adam grinned. "It is going to be simple. They're vulnerable, and we're not. They might have a few railguns down there, but shooting out of a gravity well reduces their effectiveness. On the other hand, a positron beam won't have any problem reaching the surface. There's no atmosphere to attenuate it."

To'afa's mouth formed a round shape, and his eyes widened. "I see. You're going to convince them to surrender."

"That's basically it. Should be no problem, unless they're totally insane."

AS IT TURNED out, the Lieutenant in charge of the marines wasn't insane. He was, however, intent on doing his duty.

Adam inspected his image in the vid. The Lieutenant looked young.

He considered, remembering the recent past. He'd been young when all this conflict started. He was still young in years. How had he decided that he was no longer young? Perhaps it had come through combat or commanding men. Either way, he wasn't sure he liked it.

"Lieutenant, you look reasonable. Listen closely. The NAFD is no longer in power. We defeated your forces. Most of the navy ships are destroyed. We arranged a surrender, and the NAFD is going to be under the control of a new Council composed of members of the Non-Aligns. There's no one left to hold you accountable if you surrender to us."

"Yes, Sir. I'm sure you're correct about the tactical situation, but if I surrender, my men won't like it. They'll hold me responsible."

Adam shook his head. Why were people always so set on self-destruction? It was a mystery to him, but then, lots of human behavior wasn't rational.

"What's your name, Lieutenant?"

"James Schmitt, Sir."

"Okay. Well, James, the fact is you don't have a choice. I'm going to give you a little demonstration of what we can do to the facility you're guarding. Once you've seen that, I'm going to give you precisely thirty minutes to surrender. If you do not, I think you can guess the consequences. Now, look out in the yard. Ten hulls are waiting on frames near the south end. See them?"

Schmitt was apparently near a window. He simply turned his head, then said, "Yes. They're in plain sight."

Adam activated the positron gun briefly. There was no need for a full-strength shot. The ship's cap bank hummed and the lights dimmed for a moment, but that was all. A couple of seconds later, the ten hulls and the frames and a large chunk of moon rock flashed and disappeared."

Schmitt looked shaken. "You can...How did you do that, Sir?"

Adam nodded grimly. "Didn't like that, did you? Never mind how I did it. Just know that I can do it to the entire base. You and your men, the rest of the personnel there, and the entire structure will flash and disappear if you continue to ignore my request."

The Lieutenant glanced both directions. Somehow his actions reminded Adam of an animal caught in a trap. Schmitt looked at the screen, nodded, and said, "I don't suppose we could fight you off with our railguns."

Adam laughed. "You are a good officer, son. You know that you've got trouble getting the slugs out of the gravity well. We're shielded, and they won't have enough momentum to give my ships more than a gentle love tap by the time they get up here. Now, I'm tired of waiting. Are you going to surrender?"

Schmitt raised his hands. "I surrender. I can't see any other option. I'm not going to waste my men for nothing."

"Alright. That's settled. I expect you to do this honestly. No tricks. Remember my demonstration if you will."

Schmitt nodded. "No tricks. We'll put our weapons down and assemble in the mess hall. I'll have the men wait there for your people to arrive. Just, please, remember they were only following orders. I know you took some heavy losses, but that's our job. You understand, don't you?"

"Yes, I understand. I don't like it, but I do understand. I'm not going to take revenge on defenseless men. You'll be safe. Now disarm and wait. I'll have someone down there shortly."

Schmitt had the grace to look embarrassed for an instant, then he saluted and said, "Yes, Sir."

THE PROBLEM FOR Adam was men. There weren't many. Of the ships that composed the fleet, only forty were left. Force Two had left most of its vessels at Luna, parked in orbit. There was no one to fly them since the Marines had been so effective. Force Three still had eighteen ships, and most of those only had minor damage. Unfortunately, almost all ships were minimally crewed with only two or three spacers per ship.

Once he began to count his forces, Adam quickly came to the conclusion that he could only send about five men down to the Luna Base. On the face of it, that was ridiculous. It was a tiny force to accept the surrender of the entire base. The marine defenders probably had over forty men left. Space Marine platoons were usually larger than surface platoon sizes. If they followed true to form, they would have had sixty-two men plus the Lieutenant. Five Belters, no matter how fierce and well-armed couldn't handle that many marines, even if the marines fully intended to surrender.

He gazed at the wall, searching for a solution, but there was none. The only thing he had going for him was the ability to reduce the entire base into a bit of vapor and some radioactive particles. That wasn't acceptable to him, but did the marines know that? The Lieutenant had seemed pretty sharp. He would have to suspect that Adam wouldn't destroy the base. Then again, he had cut the Ribbon. No one in their right mind would have predicted that.

He exhaled, then straightened his shoulders. He'd been slumped over, and his back hurt. They would have to go with what they had.

"To'afa, have the five available crew take the Rusty Bucket down. It's the oldest ship we have, so it won't be so painful if they lose it."

"I'll take care of it, Captain." Then in a different tone, "Adam, you look exhausted. You'd better get some rest. I can't have you so worn out that you can't function at full capacity. I, uh, that is, the entire Belt needs you."

He nodded. "You're right. I'm worn out. It's not the activity so much as the stress. I feel like I was dragged through a micro-black hole. I'm having difficulty coming to any decision where I have to risk lives. I'll be in my cabin."

The hall to the cabin seemed distorted. He really wasn't tracking well. It would be nice to open the door and find Nile in the bed waiting for him. No, he couldn't think of that, it was too painful.

He slammed the door, entered the bathroom, and looked at his face in the mirror. His eye was red, and a tear track traced down the side of his nose. Thinking about Nile always was upsetting. To top it off, he'd lost men. Flynn! Adam made an incoherent sound, slow gasping noise as he drew breath.

The mirror suddenly seemed blurry. He wiped his face with a towel, disarranging his patch.

He pulled it up. The scar underneath was white and jagged, and what was left of his eye was sunken. It would be wonderful to get a cloned replacement, but things kept getting in the way. Besides, he'd never trust an earth medic. Too many people down there wanted him dead.

He carefully moved the patch back over the blind eye as he walked towards the bed. There he sat for a minute, thinking or perhaps coming close to prayer, just being thankful that he hadn't lost more men. The faces of the dead that he knew personally floated in his mental vision.

The necessity of informing their families frightened him. Jem's death had given him an object lesson in bearing that kind of news.

He whispered, "How many more will I lose before this is done. Can I arrange a lasting peace?

He waited for a moment. No solution came to mind. He couldn't back out, and he couldn't guarantee that it would be worth the pain and loss in the end. He could only go forward, muddling through as best he could. His lack of experience weighed on him. Surely there was someone else who was better qualified...

He lay down without taking off any clothes. As he did, the thought came to him that there was no one else. He'd picked up this burden, and he was going to have to bear it until the end.

He clicked off the light, adjusted his patch, and closed his eye.

21
UNEXPECTED ALLIES

WHEN HE AWOKE, the Rusty Bucket was on the surface, resting in a previously empty ship cradle. The five members of the occupying force, Adam thought calling them that was ridiculous, but that was what they were, had been greeted by Lieutenant Schmitt and were being treated courteously.

Eloy Sanchez, the Captain of the Rusty Bucket, had assumed control of the occupying force. The other four members were miners that Adam didn't know personally. They'd had the luck, good or bad was unknown at this point, of being the only available people that weren't essential elsewhere.

Eloy had called in shortly before Adam came into the bridge. He was excited, perhaps ecstatic might be a better word. When Adam came in, Eloy was still on the comm telling To'afa about the fantastic facilities that the shipyard featured.

When Adam made his presence known, Lieutenant Schmitt insisted on speaking to him privately.

That was simply a matter of switching the call from broadband to the modulated laser system. The only way someone could listen in would be to intercept the laser beam.

"Admiral, I understand you were offline. I trust you had a good rest." Schmitt was carefully polite. Adam nodded but didn't say anything.

The lieutenant looked over his shoulder. Satisfied that he was alone, he asked, "Is there anyone on your side who can listen in?"

Adam spoke to To'afa. "Perhaps you'd better take a few minutes to refresh yourself."

The big man nodded and left.

"No. I'm alone now. What is it that is so secret?" He was curious.

Schmitt looked over his shoulder again, betraying the fact that he was nervous. Then he cleared his throat and said, "Uh. Some of us have been wondering..." He stopped, looked embarrassed, then started again. "I've polled my men. Most of them agree with me."

He stopped, looking pale, then added, "Thank you for speaking to me in private. If this got out, I'd be in bad trouble." Then he hesitated again.

Adam was getting tired of the man's tentativeness.

"Come on. Either tell me or not. I assure you that I'll consider any reasonable request. I don't want to cause you or your men any undue distress. However, it seems to me that you're in a particularly disadvantageous position. You've surrendered the NAFD's only shipyard to a scruffy bunch of Pirates as far as the bigwigs on Earth are concerned. They're not going to look favorably on that. I'd say your military career is over."

Schmitt nodded. "That's just the point. Guarding this base is the brass's way of putting us out of mind. I wasn't going anywhere before you came along. Now, if they get their hands on me, I'll be lucky to go to Leavenworth. More than likely, I'll be executed. The rest of my people are in nearly as much danger. You don't know how bad it's gotten down there lately."

He paused, breathing deeply. Obviously, this came hard for him. He took a breath, then blurted, "Admiral, would it be possible for us, I mean my personnel and me to join your side?"

Adam was startled. Nile had held an amazingly deep loyalty to the marines. Was this some trick? He leaned forward and said, "I don't see why not, but you have to understand that your loyalty to the marines would mean that we couldn't trust you. You'd have to prove yourself, and that might take time."

The lieutenant nodded. "I didn't expect anything else. I'm offering our service to you if you'll have us. We want to continue working in the way we have been trained. We're a good security and defensive force."

Adam looked at the younger man in the screen. He seemed earnest, showing no signs of dissembling. "I agree that you're a good defensive force. You killed a number of my men. You might find that their friends will hold that against you. Are you prepared for that?"

"We were just doing our job, Sir. I personally regret that anyone died. Your men killed some of mine also. I think that my people can take care of themselves if it comes to arguments. We are well trained, as I said."

Adam had made up his mind. "Okay. You're now provisional Belters under my direct control. The first thing I want from you is for you to cooperate fully with my people down there. We need an inventory of ships in progress, parts available, parts needed to complete them, and we also need a complete list of base personnel aside from your platoon. I want to see what we've got there."

Schmitt smiled tightly. "I can tell you that there are three hundred and twenty-seven civilian contractors, engineers, mechanics, electronics specialists, computer specialists, and so on. They're mixed about the idea of changing sides. Some of them have families on Earth. The ones that don't will, I think, mostly be happy to join your community. The opportunities on Earth are few, and the government controls all employment. You have to suck up to someone in power to get any work. Making a living is nearly impossible, too. We've heard that the asteroid belt is a great place to get rich. Is that true."

The words had come out with a rush. Adam grinned. "Well, you can make a valuable discovery, if you're a miner, but it's dangerous. I can say the opportunities are unlimited for someone smart. The Belters need technical expertise badly. I think anyone willing to work will be welcome. As for those who want to return to Earth, we can arrange that eventually."

THE UNEXPECTED CHANGING sides by the USSN Marine platoon said a lot to Adam. Conditions must be bad on Earth. Otherwise, he thought, desertion would never have entered the Marines' minds. Of course, there were going to be some of them who were undesirable. Perhaps some of them would reconsider their loyalty change and work against the Belt, acting as embedded spies or saboteurs. He would have to have them watched, that was certain.

All in all, it was a favorable turn of events. He could relax and begin to make the shipyard part of the belt's assets. Without the ships that had been here, and with the majority of their navy smashed, the Feds could not muster any significant attack, unless they were willing to destroy the shipyard with a nuclear bomb.

It was doubtful that they'd go so far. The facility was incredibly valuable, at least as far as any spacer was concerned. The belt's capacity for building ships was growing, but ever so slowly. If they could get the Tycho base up and running, it would go a long way to meet the increased demand for ships.

The great news was that there were ten cruiser frames already in progress. These could be finished in a few months and placed into service. The only puzzling factor was why there had been no more ships at Luna than there had been. He couldn't figure that out. The place should have been better defended.

Then there was the question about where the remnants of the Earth defenders had fled. He'd thought they would head straight for Tycho, but they hadn't. To all appearances, they'd simply disappeared. No one had tracked them. The confusion of battle had ensured that.

Adam pushed the problem to the back of his mind. They'd show up eventually. Then it would probably fall to him to deal with them. Something else unpleasant to look forward to. Well, he'd handle the situation when it came up. No sense worrying about it now.

He turned to the comm. If the Belt were going to take advantage of the shipyard, they'd need personnel. He considered for a minute. Also, an occupying force, although the NAFD probably wasn't going to get back into space quickly. The missile attacks had destroyed too much of the infrastructure on the surface to make that possibility likely. They'd have trouble keeping their populace alive, let alone creating a surface-to-orbit worthy ship that could carry a significant crew.

Launch vehicles that could climb out of Earth's gravity well had become unnecessary when The Ribbon had gone into service. The materials, parts, and technology had all gone to other efforts. There probably were no engineers left on the surface that could build such a ship. Still, there was no sense taking chances.

He started to change the frequency to that of Titan's universal band. If he sent a message now, it would arrive in about eight hours. He wondered if he'd been stupid not to send it earlier. If he had, they would already be organizing out there.

Before he could activate the comm, the active light came on. He stared at it blankly. He was exhausted, but not so tired that he would have pushed the button and not remembered doing so. No, it was an incoming call from Titan.

22

BAD NEWS

LARS NIELSON'S FACE looked pale as he stared out of the screen. The Councilman's brow was furrowed. He looked down, then began to speak, not wasting time with amenities.

"Admiral Maxwell. I hope you receive this message in time. You've got to get back here immediately."

The man's tone always set Adam's teeth on edge, and he felt his blood pressure begin to rise. Nielson continued.

"The Feds. The USSN and others, maybe privateers, I don't know who, but a lot of ships attacked. There's been a battle in orbit, and I think our defense force is mostly gone. Some of our ships got away. The Feds didn't pursue them. They are focused on the surface. They've landed, and we're unable to hold them off. They've already taken the landing facilities. Now they are shooting down the docking tubes at anything that moves on our side. My information is that they're preparing some kind of assault. Most of the combat-trained people are with you. I knew it was a bad idea to send them off on some wild goose chase. We have a small force, but I don't think that kids and grandfathers can hold off marines."

Adam's temper flared. There were several women combat vets on Titan. Why didn't Nielson include them? There were two women he knew personally who had the experience to organize a first-rate ground defense.

He clenched his fists. That was about what he expected from Lars. The man was unimaginative and probably the worst choice for the Council's leader. Nielson was a true politician and only paid attention to those he thought could help him gain and retain power. Obviously, the women vets weren't important to him.

Kendra Oligwa and Lora Dunlop could mean the difference. Kendra was adept at house-to-house fighting. She could command the defense. Lora knew about booby traps, and those would slow the invaders down.

He started to say something, but then reminded himself that the message would take hours to reach Nielson. It'd be too late by then.

On the screen, Nielson stopped talking and looked confused. Behind him, someone was shouting something. The Councilman listened a moment, then leaned forward and said, "There's a report of more ships just arriving. They are USSN cruisers. We're going to be overrun. You've got to get back with men to defend us."

It was frustrating. The transmission latency made a normal conversation impossible. The message he was watching was old.

One thing was clear, the additional ships were most likely the ones that had escaped Force Two at Luna. He'd wondered where they'd gone. Now it was becoming apparent. He'd thought there were fewer ships in Earth orbit and defending Luna than there should have been. The missing ones had been sent to take Titan. To strike at the heart of the Belt.

Nielson was still talking. "...we're holding them off for now. I'm afraid that they will resort to KEWs or nukes, and we have no defense against them. We're sitting targets on the surface. I'm ordering you to return with your entire force immediately. We need you here, or Titan will be taken."

The screen blacked out. Adam was unsure whether Nielson had terminated the connection or if enemy action had taken out the transmitter. It made no difference.

He activated the battle net. The comp linked in all of the belt ships with a slight delay. Some of them were on the other side of the moon, and the signal took a little longer to relay through intervening vessels to them.

Once the connection was made, Adam flipped it to voice transmission. It was encrypted, and he felt secure that none of the NAFD forces would be able to translate it, even if they could intercept the message.

"Maxwell to all ships. Titan is under attack. The Feds have landed a force on the surface. They hold the port facilities now and are advancing into the main habitat. There is an unknown number of ships in orbit. Our defense force has been defeated. We're leaving at once. While you're en-route, I want all battle damage repaired. We must be ready to fight the instant we get there."

The net signaled acknowledgment from each of the connected ships. Adam continued.

"I'll work out a plan before we get there. I want all experienced ground fighters ready to land. We'll use two ships for that, and the others will attack the USSN force in space. I don't have to say that speed is important here."

As he was speaking, he oriented the D-R so that it was aligned with the Titan vector. His hand hovered over the hyperdrive switch.

"All ships. I'm going to take the D-R ahead. I've got the speed to cut the trip time down. I'll do what I can until you arrive. You'll be under the command of, ah, Han Lee."

The Chinese-American Captain had been an officer in the PRC Navy before becoming a spacer. He would probably make a good commander.

The comm beeped. It was Han Lee calling on a tight band laser.

Adam put the battle-net on hold and flipped on the comm.

Lee looked sober as he said, "Admiral, I'm at your service. I will do my best, but I don't think we've got enough ships to win against a superior force."

Adam shook his head negatively, then spoke.

"Lee, get all battle damage repaired. Get the guns charged up and come in ready to shoot any USSN ship you see. I'm going to be there well in advance of you. I'll try to last long enough to send a status update before you arrive. Beyond that, you're on your own. Just remember, you're fighting for our future."

He didn't have to mention the families of nearly everyone in his force. Lee had two teenage daughters and was probably anxious to rescue them before the invading force captured them. The girls were quite pretty. Adam grimaced at the thought. The two wouldn't like their treatment at the hands of the privateers.

"Lee, you're in charge. Do your best. I'm leaving now. I'll send you the status after I arrive. Understood?"

"Yes, Sir. Good luck."

Lee's image blacked out.

Adam's finger descended decisively. There was a slight pause, then the D-R began to accelerate, the gee-force building rapidly.

To'afa didn't say anything, but he didn't have to. When they'd passed four gees and Adam didn't shut the drive off, he looked inquiringly at Adam. The big man's cheeks were sagging under the force, but his breathing was regular.

Adam felt like a buffalo had decided to take a nap on his chest. It was an effort, but he managed to say, "We've got to get there. How much do you think we can take?"

To'afa grunted. The sound was more explosive than usual due to the increased force on his chest. It came out sounding something like Adam thought his imaginary buffalo would make.

To'afa said, "Don't forget we got to slow down."

That was true. They would have to undergo similar force as they decelerated. However, Adam had programmed the comp to start the decel sooner than absolutely necessary. They'd slow more gradually, still retaining considerable velocity. He wanted to make a pass through the enemy ships at a speed they wouldn't expect.

Space battle was still new. It was sure that the NAFD's tacticians had gamed out various strategies, but they might not have come up with a suicidal attack by a single ship on a small fleet. It made sense to zip through, targeting as many of the enemy as possible. They'd be moving quickly, so unless the Feds had fired their railguns early, they'd be through before the slugs intersected their vector.

On the flip side, hitting a slug at such high speed would possibly overwhelm the plasma shield. The shield had proven itself capable of deflecting almost anything thrown at it, but momentum is additive. Adam was a little nervous over the idea. It was a gamble any way you looked at it. However, it was a bet that he was going to take.

Even with the enhanced defense and superior weaponry, the Dire Rhea sported, taking on an unknown number of warships alone seemed suicidal.

The drive abruptly clicked off. Both men took deep gasping breaths of air.

"I was kind of hoping that you weren't going to squash both of us," To'afa said, panting.

Adam held up his hand, indicating that he wasn't able to speak at the moment. He was too busy breathing. It was a joy to inhale with no effort. It even made the slightly foul ship's air seem clean.

"We're going to coast at this v for a while, then we'll start to slow down. I've optimized the calc to provide us with a slower decel. We can't afford to be wiped out physically when we fly through them."

"You going to fly through quickly?"

"Yes. We'll shoot through, blasting everything we can target as we go. With any luck, they'll miscalculate the timing with their railguns. Plasma bursts, too. I am worried about hyper-vee missiles. Those might be able to catch us if we slow too much."

To'afa nodded, his eyes wide. "We're gonna teach them something about messing with Belters. They don't seem to learn fast, do they?'

Adam laughed. "No, but I give them credit for continuing to try. I hope that we keep ahead of them, that's all."

"You've been ahead of them from the start, Captain."

BY NOW, THE other ships would be well on their way. It would take more time than he felt they had before the bulk of his command arrived. If only the D-R could hold out. If he could draw the enemy away from Titan orbit, it might give the defenders a chance to beat back the landing party. If the invaders were unchallenged, they'd start dropping rocks or railgun slugs sooner or later, and that would mean the end of the Titan settlement.

KEWs were deadly, and the unbreathable atmosphere complicated things. Any damage to the habitat would constitute a full-out emergency. He shook his head, trying to stop worrying. The best thing he could do was to work out targeting scenarios before arriving. They'd still have to solve for relative positions, but if the comp had calculated various possibilities, it would automatically take the one that was nearest to the actual situation. That would speed up targeting, possibly cutting the time between shots.

The other thing he could do was to ensure the tank was full of antimatter. It was currently about half-filled. He retasked the collection net from the drive to antimatter parameters, and the indicator started to rise.

To'afa chose that moment to say, "Don't worry Captain. We'll be ready, and they won't know what hit them."

Hours later, the tank was full, and the collector had been switched back to drive mode. The ship was coasting silently, and the two men were relaxing in their seats when the comp signaled that it was time to begin to slow.

The ship jerked slightly as the maneuvering jets turned her around. Once in position, the comp beeped. That meant the drive would come on in fifteen seconds. Both men checked their harness quickly.

The gee-force increased, but it was more bearable this time. It was more gradual, and they wouldn't have to slow to a complete stop. Adam wanted to be moving much faster than orbital velocity when his vector intercepted the enemy location.

Now, it was a matter of patiently waiting for a brief period of frenzied action.

23
REPRISAL

THE DIRE RHEA was about two million klicks out from Titan, moving quickly on a vector that would bypass the moon closely. The sensor suite alert caused Adam to start. The USSN had just used an active scan.

He waited, unconsciously holding his breath. The scan passed by and did not immediately return. The D-R might not have been detected.

The vid showed a blurry view, so he enhanced the image. The comp obligingly superimposed icons for the USSN ships that the sensors had located in orbit. Not counting ones that were currently out of sight on the far side of the moon, it was a significant force.

According to the comp's analysis of the sensor data, there were at least three types of ships surrounding Titan. Adam tentatively identified the mid-sized ones as cruisers and the smaller ones as probable privateers. Five larger ships might be some kind of battleship.

He puzzled over the problem for a moment, then gave it up as being insoluble without more data. He'd have that soon enough at the rate they were closing.

He pulled up the calc for the targeting situation that he'd deemed most likely. It was close to perfect. The Feds had spaced their ships regularly around the equator of the moon. That much, he'd planned on, but there was a wrinkle. There always was. They were separated more widely than he'd hoped. The extra distance would make it challenging to get off the four shots that the storage field would allow.

He glanced at To'afa, who caught the motion out of the corner of his eye and smiled.

"I've got the plasma cannon and the laser almost ready. I think I can get the first two as we go by. Are you going to fly her right down their line?" To'afa asked.

Adam nodded but didn't speak. He was adjusting the course and trying to induce the comp to generate a new firing solution based on the vector change. He was going to fly through the enemy line at a shallow angle. That would put two or three of the navy ships in his line of fire.

The D-R would descend closer to Titan, on its fly-by, then ascend back through the Fed line as it passed the moon. That would give them a second chance to take out more enemy ships.

Adam finished inputting the commands, then said, "Hey, why don't we give them something to think about as we go by?"

To'afa looked up. "Huh? What do you mean?"

The memory of an old movie struck Adam, and he started to laugh.

To'afa asked, "What?"

"I think we have the Flight of the Valkyries stored somewhere. Maybe in comp archive memory. Didn't Suarez used to listen to classical music?"

"Yeah. He did. The flight of the valk...er whatevers. Isn't that the music they played in that war movie? With the helicopters flying over the sea?"

Adam chuckled, "Exactly. Queue that up and get ready to broadcast as we approach. That'll give them something to think about. They really shouldn't irritate Pirates, you know."

To'afa began to laugh. "They'll think they're really in the deep stuff when they hear that, and we take some shots at them."

"Yes. I'm hoping that they recognize the context and get mad enough to come after us. I'd like to draw as many as I can away from their attack."

To'afa said, "I'll overlay some laughter on the broadcast. That might help." The islander sobered. "Do you think we've got a chance? We are better shielded, I guess."

Adam shrugged. "We can always get unlucky and catch something that gets through, but we're a lot faster than they are. More maneuverable, too. Plus, we've got better weapons, so, yeah, I think we have a chance."

He didn't put a percentage on the chance. He thought it wasn't very high. No sense in increasing his crewmate's worries.

The moon was beginning to look more like a globe than a single spot in the vid. They were getting close.

"Only about five to go. I can't believe they haven't seen us yet," he said.

To'afa answered, "Thank Jupiter for small favors."

Two minutes went by, then the active scan that the Feds were running illuminated them. It passed, then quickly came back.

"They've got us on their screens now. Go ahead and broadcast the music. That should confuse them for at least another minute. After that, it'll be seconds before we're in range. Once we're close, start shooting. Don't quit until we're out of range or out of power on the lasers."

The plasma cannon would only have one chance to get off the single shot that was stored in its tank. Then it would have to recharge. They'd be through the line before that could happen. The laser weapon, although it wasn't as powerful or as quick to do damage, could continue firing for longer.

It drew its power from the reactor. It would have to shut off after twenty seconds of continuous fire, or it would overheat and fail. However, that was enough time to hit three or maybe four of the enemy. The coherent light beam wouldn't destroy them, but they would take possibly disabling damage.

Adam said, "Be sure of the plasma shot. You've only got the one chance as we go through. Don't miss." After he said it, he realized that it had been unnecessary.

The big man snorted in response. "Don't you miss with the antimatter, either. You don't need to worry about me. I'm a good shot. I'm gonna get me one of 'em for sure."

There was nothing to say to that. The time seemed to evaporate as they arrowed in along the preplanned vector. Adam cross-checked the comp. The firing solution had changed, but only slightly.

Someone over there was paying attention. One of the enemy ships was beginning to move. They had to have alerted all of the others, too. Adam drew his lips back, exposing his teeth in a fierce grin. The ship that was moving was heading directly into their path.

To'afa said laconically, "Missile launch. I count five, no six coming our way. Looks like hyper-vee, too."

"Crap. I don't want to waste a shot on the pesky things. Let's see if we can get by with just the shielding and the point-defense. It's ready, isn't it?"

"Had it on for a couple of minutes. Anything gets close, it'll be shredded like Parmesan cheese."

"We'll go with that, then. I show optimal firing position in twenty-seven seconds. You ready?"

"Yes."

"Okay, then. On my mark. Five, four, three, two, one. Now!"

Adam's voice tightened involuntarily, and the final word came out oddly. It didn't matter. To'afa's system released the plasma bolt precisely on time. The lights flickered as the weapon drained capacitor bank one.

To'afa said, "Switching to bank two. Ready now."

"Fire as you bear."

Adam wiped his eye quickly. It seemed blurry, but then everything was clear. He glanced at the targeting display. The ship he'd picked was one of the larger ones. It was too far off at the moment to distinguish any features, but it was much bigger than a cruiser.

The display wound down. At zero, the antimatter cannon hummed as the tank vomited its contents down the barrel. The particles were boosted by the Em-Max effect and raced ahead of the hurrying ship.

The antimatter particles were invisible, except when they struck a bit of space dust. Then there was a brief spark as the dust was annihilated.

He watched intently, almost afraid to blink, although his eye seemed dry.

There were a few sparks, but nothing. Adam began to fear that the charge had missed. Then it happened. The distant ship flared brightly.

The flare dimmed, then erupted in a brilliant flash.

The display automatically dimmed as the circuitry detected the overload. Then the vid broke up totally. Adam cursed under his breath. If the stupid thing wouldn't break up every single time, he'd be happier.

"EMP just hit us. That battleship was full of nukes, and they detonated. Those asses were prepared to convert our base on Titan to a thin cloud of radioactive dust," he said.

To'afa replied, "Hope that was all the nukes they brought, but I doubt it."

"There's probably more in the other big ships. We need to get them if we can."

"Bank two firing," To'afa grunted.

The lights dimmed again, followed by the smell of ozone wafting up the corridor from the reactor.

"Reactor doing okay?" Adam asked. He was focused on the next large ship and didn't want to look at the status display.

"It's heating. We're putting a bit more load on it than normal, but it looks fine so far."

There were three ships in the line around the moon between the D-R and the next large vessel. They were now descending on a slight tangent to the surface. The big ship was going to be in line for a shot for only a fraction of a second. The chance of hitting it was slim.

Adam's finger hovered over the touch screen. Shoot or wait? The positron tank only held enough for four shots. What if he fired and missed? There would only be two left, and the outbound vector was not going to be vacant. Two ships were moving to intercept them, followed by a third that might be too far away to get there in time.

There was a flash, and the interior lights dimmed, then the D-R shuddered.

"Point defense just fired. Took out a missile. I think the others missed us. We're moving faster than they can handle. Leaving them behind right now."

To'afa had switched his display to show the space immediately behind them. There were several flares behind them, but they were becoming visibly fainter as the D-R outran the missiles.

"Hope they follow us and decide any Fed ship is an enemy," the big man said, softly.

That would be helpful. The missiles were, as far as Adam knew, capable of making a limited number of targeting decisions independently. It was likely they were set to ignore the standard USSN ship's ID broadcasts, but none of the ships in the enemy fleet were broadcasting IDs at the moment. Maybe they'd get lucky and get some help from the missiles.

The D-R passed the perihelion of its course and began to move away from Titan. The ships ahead were now throwing streams of railgun slugs at them. Most of those would miss since the angle was so high that they would be out of the way before the slugs intersected their vector.

The cruiser that had moved precisely into their path was the only one with a chance of hitting them. It had to be throwing slugs right at their bow.

Adam fired the maneuvering jets, and the ship obediently changed direction. It was only a slight change since they couldn't turn abruptly at this speed, but perhaps it would be enough.

The cruiser was being fool-hardy. Adam fired his second shot as the distant ship headed into the cross-hairs. The antimatter burst traveled at about one-quarter light. It would get there before the enemy moved out of the way.

The D-R was closing quickly, so when the burst struck the cruiser, the flash was close enough to cause the vid to dim.

"Got that one, too. How are you doing?" He asked To'afa.

"I'm working. Quiet, now. Ah."

The lights flickered again. "Cap bank three discharged. That ship is going to be gone. Damn. No, he's moving out of the way. Uh. Ah! Got him with part of the burst."

On the vid, the small enemy ship was spinning. The plasma had holed the hull, and the atmosphere venting was propelling the ship around in a tight spin.

Adam checked the immediate vicinity. No one in front of them. The big ship that was off to spinward was changing vectors. It was trying to turn quickly enough to fire at them as they went by. It wasn't going to work, their velocity was so high that anything the battleship threw at them would be left behind.

Nevertheless, the sensors flickered as the navy ship vomited a stream of rail-gun shots. There was a brief pause, then the flares of at least twenty hyper-velocity missiles showed near the battleship.

That was no threat to them since the missiles had to accelerate from a static position and had no hope of catching up.

THE DIRE RHEA was outbound from Titan. Saturn was off to the starboard, providing a beautiful view of its rings if Adam had cared to look. He did not. He was trying to figure out what to do next. Choosing their next action was complicated by the fact that there was a stream of missiles following the D-R. Behind the missiles was a cloud of rail-gun slugs. The slugs would continue on until they either exited the solar system or struck something.

The missiles were still accelerating, but their engines would burn out shortly. When the flares died, Adam would turn the D-R gradually until it was headed away from the vector the missiles were coasting along. They, too, would either leave the system or strike some mass and explode. He hoped that there was no one out in that direction. Running into that cloud of projectiles would be unpleasant at the least.

Several of the Navy ships had begun to accelerate after them leaving Titan one after the other. He had stung the Feds enough to anger them, and now they were seeking vengeance.

To'afa asked, "Do you think that Valkie music bothered them?"

Adam shrugged. "Don't know, but I hope they thought we were being insolent. An angry enemy is one who doesn't make good decisions."

24

SPACE IS BIG

THEY WERE ON a vector that would take them past Saturn, then outward towards Uranus' orbit. The maneuvering jets fired as the comp corrected the course. Saturn's gravity well was deep, and the planet pulled things toward it.

Adam barely noticed. This was normal. Ships went through minor course corrections all the time.

He abruptly stopped as his mind made a vague connection.

Retrace that thought! It had led to something else. What was it? If Saturn wanted to pull the D-R close, why shouldn't he use the slingshot technique? It was an old trick, but he could try it. If played correctly, he'd be back near Titan before his pursuers got close enough to the ringed planet to begin a similar maneuver.

"To'afa."

"Yeah, Captain?"

"This next part is going to be painful. I'm going to slingshot us around the planet. If I do it right, we'll be able to make another pass on Titan. Maybe we can convince the people in those navy ships we're a real Valkyrie."

"Uh. Aren't we going a little fast to be turning that sharply? The radial acceleration will be..." He trailed off, obviously thinking about the gee-forces involved.

Adam finished the sentence for him. "Painful. That's right. We're going to hurt some, but I think we can do it. I'm running the comp on the problem. The numbers look bad but bearable. Or..." He paused for a moment, considering. "Or, I think we'll be able to bear it. I'm going for it anyway."

"It makes sense, but won't they follow us around?"

"Yes, they likely will, but they're going a lot slower than we are right now and they won't catch us. We could continue to run. We'd be out of the solar system before they got to Uranus' orbit. That's not going to solve our problem, though. We need to stop them from destroying the base."

"Okay. If you think this will work, I'm all for it. I'd like another shot at them, too."

The D-R began to turn gradually. There was no such thing as a sharp turn at the velocity they carried. They descended slowly into Saturn's gravity well and the pull helped with the course change. The radial gees increased and increased until Adam felt his insides were going to turn to mush.

The ship held the turn, and the two men held on, passively enduring as best they could as their vision grew dim and their breathing labored.

The velocity increased as they fell into the well. After what seemed like an infinitely long time, the comp eased the turn, and they began to slowly climb away from the big planet. The D-R continued the turn as it clawed against the gravity well.

Titan crept into view around the planet. The rings were interposed, distorting the shape and color of the moon. There was no way they could fly through even the thinnest ring at the speed they were carrying. The debris density would quickly overload the shields in a way that no nuclear device could.

The comp beeped, then the course changed slightly, easing the lateral pressure.

"That's good. The hard part is over. We're on track. Titan in just a little over ten minutes," Adam said, eyeing the display in front of him.

He checked the positron holding tank. It was at one-half capacity.

"I forgot to reload! I'm shifting the collector now."

There hadn't been any time to collect more anti-particles. The drive had been running for the entire time, providing thrust to augment their turn. Now he flipped the system to the other setting and watched the gauge as the holding tank began to fill.

"Looks like it'll be at seventy percent by the time we're close enough to start shooting."

To'afa said, "That'll have to do. I've been pulling power from the reactor to reload. Plasma will be ready when we get there."

As Adam watched the vid, the view of Titan cleared. They were no longer behind the rings. The moon was still tiny, but it was growing. He turned the music broadcast back on, allowing the interior speakers to play the threatening music at a low volume.

"Man, that music sounds like the demons from hell are coming after us," To'afa said.

"That's what I'm hoping they think. If it makes them nervous, maybe they won't shoot accurately."

The moon was quickly increasing in size. Now the remaining navy ships were appearing, and flares were showing in front of them. The enemy had launched a spread of missiles in their direction.

The missiles were ineffective. Their approach speed was so high that they were past the intercept point before the missiles reached it. The hyper-velocity missiles were fast but didn't turn very well. There was no way they'd get turned around and be able to follow. They'd run out of fuel first.

There was a sudden flash ahead coming from almost behind the terminator of the moon. The plasma defense flared, and the ship shook as if it had hit a speed bump.

"That was another of those blasted nuke-pumped lasers they just shot at us! What damage did we take?" Adam asked as he concentrated on the engine output readings.

To'afa was polling the other systems. "Looks like part of the point defense went out. They missed us for the most part. We were only in the periphery of the beam, and the relative angle meant we moved out instantly."

"If they'd hit us directly, we wouldn't be talking about it now. We came out better than we should have." The bomb-laser was a scary weapon. Adam hoped there were no others in the enemy fleet.

THIS PASS WAS faster than the last one. The ride around Saturn had added speed. Adam fired once as they went screaming by. He couldn't tell if there was any effect. To'afa's plasma cannon shot struck a ship, but they were moving away so quickly, the damage was impossible to evaluate.

The D-R slowed, then began to turn in a wide radius. Adam wanted to get back quickly before the enemy regrouped. Half-way through the turn, the sensors alerted. There was another group of ships on an intersect course with them.

"What the Hades? Where did these guys come from? The Feds didn't have that many ships," To'afa said.

"Ah. Hold one. I'm getting a signal. They're ours. They've caught up to us." Adam was relieved. The presence of the rest of his fleet made the fight more equal.

It took a while for them to match velocities, then he arranged the eleven ships into a thin line coordinated by the battle network and advanced back towards Titan.

The USSN ships had grouped into a ball formation in open space away from Titan. They were hard to pick up visually against the backdrop of Saturn, but they were there according to the sensor suite.

The USSN knew they were coming. The Navy was using active scanning mode, and the D-R's sensors would periodically sound an alert when the ship had been swept by a Navy signal. Well, that was fine with Adam. Both sides knew there was about to be a battle. Neither group was likely to back-down and lead.

On the other hand, the absence of smaller ships in the enemy formation was notable. Adam pondered that for a bit, then finally decided that the privateers, that had reported as part of the Fed group, had either headed out, choosing discretion over valor, or landed to join in the raid on the surface.

The sensors couldn't detect them anywhere. Based on that, they had left orbit long before his ships had approached. What bothered him was the possibility that they might be hovering behind Titan, waiting until he had engaged with the main body of navy ships. Then they'd be able to attack from behind. That would be inconvenient.

This was when the battle net made a huge difference. With a couple of flicks of his fingers, he detailed three ships to orbit Titan. They would detect any privateers and alert him. If they were unopposed, they would come around slightly after he'd engaged the primary Fed formation, hopefully just in time to catch the enemy in a cross-fire. The three designated ships obediently moved away, heading towards the far side of the big moon.

The small Belter fleet moved closer to the beleaguered settlement. In response, the navy ships began to move outward. This was a puzzling counter, but its purpose became apparent as the cruisers gradually coalesced into a ball-shaped formation.

Adam instinctively immersed himself in the life or death game that was about to unfold. The Navy had created a defensive formation that was currently oriented as if they expected a frontal attack from his force.

The possibility of a bomb laser ship passed through his mind, but the formation facing him was tight. There was no lagging ship the way there had been the last time. The nuke-pumped laser was deadly, not only to the vessels being targeted but to any friendly ships that happened to be near when it exploded. Besides, now that he knew about the weapon, it was much easier to avoid, so maybe they hadn't bothered to build more.

The problem he faced was simple. His smaller force had to attack a globe-shaped cluster of larger ships. The Navy ships were now arranged in a pattern that left clear avenues of fire for every ship. The weakness was that the channels were oriented directly towards him.

That was a blatant invitation to attack from a different direction. Even a slight lateral vector would move his ships out of the fire lanes for the vessels at the back of the globe. Well, so be it.

The Belter force headed away following a vector that passed the Navy ships on the side away from Titan. Adam felt better having the rail-gun slugs and missiles that the cruisers were sure to launch at him heading out into space, rather than impacting the surface and possibly killing some of the small population.

As the D-R veered, the sensors picked out a much larger ship in the center of the enemy formation. It had been masked by several of the cruisers. It was odd that it hadn't been arranged along the firing avenues.

It was the sole Fed ship that had no clear shot at him. That alone was suspicious. The memory of the armory ship that had been present at the Battle of the Bubble made him wary. The blamed thing could be packed full of hyper-vee missiles. It would be best to take it out quickly.

He skewed the D-R and fired a burst of plasma at the big target. The angle and his velocity meant that it would take nearly a minute to arrive. Meanwhile, the rest of the Navy ships were reorienting. Their formation showed no signs of disarray. They'd obviously practiced this maneuver.

The enemy ships turned, tracking his fleet's path. The turn meant that the ships in the rear had no clear shot, but the comp indicated that the situation would resolve itself quickly. The globe was cunningly arranged to allow for plenty of fire-power, no matter how the component ships turned.

Adam looked more closely. The globe was maneuvering as a whole. The individual ships were not only turning on their axes but also moving within the formation to clear up their firing lanes as quickly as possible.

He glanced at To'afa. "See that?"

The big man grunted. "Yeah. They've obviously got a battle network. There's no way they could coordinate their movements that well if they didn't have one."

Adam's lips drew back in a snarl. "Makes it harder. There goes one of our advantages."

"Let's hope our weapons and speed make the difference."

"Most of our ships aren't that much faster than theirs. If they aren't going to dogfight and stay in that formation, we will have to snipe at them."

He flicked the battle net controls, increasing the formation's speed to the max.

"We'll make it as hard as possible for them to hit us, but they've probably got plenty of munitions. We're burning fuel while they just sit there and take potshots at us," he said.

In answer, the enemy formation blossomed with missile launches.

To'afa swore. "Damn, they're betting the whole game on that salvo. That must be most of their missiles right there."

Adam was ahead of him. Every one of his ships turned to face the oncoming onslaught and fired plasma bursts. The slightly glowing clouds of plasma sped off to intercept the missiles.

He flicked the battle net controller again. In answer, his ships opened fire with their lasers. The space between his ships and the missiles was covered with lines of sparks as the coherent light super-heated the interplanetary dust. The lasers themselves were not in the visible spectrum, but the dust flashed as it burned.

To'afa grunted again. "That's too many flashes. We're in thick soup here. Hope the dust doesn't attenuate our shots too much."

Adam answered, "We're in line with Saturn's rings. Some of the debris extends clear out here. The good thing is that it will offer us a little shielding also.

The sensor suite squawked a warning.

"Incoming! Looks like they anticipated us and fired a rail-gun salvo. Fire a second plasma shot along that vector," Adam snapped.

The D-R's cannon pulsed, causing the interior lights to dim. The plasma glob sped away, heading towards the enemy formation.

There were several flashes as the rail-gun slugs intercepted the plasma shot.

"That's not going to stop them," To'afa said, sounding a little alarmed.

"Yeah, but it ablated a lot of their mass. What's still coming is smaller. Our shield should hold it off. It's the missiles that follow that we should be worried about."

The Fed missiles were, in fact, taking their time about arriving. Adam suddenly realized that they were conventional and limited in speed.

"Hey! Those are too slow to be hyper-vee. They must have exhausted their store of the newer ones. We've got a chance to outrun them even if they turn to pursue us."

It was true. He checked the comp. Their passing velocity was now high enough that the pursuing missiles would run out of fuel before they arrived. The caveat was that he needed to remember where they were headed. It wouldn't do to turn and come back right into the face of the coasting flight of warheads.

Adam grinned to himself. That was a wasted effort. If he could fly around and get the enemy to exhaust their ammo shooting at him, the battle would be won easily. Then another thought hit. It was really irresponsible to shoot missiles out into space. The flight was on a direct line with the Earth and Moon. Given a long enough time, the warheads might coast right into traffic in Earth orbit.

"That's stupid on their part. They just shot that whole load directly at Earth. It'll arrive in about six weeks. I hope that it misses. They didn't think that one out very well," he said.

"To'afa answered, "Either that, or they just don't care."

That was a definite possibility. The NAFD hadn't shown much interest in the general welfare of the populace recently.

The plasma burst he'd fired at the large ship missed it's intended target, but the ship to the right and behind flared as the super-heated gas arrived and disrupted its shielding. The stricken cruiser spiraled off, out of control.

Some of the missile warheads exploded out to the side of their path. It had run into the second plasma fusillade.

Adam flicked the battle net control screen again. His ships fired another plasma burst towards the globular formation.

They were passing the Fed position now and starting to move away. He re-vectored, and the Belter ships began to turn, making the gee force rise.

On impulse, Adam spun the Dire Rhea on its axis and fired the positron gun at the huge ship. To'afa looked inquiringly at him.

"It'll take a while to get there, but maybe that will hit it. The size of that thing makes me worried. I'd rather see it gone before it gets into the fight," he commented, partly under his breath.

Whoever was in charge of the Navy ships was canny. The Belter ships were turning as tightly as they could, intent on getting back into close range when they ran into another barrage of rail-gun slugs.

These had to have been fired just before the Fed ships finalized the globe formation. Someone had predicted that there was a high possibility that the Belter ships would be in this vicinity. They had been correct.

Adam cursed as the projectiles slammed into the D-R's shields. There was a loud screeching sound that came from metal tearing, a series of loud thumps and then silence. He glanced at To'afa.

"We lost the entire sensor suite antenna and the collection funnel power connection just then." To'afa's eyes were wide with alarm.

"Great. We've only got enough antimatter for two more shots unless we can reconnect the collector. Losing the sensors means it's going to be hard to aim."

"Yeah, and we're limited to Em-Max drive without the funnel." To'afa paused, then said, "No, wait. The Em-Max is only operating at half power. Something was damaged somewhere, but the instruments aren't showing it."

They were still turning, but now they were losing ground. The remaining Belter ships were accelerating away from the D-R.

"I can't help that right now. We know the collection funnel power is out. See what you can do about that. We need it working. The way things are, we're going to be late to the fight," Adam said.

The big man jumped up and dashed down the corridor in response.

The distance between them and the other ships increased. Adam checked the relative positions of the enemy formation and the majority of the Belter fleet. His ships would be at an optimal distance for a plasma burst shortly. His finger hovered over the battle net controller, then struck downward. The ships responded by firing directly into the Fed globe.

He'd forgotten about the antimatter shot he had launched at the big ship. There was a flash as the positrons impacted. A significant part of the ship detached. He'd damaged it significantly. If there were missiles inside, they hadn't exploded, and it would be impossible to launch them now. The damage was too extreme.

As he watched, there was a series of explosions along the midline of the enormous ship. It slowly split into two chunks, the smaller damaged part moved away quickly. As the pieces separated, something strange appeared.

A gleaming, odd-shaped thing slowly emerged from the fragments of the massive ship. It looked like some hideous creature hatching from a silvery, broken egg-shell. As Adam watched, it floated free, then stretched, apparently lengthening. Then his perception changed. It hadn't extended, it had arms that trailed behind it. Now they were moving independently, waving around like a crab or spider.

It became more distinct as it cleared the wreckage. He could see a large oval central structure with jointed arms that held visible weapons at their ends highlighted against the background of open space.

Suddenly, the arms flexed, losing their appearance of lazy and slow motion. They snapped around with incredible speed, pointing at the Belter ships. The attached weapon pods fired laser bursts.

Two of the Belter ships were struck. The damage caused one to spin into an undamaged ship in the tight formation. The three ships dropped out, two totally out of control and the third limping at a slow speed.

The lasers were unmerciful. The limping ship began to glow as the anti-laser coating began to overheat. Suddenly the reactor blew. There was a burst of flame, and then the rear half of the ship fragmented.

Adam groaned in dismay. He couldn't continue to take this number of losses. There were still fourteen Navy cruisers. He had to win this, or his friends would be bombed into submission down there on the surface.

The plasma salvo finally arrived and struck the enemy formation. Five of the Fed ships suddenly developed holes and lost atmosphere. Three others were so severely damaged that they exploded.

Both To'afa and Adam yelled in triumph. The odds were far better now.

The next minute they were groaning again. The spider ship had somehow danced aside when the plasma salvo came through. It was incredibly maneuverable, and it hadn't let up on the lasers while it was dodging.

Two more of the Belter ships were showing damage, and the spider's lasers seemed to be glued to their targets. The small mining ships jinked back and forth, then spiraled in an attempt to avoid the continuous beams of coherent light, but they were only partially successful.

First one then the other suffered disabling damage.

The D-R was getting closer to the fight, but Adam judged it was still too far away and firing now would waste his two remaining antimatter shots.

Adam yelled in excitement at the vid display. Without the sensor suite, he hadn't noticed that the three ships detailed to circle Titan had arrived. The odds were now almost even.

The newly arrived Belter ships flew right through the center of the USSN formation blasting as they went. Three cruisers were fatally struck. The unlucky cruisers exploded, sending fragments flying in all directions. Two others had been struck, and their hulls were holed. Atmosphere blew outward carrying pieces of debris that Adam suddenly recognized as bodies.

The spider ship retaliated, its laser tipped arms pointed at the three mining ships and the lasers locked on to them as they retreated.

Whatever the frequency, the lasers were far more potent than any that Adam had seen before. The converted mining lasers used by the Belters took several seconds to do significant damage and then only if the target was not covered with an anti-laser coating.

All of the mining ships had been coated with a fractal silver coating that diffracted laser beams, breaking them into innumerable small bursts of light. The spider's more powerful weapons burned through the coating instantly and through the hull beneath almost as quickly.

Adam swore to himself. "Jove's beard! That damned thing is wiping us out. Got to get it!"

He flicked commands into the battle net, and the two remaining Belter ships fired plasma bursts at the spider ship as did the D-R.

Adam waited expectantly. It would take a few seconds for the plasma to arrive. Three coordinated bursts should be enough to put an immediate end to this unexpected menace.

The spider ship jinked aside in an improbable move as the first two plasma bursts passed. Its lasers were now locked tight on one of the two remaining Belter ships.

To'afa had returned from somewhere just in time to see the maneuver. He exclaimed, "Did you see that? That thing did something impossible."

It had. Adam thought quickly. There were either no humans on board, or the NAFD had invented anti-gravity. The movement had been so sudden and at such a sharp angle that any human would have been reduced to a mush of ruined organs and bloody muscles.

The thing was a drone—unmanned. If so, it had to be controlled by someone located in another ship. He began lining up for a shot at the remaining cruiser, but the loss of the sensor antenna array made it difficult. If he could take out the controller, the spider would cease to be a threat.

The spider ship danced back and forth, its lasers active, locked onto the Belter ship. The mining ship sprung an atmosphere leak and spun out of control. It was permitted to drift away as the spider focused fire on the remaining Belter vessel. The D-R was still a considerable distance from the engagement, but coasting closer by the moment.

Adam jabbed the positron gun's controls, trying to time his shot and cursing the loss of the sensors. Another bolt of antimatter launched, its velocity added to by the speed at which they were closing. The spider jumped and began to move away as the bolt neared. Adam held his breath. It was almost like the thing was psychic. It was anticipating shots before they arrived, then moving just enough to get out of the way.

This time it had miscalculated because of the difference in speed of the antimatter and plasma. The antimatter bolt arrived at the same time as the previous plasma burst he'd fired.

Two of the arms trailed behind the main body of the spider as it moved. The bolt struck them, and they flickered then disappeared. The silver ship spun out of control, but before Adam could say anything, it stabilized and began to fire all six remaining lasers at the D-R.

25

THE DEATH OF THE D-R

TO'AFA JERKED BACK in surprise as the beams flashed across their hull and whited out the vid display, then said, "I got a patch on the funnel power cable. Hit it! It should work."

"Thanks for that!"

Adam flicked the hyperdrive system, and the D-R began to accelerate. The vid was still scrambled, and the sensors didn't work, but they were headed somewhere.

The two looked at each other. The whites of To'afa's eyes were showing.

"Where are we going?"

"Not sure, but we were pointed generally towards Saturn. I'm going to turn us away if I can. You go to cargo and try to see out the airlock window. Don't get caught by a laser."

"Okay, Captain. I'll take a black piece of plastic and hold it up as a test before I peek out."

That was sensible. The airlock glass was silvered, providing a view out, but not in. That would reflect the laser to a minor extent.

Holding a piece of plastic up to the window would reveal any coherent light that was coming through. Adam tried not to think of the alternative. The beam could be heating the window to the point where it would fail. He began to rotate the ship. That would help minimize damage.

The rotation helped. The much-maligned vid system flickered then finally came back on-line as the cameras rotated away from the coherent light.

Adam's fear was justified. The D-R was headed directly toward the gaseous, ringed planet and the radius of the turn they were making intersected the planet's equator. He'd either have to brake hard and deal with the spider's fire or try and shorten the turn.

The latter wasn't physically possible. Even if the ship could handle it, the two humans couldn't. He'd have to take the lasers and figure out how to disable the spider.

The single navy cruiser that remained was now passing near the spider. Adam jinked the bow slightly and fired a plasma burst. That would be the last until they could repair the system.

The positron storage was down to a little over one shot's worth of antimatter. Perhaps he could use it. The problem was the drone's operator seemed to anticipate what was coming in time to move. There must be a fantastic sensor system over there to... Adam's mind blanked in shock.

The spider wasn't a drone. It couldn't be; it moved too quickly for human reflexes. It had to be controlled by an AI.

He'd dealt with autonomous weapon systems before. The Feds had been using them for years. His hand went to his eye patch as he remembered. He'd been lucky to live through that encounter.

He hadn't heard of any autonomous weapons incorporated into a space ship, but that didn't mean the NAFD hadn't created one. It was an obvious counter to his superior weapons and shields. That was one aspect of technology with which the Earthers excelled.

He was fine with relatively simple programming, even assembly code, but developing an AI system that had the capability that the spider displayed was far beyond his level.

The vid whited out again. They'd rotated around until the camera was in the line of fire. He increased rotational speed, and it cleared. The hull had to be taking damage. The plasma shield wouldn't do much against lasers, and the anti-laser coating wouldn't hold for long either.

Adam pressed his forehead with his hand, then began to key commands into the comp. He glanced at the vid just in time to see the remaining cruiser fly directly into his plasma bolt.

Holes appeared in the long ship's waist, and atmosphere vented out along with flames. The vessel swung slightly sideways, then seemed to shudder. The shudder was followed by a massive blast that blew white and orange fire out the holes. The cruiser broke apart, and the pieces went spinning away towards Saturn.

Anyone surviving on the pieces was going to be in for a brief and fearful ride as they entered Saturn's atmosphere. The radiation the planet threw off would probably kill them before they got that close, though.

He paused in his coding to run his fingers over the drive control touch screen. The drive created a hum that sounded as if it was straining. It was now braking, trying to slow their approach. When they got close enough, his mind would interpret it as a descent, but they hadn't reached that point yet. There was still time.

The D-R slowed, making it easier for the spider to keep the lasers focused. The strange silver ship was moving closer. It was a preview of the future for Adam. He had a momentary vision of AI-controlled ships spreading out across the solar system.

An undying artificial intelligence could travel to the stars. His hyperdrive would allow humanity to finally go beyond the solar system, but in name only. AIs might be their representatives on that journey.

The vid flickered, then turned black as the camera overloaded from coherent light. Adam bent his head and entered a few last lines of code.

To'afa called from the cargo hold.

"I'm afraid to look. We're rotating so much that I can't predict when the lasers will hit the window. You should know that it's not good down here. There's damage on the far side of the cargo hold. Those lasers are so hot, they're melting plastic even through the window. The window's looking like it might fail too. I'm getting into my suit."

"Bring mine up here. I better get into it."

"Roger."

There was that. A slim chance they could evacuate the D-R and survive. They'd be in Saturn orbit, probably exposed to high levels of radiation, and most likely they'd die. There was no one nearby to pick them up. That was if the spider didn't kill them.

There was no way to know if it would target individual humans in addition to ships. Maybe they'd find out. The camera had recovered. The laser wasn't striking it now, and the video showed stars and part of Saturn's rings.

The comp beeped. The code was ready to use. He activated it, then waited. Their rotation should bring them around so he could see the spider for a few seconds. The vid would fail again, but he'd noticed there was a brief period before it did when he could see their tormentor.

The ship rolled. There it was! Directly in line as he'd hoped. He activated the antimatter gun. The cap bank whined, and the internal systems dimmed. The shot was away.

Strangely the vid didn't white out. He watched, hoping for a hit.

The spider was moving, its lasers off. It was diverting all power to its drive. He cursed, realizing that it had predicted his shot and was trying to avoid it.

He wondered if it knew that he'd fudged the magnetic field in the barrel of the gun. His code had changed the weapon's firing characteristics. Instead of a single blast of ravening antimatter, sixteen smaller streams were spreading out in a shotgun-like pattern.

Adam's eye stared at the vid, and he snarled with a wolfish sound.

"Let's see you dodge that, you devil!" He hadn't realized he'd spoken until To'afa's voice came over the comm.

"What's that you say?"

There was no time to reply. The antimatter was intersecting the spider's position. The silver ship spun and jinked, trying to avoid the streams of annihilation. It looked like it was going to escape. His heart fell. There was no other chance.

The vid showed the spider spinning, then something incredible happened. All six of the remaining arms vanished, one by one. It had spun right into one of the beams. The enemy had lost its weapons!

His happiness was short-lived. The devilish invention stabilized and accelerated towards the D-R. It was going to ram them.

He activated the hyperdrive, but there was no response. The last shot had drained the capacitor banks, and the reactor didn't seem to be delivering power. They were stuck on their course.

Saturn loomed ahead, and between the surface and their position, the body of the spider accelerated toward them with the steady increment provided by its Em-Drive. Adam keyed the comp. The result was grim. They had a little over twelve minutes before the spider ship reached their position. If it failed to destroy them, they had three hours before they fell into Saturn's colossal gravity well.

There would be no escape from that. Even with full power, the D-R could not escape that monstrous pull if they got too close.

The spider flashed. Adam glanced at the vid. It was trying to shoot them with an anti-personnel laser. That wouldn't work. It would burn through space suits quickly, but the hull was different. Even damaged as it was, the laser was no match for it, especially given the short time they had.

He gritted his teeth and swore, then said, "Two can play at that game."

The auxiliary power supply wasn't much. It was a small, dense fuel cell that was designed for emergency use. This was definitely an emergency, so he rerouted the output to the mining lasers. The capacitors began to charge slowly. At this rate, they would be at only fifty percent by the time the spider reached their position. He stamped his foot as if that could speed things up, then aimed the weapon, using his best guess as to where the spider would be.

To'afa came running in, carrying Adam's suit.

"Get this on. That thing's coming. I saw what happened through the window. Thought you got it, but it's going to hit us. We gotta get going!"

He rose and stepped into the suit, then pulled it over his shoulders, all the while watching the vid.

This was cutting it close. He donned his helmet and sealed it. The spider's silver body was visible to the naked eye now. He glanced at the indicator. The mining laser would have one weak shot.

To'afa had headed towards the cargo lock, moving as quickly as his clumsy suit would let him.

Adam noticed but held in place a moment longer, then he fired the laser.

The thin beam licked out and touched the oncoming ship. There was a flash, then an explosion. The spider broke into pieces.

He'd won!

He'd won!

No! The pieces were still coming directly at them. The spider had died, but in doing so, it had ensured the Dire Rhea would die also.

Adam sprinted for the cargo hold.

26

DRIFTING TOWARDS DEATH

TO'AFA WAS ALREADY in the lock. He was holding two jet packs and wearing a third. The packs were bulky, but not extremely heavy in the reduced gravity, nevertheless carrying two was something only To'afa could do.

Adam grabbed a pack and slung it on his shoulders. They'd have four, and the extra two would give them a little extra maneuverability. He started to grab another, but To'afa slapped the lock control, and the outer door slid open.

The ensuing rush of atmosphere knocked Adam off his feet. He slid across the floor on his back, waving his arms and trying to recover. By the time he had managed to flip over, he was inches from the open lock hatch. He mentally shrugged and shoved hard with his legs, propelling himself outward.

There was a moment of disorientation, then things fell into place. Saturn was below, and the D-R was off to the side about fifty meters. To'afa was jetting away, trying for all the distance he could get.

Adam opened the throttle on his backpack, and the gas jets shoved at him. A few adjustments and he was following To'afa, moving precisely along the same path.

To'afa glanced back, then carefully pitched one of the jet-packs toward Adam. The pack was still moving away, following To'afa's path, but now Adam was catching up to it. He grabbed at the shoulder strap as he went by.

The additional mass threw him off balance, and he had to compensate to stay on the same vector.

He glanced at the location where the spider's body had been. It was much closer. Time was running out.

He called To'afa.

"Emergency thrust. We need more distance."

The comm was crystal clear when To'afa answered.

"Activating now."

The backpack could vent its gas quickly, but that mode wasn't used often. After the gas was gone, there was nothing a space-suited human could do to change their vector and speed.

Adam pulled the cable on his backpack and felt the resulting shove in the back. He was moving after To'afa, but the other man had a head start and was pulling ahead. That wasn't going to be a problem. Adam massed less and would get more velocity from the mass he was venting. He'd catch up, provided they survived the next couple of minutes.

The spider's body was moving closer quickly. It seemed to hover as a tiny spot for an abnormally long time, but then it appeared to gain in size in a logarithmic curve. It covered the final distance in a blindingly quick flash.

Adam could see that it was venting something. They'd damaged the hull and atmosphere...no, it wouldn't have atmosphere, but some gas or fluid was shooting out, making a stream of white particles that looked like fine snow. The AI was no longer in control of its body, but it had aimed precisely at the D-R.

Adam watched. The two ships were going to collide. There was a last jet of gas from the spider's hull that threw it off slightly. Maybe that would be enough. He waited, hoping it would miss.

The two ships came together, but not in a direct head-on crash. The spider's body impinged on the Dire-Rhea's ventral side, gouging a deep cut in the hull and causing the other ship to spin away.

Debris flew freely; silver shards of metal and plastic sparkling in Saturn's reflected light as they spun away. The impact had thrown the pieces away from the two men's path. They were able to enjoy the show without worrying about being struck.

Adam's throat tightened as he watched his ship, his home, spin wildly. It had been knocked away from Saturn's well and was now heading for interstellar space. It might drift forever out there, never reaching another star.

Adam swallowed with difficulty. He hadn't realized that his ship had such an emotional meaning. Memories of the events he'd experienced in the D-R came to him. Meeting Nile. Hurting her back when she attacked him. Then more tender moments, the two of them cuddled in his cabin.

The Dire Rhea had been a warship. A Pirate ship. Most importantly, it had been his home, and it had provided sanctuary and freedom.

It would remain in his memory forever, but now he had to see if there was some way the two of them could survive. Some tiny chance that they could find and take that might lead to more than a long fall into Saturn's atmosphere, a fall they'd never finish alive.

Adam was overtaking To'afa gradually, and it was becoming apparent that he was on a parallel course that was separated from that of To'afa. They would pass about one hundred meters apart. By now, both men had exhausted the gas in their backpacks.

To'afa had managed to remove his backpack and was struggling to don the second one but was not yet ready to use it. Adam's only means of changing direction was to throw his empty backpack, using it as reaction mass. He'd move in the opposite direction and could conceivably reach To'afa, but there was a considerable hazard to that option.

He knew from experience that throwing one-handed was an off-balance operation. Humans were evolved to throw objects in Earth's gravity well, not in space. If he pitched the mass away from himself, a large part of the reaction would be realized in rotational motion, leaving him spinning.

Pushing the backpack away with both arms would cause him to rotate backward head over heels. It would impart some lateral momentum if he was careful to push it directly away from his center of gravity.

He thought about the problem for a moment, then carefully moved his upper body so that his head pointed at his friend. Then he drew up his knees, placed the backpack against his feet and shoved as hard as he could. The effect was that of jumping off from the rather insubstantial feeling platform that was the backpack.

It shot away from him as he began to move more slowly towards the other man.

To'afa kept working at getting the jet-pack in position while trying to keep the second full one under control. He'd let go of the empty pack, and it was drifting nearby moving along the same trajectory.

When Adam jumped toward him, he looked up and commented, "Nice jump. You probably were good at basketball.

Adam snorted. "No, I never played it or any other team sport. I was too busy with martial arts, but my jump kicks are good." He paused, then added, "At least they used to be. All this low g has weakened my legs."

He was closing the distance between them slowly. It was only a matter of time before they would be able to link up.

"Hey, To'afa?"

"Yes?"

"Did you get a chance to send an emergency broadcast? I didn't. Too busy with shooting, and I didn't think about it."

To his relief, the big man said, "I almost didn't. I thought that if the USSN picked us up, we'd be taken to Earth for a hearing and execution."

"Does that mean you did send one? If they get us, at least we'll be alive for a little while longer."

"Yeah, I sent out a broadcast with our coordinates, but I don't know how powerful it was. The reactor failed before I could send it and the caps were draining fast."

They were only meters apart.

"I'm going to flip my lanyard to you. Clip it to one of your belt loops. Then pass me that full jet-pack. I'll help you get yours on. You've got one of the straps hooked on your O2-regen unit."

"So that's why I couldn't get it in position. Okay, flip it slowly. Don't want to have that give you some spin or something."

He unrolled the ten-meter long rope, letting the end with its attached spring-loaded carabiner hang loose. Throwing the cord would cause him to spin, so he held it coiled at his belly and shoved it at To'afa with both hands.

The cord snaked out, weaving as it uncoiled, the carabiner glinting at the end.

Adam suddenly realized that he might have thrown it too quickly. The carabiner was heavy enough to damage To'afa's helmet if it impacted on the faceplate.

The big man moved deceptively slowly, extending his arm and snagging the end of the cord before it could strike him.

"Talk about sports! You probably were good at baseball, huh?"

"Na. We didn't play that stuff. Wrong culture. I was good at group fishing, though. It was fun, and you could always eat what you caught." The Samoan chuckled to himself, then explained, "Plus, there were a lot of girls involved."

The carabiner was clipped to To'afa's belt, and Adam pulled himself close.

"Hold still while I get your backpack adjusted." The big man obligingly froze while Adam made the necessary adjustments. "There. That'll do it. Now help me with mine."

It took a minute to get the jet-packs adjusted. When the full pack was on, Adam realized he'd been breathing quickly. That wouldn't do. Anxiety would just burn his available oxygen more quickly. He made a conscious effort to slow his breathing, but it wasn't working well.

The sight of Saturn below them wasn't helping. It was magnificent and a view that astronomers in times past would have given their soul to see, but Adam could only see death in the swirling clouds.

They would die long before they hit the actual surface of the planet if it could be said to have a surface at all. The gasses would become progressively denser until their remains slowed and floated on some thermal layer. The speed of the fall would generate enough friction to tear them apart long before that point. Adam shuddered.

Why was it that he could face enemy action coolly, but not a fate that he could see coming and couldn't avoid? He tried to distract himself by checking their immediate surroundings.

To'afa's empty jet-pack. was diverging slightly from their path. Adam estimated it was about seven to eight meters away.

"Shove me toward that empty pack. Don't want to waste any mass. We might need it eventually."

"Okay, but I don't see what difference those twenty kilos will make."

To'afa pushed him gently towards the stray jet-pack. It was well within reach, and he grabbed it, then coasted to the end of the tether and rebounded. The momentum started To'afa moving toward him. They clasped arms when they met.

The Samoan said, "Let's not get too wild. I'm having a tough time up here, and I don't need to be spinning. It'd make it worse. There's nothing we can do but wait to see if we run out of O2 before we augur into those storms down below. I'm no good at waiting."

This admission, strangely made Adam feel better. He said, "Tell me about group fishing."

To'afa grunted. "Won't take my mind off our problem. Anyway, a bunch of us kids...I was a kid then. Haven't been back on Earth for twenty years. Might be fun to go back, if we weren't going to be arrested."

Adam prompted him. "You were a kid?"

"Yeah. There was this one girl. You know how it is. I was the biggest and the best fisherman, but I couldn't seem to get her attention. I got tired of waiting and just grabbed her one night on the beach. You know what she said to me?"

Adam shook his head. "No. What did she say?"

His friend laughed. "She said, "What took you so long? For a good fisherman, you almost missed this catch."

Adam laughed. "And, then?"

"Oh, then. Well, she got in a family way, and I couldn't get a job. I hadn't graduated. So I...I, uhh. I went to space. Guess I was trying to avoid my responsibilities or something."

He paused, then added, thoughtfully, "I'd do things differently now. It's funny how experience changes your perspective. Now, if I had the chance all over again, I'd stay with her. Think about that sometimes. Wonder how she's doing and the kid. I hope he or she doesn't hold it against me."

This was more background information than Adam had ever gotten from his friend. He shook his head, not knowing what to say.

Then he saw a flash in the far distance. It was a tiny twinkle highlighted against the velvety blackness of interstellar space. His first thought was that it was a star, but stars don't twinkle in space. Twinkling is an atmospheric effect. The stars in space are cold, hard pinpoints of various colors. This had been a definite twinkle.

There it was again. He pointed and said, "See that? There's a spot of light over there. It's varying in brightness. What do you think it is?"

To'afa looked. "Maybe a piece of debris. We scattered fragments of ships all over. Maybe it's a chunk of ice. That could flash a bit as it rotated."

"No. The flash was too bright to be reflected sunlight. Besides the angle is wrong, or at least I think it's wrong."

The comm clicked at that moment, then a faint voice came through.

"SOS, ahoy. We've got you on our scan. Hold a bit while we decelerate."

Adam's heart leaped. Someone had heard! They were going to be rescued.

The next moment he was almost paralyzed by the thought of facing trial on Earth. They'd find him guilty of something, probably piracy, and hang him for sure. No, they didn't hang anyone any longer. That was considered too cruel and wasteful. They gave condemned criminals an injection to put them out, then harvested their organs from their living bodies. That had always seemed useful to him, but now it was gruesome.

The two looked at each other.

To'afa said, "I've got a pistol."

That was all he said. Adam knew he was thinking of using it on himself. If the ship was USSN, they could both be dead before they could be brought on board.

He was calculating with no feeling of dread. The problem of survival had changed, and he was faced with potential enemies. That was something he could deal with. There was always some hope of victory, provided one was bold and decisive.

"No. Hold it and don't let them see it. Maybe there's a chance we can get into the bridge with it. Then…" He left that thought unspoken.

To'afa nodded. "Yeah. Maybe, but it's on the outside of my suit. They'll see it."

"Hand it off to me. I'll get in front of you and open my suit first, then turn. You can stick it in my pants."

To'afa snorted. "If I had thought you were going to ask me to stick something in your pants, I might not have hung around out here waiting for you."

Adam laughed. "Look, it can't be that bad. At least we're still alive, and while we are, there's hope."

The twinkling spot had ceased twinkling and was growing in size. The ship that was coming was braking, slowing down to a crawl as it approached. Whoever was captaining it was good. It looked like it would pull up within meters of their position and match their speed.

The ship gained in size until it was recognizably a mining craft. It could be a Belter or possibly a privateer. Adam's fingers clenched. If it were the latter, then he'd better be ready to fight.

27

A RIDE

ADAM STARTED TO reply to the comm message, but then just clicked his mike twice in acknowledgment. He grabbed To'afa's arm and pulled the big man close so that they could touch helmets. Once their helmets were in contact, he said, "Keep radio silence. If they're Navy, I want you to pretend to be unconscious—injured in some way. Let them carry you. That will keep two or three of them from responding quickly."

"Going to attack them in the lock?"

"That's the idea. I'll shoot before the lock closes. With any luck, I can get them before they understand what's going on." He checked the pistol. It was ready to go with a round chambered.

The weapon was an old Glock with fifteen steel-tipped 9mm rounds. No use for hollow-points in space. The steel tips were better at penetrating spacesuits.

The trigger guard of the gun had been modified to allow for spacesuit operation. The entire front of it had been removed. That created an opening large enough for a fat-fingered spacesuit glove.

He pulled the slide back partway to reveal a round in the tube, then let it snap shut.

"Ready?"

To'afa allowed his arms to spread in a relaxed position. "Yeah, I'm hurt bad, see me? When you start shooting, I'll see about grabbing the nearest one and keeping him under control."

"Okay, then. Nothing else we can do."

They separated, drifting apart, then waited.

The oncoming ship grew larger. It was apparent that it, too, was maintaining radio silence. It sent no additional signals.

There was a puff of gas jets from the ship as it adjusted its course. It was heading almost directly towards the two. Adam controlled his instinctive fear. It wasn't normal for humans to remain perfectly calm as something huge came directly towards them, threatening collision.

It was close enough that he could see it wasn't a cruiser. Not the USSN, then. It looked like a large mining ship, larger than the D-R. There were no marks on the hull, no identification at all. It could be another Belter – good, or a privateer – bad.

It gradually slowed, then suddenly it was beside them, moving slowly past. The ship rotated, exposing the open cargo bay, moving towards them. It would be easy to jet into the opening. Adam supposed that was what he'd have to do. It made no sense turning down the only ride in the area, even if it meant captivity.

He triggered his jets, the tether grew tight, and To'afa's bulk began to move behind him. He looked for suited figures as they glided into the darker area. The lock door slid shut behind them. It was pitch dark for a moment, then the lights came on.

As he blinked, the intercom rattled. "You aren't Feds. Belters or privateers? Answer now, or I'll detonate a grenade in there."

Adam mentally shrugged. The chance had been slim at best. Their captor was better prepared than he'd hoped.

"Belters." He waited for the explosion.

The comm clicked, then a deep voice asked, "Who was the Captain of the Rhea?"

Adam frowned, trying to recognize the speaker. The voice sounded tantalizingly familiar. He answered, "Suarez first, then Maxwell."

The voice came back. "You're clear. I'll bring the pressure up, and you can come on in."

TO'AFA HAD GIVEN up pretending to be injured under the assumption that they were with friends. It wasn't likely that a privateer would know to ask about the Rhea's captains. Despite Suarez's role in getting the revolution started, the belt population had expanded so rapidly that even last month's events were considered ancient history.

The two took off their suits in the personnel lock chamber. Adam glanced suspiciously at the airlock. It would be easy to open it remotely, spacing both of them, but the door remained closed.

Once they cycled into the main body of the ship, they started down the long hall to the bridge. The lights were dim, but there was still enough illumination to reveal a silhouetted figure moving toward them. They stopped and waited.

The man came close, then said, "Maxwell and To'afa! I might have known you two would survive."

Adam's mouth dropped open in surprise. "Ngombe? I never expected to see you out here. Where did you come from?"

Ngombe's bald head gleamed momentarily under one of the lights, revealing scarred skin on one side of his scalp. He laughed, a relaxed and friendly sound. "Most recently, I was in by Jupiter, checking out Enceladus. I wanted to see if it really had geysers of water."

Adam clasped Ngombe's outstretched hand. "And what did you find?"

The scarred man laughed again. "Plumes of water vapor. No life, if that's what you were interested in."

"Yeah. I didn't think so, but some of the scientists seemed convinced it was a good location to find something. Cells or bacteria, maybe."

"Well, if there's something there, I missed it. It'd have to be deep under the surface."

Adam looked at Ngombe. The radiation he'd absorbed had burned his skin.

"How about the scarring? You fully recovered?"

Ngombe shook his head. "That's a laugh. I'll never fully recover from that, but I guess I was lucky. I lived." He paused, then said, "My crew didn't."

Adam couldn't think of anything to say beyond, "War is hell."

The scarred man shrugged, then said, "Speaking of hell. It looks like you just gave the NAFD a real taste of it."

It was Adam's turn to be sober. "The knife cut both ways. I think I lost all of my command. There were a couple of ships that were damaged, but most were destroyed. Tell me about your ship. Where did you get it?"

"Yes. Well, they shipped me to Mars. I needed their medical equipment. A lot of this skin I'm wearing was cloned and grafted on there. The Martians might be odd, but their medical system is better than ours. Anyway, this is the Barsoom. It's an advanced model. They've begun building ships, and this is the first of them."

"I'd like to know about her. She's bigger than the old miners, isn't she?"

Ngombe wagged his finger at Adam. "The Martians are dead set against using gender regarding inanimate objects. They'd be offended if they heard you call the Barsoom 'she.'" He grinned. "Anyway, she is about a quarter larger than the standard mining ship. Got good shields and a more powerful reactor. They won't arm their vessels, though, so I've only got two mining lasers."

Adam nodded. "No good in a serious fight. How about help?"

Ngombe moved his hands deprecatingly. "I've got a few other miners with me. We're late to the party, but d'Antellino located some survivors in a hulk. The ship isn't flyable, but maybe he can salvage some of it. Smith is chasing another of your ships. It's got holes, and the atmosphere has leaked out. There's no response from it, so we don't know if anyone survived."

Adam rubbed his eye-patch. "What about Titan what's the status there?"

"Ah. That's the problem. The Feds got quite a few marines down there, and there's a bunch of privateers, too. Last I heard there was a lot of shooting back and forth. The invaders are still holed up in the port. They haven't been able to get into the habitat yet." He shrugged, then added, "The Council is screaming for help."

Adam nodded. "They would scream over a mouse, so that doesn't surprise me."

"No, but it sounds serious. We need to do something."

"We're as ready as we'll ever be. I seem to be short one ship, but I can still shoot a pistol. What've you got in mind?"

NGOMBE WASN'T SURE how to proceed. He had gathered a small force of seven mining ships with a total of fifteen able crew. The ships were armed, of course, but the weapons were only first-generation plasma cannons and mining lasers. The ships wouldn't last long against the larger force on the surface of Titan if those ships were allowed to regain orbit.

Ngombe wanted to drop KEWs on the enemy where they sat at the main Belter spaceport. He was unhappy when Adam practically pointed out that the collateral damage would destroy the port and possibly kill a lot of Belt citizens.

"There's no way to limit the impact, short of dropping ridiculously small masses and those can't be aimed well. The atmosphere, thin as it is, will ablate them and send them off in unexpected directions. Can the plasma cannons reach the surface?" Ngombe asked.

Adam thought about that. "Sort of. It helps that Titan doesn't have that thick of an atmosphere, but the plasma bursts will partly dissipate on the way down. You'd have to hit one ship with several simultaneous shots to disable it. Killing a ship with a single weakened shot would require an unlikely amount of luck. No. What we're going to have to do is to attack down there. Let's park four of the ships in circumpolar orbit and arrange the other three where they can take potshots at any Fed ship that leaves the surface. They won't be as maneuverable on the way up, and they'll be easier to hit. Their power will be routed for propulsion only, so they won't be able to shoot back.

Ngombe's white teeth flashed. "That would suit me greatly. I'm not a fan of being shot at."

"Yeah, me neither, but I'm going to take the rest of us down and see what can be done."

"That leaves, uh, six crew for the three ships. That'll work, but how do you intend to get down?"

"I'll take the smallest ship down. We'll drop in below the horizon and fly in below their sensors. Most of the landing cradles are blocked by enemy ships, but there is an old cradle on the far side of the habitat. It was the original landing point, but it's been out of use for a while. We can set down there, then decide how best to proceed."

The settlement was a cluster of domes and tunnels that was expanding outward from the main port area. Two docks extended in a vee-shaped formation on either side of the landing cradle field. This made for easy cargo loading and unloading. Each dock had flexible tubes that could be attached to the nearby ships.

The Feds, marines, and privateers, currently held both docks, however, they hadn't been able to get through the single extended tunnel that led from the point where the two docks joined to the primary habitat. The fighting was focused on control of that tunnel according to the information they got directly from Nielson. The council chair was on the comm, giving them a mixture of usable information and unusable commands, as he tried to assert control over their attack.

If the smallest ship, the Nelle Belle, could fit into the old cradle, they'd be able to move around the habitat outside the domes. Adam figured they could divide into two groups and approach the ends of the dock arms from outside. Once they had a clear view of the enemy ships, they'd try to attach explosive mining charges to them.

A well-placed charge could damage a ship enough to make it unable to launch. That was the goal. The situation inside the habitat and docks would then become critical for the invaders. They'd have to win or die since there would be no retreat.

That would make them desperate enough to make a direct attack, but Adam had an answer for that. His group would plant explosives on the long tunnel from the dock to the habitat. If the enemy made it into the tube and advanced, it could be blown. Both ends of the shaft had automatic blast doors that would slam shut if there were a breach that caused pressure loss. All tunnels were set up that way for safety.

If the marines were in the tunnel when the doors shut, they'd be locked in until they could crank the doors back open. The habitat side could be welded shut quickly, and that would isolate the invaders.

Adam wondered why Nielson hadn't thought of that. The Councilman wasn't someone he liked much. The guy was arrogant and seemed focused on politics. That short-sighted focus probably explained why he hadn't turned the defense over to Kendra and Lora. Adam suspected that Lars thought he was far better prepared to defend the habitat than the two women.

In any event, the attack would require extended time in their spacesuits. Jet packs were useless on the surface, so they could carry extra oxygen tanks plus explosives.

When informed about Adam's plan, Nielson vehemently disagreed.

"I want you to enter the habitat and place yourself under my command. We need help defending the tunnel. They've shot a number of my best people. I can't have you going around outside blowing things up. You might damage something critical."

Adam clenched his jaw, then responded. "How about Kendra Oligwa? Are you listening to her advice?"

Nielson snorted, "She says we need to let that Dunlop woman set booby traps, then retreat. If we do that, they'll have access to the habitat. No. We've got to hold them in the tunnel."

"Are they in the tunnel yet, or are they still on the dock end?"

"They're shooting at us and pushing barricades down the tunnel. I think they're about half-way down now."

This was bad. Adam needed to get down and plant the explosives on the tunnel first. It needed to be blown immediately.

"How about closing your blast doors, then welding them shut? You can do that, can't you?"

Lars' voice took on a querulous tone. "Too much damage to our infrastructure. That would make it difficult to reopen the port. I can't risk that."

Adam lost his temper. "Look, you idiot, the Feds are making it difficult to reopen your port. They're going to get into the habitat and kill a bunch of people. You're not prepared for a full-scale house-to-house battle. You don't have that many combat-experienced people. Have Lora set her booby traps in case the Feds get into the habitat, but first shut those blast doors, then weld them shut. If we can hold them in the dock area, they'll either go back to their ships or go outside to get at you. We'll be out there making their ships unusable, and we'll be ready to stop them if they come out."

Nielson sniffed. "I don't see what good booby traps do, but if you insist, I'll see if we can get the doors closed."

"You do that and do it immediately. It'll take us the better part of an hour to get down there. Is that old landing frame still sitting on the north end of the settlement?"

"Yes. I was going to have it torn down. We could use the metal, but it's still there right now. Get down here faster. We need help."

Adam's lips drew back. The man just couldn't accept orders. Nielson thought he was the only one who could make an intelligent decision, and he was unwilling to relinquish control. It was the same old situation. Adam had seen it before. Political power-seekers often believed their ability to garner votes and gain office meant that they were experts on everything. In reality, they were no more competent, and often much less so, than those they governed.

He answered, "We'll be down as quickly as possible. Out."

Ngombe had been listening in.

"I don't know how you can keep from yelling at that guy. He's impossible."

Adam said, "He's trying to do his best to seem important. Got to keep up appearances for the next election, you know. I can keep him under control. I've just got to get us down there quickly. Where's the Nelle Belle?"

"Uh, she's picking people up, one ship at a time. While you were talking, the four ships made orbit, and the Nelle just rendezvoused with the first one. She's headed for number two now. It'll take about two hours to get the crew off the other ships, then she's got to pick up you and To'afa. You'll be lucky to be down there in three hours."

That wasn't acceptable. "Look, let's pick up the crew of the Harley. They're near us, then we can head over and meet the Nelle Belle. That will save nearly an hour."

"Okay, we're moving now."

The ship hummed, and Adam felt the slight push of the Em-Max drive. He noted that the Barsoom was quieter than the D-R. It gave him a jealous pang. His old ship had put up with a lot. He'd fixed battle damage and modified it, so it had arguably been the most competent fighting ship in space, except for that AI thing. However, it had never been able to move with the silence of Ngombe's new ship. Maybe it was better that it was gone. This new design made the older ships seem obsolete.

THEY HAD PICKED up the crew of the Harley, then transferred to the Nelle Belle. Now they were below the horizon, moving at low altitude towards the settlement. They followed the surface, moving up and down over the slight hills.

The back of the habitat was visible, having just appeared over the horizon. The enemy ships were close to the docks, so there was no direct line of sight between them yet. That was just as well. The little Nelle Belle had a first-generation plasma shield that wouldn't withstand the impact of a hyper-vee missile or a decent-sized rail-gun slug.

The domes and connecting tunnels grew closer. Adam could see the higher center domes surrounded by smaller individual habitats. All were connected by surface tunnels except for some of the farthest outliers. He suspected that those would be connected as quickly as the owners could manage.

There was a slight valley, and the old landing cradle sat on the far edge, close to one of the outermost domes. There was no provision for a connection tube. When the cradle had been built, the standard procedure was to use spacesuits and electric carts to transfer cargo.

That suited him perfectly. He didn't intend to go inside until later.

The Nelle shuddered and wobbled as it maneuvered into the narrow cradle. Adam held his breath. There was always the question of fit. The newer cradles had hydraulic rests that moved into position to create a custom bed for the ships. This one did not, and the old rests looked alarmingly fragile.

There was a final shudder followed by an alarming crunch, then silence. Captain Rejsa checked his instruments, then said, "Might have damaged something just then. No reading, but I think one of the rests collapsed. We might need repairs to get out of here."

Adam responded. "Later. Unless we win, we're probably not getting out. Let's go."

The other man nodded.

The cargo hold was partly full of bins of nickel that the Nelle had been mining, and there was little room for the small group of men and two women who were preparing for the raid.

To'afa was standing by the lock controls, battle-ax slung at his side. He glanced at Adam and Rejsa, then said, "You should get your suits on. The rest of us are ready."

Adam grunted. "Impatient, aren't you?"

"Yeah. I've got the itch to whack a few of them Feds with Vlad."

Rejsa looked puzzled until Adam explained. "He named that horrible museum specimen Vlad for the real-life Dracula because it has the habit of drinking a lot of blood."

The other man gave a slight shudder. The miners were universally armed with pistols. A hole in a spacesuit was usually enough to kill an enemy. It was apparent that Rejsa felt the ax was barbaric.

As he donned his suit, Adam added, "Don't knock it. It works, and it never runs out of ammunition. I use a sword, myself."

He unwrapped the cloth that protected his cutlass, then re-slung the heavy sword on his waist. He paused, thinking. Something was missing from his apparel. Ah. The ragged Pirate flag. It had been left in his cabin on the D-R. He'd have to go without it.

Its absence made him feel odd as if he was missing a part of his persona. He'd gotten used to the piece of cloth. It served as a simple means of visually identifying him to his men, and it had become a sort of moral booster. He grimaced, then tightened his faceplate.

"Ready to go. Pull it." He nodded at the Samoan.

To'afa jerked the lock lever and the pumps throbbed. The hold evacuated quickly, then the lock swung open with a clash that could be heard through their feet. The ladder dropped, and they were out.

28

THE BATTLE FOR TITAN

THE NEAREST DOME was two hundred meters away to the south. Adam headed out, motioning his fellows to spread out. He leaped forward in the light gravity, bounding with each step. The distance diminished quickly.

There was a well-defined path, almost a road, formed when the old cradle was the main landing point. The ruts were filled with dust and made unsure footing. One of the others tripped and stumbled forward, landing on his hands. The larger of the two women grabbed his armpit and hoisted him back upright as she passed.

The dome loomed overhead, and the ten Belters backed against it, looking from side to side. There was nothing to see but rocks and some frost in the shadow.

Adam drew To'afa close and held their helmets together, so their speech could be transmitted by conduction. He'd insisted on comm silence before they left.

"Get four of the others and head around the settlement to the east. I'll take the rest and go west. Once you reach the dock, get out to the landing cradles and place the explosives. I'll set one in the long hallway as I go by. When you're done, go back to the dock and find a way to get inside near the outer end. I'll shoot the explosives, then we'll attack. I want to drive them into the hallway, then blow a hole in it. With any luck, the pressure doors on both ends will close, and they'll be trapped."

"What about the hole you blow? Won't they get out there?"

Trust To'afa to point out flaws in a plan. That was a possibility.

"Maybe. Assuming they're suited up. I'll leave Mary outside. She's a good shot, and she can snipe at any attempt to come through the opening."

"Best we can do, I guess. How about the residents?"

"I'm hoping that Nielson had the sense to follow my instructions. They'll have to hold their end of the tube if they can. I don't know how many men we're facing, but I'm afraid that we're way over-matched. I hope they aren't in suits. That'd make it a lot easier."

To'afa nodded inside his helmet, then turned and grabbed two of the others. He transmitted the orders to them, then grabbed the last two of his squad and did the same.

Adam pointed at the other four and waved them towards the west. The five turned and moved off along the side of the dome, circling around towards the settlement.

ABOUT HALF-WAY AROUND, Adam could hear his breath in his helmet. He was panting. The settlement had grown, and it was a lot farther around than he'd remembered. The line of linked domes went out to the west farther than seemed likely.

There was a spur of rock just ahead. It lay very near the connecting tube. He paused by the gently slanting mound and rested. The problem with the tunnels was they were too high to leap over, and they were too smooth to climb. The rock spur might give them a shortcut, provided they could get to the top. He investigated.

It was climbable. The rocks were the remains of some ancient collision that had thrown them outward. They were arranged almost like steps leading upward to a flatter area at the top. The colonists had placed the connecting tube so that it almost touched the rocks, trying to keep the path as straight as possible. The distance from the top of the rocks to the side of the tube was two meters, but its five-meter diameter meant that the center of the top was over four meters away from the rock.

The low gravity made jumping to the top of the curving tube barely possible. The rock spur had a space large enough for a two-step start. Adam had maneuvered enough in low gravity to understand that the issue wasn't going to be jumping that far, it was stopping on the top without falling down the other side. A fall of that distance wasn't necessarily fatal, but landing wrong could break bones or worse, damage the integrity of the suit.

Indicating that they should wait, he began the ascent, negotiating the rough slope. At the top, he took one look and ducked down. Two suited figures were disappearing behind a dome about sixty meters away.

From the back, it was apparent that they were Fed military. The USSN suits were distinctive and differently shaped than civ suits. Were the two exploring, hoping to find an entrance, or were they guarding against precisely what Adam's group was attempting? If he'd been in charge of the invasion, he would have definitely placed sentries to prevent a flanking attack.

The two disappeared around the curve. Adam waited, but they didn't come back, so he motioned the two men and two women to come up the sloping incline. They did so, climbing the step-like slabs of broken rock. Once on the top, they paused.

One of the men started to move forward, but Adam grabbed him before he could jump. He held up his hand, then unhooked the tether line from other's belt. The man immediately understood and nodded within his helmet.

Adam unrolled five meters of line plus enough additional for the other three to hold. The four of them would provide an anchor and stop the jumper before he went over the edge.

The man took two quick steps and leaped gracefully over the space. His feet touched down on the precise middle of the tube, but true to Adam's misgivings, he lurched forward. They caught his mass with the leash and pulled him back upright.

The other three jumped across safely with the same method. Now it was Adam's turn. The four on the tube held a line stretched between them. He could jump for the middle and catch himself, if necessary.

His jump was a little short. He landed on the forward edge of the tube and started to fall back into the crack, but flailed his arms and miraculously caught the cord. The next problem was getting down, but that was easy.

They lowered the two men down first since they were heavier. Once they were down, the two women were next. Adam glanced around, looking over the situation.

There was a line of domes connected by varying length tubes off to his left. It extended to the right, gradually curving off to the south. Tubes led from the farther domes to a second row that was about two hundred meters distant.

The dome the two figures had come around was connected on the east side, but not on the west. The layout was not favorable. They might have just lowered themselves into a trap. He could pull them back up, and they could backtrack, but time was running out. If To'afa reached his objective then attacked from the east side, the chances of success were much diminished.

Comm silence was a great idea, but he'd have to break it if he was going to keep an option open. He activated his mic.

"Gabe, go take a look around that dome in front of us. Carefully!"

He pointed as he talked. Gabe looked up, nodded, and set out for the dome, loping over the uneven ground. He was there in a few seconds.

Gabe skirted around the dome wall, leaning his head outward, so he could see farther around, before exposing his body. He held his pistol at the ready.

Adam cursed to himself in impatience. Time seemed to fly. Gabe looked like he was moving in slow motion. Adam tried to distract himself by thinking of something else, but that led to memories of Nile. He shook his head. This wasn't the place to become distracted. A feeling of despair washed over him. He'd probably never see her again. Then he was angry. Elseth had ruined every aspect of his life that she touched, even third hand. He'd been a fool ever to think that he could move in her sphere.

Ahead of him, Gabe came darting back around the dome. The three below immediately sprinted forward, seeking the dome's cover, slight as it was. Adam pulled his pistol and lay down on the tube, his legs dangling down on the backside.

There was a movement. The two figures were back. This time, he could see they were carrying rifles. That wasn't good. Long guns always trump handguns, and the distance factor made the disparity worse.

It looked like the two were carrying USSN standard-issue M8s. The NAFD's military was conservative. In fact, personal firearm development had almost ground to a standstill after the last war. Now all available funds were spent on space weapons. True, there were some hand-held laser weapons, but they required a large power pack to be truly useful.

One of the figures turned to face Adam, raising its arm to point. The other turned to see.

They were obviously conversing on a different frequency from the Belters. Adam's comm clicked in his ear as they spoke back and forth, but he heard nothing besides the static.

The two advanced towards him, raising their rifles. He prepared to slide backward. Better to fall off, then to get shot in the face. The rest of his squad slid sideways along the dome wall behind the two. When they were directly behind the advancing enemies, two of them—Adam couldn't tell who—ran up behind the two. The Belters' pistols flashed several times, and the two Feds dropped.

Adam scrambled back to the top, then sat and slid over the edge. He wanted to get down immediately.

The drop wasn't as bad as he feared. He moved until he reached the point where the tube's wall turned straight down towards the ground. He hit with a jolt, dropped to one knee, then came back up and leaped forward, arriving at the two downed marines at the same time as the rest of his group.

He paused long enough to grab the rifles and search for additional magazines. There were some in belt pouches. He liberated them, then asked, "Who can use these well?"

The first one to speak was the smaller woman. "I was military. I'm not great, but I can hit what I aim at most of the time."

The others stepped back, and he gave her the rifle. She accepted it, then checked it in a way that assured him that she knew what she was doing.

Now that comm silence was broken, he realized that it probably didn't matter much. They were broadcasting on a different frequency than the two they'd just dispatched. The habitat residents might listen in, but it was a little-used utility frequency, so even that possibility was low.

"Let's go. If those two found their way in here, then there must be a way through to the docks. We've got to get to the other side of this dome. Stay alert. If there were two, there might be more."

Gabe said, "The next tube over has a road under it. Must be for maintenance. There's some kind of isolated structure a ways out between the domes. Reactor cooling tower, I think."

"Okay. Thanks. Let's head for the road. That's going to lead in the right way, at least. Maybe the road leads all the way to the docks."

They moved quickly, spaced out by about ten meters, Adam leading.

He moved through the opening under the tube. It was short, and there were supporting struts that held the tube clear of the ground. He could see most of the space on the other side, and it was vacant.

There were three more rows of domes connected by tubes, but the road provided easy access. It went straight as an arrow towards the docks. It looked like they were going to be on time.

The dock structure was on the other side of the last tube. It angled away from the tubes and domes, forming one side of the port area.

Where the tubes had been mostly at ground level, the dock was raised on pilings. That was so cargo loaders could move freely.

Adam had left the shelter of the underpass when a puff of dust and pebbles flew up from the ground. He jumped back into the shadow and ducked behind a girder. Someone had seen him and was shooting.

The others had seen him take cover and were now behind girders of their own. He peered around the iron beam carefully. He was back in full shadow, and he hoped he couldn't be seen. The surface wasn't that bright anyhow. Titan had two sources of illumination, the distant and faint sun, and the glowing body of Saturn. Of the two, the massive planet gave off more light, and they were now rotating towards the sun. The area grew darker rapidly.

He waited, holding the M-8 at the ready. The weapon had been modified so that it was usable by a space-suited man. The stock was contoured to fit the bulky suit, and the trigger guard was open. He took slow breaths, concentrating on remaining calm.

There was a movement under the dock structure. The shooter had moved forward, his suit helmet now glinted slightly in the dim light. Adam raised the rifle, holding his supporting hand against the girder for stability, then squeezed the trigger gently. The weapon bucked slightly as it fired. The sound was audible and sounded like a quiet clap in the thin atmosphere.

Over there under the dock, the enemy jerked and tried to run back. It hadn't been a clean kill, but the guy was in trouble. The marine staggered sideways, then fell, groping for his waist. Adam moved forward, weapon ready.

By the time he'd reached the other side, the man was dead. There was a red-tinged hole over the liver. It wasn't a good way to go. The semi-vacuum had ensured that.

The others came up, and Adam waved them out towards the landing cradles. This was the point at which his plan came fully unglued.

There was a series of sparks on the supporting girders of the dock. The ships were guarded, and they'd been seen.

They jumped back into the shelter of a wall. Sandy was in trouble. The larger woman was bent over groping for a patch kit with one hand while she tried to keep her finger against a hole in her thigh.

"How bad are you hit?" he asked.

"Grazed by a ricochet, I think, but the damn thing burns like fury."

Her voice sounded strained and thin. Her suit was bleeding pressure.

Rejsa had a patch out and slapped it on the hole. The quick-dry adhesive took hold, and the thin stream of atmosphere from the hole ceased.

Adam waived people to spread out. "Stay in cover. Watch for movement and shoot carefully. We don't have that much ammunition. Sandy, can you walk?"

"Yeah. I'm good. It's not hurting so much now. Feels like it nicked my thigh, then exited. Not much damage except for the holes."

"You take this explosive pack. Go back and head toward the center of the dock. Place it on the connecting tube wall about half-way between the dock structure and the receiving dome. Flip the on-switch, then find a place to hide that's far enough away that the explosion won't hurt you. Take cover and wait. I think you'll hear when the bomb goes off. Get closer and shoot anyone who comes out of the hole it made. Understand?"

"Yeah. Give me the bomb. I'm outta here." She moved off, limping a little.

That left four of them. The incoming fire had ceased. He tried to remember how many shots it had been. Not many, but more than one. It was most likely a couple of marines. It seemed like there had been about five or six bullets that struck nearby. Maybe more. He didn't know.

"Spread out and stay covered. Susan, you look for targets. The other two of you hold your fire. Those pistols aren't going to be much use at this range."

The small woman nodded, then moved back into the darkness. Adam ran the other way, keeping girders between him and the source of fire. The men over there were probably moving also. Shooting and staying in the same position was a perfect recipe for getting killed.

He moved slowly, watching for any clues, any movement. The landing cradles weren't solid structures, but the hydraulic cylinders and pump housings provided a lot of cover.

He'd moved about fifty meters down and gotten a good angle on the enemy. The legs of one of the marines were showing. The guy was lying behind a solid piece of metal, looking down toward where Susan must be. His legs were out of sight for her, but Adam could see them from the knee down.

He rested the weapon against a girder and shot. The legs flipped out of sight, but he knew he'd hit the guy. There had been a puff of warm, moist air that left a tiny cloud floating for a moment.

Sudden action down the other way drew his attention. A second marine carrying a rifle had tried to run across the open space from an empty cradle to the dock. Despite Susan's modesty about her shooting skills, she was deadly. A still form lay in the open, arms outstretched, one hand entangled in the rifle strap.

There was a second shot, and the top of the form's suit helmet sprouted a gush of instantly freezing air.

Adam nodded. That one was dead. Was his target still able to fight, or was he out too?"

He clicked his mic. "Advance carefully."

Rejsa came out from behind a girder near the corpse. He sidled close, then picked up the rifle. That was good. Now they had three long guns. Their firepower was increasing.

There were no additional shots, so they moved out and began placing the explosives. If there were any observers in the resting ships, they made no sign.

Over on the far side of the landing area, there was a little movement. Adam watched for a moment, then decided it was To'afa's group. He clicked his mic and asked, "That you?"

Someone answered, "Yes." That wasn't helpful. It could have been anyone. Adam realized his lack of experience was a hindrance in the operation. He should have assigned recognition codes.

He clicked again. "Where's Dracula?"

The answer came back, "Vlad, please. He's right here in my hand, and he hasn't had enough to drink."

That was To'afa, for sure.

He said, "We're set. Withdrawing to next location."

To'afa answered. This time Adam recognized his voice. "Us too. See you on the other side."

"Affirmative. Start phase two, as soon as you're ready."

The shapes in the distance moved toward the end of the dock arm. There was an observation platform on each end with a stairway down to ground level. That was their next target.

29

THE DOCKS

ADAM'S SMALL GROUP was on the observation platform at the west end of the dock. They'd opened the outside airlock door. There was no locking mechanism on it. The Belters operated under the presumption that anyone working out here would be responsible and experienced enough to know what they were doing. Besides, locking an airlock when access might be needed in an emergency just wasn't done.

The chamber filled with air. Ordinarily, Adam would have removed his helmet, but not this time. If things went as he hoped, the docks would shortly be vacuum. Any marines who weren't suited up wouldn't last.

He switched his comm to the bomb receivers' frequency and entered the activation code. Outside, the cradles slumped as the explosives went off.

The Fed ships settled in ending up at angles that would prevent them from lifting. One cradle collapsed entirely and the vessel it held rolled onto its side. That one was really going to be challenging to get back into space.

The invaders had to have noticed the explosions. They'd surely be distracted by the loss of their ships. Adam motioned, and Rejsa cracked the inner lock door just enough to see down the long dock.

No one was nearby. There was a group way off near the point where the tube connected the docks to the primary habitat. Some were aiming weapons down the tube. Some others had turned to the port and were looking out the windows, waving their hands in excitement.

The dock provided plenty of cover. There were stacks of boxes at intervals down the way, and internal girders lined the walls at intervals. Each of those would give adequate shelter against rifle fire.

Adam was a little nonplussed. The Marines were armed with rifles, and an unlucky shot could penetrate the wall, creating a leak. It must be that they didn't care much. No single small hole would be enough to drain the pressure. The atmosphere system pumps were powerful enough to compensate for numerous small leaks. Besides, the walls were designed to withstand micrometeorites, even though the thin atmosphere offered some protection.

On the other hand, too many leaks and the automatic blast doors would close. Had the Feds disabled the doors in some fashion? It wasn't supposed to be possible, yet every safety mechanism had one or more unforeseen ways it could fail. Maybe they'd jammed the blast doors on this end of the tube.

He motioned his people forward. They leapfrogged along, two on one side of the hallway and three on the other. Each Belter moved quickly from point to point, while the others provided cover.

The distraction caused by the destruction outside served its purpose well. They reached a point about one hundred meters from the enemy before the marines noticed and started shooting. Everyone leaned back behind girders, listening to the rattle of bullets hitting the soft steel webs.

The marines' fire slowed to a trickle. The volume of fire had been high, so the pause likely meant that many of them were reloading. Adam leaned out and raised his gun, but a shot ricocheted off the girder beside his ear. He returned fire, squeezing off a short un-aimed burst, then leaned back. More bullets bounced off steel near his position.

Susan had stopped some distance behind them and taken cover behind a pile of what appeared to be plastic cargo boxes. Adam hoped she remembered the difference between cover and concealment. The military rounds would penetrate the plastic and might go all the way through if the contents weren't sufficiently dense.

She was fine, though. She leaned slightly out, aimed, and shot. He heard the supersonic crack as her shot went by close to his position. It wasn't as loud as it would have been on Earth due to the much lower pressure, but was still enough to make him flinch.

There was a flurry of activity in the mass of enemy, and Adam shoved his weapon around the corner to fire another burst. The return fire clanked on the truss. He looked across at the other three. They were shooting when they could.

Randall leaned out and fired a long burst, then fell, blood leaking out a large hole in the back of his helmet.

Adam snarled. He hadn't known the man, but even one Belter life was too many. He fired a burst in return, eliciting more shouting.

Something clanked on the floor, bouncing and rolling past him. One glance told him it was a grenade. He jumped to the other side of the girder, placing himself in plain view of the massed men.

They were watching the grenade and were slow to respond to his movement. He fired a full-auto burst directly into the center of the group, spraying it back and forth. His magazine was empty, and the bolt locked open when the grenade exploded.

There was a sharp crack and fragments rattled off the far side of the beam, making him glad he had jumped. The marines ahead had run down the tunnel towards the habitat, leaving a tangled mass of bodies moving painfully on the floor.

Adam looked for his friends. Rejsa was standing over Randall, picking up spare ammo. Susan was moving forward from her hiding place, but Klein was kneeling on the floor, working on patching his suit.

"Klein, you okay?" Adam asked.

The comm clicked as Klein answered. "Got a hole in my waist flex seal. I think the piece is stuck in my side. Hurts pretty bad."

"Can you move?"

Klein had finished patching his suit. "I don't know how well. Let's see."

He stood and moved toward Adam slowly.

"Not too well. I think it's in my guts. It's really hurting, and I can smell crap. I'm going to need medical help." His voice rose with the last two sentences, and he sank down against the wall, resting in the corner by a girder.

"We'll get someone here as fast as possible. You rest. Don't move, you'll make it worse. Just keep your gun close. We'll be back soon. You got some pain meds?"

Klein nodded, then made a slight moan and leaned backward.

Now they were three. The enemy was missing a few men, too, but not nearly enough. Adam couldn't continue with this rate of loss. They'd never make it.

There was a crackle on the comm, then To'afa's voice said, "Quit wasting time up there. We're here now, so let's clean out this tube."

Adam looked back. To'afa and the other four were lurking on the far side of the tube, staying out of the way of direct fire.

Adam asked, "Anyone hurt?"

"No. Not a scratch, which is better than I can say for those Feds we met." The big man snorted disparagingly.

Adam and Susan moved forward, followed by Rejsa. The bodies on the floor were still. He glanced at them, trying to discern if any were living and likely to rise up and shoot them in the back. It didn't look as if that was going to happen. His attention was drawn to a bag lying by one of the corpses.

Looking toward the tunnel and trying to stay out of direct sight, Adam hooked the bag's strap with his rifle and drew it toward him. It was heavy. He picked it up and was rewarded for his efforts. There were five grenades inside.

He hefted one, then looked across the space at To'afa. He held up the grenade, and To'afa nodded vigorously.

Adam leaned forward, keeping his face near the floor. The Feds were huddled partway down the tube, their weapons aimed back at him.

One of them fired a shot generally in his direction, but it bounced harmlessly off the wall and ricocheted away.

They were far, but not too far. Laying his M-8 down, he pulled the pin of one of the grenades, then heaved the little bomb towards the group. It arched through the intervening space, then hit the floor and bounced toward the Feds.

There was a yell and the sound of men running, followed by the crack of the grenade.

Adam and Susan both jumped out and began shooting. To'afa's group did the same. The sound of gunfire rose to a crescendo for a moment, then faded to single shots.

The remaining space marines kept on running. The tunnel curved slightly and they were nearly out of sight around the bend. Adam slammed another magazine into the well and released the bolt, but by then there were no targets in sight.

There was a clank and a rattle as the marines threw a grenade back down the tube. It rolled for a bit, but then hit a girder and stopped behind it. The ensuing explosion did no damage as far as Adam could tell. The walls of the tunnel were stronger than he'd thought. He hoped the explosive pack on the outside was powerful enough to breach the tube.

Surely, Sandy had it placed and was well away. He keyed his mic and asked, "Sandy, all ready?"

There was no answer. Either the signal couldn't get through the walls, or something had happened to her. He toyed indecisively with the remote, then shrugged and keyed in the activation code, hoping as he did, that she was no longer carrying the pack.

There was a distant boom. Air immediately began to flow from the tunnel past him, moving back the way they'd just come. That wasn't right. She should have set the explosive pack on the tunnel wall. Somehow she hadn't placed it correctly. The explosion had breached the dock seal somewhere behind them.

The blast doors! Adam jumped forward, moving into the tunnel. The blast doors were sliding closed in response to the loss of pressure. The rest of the Belters squeezed through the gap behind him.

To'afa said, "No retreat now. We've really burned the boats."

Susan answered, "No boats here. It's win or die, so let's win."

Adam moved forward, back against the wall on the inside of the curve. There was something down there, but he couldn't tell exactly what.

A few more steps, then he could see that it was a group of men pushing some kind of make-shift barricade. They were nearly at the other end of the tube and looked to be ready to move into the habitat.

Nielson! He hadn't closed the doors as Adam had asked. Now the Fed force was going to be loose inside the habitat. Where was the resistance? No shots were coming from the other end.

As he noticed that, the Feds abandoned their shield and ran forward into the reception chamber. There was a brief flurry of shots, then silence.

To'afa had come up behind him as he watched.

"That's no good. They're waiting in there for us. We'll have to fight our way in."

Adam nodded. "If they did it, we can do it too. Let's get their barricade and push it forward."

The small group of Belters ran full out towards the movable shield. They were panting when they arrived, but there had been no response from the Feds ahead of them.

"Let's rest a bit here," Rejsa said, plaintively. I'm pooped."

Adam nodded. It was times like this that living in low gravity really hurt performance. They were relatively weak and out-of-shape.

After a few minutes, they rose and shoved at the barricade. It slid along the floor on plastic skids. A few more shoves got it to the blast door.

Adam heaved another grenade into the reception room, and it detonated in the middle of the floor with no response. The marines had escaped into the habitat.

The group entered the reception area cautiously. It was vacant. The several doors along the walls were all closed. The main entrance was an open blast door that led farther into the habitat. Adam had been that way numerous times. There was a long tunnel, then a cluster of domes that formed the Free Marketplace. That was an area full of kiosks, stands, and shops where nearly anything could be purchased if one had enough credits.

"Let's check the doors on both sides. They're offices, I think," he said.

To'afa grunted and moved towards the nearest door. He pushed it open carefully to reveal an empty office. There was a desk, some chairs, and a comp, but no place to hide.

The second door was similar. Nothing there either.

Adam couldn't resist making a joke. He flourished his arm toward the last door and said, "And, behind door three is..."

Susan had the grace to laugh a little, but her eyes betrayed the fact that she was frightened.

Rejsa pushed the door open, then jumped back and fired a burst into the blackened room.

There was a thud, but no other response.

Adam moved forward, reached in to activate the interior lights. His heart stopped momentarily. There was a marine on the floor, obviously dead.

The helmet had come off, exposing a woman's short black hair.

Nile! Adam's chest seemed frozen for a moment, but when he looked more closely, this woman was older, lighter of complexion, and not nearly as pretty. He turned away from the dead woman and shuddered inwardly.

How was he to know if a marine, any apparent enemy that came into his line of fire wasn't Nile? He hadn't considered it before, but now he remembered that she was supposed to be on one of the ships that had headed out this way. What if she was one of those he'd killed? What if she were somewhere ahead of him? He shook his head and wiped his hand unconsciously across the front of his helmet in a vain attempt to rub his eye-patch.

The habitual motion failed, but To'afa was watching him and responded, apparently reading Adam's mind. He leaned close, then said, "Not her, Captain. If she's here, she can take care of herself. She's good. Now, we gotta get the rest of them."

Adam nodded in agreement. He needed to concentrate on the enemy. He tried to reassure himself. To'afa was right. Nile could take care of herself.

30
TUNNELS AND DOMES

THE SMALL GROUP moved down the connecting tube to the next dome. Usually, cargo came in at the dock and was distributed with cargo carriers from there directly to warehouses. The narrow tunnels of the habitat were not generally used for significant cargo movement.

Newly arrived spacers exited the dock through the tunnel to the reception area. There they met officials who checked arrivals and provided advice about resupply. The community was still developing trade, and lately, the officials had taken to acting as brokers. All for a price, of course.

The reception area was vacant. Now that Adam's group was following the Feds, the fighting had become disorganized. The invasion force had achieved their goal of getting into the habitat. Once inside, they had disbursed and were either hiding or attacking Belters as the opportunity presented itself.

The next dome held several electric carts parked at charging stations. Some of the stations were empty; the carts had been taken somewhere else.

The tubes were narrow but still wide enough for small electric vehicles, provided pedestrians gave way. There were lines intended to serve as a roadway for the carts. The carts could travel faster than a human could run, and that meant the marines could be anywhere in the complex.

The residents would try to stop them, of course, but both the privateers and the marines could blend in easily. Determining who was friendly and who wasn't was going to be difficult.

Rejsa asked, "How are we going to find the Feds? I thought they'd stand and fight."

To'afa snorted, then said, "Good thing they didn't. There are not many people here capable of fighting. What I want to know is how many Feds there are."

Adam considered. To one degree or another, they'd disabled sixteen ships out in the port's landing field. The ships were mining craft size.

The larger cruisers wouldn't fit any of the cradles. If the journey was short, people could squeeze into a mining ship. It would carry twenty providing they didn't breathe deeply.

These ships had come from Earth orbit, though. That meant that the atmosphere and recycling systems would be the limiting factor as to capacity and that implied maybe one half of the twenty figure. So, if each ship had brought in ten crew, and they'd killed maybe fourteen, there were still some one hundred and forty enemy fighters running around in the domes.

It was going to be difficult to tell friends from enemies until the shooting started. The best thing to do would be to lock down the complex and then conduct a systematic search. Accordingly, he changed comm frequency to the Council emergency band.

Nielson answered his query instantly. Adam grimaced. That guy always opposed anything he suggested. Maybe Lars did it by instinct, but Adam was convinced it was because the Council chair didn't like him.

"Maxwell here. I need you to activate the pressure loss emergency system. Lock down the entire habitat. No ingress or egress from any compartment. We need to find the invaders, and I think they broke into small groups."

Nielson answered with a tone of desperation in his voice. "You're wrong. There's a big group of them trying to break into our offices right now. I don't know how they got by our defenses. Get over here immediately and stop them. You have my authorization to use any means necessary."

That last wasn't required. Adam had already decided he'd do whatever was needed to preserve the habitat and his fellow Belters.

"Okay. We're on our way now. Have you got any force capable of standing up to them?" he asked, already knowing the answer.

"No. Those women you wanted me to use didn't work out. I wasn't about to use their ideas—too destructive. We had only our police force down there trying to keep them from getting out of the docks. That worked until you came along and forced them out. It was a terrible idea for you to push them into the habitat. I'm thinking of—"

Adam interrupted before the Councilman could explain whatever it was he was thinking of.

"Nielson, that was stupid of you. Lora and Kendra were your best hope. They've been in combat and know what to do. Your police force is made up of lazy people who saw government jobs as a sinecure. Risking their lives is the last thing on their mind."

Nielson spluttered, "But..."

"No buts! I'm telling you what you have to do and if you don't do it, and I make it up there, I'm going to put you outside the habitat without a spacesuit. Now listen. We're in the hall out of the reception dome. Lock down all tunnels except those that lead directly from our location to yours. Then keep the Feds occupied. I presume you're shooting at them?"

"Yes, but..."

"Once again, just listen. Keep shooting. We'll come up behind them. How many are out there?"

"Uh..." There was a conversation in the background as Lars asked someone for their estimate. "Marcel says it looks like at least fifty."

Not good from two perspectives. First, Adam didn't have a large enough force to defeat fifty in a stand-up battle. The second thing that bothered him was there must be a large number of marines unaccounted for. He started to ask for reinforcements but snapped his mouth shut.

There weren't that many people in the habitat at any one point. The entire population of the belt was estimated at somewhat less than ten thousand. Of those, at least sixty percent lived in their ships or on asteroid habitats. There were some four thousand members of the Titan community, but most of them were either too old, too young, or too inexperienced to fight. There were probably only about two hundred ex-military in the group, and most of them could be counted on to be out prospecting. Lars had only his small police force and maybe a few older Belters who were combat-vets.

Adam thought that the majority of the populace would fight, but they wouldn't stand a chance against the space marines. The invasion could turn into a blood-bath, and he didn't want that on his conscience.

"Let's go! A group of them are outside the Council offices. Keep a close watch out for others. Some of them have gone elsewhere. They might be setting up an ambush for us," he said.

His small force began to move down the tube away from the reception area, weapons ready.

The tube was littered with debris, papers, and whatnot. It looked as if the cargo brokers had taken off quickly when the Feds attacked. One good thing was accidental. Lars had kept Lora out of the fight, so there were no booby traps to avoid.

The tube was claustrophobic. Adam didn't usually feel this way, but the possibility of an attack made the place feel tiny. There were metal rings that supported the tube, but they weren't big enough to provide cover. The advance had to be made in the open.

Why the Belter force hadn't been able to stop the Feds was a bit of a mystery. They'd apparently been too busy retreating to stand and fight. He shook his head, disparagingly. Who would have thought that they wouldn't fight?

When they reached the end of the tube, that last thought was erased instantly. There had been a fierce battle here. Bodies of both Belters and marines were scattered across the area. His friends had stood their ground, but their effort hadn't been enough.

A quick scan of the open area in the middle of the dome accounted for fifty or sixty marines. What broke Adam's heart was that there were more dead Belters there than marines. It had been a brief but fierce battle.

He glanced at the bullet-pocked and heavily damaged office facades. They were riddled with holes, and a couple showed the effects of grenade explosions. It was fortunate that the domes were constructed strongly enough to resist micrometeorite strikes. There didn't appear to be any leaks. At least he couldn't detect any loss of pressure or air movement.

"To'afa, take your group and check the offices on that side," he said, waving towards the left. "We'll check this side."

It would be stupidly negligent to advance without making sure there were no hidden enemies who could open fire on their rear.

Rejsa approached the nearest door and flung it open, then ducked back quickly as a shot came from within.

He shouted, "Belters!"

Whoever was within answered, "Thank God! I'm hurt badly. Can you help?"

Adam came up behind Rejsa and shouted, "How many are on the Council?"

"What? Oh. Seven."

That was most likely a Belter. He doubted if the marines would know the Council size. He cautiously poked his head around the corner.

"Sam? Sam Gibson?"

He recognized the man. Gibson was a merchant who dealt in meal packs. Adam had purchased supplies from him the last time the D-R was at Titan.

"Adam? I've got a bullet in my guts, but good to see you anyway." Sam's voice was strained with pain.

"Take it easy, Sam. We're not prepared to evacuate you right at the moment, but we do have pain meds and antibiotics."

"Good. Give me a bunch of opiates and go get 'em. The rest escaped and headed farther into the complex."

Adam nodded. "Yeah. I hear they're outside the Council chambers."

Sam snorted, then gasped. "Hurts. It wouldn't hurt my feelings if they strung that Nielson up by the toes. He wouldn't let us organize a decent defense. We finally ignored his orders and got down here in time to try and stop them. Nielson had the police trying to hold them off, but we're not prepared for an invasion here. The police only carry pistols. I think most of them were killed."

Adam growled deep in his throat. "Nielson has got some things to answer for. I'm going to find out what he thought he was doing. I gave him specific instructions to let experienced people set up a defense. He didn't do it and this is the result."

Sam bent his head to take a couple of pills offered by Susan. He groaned again.

"Hurts. I don't know how bad I am. I'm not bleeding much, though. Probably got a perforated intestine. I'm not sure what hit me. Maybe grenade fragments. Take a look, won't you? Don't tell me if it's horrible, though."

Adam bent and pulled up the man's shirt. There was a large gash in his abdomen, but it looked as if the muscles were mostly intact.

He probed gently at the hole at one end of the wound. He moved to inspect Sam's side. There it was.

There was an exit hole near Sam's kidney. It wasn't bleeding much, though, so the organ probably was mostly intact.

"Looks like you got hit at an angle. The bullet cut a big channel in your stomach before it went inside. It came out near your kidney, but you aren't bleeding much. I think you're going to survive. Might lose a few feet of small intestine, though."

"Good. Good." Sam lay back and closed his eyes, then said, "Don't forget to send someone after me. I'd like to get back in the fight, and I'm going to need more than a few stitches to do that."

"Hah! You'll probably be on your feet in a week. Take it easy. We've got to clear out the rest of them, but we'll try and get you evac'ed to the hospital shortly."

Sam nodded but didn't say anything.

Adam glanced at the others. "Let's go. We'll close the door, Sam. I'll tell the evac team to knock three times before they open it. Don't shoot them."

The other four offices on that side were unoccupied.

On the other side of the space, To'afa's group had cleared four of the five offices and was preparing to open the final door.

Adam dropped to the floor as a burst of automatic fire came through the closed door. To'afa backed away, then moved close to the office wall.

The big man flourished his ax and said, "I'll open it. Get ready to shoot."

His voice was low, but Adam heard it clearly from where he was.

The ax flashed, striking the door latch and crushing the mechanism. There was an answering burst of fire that ripped through the plastic door panels. The ax swung again, and the door popped open.

More fire came out, then there was silence. Adam grimaced.

The occupants were playing smart and waiting for someone to make a target of themselves.

To'afa looked at Adam and made a motion with his hand as if throwing something. In response, Adam took one of the salvaged grenades he was carrying and slung it into the room.

There was a shout from within, followed by a sharp crack as it went off.

To'afa leaned forward and looked within, then straightened.

"They're done fighting," he announced.

He went inside for a moment, then returned.

"Three marines and one privateer. Two are still alive, but it looks like not for long."

Adam motioned them on toward the next tunnel. The main fight was ahead.

31
THE COUNCIL DOME

THEY'D GONE THROUGH three other links on the chain of domes and tunnels. The route wasn't direct. It first angled away, then came back horizontally before it turned toward the Council chambers.

Adam cursed whoever had laid out the complex. It seemed like they had gone out of their way to make it difficult to defend. He knew that the place had grown organically. Individual Belters or groups had constructed habitats based on their immediate requirements.

No one had planned for it to get so large, but still, someone should have had the presence of mind to think about possible attacks.

Now they were nearing the main enemy force. They could hear sporadic shooting in the near distance.

Adam took stock of his small army. There were the two that remained of his group and To'afa and his four, making a total of eight. He concluded that he was insane to go on, then shrugged. So, he was nuts. He'd been called worse.

"Check your magazines. We're not going to have time to reload up ahead."

Their weapons' bolts clicked as they checked, although it was partly drowned out by the sound of distant shots that echoed down the tube.

"We're ready," said Susan. Her expression was serious. "This is going to be bad, isn't it?"

Adam couldn't lie to her. "Yes. It's going to be bad. Take cover somewhere down the tube and pick targets when you have the opportunity. You're our best shot, and I don't want you in the middle of a chaotic firefight. Remember, cover, not concealment."

She grinned at his final, needless admonition. "Affirmative. Cover, not concealment. I can do that, but what if we lose?"

What if they lost? He hadn't even thought about that possibility.

"If we're captured, they'll probably execute us, so..." His voice trailed off.

"I see. I'll shoot as many as I can, then. They won't get me until I'm out of ammo," she replied.

To'afa grunted, holding up his ax. "Get me in their midst. We'll see how they stand up to Vlad."

Adam laughed grimly. "Yeah. I've got my sword. We'll make them pay."

The final tunnel was ahead. It ran straight for nearly seventy meters, before opening into the massive dome that housed the Council chambers.

The dome was designed as the seat of the governing body and featured an ample public space with a fountain in front of the office structure. The fountain was a recent addition, and Adam felt it was ridiculously ostentatious. Water wasn't in short supply, but the idea of wasting energy to squirt it up in the air went against Belter notions of practicality.

He looked down the tube at the fountain directly ahead. The Council offices were on the far side. Walking up the tunnel with the fountain playing made for a pretty view that enhanced the facade of the Council chambers.

There were figures huddled against the low wall of the fountain pool. Some were shooting over the wall at the building behind. So far, they hadn't seen Adam's group.

"Hang back here, out of the direct line of sight. Let's get some kind of barrier to give us cover, then we can take out those we see," he said.

They pulled some crates out of a storeroom and piled them up in a way that would provide shelter.

"Susan, see what you can do, please."

She nodded, already intent on her weapon's sight.

Adam watched as she took a deep breath, then exhaled before she squeezed the trigger.

The shot seemed loud. Up ahead, one of the figures slumped, but none of the enemy seemed to notice. They were intent on the resistance in front of them and probably couldn't determine the source of Susan's shot..

She continued to fire, dropping an enemy with each shot.

Adam held his breath, counting. Susan had emptied her first magazine, shooting carefully, and there were bodies on the floor ahead.

The enemy had moved out of their line of sight now. Someone up there had finally figured out that the tunnel was the source of the shots rather than the Council chamber building.

There was a flash followed by a bang a few yards inside the other end of the tunnel. They'd thrown a grenade down the tube, hoping to discourage whoever was shooting at them.

Adam shouted, "They're trapped up there. They can't get in our line of sight, and the people in the chamber building have them pinned down. Let's move forward. Bring the boxes."

He moved ahead, rifle held in a ready position. A figure showed at the far end of the tunnel, and he fired a three-shot burst. The figure fell back.

Susan dropped to her belly and shot, resulting in another figure falling into the tunnel. This one had been preparing to throw a grenade. There was a muffled explosion, and the body bounced as the bomb went off underneath it.

Suddenly, there was a rush. The marines ahead entered the tunnel shooting. Susan, prone behind a box, immediately started shooting back.

Adam damned the enemy and stood, firing bursts at the group. Somehow he remained unscathed, but two of To'afa's group grunted and dropped to the floor.

To'afa cursed, then rose and fast-balled a grenade directly at the center of the group ahead. It went off, dropping three. Adam had thrown another one as soon as To'afa's had left his hand and it exploded against a dead body, causing no injuries.

The two pitched two more grenades each. The explosions echoed down the tube. The rush had failed, and the survivors had retreated around the edge of the tunnel. No shots were coming from the enemy now.

Adam said, "Let's get closer then throw some more grenades. They'll go off outside the tube and maybe clear some of those clowns out."

To'afa lumbered forward, digging in his bag for another grenade. A uniformed figure appeared ahead and fired a burst. To'afa dropped to his knee, but then stood and hurled a grenade. Simultaneously, Susan shot, and the man fell backward.

The grenade went off just outside the tunnel entrance. There were yells followed by a burst of shooting as a result.

Adam rushed forward. The enemy had broken and was running. The Council dome had five exits, and the remaining Feds had disbursed into them.

There were no enemies left alive in the public space. Adam waved at the Council building and heard a cheer from within. The defenders had held.

The door opened as men rushed out, holding rifles and pistols. Adam got their attention by yelling, "It isn't over. There are still some left. We've got to find them."

He motioned toward the exits, indicating that the defenders should separate to check them.

To'afa!

He suddenly remembered that his friend had been shot. Adam turned to go back, but almost bumped his nose on To'afa's chin. The islander was standing right behind him.

"What? I thought you had been hit," he said.

"Hit Vlad. I had him over my heart, and the bullet bounced off."

To'afa held out the battle-ax, showing a splash of copper directly in the center of one side.

Adam shook his head. "That's better than body armor."

"Yeah. Didn't do anything to me." To'afa looked around. "We chased 'em out, didn't we?"

"Yes, but there's still some of them running around. We need to find them before they damage anything or kill anyone else."

The battle was won, but the victory wasn't theirs yet. Not while enemy combatants were running around somewhere in the community.

32
CLEANING UP

BELTERS SUDDENLY EMERGED from offices. Most were armed, although their weapons were mostly pistols. Adam took stock and decided that something must be done about that. If the defenders had possessed military-grade firearms, the result of the invasion would not have been in doubt. Pistols are usually fine for self-defense, but long guns are far better in an actual combat situation.

There was a buzz of conversation as the defenders greeted each other and members of Adam's group they recognized. He was suddenly isolated in a space of his own. People were talking all around him, but not focused in his direction. It was a strange feeling, being ignored. The exalting sensation of victory seemed to be mutually shared by all. They'd probably continue to talk for hours.

They needed to immediately organize and begin the search for the Feds who had escaped. Adam estimated that there were between twenty and thirty enemies who had avoided capture. They couldn't be allowed a free run of the place. There were too many critical points that could be easily sabotaged.

No one in a habitat that allowed humans to exist in a hostile environment would consider sabotage. It was too much like suicide, and that was not something the Belt community suffered from. There were too many ways to die in space. The Belters had to work so hard to stay alive that suicide was almost unimaginable to them. Further, they were too independent-minded. Everyone respected everyone else's right to self-determination. Taking an action that would endanger others without their express permission was unacceptable.

However, such points as the air recycling center, the heating plant, and the community power reactor were vulnerable to a variety of threats. These soft-points had to be protected.

Adam took a deep breath and shouted loudly. People stopped talking gradually and turned to look at him. When he had their attention, he began assigning them to groups. He intended to send a protective group to each weak point, then to use the rest of them to search for Feds.

Nielson showed up and proceeded to disrupt the organized effort. The Councilman started to give a variety of contradicting commands, splitting up Adam's groups and detailing them to begin cleaning up the mess.

Adam silently cursed as he walked over to Nielson.

"Maxwell! Where have you been? Holding back until we got the invasion sorted out, I'll bet."

"Not precisely, Nielson. I'm in charge here, and you're going to go back into your office and wait until we've got the situation under control."

Nielson huffed. "I'll do nothing of the sort. I'm the elected representative and Council chairman. You're under my orders. I intend to have an inquiry as to why you allowed this to happen. You were off yonder near Earth on your wild goose chase and left us unprotected. Luckily we're more than a match for a handful of Space Marines."

He started to say more, but Adam's fist connected with the council chair's mouth as he began to open it again. From that point on, his part in the conversation was carried out from a prone position.

"You didn't follow my instructions, Nielson. The Feds would never have reached this point if you'd done what I told you to do. Now you're trying to revoke my orders, and by doing so, you're endangering the entire community."

Nielson groaned, spat blood, then said, "We have to clean up these bodies. The status of the Council will be damaged if the citizens are allowed to see how close they came to the seat of our government."

His speech was slurred. It was probably difficult to speak with a cut lip.

Adam bent down and lifted Nielson by the collar. "I'm going to give you a choice. Either you go to your office and sit quietly until I've got the enemy completely contained, or I'm going to lock you up somewhere."

Nielson spluttered in anger. Blood was running out of the corner of his mouth, and he wiped at it, then looked at his hand in horror. "I...I'm bleeding! You struck me. You're under arrest." The Councilman raised his voice, "Guards, arrest this man."

The nearest Council guard, one of three men assigned to maintain order at the Council meetings, looked at Nielson and said, "Arrest him yourself."

Nielson began to protest, then finally understanding the situation, he clamped his jaw shut. Unfortunately, that was painful and elicited a moan. He waved his hand back and forth in a manner indicating that he was giving up, then he said, "Alright. I'm not stupid. I can see that you've got this under control. Do what you want, but rest assured that the Council will require an accounting afterward."

Adam smiled humorlessly. "Fine. I can deal with that. Right now, please return to your office. You might want to get your lip looked at, too."

Nielson climbed unsteadily to his feet then turned and moved slowly towards the Council chambers.

Adam said, "That's over. Everybody start on the tasks I've assigned. Those of you who will be searching, be on condition red at all times. The escapees are armed and may decide to shoot."

He turned to To'afa. "You come with me. We're going to the reactor. Sabotage there would do the most damage the quickest." He turned back to the others. "If you find a large force, comm for reinforcements, then wait until they arrive before trying to root them out. Understood?"

There was a murmur of assent, then groups began to depart, heading in different directions.

"Captain, you know how to get to the reactor?" To'afa asked. "I've never been down there. I think it's over by the west side, but I'm not sure."

Adam said, "Me neither. I think we walked by the cooling tower, but I've never gone there from the inside." He raised his voice and shouted, "Hey! Anyone know where the reactor is?"

One of the men that had come out of the Council Chambers answered. "Sure. I can take you to it."

Adam agreed. "Great. Let's go." He started to move after the rest, then thought better of it, turned around and shrugged with a grin on his face. "Why don't you lead? Oh, and what's your name?"

The Belter grinned back and said, "John Chen. I used to work down there. It's over this way."

He indicated an exit to the west side of the public space and started toward it.

JOHN LED TO'AFA and Adam down the passage to another hall, down it, and then they headed down a stairway.

Adam had known the reactor was below ground in a shielded bunker somewhere near the edge of the community, but he hadn't thought about stairs. Nearly every habitat in the entire Belt was on a single floor. There were few elevators and stairs were practically unheard of.

He looked inquiringly at John. The man seemed to read his mind.

"The engineer that laid out this place insisted that elevators couldn't be trusted, especially if the power failed. Makes sense, I guess. With the stairs, repair teams can always get down there."

They descended a narrow flight of stairs, turned at a landing and went down another twenty steps. The floor there appeared to be rock. The lights were dim, making the tunnel appear mysterious and threatening.

Adam followed cautiously, every sense on the alert. To'afa was following right on his heels. The big man was so close that he bumped into Adam's back when John stopped to listen.

Adam grunted in surprise. John turned around and said, "Sound carries down here. We got to be quiet from here on. If they're down here, we don't want them to know we're coming."

That was sensible. Adam nodded, then followed, his carbine at the ready.

The rock floor merged seamlessly into curved rock walls as they progressed. There were drill marks on the walls. The place wasn't well illuminated. There were only sporadic, dim light fixtures, and they only revealed a dim view of the path the men were on.

The tunnel had descended gradually, taking them slowly deep underground. It was cold. The lights were almost non-existent, and the shaft wasn't heated. There was a thick layer of frost along the edges of the ceiling. Their breath formed steamy puffs that condensed and sparkled in their helmet lights.

Adam was glad he was wearing his spacesuit. It was so cold he considered closing his helmet. The drawback would be that they would have to use the comm system and possibly be overheard. With the face-plates open, they could whisper. He settled for turning the internal heater up.

Adam asked, "They put this underground for protection. Right?"

Chen nodded. "Yeah. Can't have a micrometeorite hit the cooling jacket. Just like in a ship. That'd cause a real problem, besides there is some radiation leakage."

To'afa remarked, "I've heard that, too." He paused to check the radiation indicator on his right arm. "Nothing yet. I guess we're safe."

Adam was puzzled. "Leakage? That doesn't seem right."

"Older design. It'd cost too much to replace and, you know, what with the Feds gunning for us, parts are scarce," Chen replied.

That would change once manufacturing began in earnest. The Belt had plenty of raw materials. They were already building ship reactors with no problem. In fact, they were making better reactors than those that came from Earth. This was another thing that he'd have to address. The community deserved, no, needed, the best possible power source. There were too many lives that depended on a steady supply of power.

He said, "The Council seems to have their priorities wrong. Seems like they'd rather spend the money on something else more publicly visible."

He was about to add, "like fancy Council chambers," but Chen placed his hand on Adam's arm for an instant, then whispered, "Getting close. About another hundred meters."

Adam nodded and readied his weapon, then began to move forward, gliding along the left-hand wall. The Samoan followed, holding his rifle at the ready, the battle-ax slung over his back. Chen only had a small pistol that he had drawn.

Adam was pleased to see that the dark-haired man carried the little weapon in a way that indicated he'd had some training and knew how to use it.

The reactors in space ships were all remotely controlled. Adam figured that this one was the same. If so, there would be emergency controls located in a secondary control room somewhere.

They moved forward carefully, pausing to listen every few steps.

The secondary control room had a shielded door. If there was a problem and someone was there, they could lock the door and avoid at least some of the radioactivity. Of course, if it was an actual disaster and the reactor exploded or melted down, there would be no saving anyone within a ten-kilometer radius.

The door to the control room was partly open. The light from within shone through a small crack and reflected from the frost on the far tunnel wall. The glow was interrupted at intervals. There was someone in the room moving in front of the light source.

A few steps more, and they heard someone say, "Connect the remote to the battery. You know what to do. Do it!"

A woman's voice answered, "The antenna won't work down here. The only way to get a signal is through the reactor secondary control system. I'm trying to get that set up."

The other voice, a deeper one, said, "You want to see Earth again, you do just that with no tricks. Remember, I know you, and I know what to watch for."

She answered, "Yeah, well, maybe you do, but it's got to go from the main controls through the lines to the secondary system and then to the remote. The only other way you'll detonate the charge is with a timer, and that's just plain suicide. We don't know if we can get out of here."

The man replied with a snide, know-it-all tone. "That's not a problem. Those idiots up there haven't a clue about defense. Chances are they're chasing our late compatriots. They'll be happy to welcome us when we join the hunt. We both know enough about this place to pass as full-time residents."

She snorted.

There was something about that snort that shot straight through Adam's ears to his heart. It sounded like the noise Nile used to make when she was disparaging something stupid that he had said.

He crept forward, heart in his throat. It couldn't be her. She'd never be down here trying to blow up the city. He paused a few feet from the door.

The woman said, "Look, Jason, accept that I know how to set this and let me work."

That was the clue that Adam had needed. It was that damned Jason Klingfeldt. Nile's old unit boyfriend.

He started to lunge forward, but To'afa caught at his shoulder, pulling him back just as Chen threw the door open wide.

There was a burst of automatic fire, and Chen went flat on his back in the tunnel, a blossom of red on his face.

To'afa raised his weapon to return fire, but Adam pushed the barrel down. He couldn't risk hitting Nile. He had to know why she would change sides. His thoughts raced through imaginary scenarios.

Nile reunited with her unit. Nile reciting the oath of service to the Space Marines. Nile and Klingfeldt standing side by side. Nile and Klingfeldt kissing.

He raised his carbine, but then dropped it to hang on the sling. His hand felt for and closed on the hilt of his cutlass. The next thing he knew, it was in his hand.

To'afa had followed suit. He was holding Vlad with one hand and the carbine with the other. The two looked at each other.

To'afa's eyes showed he too had recognized Nile's voice. He looked mildly puzzled for a moment, then his face started to show signs of what Adam recognized as the berserker anger that the big man was known for.

Adam motioned for To'afa to move by the side of the open door.

The Samoan moved, cat-like, into position, his ax hand back against the wall, the ax edge glittering in the reflected light from the frost.

Adam moved up beside him, then called, "Klingfeldt, Nile. It's Adam Maxwell. You'll never get out of here. We've got the rest of your group under control upstairs. Give it up."

Klingfeldt cursed, then said in a loud voice, "We'll blow the reactor. Back off, now!"

Adam replied, "I might arrange for safe passage out, but I'll need you to disconnect the detonator."

Klingfeldt answered, "I need it to guarantee you'll let me go. Stay back, or I'll shoot your girlfriend."

Nile spoke, hurriedly. "Adam, he's well-armed, and he's got grenades. Get away!"

There was the sound of a slap, and she gasped.

Klingfeldt said, "Shut up, bitch! You don't know how much I've wanted to do that. It feels good, huh? Maybe I'll kill your boyfriend and then slap you around while we get it on. You'd like that, wouldn't you?"

Adam's temper exploded. No one could do that to her. He lost all perspective on the situation. It was as if Nile hadn't been gone for months. He forgot his feelings of desertion. Surely she hadn't left him for Jason voluntarily. There must have been some kind of compulsion. There had to have been.

He swung out and launched himself into the room. Time seemed to slow down immensely as Adam analyzed the scene inside.

Jason was standing by a desk on the far side of the room with a nasty looking submachine pistol pointed at Nile. She was sitting at the desk, with some circuitry in one hand and a screwdriver in her other hand, looking over her shoulder at Adam, her mouth open in horror.

Adam's cutlass came arcing through the air and spun across the room as he released it. At the same time, the machine pistol swung in his direction, flame shooting out of its barrel. There must have been sound from the gunshots, but Adam didn't hear it. He was only conscious of a series of blows to his chest that drove him backward.

33

THE KISS OF DEATH

TIME WAS STILL creeping slowly. Adam watched as his cutlass slammed into Klingfeldt's forearm, slicing through it. The machine pistol, hand still gripping it, tumbled to the floor with a clatter.

Nile screamed and rose, then thrust the screwdriver through Klingfeldt's throat. He grabbed at it with his remaining hand, frantically trying to pull it out as he gasped for breath.

Adam staggered backward and found himself leaning against the wall. As he watched, a large shadow moved into sight. To'afa!

The big man was yelling something in his native language as he charged across the room. Vlad swung in a glittering arc, slinging blood from Klingfeldt's neck against the far wall.

Adam started to reach for his chest, but his shoulder hurt too much to raise his arm. Nile was holding him. How had she gotten here so quickly? He tried to hug her with his left arm, but she pushed his hand away.

"Quit it, you dummy! I'm trying to see where you're hurt."

It was at that instant that time resumed its normal speed. Adam's chest throbbed, and so did his shoulder.

"Ow! That hurts!" he said slowly.

Nile looked in his eyes, then snorted, a sound that he found comforting.

"Of course it does, idiot. You've been shot. Lucky that Jason was carrying that little gun. It only shoots 9mm's, and they barely penetrated your spacesuit. Probably didn't get through the inner lining. Your eyes look fine. I think you're a little shocky from the adrenaline, that's all.

He lifted his left hand and held it out. It was shaking like a leaf. His right side had been hammered painfully. He analyzed the pain. It was dull and throbbing, but no sharp sensations, no feeling of wetness. He experimentally drew a deep breath. His lungs worked; it was just that his ribs hurt.

"Well, maybe you're right. I can breathe. It just hurts."

She looked at him tenderly, then leaned forward and kissed him.

Adam's heart beat double time, making his ribs throb even more.

"Ow! That hurts worse."

"What? The kiss? Oh, Adam, it's been so long," she whispered.

Adam looked over her shoulder. To'afa was standing there, Vlad poised for a strike.

"No, To'afa. No more. She's my problem."

To'afa looked puzzled, then the arm sagged, and the ax moved to the Samoan's side.

Nile glanced back. "Hi, To'afa."

"Hi, Nile. What were you doing? Blowing up the place?" To'afa asked.

"No. Trying to keep it from being blown up. I know it looks bad, but I was misconnecting the detonator. All it can do is sit there. No signals can get through to it. I touched the antenna to the power circuit and burned out the receiver."

Adam asked, "But, where have you been, and why were you down here with him?" He moved his head, indicating the corpse by the desk.

"It's a long story, but he forced me to come with him. He said he had someone who would assassinate you if I didn't come. The Feds got hold of me, and it was all I could do to stay alive. That ex-girlfriend of yours was going to have me executed until I promised to use my inside knowledge to destroy Titan base and return you to her."

Adam shook his head, trying to comprehend the unsaid parts of her story. "Elseth?"

"Yes, Elseth Worthington, Her Royal Highness, NAFD Queen, plus whatever else she decides to call herself," Nile spat.

He shook his head again, disbelievingly.

Nile pulled him close to her. "She really wants you, Adam. I think she's obsessed with capturing you, but I don't know if she wants to kill you or make you love her. She's crazy."

He laughed, then groaned with pain. "Agh. That hurts. I can't get a decent breath. She was always crazy, Nile. I made a big mistake getting involved with her. She doesn't want me the way you think. She wants me to worship her, love her hopelessly, then she'll have me killed and thoroughly enjoy watching me die."

"I would have killed her, but there was no chance. Besides, I wanted to get back to you. You're all I thought about. I had to lie and connive and, oh! It was awful, but it worked. I'm here, and you're okay. You'll never leave my sight as long as you live, you one-eyed Pirate!"

To'afa cleared his throat. "Excuse me, but I think that we've got to get back topside. We need to make sure that all those marines are dead or captured." He looked embarrassed. "Excuse me, Nile. I know they're your friends, but they can still do a lot of damage here."

She nodded but didn't say anything. She was trying to get Adam's arm over her shoulder to support him.

To'afa slung Vlad, then went over and picked up Adam's cutlass.

"You might be wanting this thing, small though it is. A Pirate can't be without his sword," he said as he slid it back into its sheath at Adam's side. Then he effortlessly got Adam to his feet.

Nile asked, "Can you walk?"

He took stock of himself. "Yeah. Well, maybe, but I might need you to help balance me."

She laughed. "You're transparent. You just want to get your arm around me, right?"

He grinned weakly. "You know me too well, but you don't have to worry. I'm in too much pain to do any more than think naughty thoughts."

To'afa cleared his throat again. "Hey, you two, remember me? I'm here, and it's getting kind of embarrassing. Tone it down, please."

Adam looked up at his friend. "Help me get back upstairs and then check on the clean-up. You can leave me in Nile's care. I'll try not to embarrass you any further."

Nile had moved to the desk and grabbed a circuit board. "This thing should be burned out, but I'll take it with us. The charge he set won't go off without the proper digital code. He wanted to make sure that he was out of the complex before it blew."

She kicked the foot of the corpse, moving the limp leg into a bent position, then came back to Adam. "Let's go."

The tunnel seemed longer and darker than before, but Adam hardly noticed. He was focused on Nile.

34
COMPLICATIONS

THE NEXT FEW weeks were busy. The Belters had to get the Titan port reopened as quickly as possible. Without it, supplies were relegated to cumbersome modes of transfer. The old docking cradle that had sufficed for the little Nelle Belle was in constant use. It couldn't keep up with the cargo required for the Belter industries.

The shipbuilders were swamped with work building replacements for the ships that had been lost in combat, and they needed raw materials. The miners made the best of the situation by dropping cargo on carefully calculated orbits. Huge parachutes ensured that loads of metals did not end up buried deep in Titan's crust.

Parachute material became scarce, then unobtainable, but by then a few of the damaged cradles had been repaired, and more ships were able to land. The port was gradually becoming operational again.

The Space Marines and the few privateers who survived capture by the irate Belters were put to work clearing debris and moving supplies. They had been given old space suits with just a small oxygen tank. The constant fear of running out of air, especially when the suits weren't totally reliable, kept the prisoners in check. They showed more interest in breathing than in continuing the war against the Belt.

Adam spent the first few days with his ribs strapped up. Despite his initial optimism, he had three broken ribs. By the time the bruising had faded, he was able to get around without undue discomfort.

That was fortunate because Nielson had decided that his prestige was damaged. The Council chair wanted to hold a hearing to show everyone how hard he was working to protect them. Since he blamed Adam for his fall from grace, he selected Nile as representative of the criminals who had attacked them. Some of the other Council members made the point that it had been an act of war by a political opponent, not a criminal action. However, Nielson insisted and seemed to be on the verge of getting his way.

The thought of Nile being in jeopardy to satisfy Nielson's sense of outrage absolutely infuriated Adam. In the days since the battle, they had talked extensively. They were still going over the details.

She hadn't been well treated, and some fading bruises and scars showed it. Each time he saw the marks, he wanted to kill Klingfeldt all over again. That animosity extended to all of the NAFD government, and most specifically, towards Elseth.

Nile had only seen the Queen once for a brief moment, but she suspected that Elseth had been present, though unseen, during her beatings.

"It always seemed like someone was watching from behind a screen or maybe through video. The people tormenting me sometimes looked like they were self-conscious; like they were performing for someone."

He replied, "Maybe they were. I can believe that Elseth would get her jollies by watching them beat you. She hates me and would do anything to hurt me. I'm sorry you were the recipient of that."

His hands were running over burn marks on her bare feet as he spoke.

She shuddered a little. "Hey, stop it. That kind of hurts. No, it feels...I don't know. It makes me feel nervous."

He swore, then added, "If I ever get my hands on those men, I'll make them pay for these scars."

"Oh, they weren't all men. There were a couple of women. Ugh. They were the worst. I think the men kind of felt unhappy about hurting me, but the women didn't. They were vicious and seemed to delight in finding things that I...Oh, I don't want to talk about it anymore."

ADAM REALIZED HER story was difficult to believe. She had been forced to work for the NAFD. In so doing, she had opened herself to charges that she had provided the enemy with intelligence about the Belt and Belter ship capabilities.

She hadn't, though. She'd provided information all right, but she'd lied about critical elements, doing her best to mislead NAFD interrogators. She'd suffered for it. They hadn't believed everything she'd said, and she'd been subjected to psychological and physical coercion.

They'd hired the combination law and investigation firm of Barton-Massera to represent Nile. The firm was the largest in the Belt, although it consisted of just the two principals. So far, there hadn't been much demand for lawyers in space. The Belters usually settled their own problems peacefully.

James Barton and Ali Massara were dedicating most of their resources toward her defense. It didn't make Adam feel much better. The rumor had gotten around that Nielson was set on making sure the Council would decide against her.

Nile didn't seem worried about the hearing. She had spent several days repeating her story to the two attorneys while Adam was recovering.

All she would say was, "Don't worry about it. The truth will come out."

That wasn't very comforting. He was reduced to thoughts of punching Nielson repeatedly. He told himself that a punch or two wouldn't help, but it was a great temptation. The only reason he 'didn't indulge his fantasy was that then the Council would feel constrained to charge him, too. But, the mental picture provided a degree of satisfaction and kept his mind off the possible repercussions of the hearing.

To date, the Belt had not been bothered by serious criminality. There were instances of people taking things that didn't belong to them, but they usually had an overwhelming need for the purloined items. Personal survival always came first. That was an unwritten rule among the Belters, and they made allowances for actions taken in life and death situations.

The Belt community was small, and reputation played an essential role in social standing. No one wanted to be viewed as an outcast. That was why there was no real need for a police force, jail, or legal proceedings.

Everyone knew they'd eventually have to account for every action they took. With all of space available, there was no place to run to. If someone's reputation was so bad that they were banished (something that hadn't happened yet), it was tantamount to a death sentence.

The miscreant would eventually have to return for supplies, and they'd have to justify their actions again while trying to persuade someone to supply them. The alternative of going back to Earth was not feasible. Their treatment by the Earthers wouldn't be pleasant, given the level of animosity between the two groups.

In the current case, Nielson had arranged for the Council to hold the hearing. People were angry about the attack, and he'd managed to make Nile seem at least partially responsible. His line of reasoning was that she knew all about the Titan settlement, and she undoubtedly told the Feds what she knew. How else would Klingfeldt have known how to locate the reactor?

Nielson had conveniently forgotten that Klingfeldt had spent time in the domes, too. Adam was prepared to use that in Nile's defense. He'd carefully documented the dates that Klingfeldt had been on Titan and turned it over to Barton-Massera. Barton was investigating Klingfeldt's actions, where he'd stayed, who he'd contacted, employment, and so on.

There had been plenty of opportunities for Klingfeldt to become familiar with the habitat.

When he told Nile about that, she smiled. "Don't worry about it, dearest Pirate. I'll be fine."

He wasn't so sure. Even though Nielson wasn't much of a spacer and had little respect from the hardcore mining community, he was good at bureaucratic-fu. The Councilman had a reputation of always arranging things in his favor.

The hearing might not go as smoothly as Nile seemed to think.

35
LEGAL PROCEDURES

"NILE?"

"Yes, Sweetie?"

He grinned. She had a habit of using silly endearments, and he found it charming. It was one of the reasons Nile was so dear to him.

"Adam, get that foolish grin off your face. We've already done that, and there isn't time to do it again."

"Uh, no, that wasn't what I was thinking about."

She snorted. "It's all you ever think about but never mind. I like it that you're fascinated with me." She paused and looked at him thoughtfully before continuing. "I know you've been worried about this stupid hearing thing. Nielson is a jerk. It's apparent that he's trying to deflect attention from his actions during the fight."

"Yeah. The idiot nearly gave the city away."

"Yes." She looked embarrassed.

"Nile, what is it? It isn't like you to beat around like this. You usually get right to the point."

She flushed, darkening her skin. "I wasn't sure that I'd get what I needed, so I didn't tell you. You're...sometimes you're too impetuous. You might have given him a chance to pull something."

He put his hand to his forehead, trying to curb his exasperation. "Stop it now! What are you talking about?"

"You don't need to worry about the hearing. I've got evidence that I'm going to introduce that will make the whole thing moot. I got an encrypted message last night—"

He interrupted. "I heard your comm beep. Figured it was none of my business."

She smiled. "It was, but I wanted to wait until I'd thought about it before telling you. I needed time to plan."

Adam rubbed his eye-patch frantically.

She looked concerned and quickly said, "Oh-oh, that means you're really upset. I'll tell you. Don't get angry, please."

"Nile," he growled.

She continued before he could say anything else. "It's like this. I've got friends in the communications group on Luna. They're located in Kepler, well away from the shipyard. The comm base isn't well known, and they try to keep a low profile with hidden antennas. Well, anyway, I messaged them, and they're going to send me a recording. They're not very happy with the way the NAFD has been acting, and they think that the Belter community offers a better vision of how humans should develop."

She looked at him speculatively, then continued. "It's probably not going to surprise you, but Lars was taking instructions from someone high up in the NAFD. This evidence is going to be explosive. He was supposed to make sure the Marines took Titan base in exchange for a nice place back on Earth and plenty of credits to enjoy it with."

He cursed. "That dirty Agouti! Why do I always have trouble with Swedes? I knew he was no good from the beginning."

"You were right. My friends think he's been passing information for quite a while. They were a little circumspect in their message."

He rubbed his patch again. "How is this going to help? When are you going to get the evidence? The hearing's set for 0900 tomorrow. It's a little late to go to the Council tonight, but maybe I can call someone."

She sighed. "That's the kind of thing I was afraid you'd do. I've got it all planned out. I'll read it into the record in front of the whole Council and the press. I've got a right to speak in my defense, so they can't stop me. It'll be too late for him to pull strings and have it suppressed somehow. That'll fix him." She looked at her hands, then added, "If I get the recording on time, that is."

Maybe it would. Lars was sneaky and had a lot of connections. Adam suspected that they weren't all on the up and up. The Belt community was remarkably crime-free, but there was a lot of jockeying for advantage. Even something so small as a premium position on a landing cradle closest to the docks could make a difference in income. Getting a load of cargo to the buyers before a competitor could mean a difference in the price. Nielson had played favorites before. It wasn't beyond belief that he'd call in favors.

However, it seemed like Nile's plan was sound. They couldn't very well prevent her from making a statement. Even accusing Nielson of being a quisling would disrupt the hearing. The real key would be to have irrefutable evidence, and a printed out message wasn't going to be enough.

Nile seemed to be confident that it would arrive, but that might be her way of keeping him calm. Adam rubbed his forehead. There didn't seem to be anything he could do, other than wait.

He lifted his head. Perhaps he'd better take some steps, just in case. Nile was sleeping beside him in the darkened room. He quietly got up, pulled on his pants, grabbed a shirt and his shoes, then slipped out the door.

Lying in the dark, Nile moved slightly, then smiled. She knew her man. He'd have an emergency plan in place, one that probably involved significant bloodshed. She rolled over, pulled up the covers, and closed her eyes again, thinking of what she was going to say.

THE ALARM WENT off too soon. His eye would barely open. After his nighttime excursion, he hadn't slept well. Now he felt almost hungover. His dreams were full of arguments and conflict. Nielson had figured prominently, and Adam had worked himself into a feeling of righteous anger at the man. Who was Lars to accuse Nile of anything? He felt his face flushing and took several breaths to calm down.

Nile was already up and in the bathroom, getting ready. It wouldn't do to have her see him upset. It would make her even more worried than she was. She didn't show it, but he knew she was frightened. He cursed Lars silently. If he got the bureaucrat alone, he'd...he shook his head. No good. Calm down.

Things would work out, or they'd take their new ship and head out. It was only marginally flyable as yet, but he'd arranged to have it loaded with everything necessary when he was out. Loading would be done before 12:00 today.

If the hearing resulted in a verdict to imprison Nile, and if it was done before the ship was loaded, he'd have to resort to extreme measures. He wasn't going to let her be locked up.

As for the incomplete ship, he'd assembled drives and weapons before, so this wouldn't be anything new. Once the ship was finished, they'd be able to make a living. There were plenty of places to hide. The Belt was big, and the Oort cloud was far more extensive. They could mine and trade for supplies. He rubbed his patch. They could also resume waylaying Fed ships. His plans for the new ship included modified weapons that would make it quite formidable.

THE HEARING WAS in the main Council chamber. The Belters had no judiciary and no formal courtrooms. Disputes were usually settled by a group of impartial citizens drafted on the spot by the principals. People were used to this, and it generally resulted in a fair resolution that satisfied both parties.

Since the charge was treason to the Belt community, it was speculated that it could result in a death penalty. Something so serious required the entire Council to act as a court.

Rumors and heated discussions had fueled the issue, and that resulted in the Council room being totally packed by 08:00. Nile and Adam arrived about forty-five minutes later, and he had to push through the crush of Belters to reach the table where Nile was to sit.

There was resistance at first. Then the miners suddenly realized who he was and parted for the two to pass through. The room grew silent for a long moment, then someone called out, "Here's to Maxwell and his Lady! Best of luck to you both!"

That brought a cheer, and that broke the silence. The room suddenly filled with voices discussing the possible outcome.

Adam tried to figure out the general attitude in the room. Overall, it seemed like most of the audience was on Nile's side. She had a good reputation, despite Nielson's accusations.

He looked at the doors as she took her seat. Where was that damned recording?

Nile was whispering something to him, but he couldn't concentrate. He kept looking over his shoulder at the entrance. Nothing.

The Council trooped in. Seven Belters, most of whom had never made a mining voyage. Nielson came in last, looking pleased with himself. Adam assumed that the man had been successfully lobbying the other Council members. This wasn't going to be pretty.

Nielson called the room to order then proceeded to make a lengthy speech that he mostly read. He kept looking at the two cameras, obviously hoping that the remote viewers would have a favorable view of his performance.

He finished his report on the attack. His version made it seem as if he'd been solely responsible for the defeat of the invaders. Adam was seething by the time Lars had finished.

Nielson turned to Nile and addressed her.

"We've convened to hear evidence about the treachery of Specialist Nile Jackson, of the NAFD Space Marines. She is hereby charged with high treason against the citizens of the Belt."

He paused and looked proudly around, then continued, "This charge carries the death penalty. I'm...uh...we're here to make sure justice is done, and her sentence carried out." He masked his stutter by waving his arms at the other Council members.

That was too much for Adam. He rose, shaking with anger and shouted, "You vicious bastard! You've already condemned her. You're the one who did your best to turn the habitat over to the Feds."

Nielson slammed his gavel down and shouted back, "You're out of order. Sit down and shut up, or I'll have you thrown out."

Adam didn't listen. He started to shout, but then took a deep breath and visibly calmed himself, then addressed the audience.

"Belters, you all know me. I've been responsible for beating the Feds repeatedly. The Battle of the Bubble was the first time. We recently destroyed most of the NAFD fleet in Earth orbit. We cut the Ribbon, so they're going to have a difficult time building more space ships. I've set up a provisional Council with the Non-Aligns, and they're going to monitor the NAFD. My intent was for them to moderate the situation on Earth. Millions of people are dying there. We owe it to them, to our species and our genetic heritage, to protect them, to keep them alive."

He looked around. Nielson had stopped shouting and was listening with a frown on his face. The audience had quieted and was listening to Adam. It was evident that they wanted to hear what he had to say.

Adam continued. "Some of the Feds and a handful of privateers got away. I think they were planning on attacking the Titan base before we defeated their fleets at Earth and Luna. Regardless, they and a few ships that escaped from us at Luna came out here seeking revenge. We got here in time."

He pointed at Lars, and the man flinched. "This man, Council chair Nielson, disobeyed a direct order from me to turn the defense of the port over to Kendra Oligwa. You all know her, and you know that she's one of the most experienced guerrilla fighters here. She successfully defended Atlanta in the '25 conflict. I also told him to allow Lora Dunlop to set booby traps to slow the enemy's advance. Neither of these things was done. Instead, he directed an inept defense that allowed the Fed force to advance into the docks, then take the reception area. They nearly took the entire complex. They would have, except we got here and attacked their rear flank."

Lars started to object, but Adam shouted him down. "Shut up! You'll get your chance when I'm done. You'd better be figuring out what you're going to say because you've got a lot to answer for."

Nielson yelled, "Point of order! Security, remove this man." He pointed at the two guards near the door.

One of them made an abortive movement, trying to push through the crowd, but they ignored him. He tried again, resulting in two of the miners grabbing him by the arms. They pinned him against the wall, and one of them shouted, "Let the Admiral talk! We want to hear what he has to say."

This elicited a low growl from the crowd. Adam couldn't tell if it was in his favor or merely the noise of a ferocious animal that has been disturbed.

Nielson drew back, then changed his orders.

"No. Lock the doors. I'm going to want the names of everyone in here before we're done. I don't want anyone going in or out."

The other guard obediently locked the double doors.

That was asking for trouble. In general, the miners were adamantly independent. If they got too worked up, there would be a riot in the room, and if people couldn't escape, there would be injuries.

Adam turned back and addressed the Council.

"Council members, you're here to judge Nile Jackson on her alleged betrayal. I'm saying that she's innocent. She was captured by the NAFD, tortured for intelligence, and then made to go back to work with the Marines. She was under guard when I found her. She was being made to work at gunpoint. Klingfeldt would have killed her, except he was too busy shooting me."

He rubbed his chest. It was still painful. "He forgot that she had a screwdriver. She stuck it through his throat."

One of the miners shouted, "I heard To'afa got him, not her."

Adam nodded. "To'afa finished him, but the screwdriver was first."

He turned back to the Council. "We have evidence that Nielson was leaking intelligence to the Feds. They bribed him, and he was going back to Earth to live as an Upper."

All eyes focused on Nielson. He shook his head defiantly, although his face was pale. "That's not true. He can't prove a thing," he said, pointing at Adam.

Adam looked at Nile. She shook her head in despair, then said, "Not here yet."

Adam paused. He'd jumped in too quickly again. He said, "Nile contacted some friends on Luna. They told her that they had a recording of Nielson and someone high up in the NAFD bureaucracy discussing his intelligence leak. We're waiting for the recording to arrive. We'll have it validated with AI voice recog, and it'll show that Nielson was working with the Feds."

Nielson's voice rose. "See! He doesn't have anything. He'll say whatever he can to save his little girlfriend. You all know their relationship."

Adam had a sudden self-conscious feeling as all the eyes in the room turned toward him. His relationship with her was public knowledge, and he was proud of it. He composed himself, then answered, speaking quietly.

"Yes. Nile and I love each other. I've made no secret of that. I've told you the truth. I rescued her, and she was being forced to work. She's told me about things they did to her that…Well, I don't want to go into detail. She was interrogated, and they used psychological methods along with force to get her to talk. She didn't tell them anything valuable. The true traitor here is Nielson."

Nielson shook his head. "See, the desperate lies of a man who has nothing, no evidence. You can't prove any of your assertions."

There was a commotion at the door, caused by someone pounding for admittance. Nielson ignored the racket and continued.

"But, I can prove mine. That woman—" He pointed at Nile with an accusatory glare. "That woman led the Space Marines into the heart of our community. They laid siege to the Council chambers, threatening me."

He belatedly realized that he'd left out the other people who had been at risk. He cleared his throat and said, "And all these other fine people, of course."

The crowd ignored him and turned towards the doors. The pounding was getting louder.

Nielson continued. "Then this woman led a demolition squad down to our reactor. They wouldn't have known where it was without inside information."

His voice rose almost to a squeal. "They were going to blow the reactor. We'd all have died from radiation poisoning."

Adam snorted. They would have had more pressing problems than radiation. The air plant would fail quickly, and the cold would seep in. Besides, the explosion would have ruptured the seals. Titan's atmosphere was thinner than their air, and it was composed of toxic gasses. Most of the population would have suffocated or frozen to death long before the radiation exposure killed them.

There was a sudden crash from the doors. Adam jerked around and saw a circular piece of shining steel protruding from the middle of a panel. It rocked back and forth, then disappeared. There was a second crash, and the blade came through the panel.

This time, he recognized the shape as Vlad. To'afa was locked out, but he wasn't going to remain outside long.

Two more thunderous crashes and the left door gave up. The lock broke, and the door was left hanging by one bent hinge. Both of the Council guards suddenly backed up as To'afa pushed through the opening.

The big man glanced at the two and nodded as if to say, "Good move," then he walked forward through a lane that suddenly opened in the crowd.

"Hey, Captain. I got it. It came in on the encrypted laser system. I brought it straight here."

He marched up beside Adam, then looked threateningly at Lars. The Council chairman paled even further.

"I didn't have time to listen to it. We got to do that here." He turned to one of the guards who had, for some reason, followed him to the front.

"Hi, Bill. You got someplace to plug this chip in. We need to listen to the recording on it."

Bill drew back a little, but then said, "Yeah. There's an audio system on the back wall. I'll show you where to plug it in."

Nielson shouted, "No, you won't. Get that memory chip. Lock that man up for breaking in, while you're at it."

The guard laughed. "Hey, you lock him up. I got a wife and kids."

Nielson muttered to himself, then yanked a pistol out of his briefcase.

He fired a shot in the general direction of Adam but missed. A miner groaned and slumped to the floor as two of his friends bent to help.

The crowd was silent for a moment, then a roar of outrage filled the room.

Nielson began backing toward the Council's private entrance, waving the pistol randomly.

"Stay where you are! I'll kill anyone who comes after me."

Adam put his hand on To'afa's shoulder. "Hold it, friend. It's not worth getting shot over. He knows he's done."

To'afa shrugged, dislodging Adam's grip, then hurled Vlad at Nielson.

The ax flashed as it spun forward, but To'afa hadn't thrown to kill. The handle struck Nielson in the face, knocking him down.

There was a sudden rush, and the Council chairman was buried under a pile of miners. Fists rained down on Lars, and he rolled over, presenting his back. One of the men took the opportunity and wound his arms around Nielson's neck in a choke-hold.

The crowd wasn't satisfied with that. They began shoving each other to get close enough to kick Nielson. One of the larger men, pushed in the back, fell forward and landed on the struggling pair. There was an audible crack.

The miners stepped back as the choker released his hold. He poked at Nielson's head. It moved limply.

"I'm sorry. I didn't mean to do that. When Smitty fell on me, I felt Nielson's neck give. I guess it broke." Despite his apology, he didn't look particularly sad about the event.

The vice-president of the Council, Mary Beth Rosenstein, tapped on her microphone for attention.

"Let's all calm down. I want to hear that recording. It will determine how we deal with this mess you all have created in our chambers."

To'afa and the guard consulted over the audio player for a moment, then Nielson's voice came out. "I can give you everything you want, but I've got to be sure that you'll take care of me afterward."

The room broke into an uproar that drowned out the remainder of the recording.

ADAM LED NILE through the crowd and out the door. To'afa followed a second later. He'd retrieved Vlad as he came.

"Glad that's over, Captain. You okay, Nile?"

Adam said, "Let's get out of here. They'll be busy with the recording for several minutes at least. I want to be onboard our ship before anyone gets an idea to come after us."

36
THE BLOOD MOON

THE VIEW WAS excellent. It had elements of pure beauty alloyed with moments of sheer terror. The beauty was due to the mix of colors in the surface storms, clouds, the muted colors of the rings, moons like jewels, and the pinpoints of colored stars which stood out against the blackness of space. The terror was instinctive. No matter how far humans travel from their birthplace, the heritage of gravity instills a fear of falling.

Right at the moment, Adam was floating at the end of his suit's tether. He was supposed to be inspecting the conduits, which connected the particle collection funnel to the ship's reactor. Instead, he had been caught up by the colors in the view afforded by his space suit's faceplate.

Titan was visible, a rotating globe set against the massive orb of Saturn. The gas giant was so large that it appeared to be far closer than it actually was. The rings were at an odd angle at the moment; nearly edge on, but still visible.

He shuddered momentarily. Usually, he'd view Saturn as something located off to his side and on the same level. The presence of Titan changed the perspective. Now the big moon took over the side location, leaving him feeling like the ship was plunging into Saturn's atmosphere.

That wouldn't be a pleasant journey. They'd never reach the bottom. The pressure was too high, and the gas too dense. The crushed remains of the ship would float forever on a thick layer of the planet's atmosphere.

The thought was enough to make him forget what he was doing. He drew a breath, calming himself, then floated placidly, musing on the elements of fate that had brought him, an Earther physics student here.

Now he was a citizen of the Belt community, part miner, part Pirate, and part Admiral in command of the Belt defenses. Earth, actually the NAFD, had been the enemy.

The committee that he'd set up with the non-aligned countries was supposed to be in charge of overseeing the NAFD's reconstruction, but it seemed like they had fallen into infighting, ignoring their task.

The Belt had decided to remain totally hands-off in regards to Earth. He had lobbied for more interaction. He felt that they owed Earth and they should make sure that the planet's genetic resources were protected.

The Belter governing Council and the Martian Council had dictated otherwise. The NAFD had mistreated both groups. Now, both wanted to be left alone to develop on their own terms. The Martians were cooperating with the Belt miners, although that was primarily because they needed the minerals, metals, and water the miners had to trade. The miners were interested in Martian-made equipment and Martian-grown produce. It made for a bustling trade.

Adam's comm unit beeped, then a female voice came on. He smiled. Nile's presence was still like a miracle to him. He'd thought he had lost her permanently at least three times. The memory of the hearing was still strong, as was her probable death sentence. He shook his head, denying the thoughts.

"Yes, Nile?"

"Hey, you ol' one-eyed Pirate. What you doin' out there?"

"Uh, checking the net conduits and the wave-guide."

"Looks like you're being lazy to me."

He looked around. There she was, just coming out of the cargo hatch with the ship behind her. The shiny metal of the new ship had yet to be coated with nano-carbon, and the hull sparkled with reflected colors.

"Yeah. I guess I was day-dreaming a bit."

"Nice view. I came out to admire it and maybe to lend a hand if you needed one."

That was nice. It wasn't a trivial thing to don a spacesuit. However, they'd been isolated in orbit for weeks, adding components and systems to the new ship. He glanced at the hull appreciatively.

It was nearly as large as an NAFD cruiser, which meant plenty of space for the three of them. To'afa had a suite as large as the Captain's cabin and was getting spoiled. Adam doubted whether the big man would ever go back to asteroid mining.

Mining ships were small, often only crewed by two or three people. The space inside the little vessels was tight, almost claustrophobic, but miners were stable personalities. They wouldn't survive otherwise.

The nice thing about the additional space was that it allowed him to add redundant systems and enhanced weapon capacity. There were two reactors and three huge capacitor banks. Any enemy would regret facing the ship, even if their ship was much larger. He'd also doubled the point defense turrets and the plasma shield density.

The slim lines of the ship were deceptive. It was rapidly becoming an almost unbeatable force with the capability to outmatch any of the conventional Fed ships that he'd met in the past.

"I appreciate you coming out, but I'm almost done here," he said.

She glided close, snagged his arm, then clipped them together with a short leash. Her momentum carried the two into a slow spin, and her faceplate swung around to meet his.

He gazed at himself in the reflective plate, wishing he could see her. The reflection disappeared as she switched her visor to transparent mode.

He looked at her face within her helmet and suddenly felt even more vertiginous than he had when Saturn momentarily overwhelmed him. He was sinking into her large, dark eyes.

She smiled. "Not out here, you dope. It'll wait until we get back inside."

She instinctively knew what he was thinking, even when he hadn't realized it himself. He blinked, then said, "I didn't mean that. I was thinking about how much I love you."

"I love you, too, but I've seen that look before. Usually in bed."

"Okay. Now you'll have to pay. Just wait until I get you inside and alone."

To'afa interrupted over the comm. "Hey, I may not be out there, but I can hear everything you're saying. Don't embarrass me. I'm just a poor little, lonely Polynesian."

"Lonely you may be, but you're not little," Adam replied.

To'afa chuckled, then was quiet.

"Adam?" Nile's voice was soft.

"Yes?"

The ship is lovely. What are we going to call her?"

"Her? I thought you were against assigning gender to inanimate objects."

"Don't be an ass. It's too lovely to be a he."

"Okay. She it is."

"Name?"

He hesitated, then said, "I've been thinking about that. You have any suggestions?"

She moved, turning to face the ship.

"I don't know. Not the Dire Rhea II, though."

He nodded as much as his helmet would allow. "No. That's clumsy, and nothing will replace the D-R."

She sighed and said, "I wonder if it's still out there. Do you suppose it missed the planet or did it go down and get crushed?"

He felt a pang. He'd told her about having to leave the stricken D-R. He'd fought that ship through massive battles, and it had always prevailed. Now it was gone. The feeling was like an empty hole in his personality.

"I don't know. I think it had a chance of missing. It might be heading out into deep space now. Either way, we'll never see it again. I can't use that name for this one."

"What then?"

"I've been thinking about calling it the Blood Moon."

She was silent for a moment, then he heard a giggle that turned into laughter that peeled through the comm so loudly that the auto-volume cut in.

"What? I didn't think that was funny."

She gulped, laughed again, then gasped, "Not really. You're really going to name it that?"

He said, "If you don't tell me what you're laughing at, I'm definitely going to name it that."

She giggled again, then said, "You had the Dire Rhea. Yes, I know where the name came from, but still, it was a little silly. You mostly called it the D-R, which avoided the potty humor. Now you're seriously proposing to name your new ship the Blood Moon? I mean, really?" She snickered again.

He was getting frustrated and a little hurt. "Yes. I think that's a good name. I suppose you wanted to call it the Black Pearl or some other stupid piratical name?"

"No, nothing like that. I like the Blood Moon. It has a Pirate sound to it as it should. It's going to be a fearsome foe for anyone who wants to fight. It's just that I know you, and I'm sure it won't be long before you're calling it the B-M."

He was silent for a second, then it sank in. He laughed. "Yeah. The B-M. I can hear it now. This is the B-M inbound from Uranus."

She pushed him hard, and he shot away, but the short tether caused them both to spin out of control.

"That's just too stupid, anyway the next planet out isn't pronounced that way. It's 'Your An Us.'"

"I was just trying to follow your lead."

She tugged on the leash, pulling them back towards the cargo lock. "If you like it, then it's going to be the Blood Moon. It seems to fit. Let me create some artwork, and we'll stencil it on the hull."

THEY'D BEEN BACK to Titan several times to get more material and take delivery of weapons. Adam had installed enhanced lasers and three third-generation antimatter guns that launched their positron charge with twice as much velocity as the older ones.

There had been room for only one plasma cannon, but that weapon was less effective against ships with newer plasma shielding, and he hadn't felt he needed a second one.

There was even a small mass-driver. This was a variant of the USSN's rail-guns. Instead of a specially shaped projectile magnetically launched from a rail, the mass-driver fired almost any shaped chunk of space junk as long as a magnetic field could propel it. It would be easy to grab iron meteoroids anywhere in the Belt. The mass-driver would never run low on ammunition.

THE LAST TIME they'd been back, the news was mostly about Earth. The NAFD had managed to sabotage the non-aligned

Council and the oversight system that Adam had hoped would ensure peace had broken down completely.

The North American Federal Dictatorship wasn't actively attacking the Non-Aligns, but the potential for global war was worse than ever. The Non-Aligns were at each other's throats. Adam suspected embedded NAFD agents were inciting them. In any event, the situation seemed to grow more serious daily.

The shipyard on Luna was still under Belt control and cranking out ships for the Belters. It was suspected that the NAFD was building spaceships, but no one was quite sure how or where. The Ribbon hadn't been repaired, so getting into space required surface launches and those were expensive.

Still, there was a lot of activity in low Earth orbit, and most of that was due to NAFD operations. The hands-off policy of the Belt and Mars had left a void, and it was apparent that the NAFD was going to fill it.

Adam was angry at the politicians. He didn't have the patience or temperament for that kind of thing. He was too action-oriented and too blunt. He knew those were traits which generally alienated politicians, but he didn't seem to be able to change them.

The Blood Moon was resting in a new landing cradle at the Titan port. The new nano-carbon coating was almost finished. Nile had come up with a rendition of a moon that looked somewhat like a skull with blood running out of its mouth and dripping away. She'd taken that to a printer in the domes and gotten two full-color appliques. These were now affixed to the bow of the B-M, sealed with transparent flex coating.

Adam had wanted to cover the ship with nano-carbon completely, but she'd insisted the appliques be mounted directly on the hull metal. The flex had nano-reflective particles in its mix, and Adam consoled himself with the thought that they would break up incoming laser beams enough to prevent quick damage.

37

A MEETING

THE BLOOD MOON was complete. At least he had that one bit of good news to temper the bad. A report had just come in that the shipyard on Luna had been reduced to a dusty crater. Someone had hit it with a large KEW or possibly a nuke. The report wasn't clear.

Adam had gone to the Belter Council seeking approval for a force to go and investigate. After a couple of hours of discussion, it became apparent that the Council members were stalling. They didn't want to take a position.

He pointed out that not deciding had the same effect as deciding against his request and that they were cowards who wanted everything to be easy. That probably hadn't been the most optimal thing for him to say. In the ensuing ruckus, he'd grown totally disgusted and left.

For all he knew they were still discussing the problem, but he rather suspected that they were trying to figure out how to get rid of him. That was something that they tried periodically. His thoughts were gloomy.

The shipyard had delivered several new ships to the Belt community, but they needed more. Their entire economy depended on ships, mining, and cargo. People didn't stay in one place either. It was the old problem that the automobile had solved until the government had decided that autonomous travel gave the populace too much freedom.

It had taken years for the various governments to kill the automobile, once they'd decided that it was a problem. They'd gradually made it so expensive that casual travel had faded out. It was the same in the belt.

The distances involved were so great that people were unwilling to wait for a regularly scheduled ship. They jumped in their own ships and went when and wherever they wanted. For this to work and continue to work as the population expanded, more vessels were necessary. The loss of the shipyard was a discouraging step in the wrong direction.

The B-M was currently orbiting Titan. He'd been so disgusted by the Council, that he removed himself from easy access. If they wanted him, they'd have to call. He might or might not answer, depending on several factors. If his presence were required, they'd have to wait until he landed.

Meanwhile, he was fine-tuning the antimatter guns. That was something that took concentration. It forced him to think about what he was doing and at least partially forget the shipyard. Besides, it was useful, too. The guns needed to be perfectly focused with their magnetic fields tuned so that there was no interference.

Nile interrupted him. "Adam? There's a comm from the surface."

"I don't care. Tell them I'm busy." He frowned at the interruption, then began to adjust a coil.

"You'd better come and hear this. It's Elseth. She wants to talk to you."

"Jupiter! Where did she come from?" He slammed his meter down, probably knocking it out of adjustment, then headed for the bridge.

Nile and To'afa were busy at different consoles when he came in. Nile indicated the comm system, then turned back to what she was doing. He could sense that the two were intensely interested in the comm, despite their ostensible concentration on their own tasks.

He sat and activated the system. Elseth wasn't actually calling. It was the active comm officer from Titan. He'd received an encrypted laser message and was simply relaying a digital transcript that he was going to send to the Blood Moon.

Adam gave him permission, and the comm system pinged, signaling the receipt. The file wasn't large, only a few hundred bytes.

Adam opened it and leaned forward to read. His work area suddenly darkened. He looked up to see that both of the others were leaning over his shoulders.

"Alright. You can read it, too. I'll kick a copy over to your consoles. Maybe then you won't hang over me like a couple of vultures."

Nile had the grace to look embarrassed, but To'afa just grunted.

The message was, indeed, from Elseth.

"Dearest Adam,

I've missed you. You have no idea how difficult it is to find reliable people. I'm surrounded by suck-ups and wanna-be Uppers. Even though we didn't part on the best of terms, I hope that you think kindly of me."

That was a vain hope. He didn't think kindly of her at all.

"I understand that you were the military genius who dealt the NAFD a setback. You must realize that I've been working towards peace. It's just that some of my generals have been out-of-control. They won't listen to me due to my sex.

I purged them, so that's no longer a problem. Your attack gave me the perfect opportunity to get rid of them and to consolidate my position. As a result, the NAFD is going to be stronger than ever before.

I'd like to meet with you face-to-face. Perhaps we can come to an agreement that will benefit both of us."

He considered. The only way he'd feel that he benefited was if he shot her during the meeting. He shook his head and read on.

"I propose that we meet at Ceres. The NAFD has a small base there, and my yacht will have no trouble traveling that far."

The USSN had built a base on Ceres shortly after the Dire Rhea had taken to raiding the Mars supply ships. He'd thought that it had been deserted soon after the Battle of the Bubble. The space navy had received a terrible beating there and had retreated back to Luna.

"Promise you'll meet me at Ceres. I will make it worth your while. I guarantee."

The rest of the message was brief. She specified a time for the meeting that was...he checked his data pad. Eleven days from the present. Getting to Ceres would be no problem, even though it was currently in opposition to Saturn. It was as far across the solar system as it could be.

It would give him a chance to test the Blood Moon's drives thoroughly. He had tested them, of course, but only on short runs.

Ceres would be a journey that would have taken half a year when he'd first come to space. That hadn't been long ago, but lots of progress had been made. The new hyperdrive would take only a few hours to get there, and most of that time would be deceleration.

He looked at Nile, and she nodded. "I know you're going to want to meet with her. There's only one thing I need to know before you do."

"What's that?"

"Are you going to want to take back up with her and leave me?"

He was startled to the point that his jaw dropped for a moment. To'afa laughed in response.

When he got his wits back, he said, "I'd have to be crazy to do such a thing. Believe me, baby, you're all I want. All I've ever wanted. It was just that I didn't know you existed when I thought I was in love with her."

She shook her head back and forth with a critical expression on her face. Before he could say anything else, Nile turned to To'afa. "Can I believe him?"

The Polynesian said, "I think so. The look on his face is proof of that."

She looked back at Adam. He could feel his face flushing, but couldn't decide if he was hurt, embarrassed, or angry.

Nile smiled and said, "I guess I'll have to take a chance on you." Her smile faded as she added in her most no-nonsense voice, "Just you'd better be sure I'll come after you if you go running off with her and you won't like what I'll do."

"Nile, sweetheart, I always like what you do. I'd love you even if you shot me and believe me if I was stupid enough to believe that lying spider, I'd deserve being shot."

She grinned. "Okay. That's settled. Now, what do you propose to do about her and the NAFD?"

That wasn't something that he was ready to answer. "Uh, it will take some planning. We've got to shut them down permanently if we're ever going to have something approximating peace in the solar system. If we leave them alone, they'll get back to work on Earth consolidating their power. Once they're done there, Mars and the asteroid belt are the next obvious targets. I'll be damned if I'm going to sit around and let them take over. They've demonstrated that empires don't work."

She added, "At least, not for the average subjects of said empire."

"That's right. The common people, the deps like us, have no chance. We need a new vision of getting along with each other. I think that the Belter ethos of cooperation is far better. It's going to be difficult to teach that to people who have known nothing but competition their entire lives."

To'afa interjected, "Enough, already. You two can talk politics or philosophy, or whatever when you're alone. I vote that we check to make sure we are fully supplied, then leave. The sooner, the better, too. I'm getting tired of hanging around this over-sized rock that's supposed to be the center of our civilization."

CERES WAS LOCATED about half-way through the belt. All of the miners knew the location by heart. The asteroid could pass as a small moon if it were captured by one of the planets.

The Blood Moon dove towards the Sun under hyperdrive power. The combination of solar gravity and the drive boosted the ship to nearly one-fifth light speed. Adam worried about that. No human had ever gone that fast to his knowledge. If the drive somehow failed, they'd fly out of the solar system as they tried to decelerate using only Em-Max power.

He thought about running the comp on the problem, but a rough calculation in his head indicated that they would be over three light-years out before the weak Em-Max had brought them to a stop. Then they'd have to return, slowly building up velocity. It would take years, and they didn't have that kind of time. The air processor was efficient, but it couldn't supply the three of them for more than ten months.

Besides, there wasn't enough to eat. They'd starve long before the Em-Max stopped them.

However, despite his worries, there was a feeling of elation that came from watching the Sun grow perceptibly in size. They approached almost to Mercury's orbit. There was no sense testing the hull and shielding against the Sun's corona. Several sunspots were showing and the odds of a mass ejection, a solar storm, were high. Getting caught in the path of trillions of tons of ejected particles would undoubtedly do something to the ship. No one knew what, since it had never happened before. Adam didn't want them to be the first to experience the event.

The B-M changed course slightly as it passed the Sun, then began to decelerate. Ceres had been directly behind the solar orb from Titan, but now it was dead ahead.

Their velocity was calculated carefully, so they'd arrive at a speed the maneuvering jets and the Em-Max could handle. At this point, they'd taken two days of the allotted eleven. The trip would be just a little over five days by the time they arrived in the vicinity of Ceres.

That was fine with Adam. He didn't trust Elseth and wanted the chance to look around before she got there. He had made up his mind that he wouldn't meet her on the surface. There was ample opportunity for tricks there.

Depending on the size of her yacht, he might approach it close enough for the two of them to meet on a space-walk. That would have to do.

THE BLOOD MOON was resting near Ceres. Its velocity had been shed, and it was now stationary with respect to the planetoid. They'd been there two days, and there was no sign of the yacht as yet. Adam was beginning to feel like he'd been set-up.

"What if she used this excuse to get us out of the way, while her force attacks Titan again?"

He and Nile were sitting in the kitchen, taking their time over the black fluid that passed for coffee. It wasn't very good, but it was all they had.

"Quit worrying about it. I think she's fixated on you," Nile said. Her face took on a humorous cast, and she added, "Can't be because of your looks, so it must be because you've been her nemesis. You've almost single-handedly screwed her plans up at every juncture."

He chuckled, then said, "I think it is because of my looks."

She looked like she was going to disagree for a moment, but then said, "You're probably right. You are too good looking for her. Now, me... you're just right for me."

He pulled her close in response. They sat together in silence for a bit.

Finally, Adam said, "Let's get back to the bridge. I think we should circle around Ceres one more time. Set up the scanner and sensor suite for long-range detection. Maybe we can see something."

The B-M moved smoothly, circling the big asteroid at a radius of one hundred klicks. The gravitational pull was so small that Adam had to keep adjusting their orbit. Otherwise, they would have spiraled away.

The sensors didn't alert until they reached the other side, then a series of beeps announced the presence of an incoming ship. Nile got the vid focused on it.

"It's got an odd shape, but there is a number on the bow. Looks like it's in the NAFD sequence." She looked puzzled. "But why would Ms. Queen of All She Surveys use a down sequence number? It's long. I'd expect her to have numero uno, rather than X682312."

Adam shrugged. "Maybe she wants the troops to see how egalitarian she is. I don't know why the number is so long. I'll hail them so we can get on with this charade."

He set the comm for the standard Earth-Space frequency, then called the oncoming ship.

A man's voice answered. "This is the Emperess's private yacht, The Eleanor. May I speak to Captain Maxwell?"

"This is Maxwell. Is Elseth onboard?"

There was a brief pause, then Elseth answered. "I am. I'm pleased to see that you accepted my invitation. I'm sending a set of coordinates over. Please meet us there."

"Hold on. What coordinates? I thought you wanted to meet here. I'm here, so let's get on with it."

"Ah, Adam, you always were one for expediency over form. I want to meet far enough away from Ceres that Admiral Johnson can easily distinguish our ships."

"I thought you were coming alone."

"I never said that. In fact, I never implied that I'd be alone. It would be the height of folly for me, the leader of the NAFD, to risk myself with no back-up. But, don't worry, Johnson has specific orders not to approach unless you take aggressive action against The Eleanor."

"He must be too far to get here quickly. I haven't picked him up."

She laughed—a surprisingly pleasant sound. "Do you think that Earth is washed up? My scientists have been constantly busy. Johnson is close enough that you wouldn't be able to kidnap me before he arrives. His ship has our new stealth system, and you've just proved to me that it works better than expected."

Nile had been busy with the sensor suite. Now she motioned to Adam, then whispered, "I've got him. He's some 200,000 kilometers off lined up on the vector to Mercury. The Sun makes it difficult to pick him up."

Adam smiled tightly. "You know, Elseth, hiding with the Sun at your back is an ancient trick. I believe it dates back to the beginning of air combat, or perhaps much earlier."

She looked flustered for a moment, then answered, "So, you picked him up. I'll have his...no, I'll have to crack a whip on the scientists. They need to do better." She looked back and addressed someone off-screen, then turned to the camera again.

"Adam, please oblige me and meet me at the coordinates I've sent to your navigator. If nothing else, it will make Johnson happy. I promise you that I'm not wasting time out here."

He nodded curtly. "Okay. We're moving now. When we get there, assuming that you want to actually meet face-to-face, take a suit and meet me between our ships."

"I was expecting you to insist on that. I've got my suit ready."

THE TWO SHIPS approached the designated spot. The Blood Moon was considerably closer than The Eleanor. Adam slowed to a complete stop, then rotated his ship, so that it was facing outward, away from the ecliptic. If they had to leave suddenly, he wanted to head for empty space with no obstacles preventing rapid acceleration.

He climbed into his suit, listening to Nile nag about how stupid this whole thing was.

"You go out there with her, and she may try to have her men capture you. You'll be vulnerable, too. A single laser could take you out. Do you really have to do this?"

"Yes. I don't think she'll try that, but if she does, keep her in your sights. If I get shot, make sure that she doesn't escape."

Nile looked angry. "If you get shot, I can guarantee that neither she nor her idiot Admiral will get away. But you'd better not get shot. I...I couldn't live with that."

HE COULD HEAR the air circulating in his suit. The jet pack pushed him slowly to the precise coordinate spot Elseth had specified. He could just see her ship approaching. It was a tiny fleck of light that seemed to be coming closer. It would be several minutes before it came close enough for Elseth to space-walk over to him.

Something went by fast, just catching the corner of his vision. He turned to look, but whatever it had been was gone. He shook his head. Maybe he was having some kind of hallucination.

To'afa's deep voice interrupted his thoughts.

"Adam, get back here. There's a swarm of objects coming towards us. One just went by. They're meteoroids, or...no, they're rail-gun slugs. They're shooting at us!"

Adam jetted back towards the B-M. The open hatch was lit invitingly.

"Nile, get the ship ready to move and power up the plasma shields and point defense."

"If I do that, you'll be the first target. I'm going to wait until you're inside."

He squeezed the jet-pack. throttle until he was moving as fast as he dared. Any more velocity and he'd hit the backside of the loading bay so hard that he wouldn't survive. The B-M's open-door grew larger, but time seemed so slow.

A cluster of objects zipped past. They moved so quickly that the only thing he could see was a brief after-image caused by reflected sunlight. Elseth must have planned this out carefully. They'd fired the rail-guns long before he was in position. The coordinates she'd given him were the target. The place was going to be full of slugs any second now.

Sparks flew off the B-M's hull. A slug had struck a glancing blow. It looked like the sensor antenna array had taken the brunt of the hit.

The hatch was directly ahead, and he began to brake. He was going too fast for a safe entry.

Nile was saying something over the comm. His subconscious interpreted it as: "Hurry, Adam, oh, hurry!" However, he was totally focused on getting inside.

The hatch grew bigger, then he plunged through. The lock instantly shut after he passed, then Nile came on the comm.

"Point defense and shields up. Take hold. We're moving now."

There was a series of folding eye-bolts that served as cargo tie-down points. He fumbled his tether out, clipped it to one, then locked the reel so that he was on a short leash. The ship shuddered, then he flew out, hit the end of the rope and swung hard against the deck.

His vision flashed from the fall. After a moment, he understood that he was pressed in an uncomfortable position with the rope pulling across his left arm. He moved slowly to untangle himself.

By the time he'd gotten back to his feet, the acceleration had stopped. They must be moving quickly now, the acceleration had been hard. He hoped the new hyperdrive had been up to the task.

"Adam, are you okay?"

It was Nile, and she sounded frightened.

He spoke slowly. "Yes. I think so. I hit the deck pretty hard. Are we? I mean is the Blood Moon okay? Still in danger? I'll be up as quickly as I can."

"We're moving away quickly. I don't think they understood how quickly we can move. The bad news is that we were hit twice. The first time took the sensor suite, the second one damaged the hyperdrive."

"Bad! What happened?"

"I think the funnel routing field was damaged. We're still getting virtual particles, but not as many as we should. We're going to be limited in speed until it gets fixed."

"Not good. Can you get Johnson and Elseth in your sights?"

"That damned yacht has got some crazy engines in it. It went past like a streak and now it's hiding behind Ceres."

"Status of our shields?"

"Eighty-four percent and holding okay. That's because they quit broadcasting.

They were sending a mix of jamming frequencies that would crash the comm system of a normal ship. The B-M survived because they'd never seen anything like it before. Best to be careful. They outnumber us, and they're well-armed."

HE CAME INTO the bridge, balancing himself with one hand on the wall. His head throbbed from the deck.

Nile took one look at him, cursed, then said, "Get over here and sit down. There's blood coming out of your ear. You're probably concussed."

"No. I don't think so, but something happened to my balance. I'm getting better, though." He gave the lie to that statement with his next step. He overbalanced and pitched forward.

To'afa's large arm interposed itself, catching him before he went to the deck again.

"Just let me strap in at my station. We're going after those treacherous bastards."

The B-M braked, then rotated, so that it was heading back towards the enemy ships. The guns were now pointed in the correct direction, even though they were still receding from the rendezvous point.

Adam asked, "Got Johnson's group in our sights?"

To'afa grunted, then said, "Wait one. Okay, now got 'em."

"Start shooting. Positron guns. Let's see if they have any shielding that will save them."

Nile interjected, "Johnson is moving. Heading to surround Elseth with his squadron. Looks like he's trying to protect her."

"I don't care. Shoot at her. If we get her, it'll save a lot of trouble in the future. She's pure poison," Adam said. His ear hurt, and he rubbed it. He might have ruptured his eardrum judging from the tinny sound of the other voices.

The capacitor banks hummed, and the lights dimmed three times in quick succession.

Nile looked pleased. "We couldn't have done that with the D-R. Damn, I hope we got 'em."

They waited. The rail-gun slugs were way off on another vector and Johnson hadn't launched any missiles.

Suddenly the vid showed many flares originating from the vicinity of Ceres.

"Missiles! They tossed some out and left them to lie dormant. They're tracking us now. Uh-oh! They just went hyper-vee," To'afa said.

The flares had brightened. The swarm was locked on the B-M and coming fast.

"Plasma cannon. Wide dispersion," Adam snapped. There was a click, then the lights dimmed again.

"Burst away. If that doesn't get them, the point-defense will have to," Nile said.

"Keep the hyperdrive on. We'll fly right through the swarm. If we're moving fast enough, they won't be able to react in time." Adam checked the drive. It was boosting at full acceleration. He could hear the twin reactors humming through the bones of the ship.

The flares grew bright as the missiles drew closer. Up ahead of them, the plasma burst caught several missiles, causing them to detonate.

The blast caused the vidscreen to white out and roll with static for a moment. When it cleared, the rest of the missiles were spread out on either side of their course.

Adam said, "We got through. They won't be able to turn in time, and we're faster anyway. Let's get Johnson."

The NAFD ships were dead ahead, moving slowly in comparison to the speeding Blood Moon.

Nile shouted, "We got them dead in our sights."

One of the NAFD ships dropped out of formation, followed by a second. The positron charges had taken their toll. The other vessels moved to screen The Eleanor.

Elseth's ship was headed away under full acceleration. Adam was intent on catching up, but the Blood Moon was coasting. He checked the hyperdrive output.

"Ugh. Something's wrong. That last missile blast did something. We've got power, but no output. The drive's fail-safe has shut it down. We're restricted to Em-Drive only. I think that unmitigated bitch is going to get away."

He rubbed his eye-patch in frustration. Then he raised his head. "Let's see if we can get a lucky shot in."

Nile's hands flew over the keyboard, then the cap bank hummed again. They were much closer now, and it didn't take long for the shot to reach the enemy.

The largest ship in the small squadron, presumably Johnson's command ship, was struck. The positrons annihilated the ordinary matter, burning through the ship and breaking it in half. The three remaining cruisers turned and fled. They'd apparently had enough.

The Eleanor was far away, still accelerating. They might catch her, but it would be a long stern chase involving two ships with roughly equal speed.

Their damage demanded repair, and Elseth was probably screaming over the radio for reinforcements. If he pursued, there was a significant chance that she'd have more ships by the time he began to get close.

He hesitated, then shook his head. "No. We've got to get our damage repaired. Let's head for Titan. As soon as we're clear of the Sun, we'll send an encrypted laser message. It'll get there long in advance of us, so the Belters can begin preparing. Elseth doesn't take losing well. She'll be planning another attack. I know her too well."

Nile nodded, solemnly. "She's lost you. That's her worst mistake, but it's my biggest blessing. I've found you. By the way, Captain Maxwell, is it legal for a space ship Captain to conduct a marriage ceremony when he's marrying his own crew member?"

To'afa laughed. "Probably not, he shouldn't be hitting on a crew member. There's a power difference. Some people would say he was taking advantage of her." He laughed again, then added, "But, we never worried about legality in the past. We've been Pirates, revolutionaries, Pirates, and...uh...Pirates."

Nile smiled and said, "I happen to like Pirates, especially one-eyed ones."

Adam looked at Nile's dark hair and complexion. Her skin was smooth and fitted her frame perfectly. She was the woman he'd always dreamed of and never thought he'd find.

"I guess I can promote To'afa to Captain temporarily. He can marry us, then resign in my favor." He looked at her and smiled. She smiled back.

To'afa snorted and said, "Calm down now. Let's just calm down. I don't want you to embarrass me."

38

FRIENDLY – NOT!

THE BLOOD MOON was limping back to Titan. The journey across the entire solar system was taking a long time at their reduced speed. Adam and Nile had little to do, but sit, watch, and learn more about each other. To'afa was an ideal companion, considerate and inclined to give them as much privacy as possible.

They'd reached a point where Titan was in the direct line-of-sight. The sun was off to the stern on one side. They'd sent the laser message to the belt many hours ago. Now it was time to listen. They were approaching the window where a reply could be expected. It all depended on how fast the Belter Council could respond.

The beginning of the window passed, and the hours slid by. They were beginning to think there was no reply coming.

Nile was at the comm station when the unit beeped.

"It's a response!" she said.

Adam said, "You capture it?"

"Yes. Decrypting now."

THE COMP WOULD take a few seconds to decode and verify the message. They waited for what seemed to be a much longer time, then the screen display changed to show the message.

"Belter Council to Blood Moon. Your message received and taken under advisement. We're debating how to allocate resources. Retrofitting of available ships has begun. If the NAFD returns, we are planning on being ready.

There is a serious problem, though. The scientific mission that was sent to Eris to salvage the alien ship is overdue to report. They were to send daily reports, and they missed the last one.

We just received a fragmentary message from them. The alien ship owners have returned to our solar system. The scientific mission's message ended with: 'We have company, and they are hostile.'

As of this time, contact with them has not been reestablished. Our analysts think that the scientific mission has been destroyed.

We need you back as soon as possible. We may shortly be fighting a war on two fronts."

The three looked at each other for a moment, then To'afa said, "No one ever promised us that a Pirate's life would be easy."

ABOUT THE AUTHOR

Eric Martell has a doctorate in experimental Psychology. He says that the primary benefit of his graduate degrees was that he learned to learn.

He is the author of several other science fiction books and a number of short stories for various anthologies. He is a longtime student of the spiritual, holds a black-belt in Tae Kwon Do, is a licensed Heart Math™ provider, and has been trained as a Quantum Energy Healer and medical intuitive. Eric also plays guitar. His taste in music runs from Country through Reggae and Rock to Jazz and New Age.

Eric stumbled into real estate after a successful stint in software that covered everything from early childhood education to military training and consulting. He has 30+ years of experience in real estate investment.

Eric's passion is writing novels and short stories that are intended to both entertain and give readers material for thought. He makes the science in his stories as close as possible to that of the real world given the constraints of the plot. His stories are realistic and, although he does not go out of his way to offend, he sometimes uses difficult or sensitive topics to advance the plot.

BLOG INFORMATION

If you enjoyed this book, please follow my Author Blog at EricMartellAuthor.com for information about my other books. You'll find free short stories there, occasional preview pages for new novels in progress, and blog posts about things that I find interesting (most lately Artificial Intelligence).

I welcome comments and enjoy discussions with readers.
You can also follow me on Facebook at ESMartellbooks.
My Twitter handle is @emartell.
You can email me directly through my Author Blog.

LINKS FOR THE TIME-EQUATION STORIES

Heart of Fire Time of Ice
http://bit.ly/HeartofFire
Paradox: On the Sharp Edge of the Blade
http://bit.ly/ParadoxBlade
All the Moments in Forever
http://bit.ly/MomentsinForever

LINK FOR THE GAIA ASCENDANT TRILOGY

The Time of the Cat, Second Wave, & Confederation
http://bit.ly/GaiaAscendant

LINKS FOR THE CYBER-MAGIC STORIES

Cyber Witch–The Origin of Magic
http://bit.ly/Cyber-Witch
Nano-Magic
http://bit.ly/Nano-Magic